BROKEN PRISON

Prisoner Series: Book THREE

M.J. THOMPSON

Crystal Eye®
Absolutely Unprofessional®

Print and distribution through IngramSpark at ingramspark.com.
Paperback Printing: 2025
ISBN 979-8-9879116-8-6
Crystal Eye®
crystaleyepub2022@gmail.com
Absolutely Unprofessional®
absolutelyunprofessional.com

I am so thankful for my family's patience during this
tumultuous writing season.
My co-publisher, editor, and book designer has been more
patient than I could've asked for…
Thank you Rick!
I'll give the glory for this final book to my mother, who
taught me to be strong, patient, and courageous. Her traits
are found in the woman who started it all in this novel.
She is the heart that kept our family beating strong and the
one that gave me the idea to write in the first place during
my days of silence after my accident.
If it wasn't for her, these books wouldn't exist.
Love you mom.

Prologue
Where Is She?

Sanford, NC | 2010

"Where's Memé? Aidan, honey, where did she go?" Maya's hands cradled the toddler's face, trying to pull his focus back to the present.

Aidan couldn't speak. His nearly two-year-old mind kept replaying the big black van driving up and those two men pulling his grandmother inside.

"Hey, I need you to look at me Aidan." Her face only inches from his, he saw her lips moving, but he heard no sound.

He felt himself go weightless before being cradled into his mother's arms. She was breathing hard and yelling over the sound of sirens getting closer. The suffocating July heat smothered him.

The sound of a man's voice was muffled in his ear as though

underwater in the bathtub.

Suddenly, he jerked back as a strong peppermint scent burned the inside of his nostrils. With his ears ringing, he could see his mother, Maya, standing at his side as tears broke like a dam, falling in waves down his dirty cheeks. "Mommy?"

Maya sat him in the back of an ambulance and crouched down to look into his eyes. "Baby? Honey, you're okay. You're okay." Her hands touched the sides of his cheeks again as she focused his gaze on her. "Can you tell me what happened to Memé? Did you see where she went?"

"Ma'am—" a paramedic started, but she waved him off.

"We really need to get him to the hospital to be looked at," said a police officer to her left.

"I'm a nurse. He's shaken up, but he'll be okay." Maya gritted her teeth as she spoke. She knew her son would be fine. She'd make sure of it, but she needed to know what he knew.

"Okay, baby. Listen to my voice. Did you see Memé leave on her own?"

Aidan took a few breaths before shaking his head slightly between the grip of her hands.

"No? She didn't leave alone?"

He shook his head again but, this time, found a few words to go with it. "There was a van."

Maya nodded. "A van? Do you know what color it was?"

He squinted his baby amber eyes. "Black. It was black. The men grabbed her… she screamed."

Maya could hear mumbling behind her. *I can't believe the kid remembers… he speaks so well for his age… what is he, like, two? Three?*

Ignoring them, she remained focused on her son. "Do you

know which way they went?"

He blinked a few times, eyes shifting all around, then raised his arms. Maya pulled him into hers, and just as quickly, he wiggled for her to let him down. Everyone watched as this tiny little person wandered back to the grass before turning back to face the parking lot. He recalled his memé going back to her car to get him a water bottle. Squealing tires made him turn his head just as two men jumped out and grabbed her arms. She had managed to get out a scream before one of them covered her mouth. They went to the stop sign and turned, driving away from him. Lifting his pudgy little arm, he pointed in the direction he remembered seeing the red lights disappear.

"Good job, honey." She stood and faced the officer. "Can you put out an APB—"

The officer put his radio to his lips before she could finish her sentence, then dashed to his car.

The paramedic touched Maya's arm as she stood blankly watching the police vehicle leave the parking lot.

"Ma'am?" The paramedics' voice was quiet. "Ma'am, do you want us to take your son to the hospital?" The medic was about a half foot taller than her and probably about her age, maybe a year or two younger.

Maya pulled in a deep breath as her mind raced. Turning back, she saw Aidan standing there, crocodile tears on the verge of sliding down his cheeks. "Aidan," she breathed out. Scooping him into her arms, he laid his head in the crook of her neck. "You're alright, honey. You're okay. We're going to find her," she repeated, rubbing his back. His shirt was drenched with sweat, and she realized she needed to get him out of the sun.

"I'm sorry, Mommy." His mumbled words were barely audible.

"What? No, Aidan. Why would you be sorry?"

As she spoke, the paramedic watched in surprise. She spoke to Aidan as if he were an adult.

"I saw them take her and didn't help."

"Aidan. What do you mean?" she replied, shocked. "You couldn't have done anything. Those men were too big. You don't have anything to worry about. The police are going to find Memé."

He shook his head. "No, I saw them in my dream, and I didn't tell Memé. I saw them with my eyes closed. When we came here, I didn't tell her." His nose scrunched up as tears rolled off. "I just wanted to play with my friends."

Maya stared at him, motionless. "Oh, Aidan. This is not your fault." She pulled him to her chest and held him tight.

The paramedic was speechless. He had no idea what was going on, but it was clear this was no ordinary child. Finally finding his feet, he motioned for Maya to sit in the back of his ambulance so he could take a look at Aidan. She did as she was told, never letting go of her son. The cool air conditioning hit them both, soothing the sun's sweltering heat.

The paramedic didn't force Maya to put him on the gurney. He checked Aidan's vitals and gave him a Pedialyte with a straw. "Do you want us to take you to the hospital now, ma'am?" His words were kind, but Maya could tell his mind was spinning with questions.

Realizing she was going to have to pull it together, "No, uh…" she paused, "he's okay. Just scared. We'll be alright. Thank you for your help."

The man looked like he wanted to protest, but as Aidan lifted his head from his mother's shoulder, a glint of light struck his eyes, creating a crystalline flash so distinct it caused him to falter backward, quickly righting himself.

Maya was getting out of the ambulance and turned to see the surprise on the paramedic's face. "Are you alright?" she asked, brow furrowed.

Blinking a few times, he thought maybe the heat was getting to him as well. "Uh, yeah. Yes." Pulling two water bottles out of the small fridge, he handed them to her. Concerned, he said, "Please keep the both of you hydrated. This heat will get the best of ya."

When she reached for the bottles she noticed his name tag. "Thank you. Thank you, Thomas. I really appreciate the help."

He didn't immediately let go, feeling as though something worse was coming. An odd sense of protection washed over him as he finally released the waters and watched both mom and son hurry to their vehicle.

"Tom! Tommy!" He turned around to see his partner twisting back from the driver's seat. "We got a call. Wrap it up. Cardiac arrest on Carthage."

Without another word, Thomas grabbed the inside handles and swung the doors shut. The last thing he saw before the space between the doors closed was Maya lifting her eyes to his. The sun's rays hit her just right, causing another flash of light to catch him off guard.

Chapter 1
Storm

New House - Sanford, NC | May 29, 2030 | 3:00 a.m.

The crack of violent thunder jolted Lexi's body from her bed before her eyes opened. Disoriented by the waves of the lingering boom, vertigo forced her to grip the bed to steady herself.

As she waited for her vision to return, she realized she couldn't hear the gentle sound of her sister, Zuri, breathing. Reaching across the covers, she only felt the flat mattress and bunched-up blankets tossed to the side.

At any other time, she would've assumed Zuri had gotten up for a drink or to use the bathroom, but the buzzing of her skin told her otherwise.

Macie was sitting in her bed, and when Lexi turned her direction, she pointed with shaking fingers toward the door.

Lexi grabbed her hoodie and shoved her feet into flip-flops. Opening the bedroom door, she stepped right into Joanna and Adeline.

"Oh!"

"Lexi." Adeline's voice was hoarse.

"Zuri's outside," added Joanna.

Lexi didn't need any more information. She left them in the hall and ran through the living room, the kitchen, and out the back door just as a lightning strike lit up the field beside their new home. There was Zuri, arms outstretched, face toward the sky, with her diamond eyes flashing just as bright as the lightning. Her long hair was drenched and stringing down her back as she stood statuesque in the middle of their three-acre property. Cracks of thunder jarred Lexi's brain, causing her ears to ring as the heavy rain and black night were broken only by the shine of Zuri's eyes and incessant lightning strikes.

The field was surrounded by trees and provided a natural barrier to anyone who happened by. However, with this early-season tropical storm pushing through, the trees maliciously swung back and forth, daring the winds to break them.

"Where is she?" Aidan's voice broke through the pounding rain.

Lexi jumped at his words, then pointed to the center and brought her face close to his so he could hear. "Did you know she was out here?"

"No. I heard some commotion downstairs and found Addie curled up in the hallway, disoriented. Joanna ran to get Maddy to help calm her down."

Lexi looked back at the house. She knew Addie and Macie would be shaken to their cores by the lightning and loud thunder assaulting their senses. While she felt for them, Zuri was the one in danger.

Conditions worsened with every passing second. Lexi began to move for her sister when Aidan gripped her arm. "Wait."

"What? No—"

"Just wait!"

Aidan's face was the most serious she may have ever seen him. Looking back at Zuri, she could feel her sister pushing out an exorbitant amount of energy, trying to steady the trees despite the wind.

They were both in awe as the force of the wind eased, so much so that it felt as if the air had entirely ceased to move. The sensation grew until even breathing became difficult, as if the oxygen around them was rapidly being depleted.

Locking eyes, they watched one another as their faces grew equally frantic. Lexi struggled to speak, muttering, "We have to stop her."

As the words left her lips, a vicious bolt of lightning struck a tree some twenty yards from Zuri. Breaking through the pressure, Aidan raced across the field at a speed Lexi wouldn't have thought possible.

Just before he grabbed Zuri around the waist, her face twisted toward him with a look he knew meant she'd had a vision. She'd seen something beyond the obvious storm. Still, there was no choice but to break her connection as his momentum took them to the ground only inches from where the trunk of the splintered tree landed.

In the chaos, Lexi witnessed a crystalline amber flash of light intermixed with Zuri's diamond glow, though struggled to find the source. Aidan, shielding Zuri from the branches in anticipation, was relieved not to feel the crush of the limbs until he turned to see a branch three times his width suspended just overhead.

Their skin tingled with the all-familiar feeling that came upon them when one of the women surged energy. He turned to see Lexi, eyes bright as a summer sky, glistening from where he'd left her. She was holding the tree in place.

"Come on!" He yelled, hoisting Zuri out from under the branches, picking her up around the waist, he raced back to the house.

"I can run, Aidan!" Her small voice barely audible over the rain.

Dropping her in motion, he refused to release her hand as she struggled to keep up behind him.

Once inside, the back door slammed behind them as rainwater dripped onto the old wooden floor in the laundry room.

"What do you think you were doing?" Aidan's dad-like voice boomed despite the early hour.

"I just wanted to practice. This was a perfect opportunity to test my strengths." Her words were calm and clear in stark contrast to his.

"Not *alone*! What would've happened if we hadn't found you in time?"

"I—"

"Dead! That's what you'd be! That tree would've crushed you, and we'd have found you in the morning in pieces!"

"But—"

He held up his hand. "Nope! You don't get to have reasons right now while I'm yelling. Only I get to—"

Lexi's hand on his shoulder stopped his brewing lecture. Stepping in front of him, directly into Zuri's line of sight, she stared at her sister.

After a few moments of silence, Zuri said in a hushed voice, "I'm sorry, Lexi." Lexi didn't respond with words, but Zuri answered, "I know. I should never have gone out there alone. I didn't mean to scare you."

Again, no sound left Lexi's lips.

"I just wanted—. Yes, I promise not to be reckless again."

Aidan watched the exchange with wonder, frustrated that he couldn't hear Lexi's side of this argument.

Several more seconds ticked by and Lexi's face softened. Breaking her silence, she pulled Zuri close and, in a muffled voice, said, "I've almost lost you too many times for it to be a tree that takes you from me."

"I'm sorry. I didn't mean to scare anyone." Her soft voice gave away that she could sense how badly she'd shaken them. "Lexi? I saw her."

"Who?"

"The last one."

Lexi held Zuri at arm's length to examine her sister's face.

"I couldn't tell where she was. I think she was sleeping, maybe? It was like… I'm not sure… like trying to break through a wall to get to her." Zuri tried to pull the images back into her mind.

"Is she trapped?"

"I don't know," Zuri whispered, bowing her head. "It seemed like I surprised her. As if she could actually see me there with her. Just before the connection was broken I felt something else. I'm not sure how to describe it." She paused, trying to go back to that moment in her mind. "If only I'd had a few more seconds," she exclaimed, her gaze raised to Aidan.

"Hey now! Your connection would've been broken by that tree if I hadn't gone—"

"Aidan?" Zuri cut in, taking a step toward him and reaching for his face.

"Nope!" he declared, grabbing her hand out of the air. "I'm not ready to forgive you yet. Just *let* me bleed!"

"What?" Lexi turned to examine the wound. "Crap, Aidan! How did that happen?"

"Uh, my guess would be the large *tree* that tried to eat me as I was heroically saving the princess."

Zuri rolled her eyes. It was a spot-on imitation of Aidan when he was annoyed.

So that's what it's like to be on the other end of one of those, he thought.

Lexi turned to the table where some folded washcloths sat. Reaching for one, she froze, feeling the overwhelming pressure of fear emanating from the other room.

Macie and Adeline!

Chapter 2
Just a Dream

Florida | May 29, 2030 | 3:05 a.m.

The ground changes from cold, hard tile on my cheek to the grit of sand and dirt. Pushing my body up from the ground I can feel the bruises and cuts on my skin. I want to cry, but there are no tears. My eyes adjust to the dark just enough to finally see the others, so close I can touch them. Yet our hands never seem to clasp together. Always just inches away before they disappear like smoke in a breeze.

Spinning in crazed circles, I search for their faces. Faces I've seen so many times behind closed eyes and know they aren't figments—know they are out there, hurting, searching. The darkness shifts to bright flashes of light. Bolts of lightning surround me like an electrified prison, sizzling the hair on my arms. Spinning, abandoned, I wait for that final strike to hit.

Diamonds. Crystals with colors glistening radiate before me as I lock eyes on the young woman. Arms outstretched as the winds whip her fiery hair. Our movements mimic one another.

What is this? I strain to ask but my mouth refuses to form the words.

Her eyes shine brighter. I can tell she sees me with our arms outstretched and fingertips drifting ever closer together as bright white bolts of electricity strike all around, enclosing us in a prison of light.

Just as our fingertips are seconds from touching, her focus is wrenched away.

"No!" Dakota jerked upright, arms flailing, grasping for the woman that had evaporated behind her eyes. Her mind raced through the dream again, struggling to hold onto details. Grabbing a notebook and pencil from the nightstand, her hands moved furiously as she began drawing every detail she could recall from the scenes that had played out.

Of course, she sensed it was more than a dream. Maybe memories intermixed with something else. Something happening in real life. In real time. She'd known for six months now that she was being sought out, though not convinced she wanted to be found. After all, wasn't the devil she knew better than the devil she didn't?

Dakota looked around the barren room. Sometimes she wondered if she was living in Hell or purgatory. Any space lit up by the flickering of fluorescent lighting was by no means Heaven. Cold, hard concrete under her feet had long since been normal. Cinder block walls made creating that 'homey' feeling a bit challenging, but she told herself she didn't want any of that anyway. She wanted to block every hint of comfort from her life because safety and comfort always proved to be nothing more than a mirage.

It seemed a lifetime ago that she had worn a dress. Or stepped into a walk-in closet full of clothes, shoes, and jewelry. All gone. The big house brimming with people and parties, everyone treating her with wonder and admiration? Nothing more than a distant dream. A delusion.

Dakota had never been one to ignore the truth. Those comforts had been real enough, but thinking about them wouldn't bring them back. She'd been a prisoner back then, too, only it was a luxurious prison. She had attempted several times to sketch out those memories, the problem, however, was that it made her desperate for the safety and love she was working so hard to keep at bay. Rather than comfort, she would find herself having to claw her way back from depression.

With a deep breath, she let her mind drift back to when she was a little girl.

She traced pieces of memories like moving waves on a pond. The doctor with his seemingly kind eyes and dark skin like hot cocoa, lorded over them. The girls, scared, huddled together when they realized his kindness masked something sinister. Snapshots of being pulled from their beds, confused, unaware that those stale white walls and clean floors would soon be longed for. Forced to travel long distances inside crudely made wooden crates to a hot, dirty, unfamiliar place. The doctor protected them in that sandy, windowless hut. Keeping them hidden until he could move them somewhere safe to continue his work. Intuitively, she knew that he protected them the way one protects an investment, not out of love, but out of selfish gain.

Too young to understand the finances, she did, however, understand that he would have to get rid of one of them in order to stay below the radar. Dakota also knew he would choose her. After all, she didn't cry like the others. "More malleable," is how he described her. So when he needed funds to complete his research, he reluctantly sold her.

Dakota's mind drifted forward in time, watching as her tiny body was handed over to a clean-cut older man. Whispering in her ear, the doctor said, "I'll find you. This is only temporary."

He was partially right. Everything was temporary, but he never did find her again.

Snapping back to the present before the past took her to that dark place, she stood up and gazed into the cracked mirror above her sink. Her eyes sparkled, even in the dim light of her room. Staring into her bright, gray eyes, the fluorescent lights reflected off the silvery, jagged edges of her irises. A silver that had amplified over the past year.

She felt trapped.

From one stranger's prison to another, she thought, as memories crept back in.

She saw the rich man and his wife who had purchased her in Uzbekistan. They doted on her. Gave her everything she could ever want with the caveat that she would make them wealthy beyond their dreams with her magic, or *sehr*, as he called it.

Dakota breathed deeply at the memory of civil war breaking out. She watched through the grate of a hidden compartment in the living room, wincing as her new family was slaughtered. She could feel the crisp night air on her cheeks as she escaped into the night. Their screams tormented her youthful mind. She recalled the lonely desperation of life on the streets until an elderly woman named Ellie took her in.

Her time with Ellie was the most she had ever felt love. When it ended, she was more distraught than ever before. The woman cared for her like a granddaughter and would often say that she had saved her, not the other way around. Not long after her arrival, their small safe space was raided. Dakota relived the scene, abducted once again as Ellie died trying to protect her.

Dropping back down on the edge of her bed, she envisioned the American special forces team that overcame her abductors and whisked her back to the United States. She felt her stomach turn as she watched that little girl learn the fate of her parents, killed during her abduction, years prior. But instead of collapsing in despair, she watched as her younger self resolved to grow stronger. Work harder.

Though nice, her new foster parents didn't have a clue what to do with such a strange, broken young girl who barely spoke English. Her foster siblings, though, weren't as kind. They relentlessly bullied her behind their parents' backs.

Dakota, though little more than eleven years old, had learned how to survive and decided to leave the semi-safe environment of her foster home. Without a plan, and little understanding of her gifts, her days were spent hiding from the world, only daring to search for provisions after dark. One day, however, too exhausted from lack of food and fresh water, she'd decided to risk using one of her developing gifts to find supplies. To her surprise, it worked. And it led her to a gold mine of rations in what appeared to be an abandoned shack.

Squeezing the notebook, she pursed her lips at the memory

of her young self learning so much at such a young age, almost instinctively aware that all she had to do was think of something, draw it out with paper and pencil, and her special senses would guide her to it. That shack with those rations proved to be a turning point.

That's where they found me, she recalled, whispering aloud, "Breakers."

Sanford, NC  3:20 a.m.

When Lexi and Zuri entered the Library they expected to see Macie and Addie huddled together in a state of shock—and they were. What they hadn't anticipated was Maddy tending to Joanna who was lying on the couch, struggling to breathe.

"What happened?" Lexi asked, kneeling down beside the couch.

"Joanna said her chest hurt. She said she saw flashing lights behind silver-colored eyes," said Maddy, rubbing Joanna's forearm. Her voice was calm and professional but urgent.

Zuri sat by Joanna's feet. "This is my fault. I think I cracked open whatever wall has been blocking us from finding the eighth."

"I think so too." Addie stated. "I can see it. A faint strand of colors, blue and onyx, tethered to Joanna. I've never seen them before."

"Hurt and sadness," Zuri whispered, keeping her eyes on Joanna.

"It's like… something… is sitting on my chest," Joanna said in a raspy voice, laboring to breathe.

"Can you tell where she is? Or what's happening to her? Is

she in pain?" Lexi blurted, rapid-fire.

Joanna shook her head no before saying, "I see… a little girl. She's in a... small wooden building surrounded by food. She's dirty... and tired. I don't know… it's strange."

From the doorway, Aidan wondered, "Maybe the eighth is the one blocking the connection. Maybe she doesn't want to be found?"

The room went silent.

"What?" he said with a shrug, "sometimes people don't want to be found."

Chapter 3
VISP

Maya's chest tightened as she made her way to the operations cell in the recesses of the VISP bunker. She could feel a pressure in her brain that was more than irritating, but not so concerning that she needed to see a doctor. It had been increasing and waning over the last year like a low grade migraine that wouldn't cease. Her job kept her busy enough that she could ignore it the majority of the time, but for some reason it had gotten so bothersome in the last few hours it kept her from sleeping.

She needed to check the weather anyway, so she'd crawled out of bed hoping moving her body would ease the strain. A tropical storm was impacting the East Coast, luckily they were nowhere near the storm's impact in their Pennsylvania location.

As their organization often sent people out in search of targets, her job as their resident meteorologist meant she needed to pay attention to all significant weather events.

Maya was responsible for the safety of all the expeditions VISP sent out. The Director had also tasked her with searching for any abnormal weather patterns that seemed out of place or that could be detrimental to their location or their team out in the field. The weather radar had picked up some interesting signatures within the tropical storm she thought may be of value. There was also a weather disturbance along the western coast of Africa she believed had potential to batter the East Coast again in the coming weeks as a hurricane. Nothing to fret about yet, but the conditions were ripe for a significant storm. The early season heat wave only exacerbated the weather in the tropics.

Voices filtered down the quiet hall despite the early morning hour. Her mother used to say she had the hearing of a bat. Her parents couldn't even *whisper* in the house about Christmas presents.

The familiar voices of two men caught her attention and slowed her steps.

"This is the signature, sir." The intelligence analyst pointed at his computer screen, showing anomalous heightened signatures around a property in central North Carolina.

Dr. Harold slammed his hand down on the table. "It's *got* to be them!"

"We can't say for certain, though, sir. The lightning storm in that location is intense. We don't have eyes on it."

"Well let's get some out there then. We can't afford to lose this opportunity."

"Yes, sir." The analyst immediately picked up his phone

and began giving orders to someone on the other end, saying, "Possible lock on target. Prep the bird for launch…"

The sound of Dr. Harold's voice still made Maya's spine cringe when she heard it. When she came to work for Valuable Interests of Special Persons, VISP, in 2025 after her son passed away, she had no idea Dr. Harold was part of the organization. It wasn't until they were forced into the bunkers nine months and seventeen days ago, *she was counting*, that she saw him for the first time. Shock didn't quite fit the bill for how she'd felt.

He'd been an OBGYN in their previous life before the fall of the power grid in 2023. Maya was a nurse, and they worked together for almost seven years between 2003 and 2010, right up until he suddenly retired, never to be seen by her again. Yet, there he was, the new director, and she was still unable to connect the dots as to how he, of all people, would be working at VISP, let alone having assumed Director Jones' place.

They had an awkward reunion when she'd seen him that first time in the bunker. The only reason he gave for being there was that VISP had approached him, seeking someone with both medical and military training to be a part of leadership in the organization, and he'd agreed to help.

She had never forgotten the change in his demeanor that day, twenty-one years prior, when, as a nurse, she'd walked out of a birthing room with a lifeless baby girl, only to walk back in with that same infant, minutes later, alive and well. The moment was imprinted in her mind. Pregnant herself, the lifeless child in her arms cut her to her very soul. With tears streaming down her face, unable to remain professional in the nursery, it was then that the little angel took a breath and opened her eyes wide, looking into Maya's face as if she recognized her.

Upon placing the vibrant child into her mother's arms, she watched as Dr. Harold's eyes morphed from shock to calculation.

After that day, she listened intently during his meetings with expectant mothers. She noted how his questions inched toward the bizarre. When she would ask him about it, he'd brush her off with half answers, only making her more suspicious.

For the next year, she watched as Dr. Harold feverishly worked with parents and children in private, refusing to share his work with anyone. Children who should have been seeing a pediatrician, not an OB, regularly visited the office.

Then, one day, he was gone. The administration notified his staff that he'd dropped his retirement paperwork and would not be returning.

While her chest constricted and her mind raced, she began to think of the day her mother was abducted. They had both worked with Dr. Harold, and her disappearance came only a few months after his mysterious retirement. While she couldn't see a connection and had worked hard to move forward, the pain was all the more fresh with his entrance back into her life.

Shaking her head and breathing slow and deep, she pushed the memories to a little box in her mind and slammed the door.

Maya paused outside the door before walking into the office, watching the interchange between the analysts and Director Harold. It wasn't long ago that it was Director Jones standing there.

His death shocked them all, and she still questioned the how of it. The medical team stated he'd suffered a heart attack during the discord of moving to the bunkers. It seemed reasonable enough, after all, he was a big man, yet something about it stuck like a thorn.

The entire situation had been organized chaos, but Jones' dying was a grief she felt more than most. He was a difficult man to work with, but somehow always had a kind word for her. After her son's passing, with children of his own, he treated her with a softer edge than the rest of the personnel.

"Maya?" Dr. Harold said with surprise when he saw her standing uncomfortably still.

"Yes? Oh, yes, sorry."

"Everything okay?"

"Of course. Yes, I was collecting my thoughts about this storm." She made her way across the room. "I thought I heard someone say you were prepping to put an unmanned up? Is that for today?"

"Correct. We think we have a lead on…" said one of the analysts with an awkward pause and a glance toward the director, "some individuals. We need to get eyes in the sky over their location."

"Okay, what area?" replied Maya, quickly compartmentalizing any further questions and shifting into mission mode.

"Central Carolinas."

She stared at him as if he had a horn growing out of his head. "You did hear me at last night's briefing right? There's a tropical storm over that area and flying won't be possible for the next," she looked at her watch, "thirty-one hours at this point."

The analyst blankly stared back.

"I showed you pictures? Big rotation of clouds impacting that area? Lots of red on the screen?"

Still nothing. *Is there a brain behind that facade?*

She blinked hard before saying, "James, there's no flying.

Aircraft cannot be in that area until it passes."

"Isn't it your job to forecast the weather? Can't you find us a break?"

She cut a look to Dr. Harold. "You know this is Mother Nature, right? It's not like you can *order* weather on command." Turning back to the analyst and speaking slowly, "It's a tropical storm. It's slow-moving. The Carolinas are taking the brunt of it. You can't fly your bird through the rings of the storm. The Hurricane Hunters out of Keesler AFB, Mississippi were the only ones that could fly through that. They don't exist any longer. To take advantage of any breaks in your target area, you'd have to physically be on the ground near the target to launch and receive your bird rapidly."

Director Harold nodded, taking in her concerns.

"But, as always," Maya continued, "the call is up to you. I'm just the messenger. If you really want eyes out there, you'll have to put someone on the ground. Even though that's also a terrible idea because there's likely flooding and downed trees en route." Her condescending tone was not lost on the gaggle of men.

Without a word, James turned around, snatched up his phone again, mumbling, *"Wasn't that your job in the service? Maybe we should just send you."*

His attempt at spite inadvertently created a window of opportunity for her. "Honestly? You're exactly right. My job was to stake out a target area first, then call in weather updates." She looked directly at Dr. Harold and, without sarcasm or condescension, said, "I'd be more than happy to go out there if it helps the mission." James may have been joking, but she sure wasn't.

Dr. Harold laughed nervously, tossed his hands in the air, and said, "Okay, no, no. That's not on the table. We can't risk our genius meteorologist. You're too important around here!"

James, in the peanut gallery, mumbled, "Genius? Must be nice having a job where you can be wrong and still get paid."

"Good one, James," Maya shot back. Turning to Dr. Harold, "I didn't realize we were getting paid. If I can be fired, that must mean I can quit, right?" She'd never been one for sarcasm, ever the professional, but it'd gotten harder not to be jaded by their forced imprisonment underground.

The director put his hand on her shoulder and steered her toward the door. A nervous laugh left his lips. "Maya, I am always amazed at the spitfire woman you've become since I knew you as a young nurse." His patronizing tone grated on her as he quickly changed the topic. "Before I forget! We've decided to leave the bunkers."

She was about to shrug off his touch, but the news was something she'd been waiting to hear. "When?"

"I'm going to make the announcement today. We'll start transferring up tomorrow. The security team and engineers should be finished this afternoon with the additional security measures I've ordered."

The relief in her bones was palpable. "That's great news. I'll start gathering my belongings together then."

"Perfect! But first, if you could get us a solid timeline for when this weather will break it'll help us get a plan together." His voice was tender, and eyebrows raised as if pleading.

Realizing his hand was still on her shoulder, Maya rolled out from under his touch. "Sure thing. I'll have it to you at the nine a.m. meeting." Exiting the room, she was halfway down the hall when her shoulders relaxed with the first taste of excitement in years. She'd finally get to see the sun again.

Ugh! she thought, suddenly recalling her reason for seeking out the director in the first place.

Whipping around, she stepped up to the door once again. Before entering, her ears picked up a name she hadn't heard in a very long time. Frozen in place, the whispered words that should've been too quiet for her to hear floated through the air and gripped her heart.

"... Zoey, Joe, and Aidan... Sanford, North Carolina... location makes sense... need verification..."

Aidan.

Sanford.

Aidan?

Could they be talking about him? Her Aidan? But he died. It couldn't be.

She turned back and raced down the hall to her desk. Pulling up the radar on her laptop, she found the abnormal signatures and zoomed in, recognizing the location. *Sanford, NC.*

Why didn't I think to look closer before? Could it be her hometown? Where Aidan was born? They said his name! It can't be.

Maya's face went numb, followed by her hands. She could feel her chest heaving, struggling to pull in air, but the air wasn't turning to oxygen in her lungs.

Standing up, she stumbled down the hall to her room. Her thoughts chaotically racing in staccato bursts.

Once inside her small, cinder block quarters, she fell to her knees. The unsettling darkness of tunnel vision began to consume her, and though the cold cement under her palms helped calm her, it was too late. That's when the memory broke from that secured box in her mind.

Maya stood in the kitchen watching Aidan on the other side of the island faking left then right. Tag had been their favorite game since he was a little boy. She was waiting for the cinnamon rolls to bake when they felt the vibration. The earth seemed to shift under their feet, though she noticed that nothing in the room was moving. Suddenly, Aidan fell to the ground. She tried to reach for him, but her grip on the counter for balance kept her in place.

The air felt thick, and an incessant droning sound grew louder and louder until there was a deafening pressure on her brain. Her son crouched on the ground, covering his ears from what sounded like a tornado barreling down on them.

Unsure of what to do, she tapped the Emergency Call button on her phone before dropping to her knees, Aidan was on his back with eyes wide open.

Battling the vibration and muscle-wrenching pressure, she crawled to his side. "Aidan?" she said, pushing through the unseen pressure to touch him.

The moment their skin connected, a bright white light pierced her mind, knocking her unconscious. But, not before she saw them. A series of faces. Young girls in various stages of fear. And then darkness.

When she awoke, paramedics were speaking incoherently as her son was being wheeled out of the room on a stretcher.

"We're taking him to the hospital," a disconnected voice said. "Are you okay to walk?"

Everything happened so fast after that. She sat in the ambulance as it barreled toward the hospital. Then sounds of crushing metal. Dizzying fear as the ambulance tumbled off the road. Debris hitting them from every direction. The back doors flew open as a kaleidoscope of bodies and medical supplies slammed together and tossed from the vehicle.

She remembered seeing the ambulance engulfed in flames. Limping toward it, screaming Aidan's name over and over, she fought to get close enough to see anything, hear anyone inside.

Someone stopped, man or woman, civilian or official, she couldn't recall, but they pulled her away from the burning mess.

Once again, darkness.

When she awoke in the hospital, they told her no one survived. The world hadn't yet realized the cataclysm of events that was about to happen with the grid failure, but it didn't matter, her world had just been shattered.

Sanford, NC      5:05 a.m.

Aidan sat up in bed, soaked in sweat, breathing hard as if he'd been holding his breath under water long past what his lungs could handle.

It was still night. The sun hadn't yet graced the day with its presence and likely wouldn't with the storm. As his eyes adjusted to the room around him he could see Joe, Grant, Brandon and Justin sound asleep. The air was stuffy in the workshop-turned-living space.

Though he hadn't suffered the nightmare in years, Aidan remembered it all as if it were yesterday. Wiping his forehead, the details rushed back.

He saw debris inside the ambulance moving through the air around him in slow motion. The violent jolts of the vehicle overturning. Holding his mother's hand until it was ripped from his. The crush of metal as the rear end met the ground, throwing his body from the spinning death trap.

When he woke, bruised and cut from head to toe, he could see the last bits of smoke rising from the charred vehicle in the distance. Confused, he just wanted to go home and find his mom.

As he made his way to the smoking ambulance he searched for his mother. His young mind refused to believe she was still inside. Looking around, he recognized the street and thought it odd that no cars were passing by. He stood for what seemed like hours until an SUV raced down the road toward him. With an abrupt stop, the man behind the wheel locked eyes with him.

He was heavyset, maybe in his twenties. A little younger than his mom. "Hey kid, are you okay?"

Aidan couldn't speak. He just nodded.

"Were you in there when that happened?"

He stared at him blankly.

"Can you hear me? Are you okay?" Touching the boy's shoulder stirred him from the shock.

"My mom. My mom was with me." Tears pricked at the corners of his eyes.

A sadness washed over the man's face as he turned and walked several steps toward the ambulance. Looking in he could see charred bodies.

"Maybe we should get you to a hospital? Are you hurt anywhere?'

"Is my mom in there?" Aidan had always been observant.

The man didn't want to lie to him, and could see the kid had already suspected the truth. There wasn't much time either. With the power grid failing, the man knew it wouldn't be safe to stay out in the open. He needed to get back on the road, to get provisions, but now he had this young man who clearly needed help.

An indiscernible look washed across this stranger's face. Aidan couldn't make sense of it as he watched him look both ways on the road. No other cars, no people. Just an unnatural silence that Aidan wouldn't understand until months later.

"Okay," the man said. "I… this probably won't make sense right now, but let's head back to your house and get some things for you. Is your dad there?"

Aidan stared at him before he found the words. "My dad died."

The man's face fell further, and looked down the road again. "We need to get somewhere safe. Do you know where you live?"

"Safe?" Aidan's teenage brain didn't understand.

"Something, uh, kind of strange happened today. We need to find you a safe place for a while. Do you have family nearby?"

Aidan shook his head.

"I know I'm a stranger, but I won't hurt you."

Wiping the tears from his face with his dirty forearm, Aidan stuck his hand out as his mother had taught him. "I'm Aidan."

The stranger was shocked by the polite nature of the kid. With a subtle smile, the man gripped Aidan's hand and said, "Nice to meet you, Aidan. My name's Joe."

Chapter 4
Nerd-Pack

"You know she loves you to the moon and back, right?" Grant, the same man who once held her prisoner and yet eventually saved her life, startled Lexi. She hadn't seen him enter through the back door.

"And?"

His smile widened. "And you don't have to be her mother anymore. You can just be her sister *and* her friend." He watched as she stared through the kitchen at Zuri joking with Aidan in the living room. After the previous night's activities with the storm, it was clear Lexi was wrestling with the reality that Zuri needed a little room to grow.

Everyone had seemed to adopt Aidan's eye rolls, and after giving Grant a doozy of one, she responded, "Maybe not.

But she missed all the critical teen years where making those mistakes is a right-of-passage into adulthood."

"And you didn't?"

"It's not the same. I might've missed everything, but I *heard* everything during those years in that glass box. Thankfully, she slept through most of that. It just means she's got a lot of catching up to do."

Grant cringed at the thought. He was one of those people she'd heard all those years—guilt he still held onto. "Maybe not, but I think you're scared she's too naive to recognize danger," he said with a wink. "She's experienced enough in that to last a lifetime. I think she might know the difference, at least just a smidge more than you give her credit for?"

"I know," she sighed. "But even with what she's been through, there's still a lot left for her to learn."

"And likely more danger. We still don't know where your other sister might be. Let's not forget, VISP may yet become a problem, too. Who knows what or who else is out there that might try to come against your group of *Avengers*," he said, in awe of his witty comparison, smiling at her attempt to contain a laugh.

While they weren't all blood relatives, Lexi knew the girls would always be sisters. And not knowing where their final sister might be was like having a small black hole in her heart growing larger by the day. Last night, Zuri believed she'd seen her, the eighth, and this fresh vision only made Lexi more protective.

Bumping his shoulder into hers, Grant said, "I think we all have quite a bit left to learn." Their eyes locked, but the spell broke when Zoey abruptly entered.

"Hey! There you guys are. Is the nerd-pack in the shop?"

Zoey coined the term *nerd-pack* right after they'd found their new home. A few weeks after rescuing Adeline and Macie, they decided the apartment complex wasn't going to work for Macie's wheelchair and Adeline's disabilities. Not to mention, they had no room to begin working on their gifts. That's when Joe recalled that an old family friend used to own a house on several acres in Sanford. Land that had been vacant since the grid failed.

When they moved in, the property was in dire need of maintenance. It was old, built in 1908, yet still in good shape. The land was flat and cleared, surrounded by trees and brush, which offered a natural barrier for their antics. Granted, Jahnsen, the leader of LIMIT who had helped Zoey, Joe, and Aidan rescue Lexi and Zuri, kept an eye on them occasionally with his eyes-in-the-sky.

There were apple, pear, plum, walnut, and pecan trees, as well as blueberries, grapes, and dewberries. A chicken coop that needed some love sat off to the side of one of the two big workshops on the property as well. It could not have been more perfect.

The house had been renovated just before the grid failed. Having four bedrooms, three bathrooms, and easy access for Macie and Addie, it still didn't contain enough sleeping space for the entire group. Lexi, Zuri, and Macie shared the master bedroom on the first floor since it had a wheelchair-accessible bathroom. Zoey and Madison shared a room upstairs. Adeline and Joanna had the second upstairs bedroom. Sheila had the third to herself. They had added two tiny homes to accommodate some of the girls they'd rescued from Oakley who had nowhere else to go. The tiny homes sat on either side of a sizable garden where they grew medicinal herbs and vegetables for canning. Maria and Gavin found an old mobile home on an adjacent acre and rehabbed it for themselves.

Thankfully, the property had well water and septic. And Joe, always one step ahead, brought his generator, or *Gennie* as he called it, to power it all until they completed installing solar panels.

Behind the main house was a woodshop they'd converted into a lab. The nerd-pack worked there most days.

Twenty yards back from the nerd-pack was a much larger metal building they'd turned into a workshop/residence. This was where Justin, Aidan, Joe, Brandon and Grant stayed.

Despite having their own sleeping quarters, more often than not, they all fell asleep in one place or another in the main house.

"Hello? Nerd-pack?" Zoey called out.

"Sorry!" Lexi replied, pulling her eyes away from Grant and shaking off the stirring memories. "Uh yeah. I think they're all out there."

"Except for me. I take offense to being part of a so-called *nerd-pack*." Grant tilted his nose in the air.

"Oh, please. You love it." Zoey's eyes shined at him. Her sarcasm usually amplified the hazel crystals in her eyes.

"What are they working on today?" Lexi asked.

"They think they've found a similar gene, cell, mitochondria, heck, I don't know. They throw those words around like anyone outside the pack has a clue."

Grant's head dropped to his chest at her words. "I swear we've talked about this a thousand times. We're looking at segments of your DNA."

"Right. Yes. Clearly, that's what I meant."

Lexi tried not to laugh.

Losing control of her serious look, Zoey laughed, grabbed her rain jacket, pulled the hood up, then hustled out the back door. Without a word, she sprinted through the downpour to the makeshift lab.

"Guess that's my cue." Grant nodded toward the door. "You heading over?"

"Shortly. Gonna check on Macie and Addie. Storms seem to really affect them. I think Sheila and Maddy are with them in the library."

"Alright. It's going to be okay, Lex," he said, placing his hand gently on her shoulder.

Lexi had grown fond of him over the past several months. While there was a growing connection between them, her heart remained covered in a hard shell she wasn't sure would ever crack.

Making her way from the kitchen through the living room, she headed toward the library. The walls were lined with books, and the couch, intended for reading, doubled as a bed most nights. Macie seemed to enjoy that room most, diving into novels and distant worlds in hopes of escaping her own memories. She and Addie had become close, snuggling as they read. Despite Addie and Madison's unique connection, Macie and Addie had become two peas in a pod since their rescue. Their individual traumas resonated with one another, which somehow allowed them to develop their own unique bond. Just as Lexi was connected to Zoey and Macie to Zuri, this new development had the nerd-pack on their toes, working overtime and solidifying their original theory that it was shared trauma that connected each pair of girls.

Macie had finally begun talking, whispering mostly, though only while reading to Addie. Addie enjoyed playing through the images like a movie in her mind. Macie had yet to speak actual thoughts aloud, choosing to write them down when she felt she had something to say. She could speak the words while reading from a book, but speaking her own thoughts seemed an impossible hurdle.

Lexi pointed at the library door. Joe, sitting on the couch across from Aidan, raised his eyebrows and nodded before quickly looking back at the screen. She laughed at the sight. It was rare to see Joe with his feet up, snacking on dried fruits. He had managed to rig the TV to play movies from an old Xbox. And they never lacked for something to watch after finding a cedar box beneath the stairs packed with DVDs. Most of the time, she would find him working on one project or another between their living spaces, the nerd-pack's lab, Sheila's garden, and arguing with Aidan, which seemed to be his favorite pastime. But with the heavy storms, he simply sat back, taking in the *Twilight* series. She guessed he lost a bet with Aidan.

"That's my favorite movie," she mouthed. His grimace said it all.

Before even opening the library door, she could feel a steady current of electricity in the air emanating from Madison. This particular vibration was meant to calm those in its vicinity.

Nerd-Pack Lab

"No matter which way you slice it, none are the same." Maria wanted to throw her clipboard.

Gavin removed his hand from his pocket and rubbed his

eyes with the heel of his hands. "Which makes no sense," he muttered. The grit in his voice was evidence of another early morning reviewing and re-reviewing all the blood samples. They'd finally found blood chemistry, hematology, and genetics analyzers thanks to Aidan's recent raid of some local clinics and the hospital. "You'd think, at the very least, whatever's causing their eyes to crystallize would show similarities in some biological way, shape, or form."

"We know the trigger isn't familial, though," Grant added.

"Which means an external modification of some sort altered their DNA," said Maria, something she'd been saying since the beginning. "There's still the possibility that Aidan's mother, Maya, or her mother, Josephine, had something to do with it." She looked around the room contemplating.

"But if it was in their DNA, you'd think it would show up in his blood as well," Gavin countered. Early on, the whole team had submitted blood tests to compare to the girls'.

"Maybe it skips a generation, or maybe it's only in females?" Maria lifted her brow as if to say females were clearly superior.

"And let's not get crazy. Aidan's head doesn't need to get any bigger," Zoey chimed in. She knew that if it turned out her brother-by-choice had superpowers, his head might literally explode.

"We've already been through all this," Justin reminded them. "Like the girls, his blood didn't show anything. The connection has to be somewhere else."

Maria spun around. "Or! What if... guys, what if their DNA *has* changed from its original form, but only in relation to itself? Meaning, whatever altered their DNA wouldn't reveal a common source between them. What if each one morphed uniquely in line with their original source code!?"

Gavin stopped pacing to stare at her. "Babe, you're a genius!"

Maria paused. "Babe?"

Gavin shrugged. "Yeah, sounded weird when it came out."

Justin interjected, "Hold up. So, are we one hundred percent sure they weren't born with some sort of gene mutation?" Justin had looked over the results many times, and nothing irregular was found.

"I think we have to cross it off the list," Grant offered. "We'd see the mutation in the blood work if there was one." At the whiteboard, he grabbed the red marker and officially crossed off *Birth Defects*.

Gavin began to walk his thought-process-marathon like he used to do in the VISP lab. "We know that they've had this since they were toddlers based on the rescue mission back in 2011," he said, pointing at Phil, visiting once again from Ohio. Phil had been on the team that rescued the girls when they were young, alongside Jahnsen, the leader of LIMIT, and Sheila, their resident doctor and mother hen. Phil was spending more time in Sanford than he was back at LIMIT. Traveling back and forth, he provided updates on their tracking of VISP, as well as the Breakers, the organized militia-styled nuisance whose activity had started to wane over the previous six months.

Jahnsen had reconstructed cell phones that could reach from LIMIT headquarters in Ohio to their small property in N.C. More often than not, Phil chose to update them in person, which was mostly an excuse to spend time with Sheila.

"Likely, there was a catalyst in the first few hours or days after birth," Gavin continued, "but not in the womb if we go with the theory that Aidan's maternal bloodline had something to do with it. Let's walk through it again."

"We know that Dr. Harold, Josephine, and Maya were either present or on duty when each girl was born," said Maria.

"Those we know were born at Central Carolina Hospital anyway," Justin interjected.

"Correct," said Phil. "And although we don't know for sure, we can speculate that Dr. H., the doctor we were never able to capture, is 99% likely to be this Dr. Harold since we now know that Harold was a military doctor once moonlighting at Central Carolina for six years. It's plausible he either did something to these babies at birth or something happened during their births that caused him to recognize these girls as uniquely different. The timeline makes sense as to why he fell off the grid at the same time as the girls' abduction."

"And there's no documentation on where he went after he retired?" asked Thomas, an old friend of Brandon and Joe's who lived in a mobile home in the woods near Brandon's old cottage. About once a week he'd swing by to help out around the property.

"After retirement, Dr. Harold ghosted. We do know, at least according to Aidan's memory, that he retired just a few months before Josephine's abduction."

They were reflecting on the sequence of events when Aidan and Joe came bounding into the room, shaking off rain water like shaggy dogs. "Dang! Sheila won't have to water the garden for a month!"

The group stared at them in silence.

"What?" asked Aidan, scanning the room. "Do I have something in my teeth?"

"Aidan, how old were you when you lost your mom?" Maria asked.

He hated walking into these questions. His chest constricted as he pretended it didn't bother him. "Uh, probably thirteen or fourteen I guess?" He grabbed half of her sandwich as she looked away, then plopped into a chair nearby.

She made a few notes, then fired off her next question. "What about your grandmother?"

"Uh, I don't know. She was old."

Maria rolled her eyes. "No, you dummy. How old were you?"

Shifting his position, he pretended to think about his answer. "I was, like, almost two when she was taken in the park."

Thomas's head snapped up from staring at the pages in his hands. Not that he knew what he was looking at, but Aidan's response cut through his mind like a knife.

"What can you remember about the people that took her?" Maria continued, oblivious to Thomas' reaction.

Clearing his throat, Aidan repeated what he knew for the umpteenth time. "Not much. Like I told you, they wore all black. Jumped out of a big van and grabbed her."

Thomas was now sitting at the edge of his seat, viewing Aidan in a whole new light. He usually spent his time helping Joe around the property and listening to stories about the girls and what they'd done to save one other. This, however, was a story he'd never heard before.

"Aidan?" asked Thomas, realizing he'd known Aidan from before the grid failed. Before he'd met him alongside Zoey and Joe.

Aidan's eyebrows pinched together, confused by the

astonishment on the man's face. "Thomas?"

"Did this happen at Kiwanis Park? Downtown Sanford?"

"Yeah? How did you..." Aidan's voice trailed off as a warmth touched the back of his neck, and the name Thomas skipped through his memories. He shuddered.

"That was you. You were the kid whose grandmother got abducted and was never found."

"Thomas, were you there?" asked Maria after a heavy silence fell over the room.

Without taking his eyes off him, Thomas vividly saw Aidan as that toddler in that park. He nodded his head and said, "I was a paramedic back then. Called to the scene to check out a young child involved in a kidnapping." Seconds passed as he processed the memory.

"What are the odds?" Aidan's loud voice brought them all back to the present.

"I thought you were in the military," said Justin.

"I was. I did the paramedic gig for a few years before I joined." His eyes flicked back to Aidan, still trying to comprehend how he could've ended up with this kid back in his circle after all these years. "That particular incident was just one I never forgot."

"Why?" Maria prompted, leaning forward with an iron stare.

"I guess it was just that the boy... well you, Aidan... spoke with a clarity I'd never witnessed in a child that age." He wanted to mention the shimmer of light he'd seen in both Aidan's and his mother's eyes that day, but after all the time that had passed, he was no longer positive of what he saw.

"I know. Wise beyond my years," said Aidan, taking a

sloppy bite of Maria's sandwich.

"Did anything else happen that you can remember, Thomas?" Justin asked.

"No, not that I can think of. No one was physically hurt, so we didn't transport anyone to the hospital."

The group watched Maria closely as she analyzed the new information. Her face was always so animated they could almost hear her thoughts. "Okay, well, interesting. Unfortunately, as wildly coincidental as it is, doesn't help us in any meaningful way right now." Spinning in her seat back toward Justin, she said, "So where does this leave us? What's our next step?"

"We need an MRI machine, is what we need," he said with a deep breath. "If we could get a good look at their brains in action like we did at VISP… if we could compare each of them against one another, and even maybe against us mere mortals, that may provide some answers."

Maria's eyes lit up. "Any chance the hospital still has a functioning machine after all these years?"

"I guarantee we can get one working if we find one," Grant said with confidence.

Thomas cleared his throat and, still trying to adjust to the reality of Aidan's presence, said, "While that piece is getting figured out, we still need to decide what to do with Oakley and his men. I'm not much for babysitting."

"Dang, I'd almost forgotten about them," Aidan piped in, finishing his sandwich. "I mean, there is one way…"

"Seriously, Aidan?"

"Maybe we could drop them at VISP? *They* seem to have the ability to make people disappear," offered Gavin, raising his shoulders.

"True, but somehow, I don't think that would end in our favor," said Justin. "What about Jahnsen? LIMIT might have a use for them."

Phil shifted in his seat. "We've discussed it a few times and it is a possibility. There's a facility near LIMIT that Jahnsen's already got a few folks housed with guards. It's hard keeping that post staffed, though. As Thomas said, it's a glorified babysitting job and the idea of adding more mouths to feed doesn't sit well with our staff."

"Maybe the girls could use *them* for practice? You know, a little tit for tat?" said Aidan under his breath followed by an uncomfortable silence.

Just as Aidan was beginning to believe they might consider his idea for once, Maria cut in. "Okay, as enticing as that sounds, we aren't those people either, right?" she said more as a question than a statement.

"No, no. That's not the answer here." Justin stood up and shook out his arms as if shaking off his negative thoughts. "Phil, if Jahnsen will take them, even for a little while, maybe we can come up with a better solution."

"What about the kid?" Thomas asked.

Justin turned to him with a questioning look.

"The one that said he was trying to help the girls escape."

"He stays. He was there. He was part of it. Likely, he's lying to get out of there." Justin said without hesitation.

Maria added, "He might be telling the truth though. Addie said there was a man who came in and tried to help her at one point. At least, she believed he did. Maybe—"

"Maybe. Or *maybe* he's as psychotic as the others and we'd regret it the moment he was out." Gavin slid up beside her and put his hand on her shoulder, while subconsciously his other hand touched his pocket again.

"He's told me several times he works with the Breakers," Thomas countered. "They'd found Oakley through one of their recon missions and had sent the kid in undercover. He had no idea what he was walking into until he got there. He decided on his own to try and help get the girls out but found it more complicated once he was in."

"And you believe him?" Justin asked.

"Well, he makes it a point to tell me when the others aren't close enough to hear him."

"Maybe because he doesn't want them to kill him for being a traitor," said Justin.

"Okay…" said Grant, thinking out loud. "What if we brought Zoey and Addie over to see him?"

"Yeah, I could—" began Zoey.

"Hard no!" said Joe, unwilling to let that thought linger. While his love for her had slowly shifted away from a romantic one, there was no doubt he would protect her like a sister.

"It's not like they'd be alone with him. Just have a quick conversation to see if he is what he says he is." Grant usually didn't seek confrontation, but he also didn't want to see a man pay for the crimes of another.

"Nope. End of story." Joe stood up and walked out the door back into the rain.

"Alrighty, let's table that discussion for now. Honestly, I think it should be up to the girls, but for now, they stay where they are. Can you hold out a little longer, Thomas?" Maria hated they'd laid the responsibility of babysitting Oakley and his men on him, but they didn't have many options.

Thomas nodded.

"Okay, so about that MRI?"

Chapter 5
Boss

Dakota's nightmare dissolved as her body trembled. Muffled words slipped through her subconscious.

Wake up… there's no one else here… Dakota? Can you hear me? Jolting upright, she smacked Elias in the cheekbone and his cry startled her awake.

"Dang, Boss. Seriously?"

Her confusion cleared as she felt the sting in her hand where it had connected with his face. "Oh, crap! Sorry, Eli." Shaking her hand, she stood to inspect his face. "Are you okay?"

"Yeah, yeah. I'm good. You okay?" More and more, Eli seemed to show a degree of concern for her she wasn't overly comfortable with.

"Fine. No worries. Uh, what's going on?" she asked,

walking to the sink and splashing water on her face.

"The team thinks they found something. Want you to take a look."

"Sure, just give me a minute and I'll be right out."

"No problem, Boss. I'll let 'em know you're on your way." Eli took a step toward the door before pausing.

"Was there something else?"

Shuffling his feet, "Uh, it's just… you might want to put your glasses on."

She pulled her eyes from him and looked in the mirror. The silver sparkle shining back at her caught her off guard. Her nightmares made her eyes stand out, which tended to be disconcerting for those around her. Grabbing her tinted glasses, she shoved them on her face and turned back to her second in command. "Thanks for the heads up."

Eli stumbled back toward the door, timidly replying, "Yup, no problem."

Dakota wasn't sure if he was shocked by her appearance or afraid. Likely, it was both. He was the one who;d found her so many years ago and brought her into the fold of the Breakers. Since learning of her abilities, their roles had reversed, and she had become the one in charge. No one ever challenged it.

Throwing on jeans and an ancient 5K Mud Run t-shirt, she walked out into the hall of what they called *the Station*, mainly because it was the old Florida East Coast Railway Station that sat across the bridge from Cape Canaveral.

A buzz was in the air which she attributed to her team's excitement. Usually, it meant they'd located an area where communications had been restored and they were devising a plan to take it down. In the beginning, it felt like a purpose. As if the universe had brought her to them because her abilities could make their mission stronger. However, after all these years, it just felt wrong.

She never shared this brewing sentiment with the team. It wasn't something she'd generally do anyway, but it was getting harder and harder to feign vengeance on the world after it had already suffered so much.

"What's all the fuss?" Her words sounded forced as she entered the Station. Eli turned when he heard her voice.

"Come check this out," he stood next to a man with wildly long, curly hair, dark rimmed glasses and a generally pessimistic attitude. It didn't matter what time of day it was or what was going on; any question asked of him received a negative response.

Dakota made it a point to avoid asking him anything if she could.

"Levi, tell her what you told me," Elias said, casually reaching for Levi's shoulder but quickly thought better of it, dropping his hand.

Levi pulled a chewed-up pencil out of the corner of his mouth. "Okay, so I was hacking into the VISP secure link. They always have the most accurate weather data. When I pulled the radar imagery, I also managed to pull some images that had been manipulated by one of their analysts."

"Nice," said another team member with reverence.

"Easy stuff," Elias shot back, his self-confidence never lacking. Dakota really didn't like this guy. "So what we have here," he pulled the image up on the screen showing the circulation of a large tropical storm entering the eastern coastline, "is the storm itself. As you can see, someone drew several circles on the image."

"That's odd. Why didn't it hit us first?" she asked, turning toward their resident meteorologist.

"Tropical storms follow the edge of a high-pressure system. The high itself is oddly shaped because of a trough in the Gulf of Mexico. It kept this storm further north than a typical tropical pattern," he said.

"I'm going to pretend like I understood most of that, Jon," Dakota said. "Okay, so it missed us and hit the Carolinas."

"Yes, ma'am. There's another disturbance off the African Coast. As of now, the conditions for hurricane formation are pretty solid. However, it's still a question about where exactly it will hit after crossing the pond."

Dakota leaned forward to get a better look at the current storm over the Carolinas and noticed the colors within those circles were unlike anything she'd seen on a radar before. "Isn't the heaviest part of the storm usually orange or bright red?"

"She's getting it—" Levi began, before Eli cautioned him with a tap on the arm. Annoyed, Levi glanced over his glasses before returning to his computer. "Yes. But as you can see, clumped in this one little area there are spots of white with a black edge around the centermost points showing the strongest returns."

"Returns?" Dakota wasn't a weather specialist but she had seen enough briefings to know the colors on the screen weren't normal. Since it didn't seem to be related to hitting a target, she felt less of an urge to dip out and walk to her favorite place along the beach.

"Radar returns," he repeated. "It's how these images are created. By the strength of the returns from the radar frequencies themselves."

"Could it be some kind of error? I mean, that weather equipment has been out there for years, and I doubt anyone is maintaining them," said Eli.

Levi shrugged. "Sure. Anything's possible. But since it was noted by whomever is analyzing this data, I'd say it's probably more than just an error. And look, it lasted over a thirty minute period of time, fluctuating in intensity. Even as the storm itself continues to move northeast, those returns remain in the exact same location."

Dakota stared at the screen for a moment before standing upright. Looking around the room, she tried to think of something clever to say as the team looked to her for answers. "Okay, well… keep monitoring and if anything of interest happens moving forward, let me know." She felt their eyes on her back as she turned to leave. Despite the odd imagery, she wasn't going to give the approval to plan a raid with such limited information. She knew they had anticipated a motivating speech to rile them up, but she could hardly motivate herself, let alone her team.

She was exiting the room when a thought occurred. "Levi, can you tell where those signatures are located?"

Spinning back to his screen, he zoomed in for a closer look at the map and called out, "Sanford, North Carolina. Actually…" his words trailed off before clicking on some files to pull up an old image. "We've had some abnormal signatures in that area since last fall. I'm wondering…" his voice trailed off as he clicked some more keys. "Yup! In August, on a clear night, we had multiple strange signals in that same area, but we *did* think it was an error at the time because there was no weather to speak of."

Sanford? The name seemed to knock the wind out of her. Suddenly, pressure mounted at her temples, and the sound of a wind only she could hear began to rage inside her mind. No one said a word as they watched the color drain from her face.

"Dakota?" Eli finally said, taking a step toward her.

She had spent years concealing her inner thoughts and feelings. Despite the deafening sounds of an ethereal wind, she managed to raise her hand and say gruffly, "Let me know if you see anything new. I'll be outside."

The air was muggy as the morning sun cast a rainbow of colors across the Florida sky.

Sanford.

"We need to talk about this," Levi said, once Dakota was out of sight.

"About what?" Elias avoided eye contact.

"About the fact that she's changed. That she's not invested in—"

Elias grabbed his arm and pulled him out of his chair. "Not here!" he grit between his teeth, and walked out the door gesturing for Levi to follow.

With the door shut and the hall empty, Levi picked up where he left off. "She's not invested in us anymore. Our cause."

"That's ridiculous and you know it. She's been with us since the begi—"

"*And* she's done way more damage than we ever intended. But you know what, that destruction set us on this path and we can't stop now."

Elias, not a violent man, wanted to punch Levi for even

suggesting such a thing. However, he also knew Levi wasn't wrong. Over time, Dakota had softened. While he was secretly pleased with the change, not all Breakers were. "She was eighteen," said Elias, defending her. "We'd never seen her do something so catastrophic, so that's on us!"

"Either way, we've committed since then. It doesn't matter that we only intended to take down the one power plant. It doesn't matter that we just wanted to show the world it could be done and that the population needed to become better humans." Levi's blood was boiling. Every Breaker agreed on these points and Elias should have known better. "*And* to show that security systems in tech needed to be beefed up against terrorists lusting to cause irreversible damage!"

"*We* are the terrorists!" Elias shouted, sickened by the reality. "We earned that title by default doing what we did! Just because it wasn't our intention doesn't make us any less culpable. And we've leaned into it ever since." He could feel every heartbeat pulse through his chest and into his brain. "The world as we know it was *not* the plan we had in mind."

"Maybe, but that doesn't make us terrorists. We saved this planet. Us. We did that. We showed everyone that the way they were treating our world was going to kill us all eventually."

"Yeah, well, we sped up that process, didn't we?" said Elias, his voice low and raspy.

Their act of blowing up the power plant killed untold numbers of the population and they couldn't take it back. There were some in their organization that were happy with how things turned out, and they continued to push the envelope to keep it that way. Made them feel superior. Others, however, were devastated by the collapse of civilization but were too weary to change course. Those that were scared to instigate change were scared of one thing. Dakota.

"You need to talk to her," said Levi, diverting back to his original point. "She still hasn't given us the go-ahead to investigate the power surges we're seeing in Pennsylvania, Ohio, and now this new one in North Carolina. If someone is out there working on bringing power back to the masses, we need to find them."

"We already know about VISP in Pennsylvania," Elias replied, taking a deep breath. "They've gone underground, so there's nothing we can do about them until they resurface. And let's be real. We've been trying to figure out a way into their compound for years. They're too fortified."

"You're probably right. But what about her?" asked Levi with a straight face. "Maybe we need to do something about her."

Elias took several more deep breaths before looking Levi in the eyes. "Nothing happens to her, Levi. Do you hear me? I'll talk to her, but you need to remember we are nothing without her." His eyes bore into Levi's with a ferocity he hadn't felt before. Dakota had become like a little sister to him. He'd protect her at all costs. "Do we understand one another?"

Levi nodded. Elias could tell his mind was ticking, but he also knew Dakota could handle herself. If Levi wanted to go up against her, that was his loss. Regardless, he planned to bring it to her attention. A change was coming. He could feel it, and it felt like the storm of a century.

Chapter 6
Connected

Joanna sat curled up next to her sister Addie on the overstuffed recliner. "Can you tell me again? Y'know, what you see?"

Addie hadn't been the same since the rescue. Her once bubbly, sarcastic nature had become reserved. Though, now and again, when just the two of them sat comfortably together, a glimpse of her old self would shine through. "Seriously? Again?" Addie scoffed, feigning annoyance. In truth, she loved having her sister beside her, hand in hand, knowing they were both alive and safe.

"The way you describe it is so mesmerizing. I wish I could see things the way you do." The moment the words left her lips, Joanna wished she could retract them. She still didn't know the depth of torture Addie had survived to receive her new ability. Though she had tried to catch a glimpse of her sister's past using her own gift, somehow, Addie was able to block her attempts.

Addie felt her sister's slight shift in weight and squeezed her hand. "Let's see what's around us right now," she said, closing her eyes. Though she didn't need to, Addie made a show of turning her head from side to side as if viewing the room. Weeks back, she'd finally been comfortable enough to remove the eye patch over her left eye. The brokenness and bruising had healed, but the black coloring of her iris, along with the blindness, remained. Her right eye, feeble though it was, was aided by a pair of glasses Sheila managed to find. Regardless, it was the love she felt that helped her overcome the embarrassment of the deformities incurred from her imprisonment.

"Mostly I just see bright emerald green ropes being shared between us. They are twisting from your chest in thick braids that wind around us. Several thinner strands like vines are veering off and maneuvering their way through the library door and…" she gave a small smile.

"Yeah, yeah, I'm sure I know where they're going," Joanna said, giggling. Brandon was probably outside doing woodwork. He'd gone back to his old cabin the week prior, after the storms passed, to gather a load of lumber. There was so much she still didn't know about him, but every day she loved him more.

"Well, just so you know, a darker shade of emerald is winding its way back to you at the same time," said Addie. It was a miracle to find love in the state the world was in, and yet she could see tendrils of green around everyone in her life. Different shades for different types of love. The ropes from her to her sister were a light color, signifying familial love. Friendship love had a lemon hue to it, which was abundant on the property. For her, though, those dark emerald strands were non-existent. And she felt pretty confident that a deformed young woman such as herself wouldn't be chased down for romance any time soon.

Joanna could feel Addie's pain. It moved like an undercurrent beneath them, causing her to squeeze her sister's arm a little tighter.

Addie noticed Aidan's tell-tale turquoise and flamingo pink ribbons start to wriggle into the room. He was the most joyful and excited person she'd ever met. The more excited he was, the brighter the pink shade exuded from him. However, after informing him that his color was similar to the awkward Floridian bird, he insisted on calling it *salmon*.

There was also a purple haze that hovered around him more often than not. It wasn't a rope or vine like the others, just a smudge in the air near him that would glow brighter when he seemed unhappy. Addie sensed what the source might be, but even with everything they'd all been through, she struggled to believe it could be the essence of another person with abilities lost sometime in the past and attached to him.

The door burst open as he yelled, "It's *gorgeous* outside!" Holding the word gorgeous out longer than necessary. "You two need to get out there and feel the sun on your face. Get some vitamin D!"

"But we're so cozy and warm right now," Joanna said, laughing at his puppy-dog face.

"But it's June, in North Carolina, and like eighty degrees out there!" Leaning down, Aidan placed his hands on Addie's shoulders and looked her in her one good eye. Aidan was the one person she felt most comfortable around because he treated her like a whole person. "You need some sunshine, and…" he paused, waggling his eyebrows, "I have a surprise for you!"

"We have a surprise for you," added Brandon, his heavy boots thudding to a stop inside the doorway.

Rolling his eyes, Aidan admitted, "Okay, yes, we. But it was my idea!" Jumping up, he helped Addie to her feet as Joanna pushed slip-on shoes in front of her.

"Alright, fine. Let's check out this surprise." Addie's pain had all but ceased, but there were still moments when nerve damage caused agonizing spasms. While the others typically gave her plenty of space to do life independently, they remained close enough to allow her to use an arm when needed.

The house was empty as they made their way out the back door and down the ramp Joe had installed. Joanna's excited gasp guided Addie's search for the mysterious gift.

It took a moment for her to physically see beyond the colors of the rainbow surrounding her. All of the people she'd grown to care about stood in a gaggle in front of a wooden structure. A beautifully constructed gazebo, complete with a wheelchair ramp and railing, stood about twelve feet high. She could feel the carved vines winding around one another as her fingers moved along the smooth, soft wood. On each post, she could feel the features of a woman's face carved with care. Eight posts in all, and she knew it was for her and her seven sisters, including the one they had yet to find.

"It's beautiful," Addie whispered.

Joanna, taking in the incredible detail throughout the artistic structure, caught Brandon's eyes and, with tears in her own, mouthed, "Thank you."

Without hesitation, he pulled her into his arms.

"I can't believe you did all this. It's absolutely stunning," Joanna said softly.

The eighth post had the beginnings of a woman's face, but no true detail. Addie ran her fingertips across the smooth surface.

"We'll find her. And when we do, I'll finish the last one," said Brandon, kissing Joanna's head as Addie ran her fingers over the unformed face on the final post. He watched as the women gathered around Adeline on the center bench beside Macie in her wheelchair. Snuggling up, a familiar hum began to emanate from them, causing the hairs on the men's arms to rise from the vibration in the air.

That's when the girls felt it.

The pull. The pain. The despair.

Zuri could feel the heartbeat of the wood carved with love and knew it amplified their collective reach out into the world. There was a reciprocating heartbeat coming from a long distance off. It was clear and felt by all. Only the rhythm was off from their own collective beating.

Suddenly, Lexi gasped.

"What's wrong with her?" Zuri asked, squeezing Lexi's hand tight.

The arrhythmic palpitations took them all by surprise, even causing Joanna to grip her chest as if struggling to breathe.

"She's out there," Zuri whispered.

"Something's not right," said Madison, squeezing Zoey's shoulder.

Macie's wheelchair squeaked as it shifted backward several inches. Joanna, touching the back of Macie's hand, gasped as a frozen chill raced through her veins.

"Joanna?" shouted Brandon, rushing to her side as her knees buckled. "What's wrong?"

"I see… darkness and a wall," she whispered, squeezing her eyes shut.

Standing in the center of the beautiful gift, all seven were interchangeably seeing and feeling two separate forms of pain rapidly twisting together, making it difficult to determine what or who they were seeing.

Zuri gripped Macie's hand tighter as she focused on separating everyone near her from the thread of their missing sister. It had been easier to do the other night alone in the storm. Here, it was more difficult with so many people and their emotions masking the trail.

Releasing her grip, she stepped into the center of the platform. "This doesn't make sense," she mumbled, trying to tease out the different energies. "One is so familiar, but the other... it's something else entirely. Difficult to grab hold of."

Addie watched as ribbons of color were pulled and then pushed away from Zuri. Checking and sorting them one by one until the only threads near her were red, blue, and black. The red and blue were anger and sadness, twisted and tied up in knots and wrapping around Zuri's right hand. Addie could see that it led south, disappearing out of sight. The black came in a steady wave until it wrapped around Zuri's left hand. This thread was thinner and came from the north.

"I can see them," Addie whispered. "There are two strands."

"Two women? I thought there were only eight of us," asked Maddy, who could feel the energy Zuri was struggling with. All the girls could. It was a person, definitely, maybe two, but it wasn't the baseline signature of one of them.

"It feels like it has its own vibration pattern, its own character, unlike anything I've felt before."

The men watched in silence as the air crackled with power.

Aidan watched in awe, his heart racing and mind spinning. Something about the sizzle in the air stirred up long-lost memories, causing him to freeze in place as a tornado of images flooded his mind. For the first time, he had trouble pulling them into that box in his mind.

As if breaking through a wall, Aidan released a guttural sound from his abdomen that seemed to break the spell of what was happening among the girls. The ropes in Zuri's hands dissipated, the colors faded away from Addie, and the heaviness in the air eased.

Exhausted, everyone's gaze shifted toward Aidan.

Quickly centering himself, combing his hair and straightening his shirt, he broke the awkward silence by clearing his throat. Then, with a nod, he simply said, "Cool. So there's a ninth witch?"

Chapter 7
View

Maya's entire body went rigid. Images of people and places she didn't recognize washed over her eyes. All but one.

Aidan.

His familiar scent wafted in the air as she reached for him. *Could he really be alive?* He looked so different, taller, muscular, his face squared off compared to the rounded young teen he was when she saw him last. *All these years?* His red hair, beautiful amber eyes and freckles, however, hadn't changed one bit. *Wouldn't I have felt him? Known my own child was still alive?*

She grew dizzy, struggling to comprehend if what she was seeing was real or a vivid dream torturing her. Had the walls she'd erected to protect her emotions also closed off her ability to connect with her only child? *I saw the charred ambulance. It had caught fire with him inside. Hadn't it?* She winced at the thought of the unrecognizable bodies in the wreck.

It was as if she was viewing him through someone else's eyes. Then, just as fast as it washed over her, the connection was gone. The cinder block wall appeared in front of her as the whirring of her computer on the nearby desk filled her ears.

Aidan.

For months after the grid fell, chaos ensued, but she couldn't process it. She'd been numb to the devastation of the world because her world had already been shattered.

Then, one day, out of nowhere, a man named Jones appeared at her door. Director Jones asked her to join his team. The organization consisted of the military, doctors, scientists, engineers and so on with a mission to find select individuals with consequential skills that would help restore civilization. *People like her,* he said. After the disappearance of her mother, years before the grid fell, she joined the U.S. Air Force as a combat meteorologist. The military fell apart after the loss of electricity, devolving into smaller factions around the world. She managed to survive on her own until Director Jones showed up. He claimed she was the perfect fit to help their mission succeed. While she didn't care much for the details of the mission at the time, she knew she needed to do something, anything to bury the excruciating pain eating away at her.

Even so, there remained some small piece of her that genuinely wanted to help humanity. At the very least, pay homage to her son's life.

After all this time, she was unaware of those she might have helped save. Everything had been so compartmentalized in VISP that she only ever knew of locations. They'd find a person of interest and then give her a location to forecast for, but never any personal data. For nearly seven years, she had remained closed off from the rest of the world.

Closed off to everything but her dreams. Violent nightmares that once ravaged her sleep had subsided, replaced with odd dreams she struggled to recall upon waking. Remembering bits and pieces from time to time, though rarely making any sense of them. Only in the last year was there a shift.

Her dreams had grown uncomfortably realistic. At some point, she'd taken to recording them in a notebook she kept under her mattress.

Last August, when they'd been forced into the bunker, it seemed she went from being a worker bee like the rest of the team to a prisoner. At times, she noticed that Dr. Harold, who'd replaced Director Jones, would look at her with great anticipation. It was as if she was supposed to be doing something more than forecasting the weather. But what, she didn't know.

Her time in the service as a meteorologist was spent behind walls, just like those around her now. When she'd chosen weather forecasting after her stint as a nurse, she envisioned being outside, under the sky. The naivety of that made her want to both laugh and cry. She'd spent a lot of time in block buildings without windows, forecasting the weather all over the world. Rarely seeing the sky itself.

Of course, all the locations and equipment that once provided instantaneous weather updates, especially the people who kept their eyes on the current conditions, no longer existed. Some tactical weather equipment remained simply because it was solar-powered. Satellites continued to circle the globe, maintained by the NASA folks in VISP, and that's where the bulk of her data came from.

She had trained some of the operators how to set up an IWOS (Integrated Weather Operating System) when they were out on missions so she'd have additional data to pull from. An IWOS could take continuous observations of the wind, temps, pressure, and sky conditions and then instantaneously relay it back using satellite triangulation from which she could pull.

Primarily, all VISP leadership cared about was whether their remotely piloted aircraft could safely fly and whether their operators on the ground could make it to their targets and back.

She would have given anything to be part of the action. To go into the world and collect data firsthand before sending it back to some desk-jockey. Once upon a time it had been her favorite part of the job.

But she knew better. Supposedly, they needed her. In reality, she was beginning to believe they thought she'd run.

Until recently, running had never crossed her mind. Where would she have gone?

But if Aidan was alive… if there was even a one percent chance her son was out there, nothing would stop her.

His gentle face came to mind once again. Soft freckles sprinkled across his nose, sunshine red and blond hair glinting in the sun. She sighed. So many years.

Maya stared at the water pulsing from her bathroom sink spigot. She didn't remember turning it on. She didn't remember moving from her couch to the bathroom. The sound of the water splashing as it hit the porcelain basin was soothing, clearing her mind as her eyes slowly shut.

With her heart rate down and her mind settled, she noticed a gentle tingle moving across her skin. It was a sensation she hadn't felt in years. In fact, she had completely forgotten about such sensations.

As the feeling grew, beautiful faces blossomed behind her eyes. Newborns with their eyes scrunched, and soft breathing sounds leaving their puckered lips. Then, small children, scared and afraid. She watched them grow, noticing more and more details of these babies she'd once held in her arms.

At that moment, she knew she had to start believing the visions were real and that maybe she had another purpose, something greater than simply forecasting the weather for VISP.

Maya felt them before she heard them. His steps were silent as he came down the hall. She could *feel* him. Something inside her had awakened.

The knock at her door made her fingers grip the sides of the sink as her eyes opened to see her own reflection in the mirror.

Air froze in her lungs at the sight. Crystals of every color wove a pattern through her irises.

Chapter 8
Who Do You See?

Sanford, NC | June 13, 2030

"Okie-dokie, ladies," said Justin. "We're going to take this nice and slow. It's not a race. It's a marathon."

"Ugh, that could take hours! Can we eat lunch first?" Aidan whined.

"It's only nine a.m. You just had breakfast!" Zuri chided.

"Alright, my beautiful, strong women," said Maria. "Let's get this party started. Safeties, stand behind your partner." Her voice was almost sing-songy despite the nerves stirring up her stomach. For each of the girls in the circle, one non-gifted member of the group stood behind as a safety in case anyone fell out.

This was their third attempt to move the tree that had fallen in the storm. The first two didn't fare well, though they learned quite a bit about timing and technique. They discovered it was best to start out holding hands. Doing so would allow them to build up enough energy they could then transfer to Zuri through the golden ethereal ropes only Addie could see. Once these were in place, Addie would give Aidan a nod. Aidan would then gently tap Zuri on the shoulder to let her know she could begin.

Even with the abnormally chilly June morning, sweat trickled down Lexi's spine, pooling at the small of her back. Justin, comfortable in the cool air, was still nursing a small wound on his arm from one of the prior training events. Fear had led him to jump in to assist, only to end up injured.

The men had prepared for the experiment by chopping off the wayward limbs of the fallen tree, leaving the trunk at Lexi's request. With all seven holding hands, the goal was to combine their unique skills in support of Zuri as she raised the tree from the ground, maneuvering it mid-air to a location prepared by Joe where he and Brandon could utilize the timber.

It wasn't so much that the task itself was too ambitious. It was the attempt to work together, harnessing their abilities for a common good, that made it potentially explosive. And each one felt ready.

Lexi was ready to offer protection should the tree fall during transport. Maddy, who could create a sense of calm in the most precarious environment, would work to keep the group, particularly Zuri, calm, hopefully allowing her strength to endure. Joanna's gift, the ability to see a person's past through touch, was more subtle and didn't directly translate to the exercise. Still, her presence, as they had discovered since finding one another, made all the difference in strengthening the group as a whole.

Of all the girls, Macie had the most to offer the exercise, other than Zuri. According to Addie's recollection of Oakley's comments, Macie could see into the future and, more notably, had telekinetic abilities. Despite her incredible powers, Gavin, her brother, remained cautious, shielding her from even a hint of overindulgent expectations. With a pen and paper in case she had an unexpected vision, Macie was encouraged, if it seemed fitting, to assist Zuri in moving the tree.

Zoey, on the other hand, carried a small degree of guilt that she couldn't offer anything more than her presence in closing the loop, which, of course, was essential.

Addie's objective was to better understand how the ropes of color maneuvered as they worked together and how these impacted their united abilities. She recalled the closed loop of colors when they rescued Lexi during the building collapse at Oakley's compound. If all went well, she desired to be able to explain her observations so the nerd-pack could analyze it all.

Aside from learning how to work together, the exercise also had a secondary goal. The previous two attempts had opened up their ability to seek someone at a great distance. It was something Zuri was capable of doing on her own. However, with the group, like a more powerful radio tower or satellite, her reach was exponentially farther. They knew they could find the eighth girl if they could harness it, but they had also become aware of someone else. It was a signature so different from the girls that they weren't yet able to grasp who or *what* it could be.

Maria and the others had theories, but there was nothing concrete.

Just as soon as they had settled their hearts and minds, the girls began to generate enough energy to release Zuri from the circle. With Addie's nod, Aidan touched Zuri's shoulder and whispered, "You're up."

Releasing hands, Zuri stepped forward into the circle. Colorful ropes began rotating around and through them as she stretched out her arms and then fingers, allowing the strands of colors to curl and wind about. Turning her focus to the fallen tree, it groaned and cracked as it rose from the ground.

A red and blue thread twisted around Zuri's left hand while a black strand wrapped around her right. Off in the distance, Addie watched as a shimmering tornado of colors raced toward them.

"I can see them. The colors from the north and south," Addie said. "Zuri, you have them in your grasp. Can you tell the difference between what you feel in your right hand versus your left?"

"It feels... it's like... like it has more weight to it. Like a heaviness. Hard to describe."

The black rope intertwining Zuri's fingers rapidly thickened. The thicker it grew, the more Addie could see it wasn't black at all. She focused all her effort on it until it became clear that it was a mix of all the colors. The entire light spectrum twirling and thriving. Initially, she believed the black rope was made of vengeance, pain, and fear. Dark and painful emotions. The more she observed, however, the more she was convinced it wasn't so malicious after all.

"These aren't dark emotions flowing from just one person," Addie's voice cracked. "It's like it's—"

"It's all our emotions combined," Macie quietly interjected.

There was a collective gasp as eyes flew to Macie. It was her first freeform spoken phrase, beyond the reading of a book, and it seemed to empower them all the more. With a burst of energy, Addie propelled their focus north, following the black vine. She could see in the distance, at its source, a brilliant crystalline stream that changed colors as it stretched out, morphing into all the colors combined.

"What do you see?" whispered Joe.

"It's... it's beautiful," Addie stammered. "Crystalline... a... a three-dimensional rainbow."

"I can feel her," said Zuri as the red and blue strands grew. "The eighth. She's not hurt like we thought. I think… I'm not sure... I see train tracks and water." Her face scrunched as she sought more detail.

"Joanna?" Zoey watched as the color drained from her face.

"She's not hurt," Joanna said in a hushed voice as her breathing grew shallow. "But she's in danger... she... she just won't let go."

Without warning, an explosion of light and heat sent a shockwave that knocked each and every girl backward. The heat stole their breath as the punch from the blast disoriented them. Without hesitation and less-affected by the eruption, their safeties jumped into action to ease the fall of each girl.

"What happened?" Justin shouted, his own voice dull and distant.

"Zuri, can you tell what happened?" Lexi called out, breathing heavy but clear-minded.

"I felt a pulse in the white light at the far end of the black rope," she replied, her head still spinning.

"It happened so fast," Adeline added. "Like a tsunami, it increased ten-fold as it rushed toward us."

"Whoever it is, they aren't like us," Macie offered, matter of fact. "They're... I don't know... some combination of *all* of us."

Gavin, kneeling beside her, asked, "What do you mean, all of you?"

She couldn't explain and the pressure inside her head and chest intensified at the thought.

"Stand back," Sheila called out, pushing past Gavin. "It's okay, honey. Just breathe." Glancing at Gavin, she said, "Let's get her inside to rest."

Maddy, shaken, followed them in as the rest struggled to grasp what took place.

"What do you think she meant?" Grant asked, holding Lexi's hand.

"It seems insane. Just doesn't make sense," Zoey said, rising with Justin's help.

"Zuri," Aidan asked, stretching his cramped legs out in the grass, "could you feel the person on the other end?"

Nodding, she quietly said, "Yes, but it was different. None of those emotions were hers."

"So it was definitely a woman?" Grant asked gently.

Nodding, she struggled to describe it. "I think so. It's usually just something that I know when I feel out for someone. But it was different. She can't do what we can, at least, that's what I sense. Yet somehow she feel's more..." She paused, trying to collect her thoughts. "I don't know. We need to try again so I can figure this out." Jumping to her feet, she stumbled over debris, grasping for support.

"Whoa, now. You guys are wiped out. Let's wait until you—" Aidan tried to be the voice of reason.

"No," Zuri pleaded, her voice sharp but her eyes gentle. "I need to do this now."

With a deep breath, Aidan resigned, "Fine, I—"

"Not yet," said Lexi, grabbing Zuri's hand. "Aidan's right. We need to rest, recover our strength, think this through."

Zuri's puppy dog eyes weren't as effective on her own sister.

Aidan looked up at Lexi. "Not to overstate the obvious, but we're not moving the tree today, right?"

Chapter 9
Breakers

"You need to listen to me, Dakota." Elias pleaded. He could see her mind was a million miles away. "Some of the others are talking. They're concerned you don't want to fight anymore."

"And?" she said in a hushed voice, staring through him.

"And they may try to…"

At his pause she pulled herself back to the present."They can't hurt me. They know what I'm capable of," she shot back, her voice low and distant.

"But it doesn't mean they *won't* try if they think you've turned."

"Seriously? Why? Because I want to rationally process the best strategy before pouncing on every human attempting to live a better life? I barely knew what real life was before all this, but I highly doubt society can go back to whatever it was overnight. If ever!"

Eli stared at her. She was right, but that didn't mean the most loyal Breakers wouldn't try and somehow hurt her or worse, use her to continue their mission of keeping the world on its knees.

"Does it even matter?" Dakota asked, jumping to her feet.

"Of course it matters. What are you..."

Brushing past him, she pulled open her bedroom door and made her way down the hall with Elias on her heels.

"Where are you going?" he demanded in a hushed but gruff voice, growing nervous as she headed toward headquarters. "Shouldn't we talk... Dakota?"

Pushing open the door, she noticed four people leaning over Levi's desk: two analysts, the medical officer, and the lead missions operator. "What's that?" she inquired as the room went silent.

Levi took a second too long to remove the image from his screen. She'd already taken notice of it.

"What is that?" she repeated, pushing past one of the analysts.

Levi swung around in his chair to face her, stammering, "I... we... we were just discussing the abnormal radar imaging in the Carolinas." Had it been almost any other day, she might have believed his innocent-like demeanor.

"Great. Pull it up and let's take a look."

His cheeks turned red as she nodded at the computer screen. Turning around, he quickly pulled up a secondary window with similar satellite imaging.

"Stop," Dakota commanded.

"I'm sorry?" Levi said, feigning ignorance as the hair on his neck stood up.

Grabbing the mouse, she clicked on the diminished tab at the bottom of his screen. When it popped up, the two maps sat side-by-side. One looked like their standard travel map with a path connecting their position in Florida with a fixed point in Pennsylvania. The second was the blueprint of a building marked with identifying annotations for a targeted room. Likely a communications room.

Dakota pointed at the screen. "What is *this*?" she asked, though she didn't wait for a reply. "It's a full mission brief with a timeline for two weeks from now."

Each one stood stiff, breathing shallow.

"Looks to me like this is the target we decided *not* to infiltrate."

"Not we, *you*. *You* decided against it!" Levi replied, his cheeks bright red and his voice trembling. "There's something going on beyond what we already know about VISP. We need to get up there and investigate."

Taking in their emboldened defiance, she had two options: agree and move forward to avoid risking a coup against her or refuse to allow it and risk the consequences. There was a deep burn in her chest. A feeling of darkness washed through her. She'd felt it before, but not to this extent. The burn prodded her to engage and she couldn't hold it back.

"So you're in charge now? You? A weak man that's never stepped outside that door? Never—"

"Dakota. Hey—" Elias touched her shoulder.

She rounded on him with fire in her eyes. "Don't touch me!" Her hand swiped away his and he felt a jolt of electricity at her touch.

She turned back to Levi, putting her face right in his. "You won't do a damn thing without my say-so."

"Or what?" Levi held her gaze, trying to hide his trembling hands.

In a flash of rage, Dakota grabbed hold of his shoulder. Immediately he felt a sizzling pain on his skin. He tried to jerk away, but her grip held him firmly in place.

"I don't think you want to know," she gruffly whispered. And with a last push of pain into his shoulder Dakota wrenched her hand away, stood tall with her shoulders back, and glared at the group. Silently, they trembled at the flickering light in her eyes emanating from behind her dark sunglasses. Fear washed through them as they'd never seen this side of her.

Eli had known her longer than any of them. He was only twenty-two when he caught her via his security feed sneaking into their storage. Patiently, he observed as she scoured the room until she saw the very camera he had been viewing her through. He watched as she pulled a small pad of paper out of her pocket and began drawing. Almost immediately, the camera lens cracked. Abandoning his post, he raced through the empty halls, out into the night, and to their shed. There she was, kneeling on the floor, hastily shoving pre-packaged crackers into her mouth while filling her bookbag with canned goods.

At the time, he couldn't understand how she had managed to break the camera without touching it. He only knew there was something special about her.

As he watched Dakota, now fierce and commanding, he knew something had changed. In fact, she had been changing over the past year. Night terrors. Shivers in ninety-degree heat.

Now, something about her entire being had shifted. Whatever it was, she was not the same person she had been even a few days ago.

Dakota gave one last look at Levi before walking out of the room. Eli knew where she was going. Out to the water. It was a place of peace for her. The slight hint of regret in her eye when her final gaze landed on him told him she knew she'd gone too far.

Sanford, NC 

Joanna sat on the swing under the pecan tree, imagining the person she could feel on the other end of the tether. It seemed so different from how the others described their connections with one another. Everyone else seemed to have felt pain or discomfort in between them. Maybe this woman wasn't in crisis. Maybe she was actually happy where she was.

That thought somewhat faded as she felt a different sort of sensation. Not joy, but… anger? She was angry.

Almost menacingly so.

Was she in need of help? Should they go get her now?

Or is she… Joanna didn't want to imagine the worst. But maybe they shouldn't find her.

They had been paired for reasons they didn't yet understand. The running theory was that when they were first abducted as children, they were paired up during the experiments, and this pairing inexplicably linked them to one another. Lexi to Zoey. Madison to Adeline. Macie to Zuri. A theory that seemed more plausible as they watched Macie and Adeline's connection grow after their shared trauma under Oakley's hand.

Until now, Joanna had felt little of whomever she was tied to.

Is it right to uproot this woman's life if she's in a safe place? Is it fair to pull her away from a life that's comfortable? Do we have any right to thrust her into our chaos, fearful of being captured or imprisoned? Or, is she someone we may not want around.

Her chest tightened at the thought. She didn't even want to consider it. Wouldn't.

Looking across the field at Brandon, she smiled. He truly was a source of happiness and peace, much like her sister Addie and the incredible joy of being reunited. Regardless, there was a void.

Maybe I just want to find a reason to save her so we can be together. Maybe we're being shortsighted. Maybe I'm being selfish.

Without realizing it, Joanna found herself standing at the shop entrance. Pushing it open, she found the nerd-pack working on various projects.

"Joanna?" Maria asked, noticing her rigid stance and distant look.

"I think we need to stop attempting to connect with her... to leave her alone."

Chapter 10
Discussion

"Devil's argument," said Gavin. "First, let me clarify where we're at."

For the first time since all of this began, the question wasn't *how* to rescue one of their sisters, but *should* they attempt a rescue?

"We're saying that maybe she's in a safe place. Possibly happy. And maybe even with a gift not quite strong enough to think it's anything more than heightened intuition. Correct?"

"Yes," said Joanna, looking around the shop at everyone gathered.

"We know it's been difficult to reach this individual, right?" he said, pausing for approval. "Well, couldn't it also be said that maybe she's strong enough to design a barrier to remain hidden? After all, we did experience what can only be described as a reverse surge of energy the other day in the gazebo, right?"

"I don't think that surge came from her, though," said Zuri. "I mean, I guess it could have, but I could feel two distinct lines pulling me in opposite directions. It felt like that blast originated from the unknown source, not from her."

"Agreed," Addie interjected. "I'm fairly certain what I saw came from the black strand."

"I see what you're saying—" Gavin started.

"I think I know where Gavin's going with this," Maria chimed in. "Even if the eighth didn't produce that surge, when it was just Zuri straight out of her induced coma, she was still strong enough to feel out for Lexi and Zoey. With all of you combined, her reach is a force to be reckoned with. Even if the eighth's gift is weak, just a regular person like me, you'd be able to find her. Yet, somehow, she's keeping you at bay. Seems it would take a lot of energy on her end to keep Zuri, let alone all of you together, from seeing her clearly."

"First, you're not a regular person, Maria. You are a force!" Addie laughed. "But you have a point," she added. "Wouldn't we want to have her here with us then? If she is that strong?"

"Whether she's strong or not, maybe she doesn't want her gifts," Grant offered. "Or… like Joanna said, she might be happy where she is. Who are we to rob her of that?"

"Or maybe," Aidan said from the back of the room, "it could be she's not like you. Maybe she's gone to the dark side, Vader-style."

His words rang out in the silence of the room. A thought only Joanna had considered, but wasn't ready to share.

Dakota stepped hard and fast through the woods. If steam could come from her ears, she imagined it would scorch leaf and limb as she passed. With red cheeks and a rising heart rate, she fumed at the traitorous actions of her team. *Have people always been this unfaithful? I may not have had a normal childhood, but to just go behind someone's back like that?*

Just like when she was a child, they wanted to hurt her, confine her, use her. *They aren't my family. All these years I believed they cared about me, but I've been nothing more than a tool.*

She woke up that morning even more furious. Everything she'd done. For them. For their cause.

On autopilot, her march through the forest brought her to the beach. The Atlantic spread dark and wide before her as a storm cell raged off the coast. It looked as beautiful as it did menacing, with flashes of lightning and a distant water spout moving north. Dakota hardly felt either the wind or the rain on her skin from her vantage point. Clenching her fists, she wanted to feel the needling pain of driving rain and the surge of wind too forceful to stand.

She never had the capability of altering biological or atmospheric things, but burning vibration on her skin and intense pressure in her brain was fueling a rage within her. Without thinking, she pulled out her notepad and pencil and began to sketch out the scene. She drew herself standing on the beach, waves lapping against her knees. She penciled palm trees bent and broken and lying on the ground. She sketched the pier in the distance being washed away. Her ferocity ripped the wet page with the sharpened granite.

Staring at the storm in the distance, she focused all her attention on the scene playing out before her. Clenching her notebook in one hand, she slammed her hand on the image and swiped across it with a ferociousness that tore and ripped the page further.

The action amplified the pressure in her brain, squeezing like a vice. Her hands flew to the sides of her head, pressing in on her temples, her vision began to blur as the pain intensified.

Without warning, a furious wind sent her flailing back onto her right arm, bending her forearm at an angle it wasn't meant to. The snap of her arm, along with the searing pain shooting from her head down her spine, was more than she could handle.

Her scream, however, was drowned out by the incoming pelting rain and the crashing waves. Scrambling up the embankment, she pressed behind a fallen palm tree, hoping to block the onslaught.

As she listened to the pier snap into pieces by the waves, her rage and pain turned to fear, warping her view as her surroundings grew darker and her hearing muffled as if the waves were overcoming her. That's when she saw them, cinnamon-colored eyes sparkling so bright they cut through the deafening darkness.

She whimpered as her mind shouted, *Help me! Please, someone. Help me.*

Sanford, NC 

Joanna sat beside Brandon, quietly listening in on the gang's back-and-forth. They had taken their discussion into the house so Maria could make her famous paninis. Trying to stay engaged, her skin prickled against the blanket she was wrapped in. Cautiously rubbing her arm, it began to sting as her friends' words morphed into the cacophonous sound of waves rushing in.

Grabbing her left arm and letting out a high-pitched gasp, Joanna jolted upright, catching Brandon off-guard.

"Joanna? What's going on?" Brandon's voice was distant and muffled, like a whisper being swallowed by the wind.

She felt loving hands grab hold of her stinging skin as the cold, harshness of East Coast waves washed over her body. The others panicked as her body seized at the crackling flash of lightning so bright it imprinted a ghostly set of silver crystalline eyes into her mind.

"It's... it's her!" Joanna choked out. "I can see her. She's... she's by the water. She's hurt!"

Zuri, pushing through the crowd, grabbed Joanna's hand. Instantly she felt the prickling rain, the cold water, and the crystalline eyes engulf her.

"The walls have come down," whispered Aidan, his eyes aglow with an amber glimmer bright enough to refract crystal sparkles across the walls.

Maddy gasped at the sight, which caused the others to shift their focus from Zuri and Joanna to the unexpected source of light.

"Aidan?" Lexi asked, touching the side of his face as Zoey carefully removed the sunglasses he had been wearing more and more as of late. "How long have you known?"

Chapter 11
Confrontation

Getting into his office was easier than she anticipated. While Dr. Harold was meeting with the intel analysts, she waited less than patiently for his assistant to go to lunch. Maya only had a handful of minutes. Regardless, she fought the urge to toss the room as she searched for anything that would clue her in on what Dr. Harold was actually working on.

She had never snooped in either his or Director Jones' office before but knew that waiting for him to be forthright would never happen. As she searched every shelf, binder, and drawer with no luck, Maya wondered if maybe he kept everything incriminating offsite. Or that maybe she was wrong altogether.

Her heart was telling her she wasn't wrong about this. Aidan was alive. For the first time ever it was as if she was starting to feel him out there.

Reaching for the bottom-most drawer of the final filing cabinet, her hand met resistance from an engaged lock. Her head swiveled, scouring the room in search of a key, sure he would have had it on his person.

"Okay, the hard way then." Maya had just grabbed hold of a paperclip when she heard a click. Her breath hitched in her throat as her eyes flicked to the door, frozen as she waited for the handle to turn. When nothing happened, she went back to work on the filing cabinet. Something was off. The keyhole was now horizontal. Her eyes saw a hint of purple flicker and she leaned back, blinking a few times to clear her eyes. *Great, what am I having a stroke?*

When she bent forward again to insert the paperclip the lock was now horizontal. *I could've sworn it was vertical only seconds before. I know it was.*

Tentatively reaching for the handle, she gave it a light tug and the drawer opened.

Shaking off her confusion she took a deep breath and began skimming the headings of each folder. They were all labeled with the names of flowers: Rose, Calla Lily, Lantana, Iris, Oleander, Valley Lily, etc.

What is this? she wondered, thumbing from one to the next.

It didn't make sense. Why would he have a drawer full of folders about plants? She pulled out the one labeled Calla Lily and opened it to find several photos. The first was a baby. The second of a toddler. The final photo was of a pixelated woman, the sort of picture quality their drones could achieve. The baby photo triggered a memory. Shaking, she pulled the photo from the folder and studied it.

It couldn't be.

She imagined herself holding this newborn girl, those lifeless fingers curled into a ball as her rosy skin faded to gray. Maya recalled the feeling of indecision when she brought the listless child into the nursery. She had been pregnant with Aidan at the time, and the horror of holding a lost little soul had been overwhelming. She should've been washing the baby, preparing her for the arrival of morgue personnel. Instead, she sat quietly with the still child.

Putting her lips to the baby's head, tears spilled over her cheeks. Before lifting her lips, Maya felt a shudder. Pulling back, she gasped at the sight of two beautifully bright diamond eyes seeking her own.

It didn't make sense. The baby had passed over thirty minutes prior. Yet there she was, squeezing her little fingers and nuzzling at Maya's chest for food.

It was a miracle. The baby girl was a miracle.

Maya wiped the sting from her eyes and examined the first document in the folder containing the girl's name, Zuriella, birthdate 2009, parents' names and so on. All familiar. She remembered the mother Veronica, heart broken, quiet sobs wracking her chest as she cradled her lost daughter. Then the fierce joy when Maya brought the baby back to her. Alive.

Placing the folder on the desk, she grabbed the next one titled Lantana. Once again, the baby photo was familiar, but the other two images she'd only witnessed in her dreams. The child's name was Adeline. Born April 9th, 2003. She remembered that time frame because that was the first miscarriage she had endured. The first of several. Maya had lost her first child four months into her pregnancy in May of that year. Right after

Adeline was born.

Her breath quickened as she removed the third file: Rose. The baby's name was Alexi, born in 2006, once again just prior to another one of her own failed pregnancies.

Her cheeks flushed and the air grew thick as she opened one folder after another. Each baby she recalled, and all of them were born at a time correlating with one of her own heartbreaking pregnancies.

Maya sat staring at the final folder in the cabinet. Eight folders sat on the desk beside her. Eight folders, eight babies, and all born during the exact time frames she had miscarried, all except the final two: Zuriella and Macie.

She hesitated to grab hold of the ninth folder, sensing in her bones that it was somehow different. With trembling, clammy fingers, she grabbed hold of it. Her eyes blurred with tears the moment she opened the cover to see the most beautiful, fiery-haired baby boy looking back at her. Once again, three photos. The first two she knew well. But it was the pixelated adult image of the boy she once knew that choked in her throat. A man she had never set eyes upon but knew like a parent deep in her gut.

Aidan.

5:30 p.m.

"MJ? MJ, you okay?" Director Harold was snapping his fingers in front of her face. "Maya? Can you hear me?" Her eyes were red and glazed over, focused on something distant and unseen. Leaning close and checking for air, he gasped at the shimmer emanating from her irises, bright enough to see through her tinted glasses. Both excitement and fear raced like a shiver up his spine.

She'd been holding in her rage since discovering the files. Though she wanted nothing more than to confront him with the first sharp object she could find, she restrained herself. But the moment he walked into the briefing room, her adrenaline rushed to her brain, causing her to freeze in place like icy waters in a blizzard.

However, it wasn't until it was her turn to brief the group that anyone realized something was off with her. After a quick check from the medic, he ordered, "Grab her arm. Let's bring her to the med bay."

Director Harold followed close behind. Maya was able to walk, though was clearly unaware of her surroundings.

Knowing what the medics were likely to find when they examined her, Dr. Harold stepped in front of them asserting, "Her apartment is closer. Let's bring her there instead." He wasn't ready to give up what he had waited so patiently for.

Confused, the aide replied, "Sir, something's clearly wrong. We've got to..."

"I'm aware. I'm a doctor, first and foremost. Her room is up here on the right, so let's get her in there, lay her down, and I'll do an assessment." Thinking quickly, he added, "Maya's been under a lot of stress lately. It's likely she just needs to rest. If I think it's more, I'll have her brought to the med bay for further examination."

The medic slowly shook his head then followed orders. Arriving at Maya's room, they used the keycard dangling from her pocket to enter. Once inside, they immediately laid her on the couch.

"Sir, are you sure about this? We can easily—"

"I've got it from here, thank you," said Dr. Harold, waving them off. "Please close the door on your way out. She needs rest." When the door clicked, he sat on the coffee table and stared. She was lying there, hands crossed on her stomach, motionless. Her eyes, however, were wide open behind the tinted glasses.

"Maya, can you hear me? It's Dr. Harold. If you can hear me, blink." No movement. Carefully he removed her glasses. Like a giddy child he smiled at the sight of her sparkling eyes. Flashing a light in each, he waited for her pupils to contract, but they held as large black saucers surrounded by glistening rainbow colors.

"Your pulse is steady and your breathing regular," he said, assessing the rest of her. "You don't seem to be in any pain."

Excitement coursed through his veins. He had waited for so long. For a time he thought maybe he had been wrong, but now. This was confirmation that she was somehow intertwined with his work all those years ago.

Too provoked to stay seated, he walked the room in search of anything that might clue him in to who or what she really was, half-heartedly observing her minimalist life. The only personal touch was a photo of her with her son on a shelf beside the TV.

Pulling a thick book from the same shelf, he stepped back to the coffee table, letting it drop with a violent thud on the wooden top. She didn't flinch, just laid there, seemingly comatose.

"You know, I never could've imagined years ago that we'd one day be working together again like this," he said, glancing at her as the sunlight streamed in, warming his face. "I know you had a lot of questions that I never answered that last year before I retired. "But if you knew what I did for you, you'd thank me."

Snapping his fingers in front of her eyes and noting her lack of awareness, the doctor continued his walk.

"When I left the hospital, I had such great plans. My research was everything. Any scientist or physician worth their salt would have agreed. The opportunity to enhance the human brain? Make great strides for humankind? It was right at my fingertips." His voice sounded forlorn. "Then it wasn't," he growled, clenching his fists just thinking about all the work he'd done, only to have it ripped away.

"I never planned to hurt any of them. If they hadn't been taken from me, they would've lived incredible lives. Maybe the grid would've never failed. They'd all be healthy and happy and doing unimaginable things in this world. *For this world!*" Swinging his arm, he swiped everything off the shelf, including the frame with Maya and her son, which shattered on the floor.

Maya lay still on the couch—no acknowledgment of his outburst.

He took a steadying breath. "Your mom though, she was an angel. I went back and forth between you. But with you having a son and considering joining the military, it made more sense to select Josephine." Stepping over the debris on the floor, he paced, lost in his monologue.

"So see?" he continued. "You should be thankful you got to spend the years with your son that you did. I reasoned that if it were you who gave the gift of life to Zuriella that day, it would likely be in your bloodline, and of course, if your mother didn't have it, I would've come back for you. Brought you in on something so incredible. Something I *knew* you'd agree to. I mean, look, you're here! When I sent Jones for you, I knew you'd want to be part of something bigger than yourself."

Reaching down, he picked up the broken frame. "Especially after your son… well. I would never have wished you to lose a child by any means." Dr. Harold removed the last bits of broken glass and put the frame back on the shelf.

Cleaning up the rest of the glass, he dumped it in the garbage can. "Those girls were my everything. My path to greatness. Losing them..." he sighed, "losing them devastated me. You need to know. I loved those girls like my own children. I only ever wanted to see them flourish. Now, perhaps, I'll get that chance once again. When you help me bring them back, they'll be my redemption. They'll help us revive society. You can't tell me they aren't longing to live in a safe place with fresh food and water. Saviors of the world! And, of course, they'd have each other. And you."

He turned his back to the room, looking out the window at the deadened landscape. "If nothing else, I have you. You hide your eyes behind those glasses, but I know. The crystalline shimmer in a certain light. Your sixth sense about people and the weather and just about everything, really. To be honest, I'm surprised. I mean, isn't there such a thing as a mother's intuition? Or did the supposed loss of him short-circuit that connection? I thought about telling you many times but knew you'd want to leave. Obviously, I couldn't have that."

Leaning on the windowsill, he paused, grit his teeth and said, "Jones was a traitor to our cause. He helped bring your son here along with the others, trying to save Calla Lily and Rose. If it weren't for your seclusion, which was for your protection, he might've ruined everything had the two of you crossed paths that day."

Feeling a warmth on his neck, Dr. Harold was shaken from

his reflection. Turning, he saw Maya standing mere inches away with a glare in her eyes radiating with color. Her face was cherry-red, and her voice gruff as she whispered, "Get a good look, doctor? It's the last time you'll see anything in my eyes."

In a move he didn't anticipate, Maya swung the heavy book Dr. Harold had left on the table, smashing it over the side of his head. "Time for you to protect yourself, you son of a bitch."

Chapter 12
The Beginning

Aidan said he needed to eat before getting in too deep. In truth, he just wanted time to think. Having powers is something he had always wished for as a kid. Every little boy wanted to be Superman or Thor. Over the past year, he began to wonder if it could be possible. Regardless, he was convinced he was imagining things and kept those thoughts to himself.

His eyes had given him away in the end.

Not to mention, he wasn't able to do what the women did. They were beyond exceptional.

He spent the afternoon delaying the inevitable. First, he went for a run. Next, he needed a shower. Soon after, he followed with a nap. When he couldn't put it off any longer, Aidan made himself a sandwich and sat in the living room. No one pushed him to speak, though their deep sighs, sideways glances, and subliminal energy shift spoke loud and clear. Which, incidentally, he could feel. He'd felt it from that first day he'd met Zuri. Walking in circles in the foyer of VISP, he felt it—the energy flowing from her. Since then, he knew something deep within had come to life.

He knew they were waiting for him to begin, but he hadn't the faintest clue where to start.

"Fire away, friends," Aidan said in a poor attempt at humor, his eyes telling a different story.

No one wanted to start. Glancing around the room, he was just about to crack another half-hearted joke when Maria broke the silence. "How long?"

"Have I been special? My mama said I was born special." He smiled, though Maria didn't. Clearing his throat, he continued, "Uh, honestly, I'm not sure. I noticed my sparkling eyes becoming more sparkly around the time we found Adeline and Joanna."

Zoey added, "Before that, when it was just the three of us, I remember you'd throw out dumb jokes about magic eyes and super-sight, always humorously speculating about something. But what you joked about turned out to be true."

"It could also be that my jokes and speculation are a sign of observational brilliance." Looking down his nose at her, he added, "And that I'm right even when I'm not yet aware of my rightness."

"Uh-huh. Yeah, you know what? No," Zoey replied, shaking her head.

Zuri chimed in, "I could tell something was different about you every time you touched my skin, like holding my arm or my hand." She gently placed her hand on his. "Your energy isn't like the other men. It's not like ours either," she said, looking at the others in the room. "I can feel it now. It's a less rapid vibration than when I touch Lexi, but more significant than touching Justin. It's actually... a cross between them? It's hard to describe. Whatever it is, the electricity is definitely powerful."

"Addie?" said Grant, chiming in. "What do his colors look like? Is there any difference there?"

Sitting up straight in her chair with head tilted slightly as if already deep in thought, she said, "Each of you have your own colors that sort of wrap around you, which I've grown to associate with your personalities. The stronger your emotions, the brighter the colors. However, they're fluid, meaning they shift with your moods. Aidan has a strong pink, excuse me, salmon color, which I associate with joy and excitement. Lately, though, I've noticed a few threads of blue intertwined with the pink, and..."

When her voice trailed off, Aidan leaned forward. "And what?"

"It's not a thread or a rope-like strand, but there's a purple hue, like a smudge or a fog that tends to hover near you. The more blue threads there are, the stronger the purple."

"What's the blue mean?" Joe asked.

"Sadness," Joanna said in a hushed voice.

"Maybe blue means something different with me. I don't really get sad," Aidan cut in, his voice thin and without conviction.

"Okay, so what's purple mean?" Maddy said, motioning the crew to move it along.

Though Aidan usually ate it up, she could see he was

struggling with being the center of attention this time.

"Typically, I see purple when someone is both angry and sad. The red and blue vines wrap around each other, squeezing tighter until those emotions radiate a purple hue. But this? This is a stand-alone color. It presents itself similarly to how inanimate objects appear in my alt-vision."

"Alt-vision?" asked Justin.

"It's what I've started calling what I see without the use of my eyes. Alternate vision."

"That's so cool," Aidan said, wide-eyed with excitement. Momentarily forgetting the purpose of their discussion.

"This purple hue you see, does it have a particular shape?" Joe usually didn't get involved in these conversations, choosing to observe instead. Lexi, noticing his pointed question, knew more than most how much he loved Aidan like a little brother, even if he would never admit it.

"I… I..." Addie glanced around the room, unsure how they would take what she had to say.

"It's okay, Addie," whispered Zuri, reaching over and wrapping her pinky around Adeline's.

"This might sound crazy, but I think it's a person. Or what used to be."

"Like a ghost?" Aidan blurted out, sitting up straight, excited at the prospect of seeing apparitions.

"Maybe," Addie gently replied. "It's not just the color or shape. There's a feeling I get when I see it. A sort of warmth."

"Like love?" Macie asked of her own volition, causing the group to fall eerily silent.

Addie, locking eyes with her, nodded slowly. "I think so. Who or whatever it is feels protective."

Aidan sat back. Memories of his memé filtered through his mind. In every image, she wore something purple. A loose sweater or dangly earrings. Purple Crocs to match the violet bangles on her wrist.

"Purple is the color of an artist—someone a little eccentric at times. Spiritual even," Joanna added. She and Addie were familiar with things like that, not just since Addie's gift had come about, but even earlier on it had been an interest of theirs.

"I mean, she definitely could've been considered eccentric." Aidan laughed, shaking his head.

"Who are you talking about?" Zoey asked him.

Swallowing the lump in his throat, he said, "My memé. My mother's mom. She loved that color. Always wearing it in some way." He looked up at Addie. "I mean, can you see her now?"

"Yes. The outline is growing brighter as you speak." Everyone stared at the space around him, hoping for a glimpse of someone or something to feel. "Can anyone else sense it?" Addie wondered, holding her breath. No one answered.

"Maybe this is only something you can see," said Lexi. "Like the ropes and colors."

"Other than uncanny speculation," Justin cut in, "is there anything else, anything different you've noticed about yourself?"

"Besides my incredibly good looks?"

"Aidan," said Joe, straight-faced.

"Well, I mean, I don't see dead people. So there's that."

"I think he's able to sense just beyond what the rest of us can," Zuri offered, squinting as she stared at him. "I've noticed when we're talking about something we can feel or see, it's like he can tell us what it means."

"Enhance what we're doing?" Maddy wondered.

They looked directly at him as if waiting for a response. The silence brought by the question was interrupted by Maria. With raised eyebrows, she asked, "Aidan, are you up for some practicing of your own?"

"Well," he said, huffing and sliding his feet back and forth, feigning lack of interest. "I guess. I mean, if my awesomeness can make you guys more awesome, well, a man's gotta do what a man's gotta do." He stood up stretching his body as if he didn't want to. Then stepped toward the kitchen before turning back. "So there's one last question I know you've been dying to ask. Am I now a Warlock?"

Pausing for dramatic effect, he continued, "The answer is an emphatic *YES!*"

Chapter 13
Time to Leave

VISP | June 14, 2030 | 7:00 p.m.

Years of fantasizing about leaving didn't measure up to the act of doing it. Maya had jogged the grounds daily since her arrival years ago. She knew the schedule of the maintenance crew and had grown friendly with all those whose paths she crossed regularly. Everyone was familiar and everything monotonous.

She had also taken note of the unwatched stretches at various points across the compound where she would be alone.

In her daydreaming, her adrenaline would skyrocket at the thought of stepping beyond the compound walls. Now, here she stood, preparing to do it. It was real this time. And so was the fear gripping her heart.

You can do this, Maya. Just breathe.

Inhaling the evening air, she paused to scan the area. She wore workout clothes so prying eyes would think she was out for her evening jog and nothing more. The backpack, however, was an odd addition to anyone used to seeing her, but most people don't catch such details in the moment. Regardless, she planned to play it off as additional weight to her run, hoping to lose a few pounds. It was the best she could come up with.

"Hey Maya, how ya feeling?" James, one of the analyst guys, stopped to ask.

"I'm good! No issues here." Her voice was too high pitched and she cleared her throat.

"Should you be jogging after what happened earlier?" His concerned questioning tone surprised her. She'd passed him a million times over the years with nothing more than a cursory nod or smile.

"Yeah, no, I'm fine. Just a little stressed. That's why I'm out here, jogging. Decompress you know."

He nodded again and began walking past, "Well take it easy." His words hung in the air as she stared after him.

She needed to move before he said anything to anyone about her.

If she was lucky, Dr. Harold would still be out cold on the floor in her room. She'd packed the necessities and swung by the cafeteria for some provisions. Paranoid, she felt everyone was watching her. In reality, it was another day in purgatory. Even James barely cared enough to push the issue of resting after her fall out earlier.

Maya had memorized the best routes to Sanford, N.C., but after all these years, had no idea what was truly going on in the world. If she had to walk the entire way, it would take her at least a week, especially without knowing who or what she might have to hide from. And she highly doubted she'd find a working vehicle. Anticipating and accepting the worst possible scenario was the only way she knew she'd survive it.

Of course, the worst outcome was death. Short of that, it was that VISP would come after her, which she knew they would after attacking their fearless leader.

"Well, what's a little fear of death when it comes to your kid right?" she said under her breath. "Talking to myself probably isn't a good sign. I haven't even left the compound yet!"

She made her way to the furthest compound wall. Standing there assessing the best way to climb over it, a tingle shimmied up her spine.

"Maya?" His voice was low and her heart stopped at the sound of it.

Dr. Harold stepped from the Gator only twenty feet away. Even in the evening light, she could see dried blood on his white shirt collar.

Standing firm, she watched his LSO, Lead Security Officer, Commander Fisher, and two other guards appear and encircle her.

"Is this you trying to leave?"

"Is this you trying to stop me?" Her eyes flicked back and forth between him and the others.

"We never imprisoned you. You came here on your terms."

"And I'm now leaving on my terms."

"Where do you think you'll go? There's nothing out there for you anymore. Your son—"

"Do *not* talk to me about *my* son," she growled, fists clenched.

Dr. Harold stepped forward, palms out. "You're needed here. You're a vital part of our success."

"Success? In what exactly? I've been here for years and I'm only now starting to understand what you do here."

"We find special people. Like you. We can't bring our world back without each of us, including you, playing our part."

"The world is dead. The world we knew is gone," she said, breathing heavily. "What exactly is our goal? I've seen nothing that leads me to believe we're doing anything to bring it all back. And it can't be about money. Money is meaningless! So that leaves us with what? Power? Control?"

She could tell he wanted to share something as he shifted his eyes toward his entourage. There was something he couldn't say in front of them.

"How could you not tell me he was alive?" Maya's cheeks turned blotchy red as she squeezed her fists all the more tightly. She knew he didn't want to have this conversation in front of anyone else. "All these years I believed he was dead. You led me to believe he died in that accident. What kind of monster are you?"

"Let's go back inside," he said, reaching out to her. "I'll explain everything."

"No! Now. Right now! Go on. You'll explain why we had to go into the bunker. We all know it wasn't an imminent bomb threat. That wouldn't have kept us down there for the last ten months." Maya took a deep breath, but her sight was beginning to narrow and cloud over. "How could you? How could you take me from my son?"

"I did what I thought was right!" Dr. Harold shot back, cold and crass.

"My son is out there. Alive. And I'm willing to bet he's at one of the locations you've had me forecasting for. After all, there are only so many interesting things out there, at least after what you've done to the world."

"I didn't do this!" His arm swept the horizon. "I didn't make the mess. I'm the one trying to clean it up!"

Growing dizzy, Maya turned to see Commander Fisher directly behind her with a syringe. She had been too incensed to feel the needle enter her arm and knew she was fading fast.

"Who are they?" she said, legs wobbling.

"Who?"

"The people... the ones you're looking for. Who are they? What... what do you want?"

He stepped close as her knees began to buckle and pulled her to his side. Low on his breath he whispered in her ear, "I'm surprised you don't know. It was you who made them. Wasn't it?"

"Made?" Her knees gave way and he held her tighter.

"Those children. Those babies you held so close right out of the womb." Dr. Harold's face began to twist in her vision as the drugs they injected spread through her bloodstream. "I found the drawer unlocked in my office. I know you've seen them. The files on the girls. On your son." He took a breath. "I pulled your medical records and, for the first time... after all this time... it finally clicked."

Her dead weight had Dr. Harold slowly lay her to the ground. Visions of babies cooing in her arms flashed in her mind. "I don't understand."

"You were pregnant."

She struggled to listen as he put the pieces together.

Something she'd noticed that afternoon when she discovered the timeline but couldn't quite grasp the relevance.

"There's work yet to be done to understand the details, but there's a definite connection. You. And if you think about it, all of this is really *your* doing," he said, glancing out to the barren trees that should've been filled with greenery. Kneeling beside her, he pressed his lips against her ear, ensuring she could hear his every word. "I believe, Maya, that you're the reason those babies had gifts. You were pregnant during each and every one of their births. You lost each of your own babies shortly after holding those newborns. All but Aidan."

Squeezing her arms and pulling her even closer, he said, "If I had truly known from the start that it was you, I would never have taken Josephine." He clarified, "I would've taken you… and your son."

At the mention of her son, adrenaline coursed through her veins. With eyes lightly shimmering, Maya's head snapped up along with her hand, which made sudden and violent contact with Dr. Harold's chest. She watched as his body flew away like a rag doll, hitting the ground several feet away and hard, though not enough to knock him out. As her eyes fluttered closed, she heard his pained voice say, "Bring her to nineteen. We have some work to do."

Chapter 14
Purgatory

Dakota only partially listened to their final briefing in preparation for their trip the next day. She was preoccupied with how she had manipulated the weather. No one knew how she had broken her arm. She simply claimed to have tripped on that hike two weeks prior. No one had any reason to question it.

She already knew the plan. They were to make their way to Pennsylvania over the next two days. They planned to camp outside the target location to do some reconnaissance before infiltrating and disabling VISP's communications. Typically, this involved confiscating anything that could be used for their own benefit. The plan had changed slightly with her arm now immobile, though being left-handed meant she could still draw if the need arose.

Staring off, a pressure began building behind her eyes. Leaning forward, she touched her head with her hand, attempting to massage away the impending headache.

"Dakota? You okay?" Elias asked, taking notes.

"Yeah, I..." Before she could finish, a wave of electricity tore up her spine while an image of a trapped woman, scared and enraged, burned into her mind. Screaming in pain, Dakota slid from the chair onto the floor.

"Help! Something's wrong!" Elias grabbed her beneath her arms and pulled her away from the table. "Dakota? Hey Dakota, can you hear me?"

She could hear everything. See everything. Present and imagined. Flashing behind her eyes were so many faces. Faces she had only witnessed in her dreams now passed like a carousel in her mind. And full of agony. So much pain coursing through her entire body.

Elias, squeezing her hand in panic at the sound of her whimpering, whispered, "Hey, I'm here. Everything's gonna be okay."

Her wide-open but motionless eyes cut through him. Watching his leader in a state of helplessness he had never witnessed before shook him to the core. "Everyone out! Close the door!"

Sanford, NC 

The living room went from laughter at Aidan's obnoxious storytelling to dead silence.

"What's going on?" said Joe, taking in the odd scene. Their

blank stares gave him chills.

"Her heart rate is high," said Grant, checking Lexi's pulse. "Lexi? Can you hear me?"

Justin, grabbing Zoey by the shoulders, shook her gently. "Where are you Zoe? What's happening?"

Without a sound, the girls, one by one, curled up in the fetal position, wincing in pain. Aidan could feel the crushing weight they were experiencing, though remained physically unaffected.

Brandon reached Joanna just as her body slid to the floor. He managed to get his hand under her head, pulling her into his arms. "What's going on?" Scouring the room and then the length of her body with his eyes, he noticed that her shirt had ridden up as she slid, revealing a bright red patch on her stomach. "What on earth..."

"It's happening again," Joe muttered, staring at her red skin.

Aidan followed Joe's line of sight and gently pulled Zuri's shirt an inch or so up from her waistband. He watched as bright red vines slowly crept across her abdomen. "No, no, no!"

Aidan looked across the spread of bodies huddled on the floor. He could feel the electricity coursing through the room. He felt it course through their bodies and even into his own. Grasping Zuri's hand, he instantly felt the connection tying them all together.

I can see her.

The woman had more creases lining her face and a few silver highlights running through her auburn hair. Still, Aidan knew her immediately with an ache in his heart that undeniably confirmed their connection.

VISP  

Staring down at Maya inside the glass chamber, her eyes burned into his. "Subconjunctival hemorrhaging. Evident in both eyes." Blood vessels had ruptured, making her glare that much more intense. Her bloodshot eyes, however, were nothing compared to the bruising that had formed in relation to the significant pressure they'd put on her body.

Turning away from her glare, he felt a tug at his heart. He'd never intended things to spin out of control like this, hoping instead that finding the girls would remove the necessity for it. That, and, until a few weeks ago he hadn't seen anything to suggest she had any additional abilities vital to his mission. He assumed that either Maya or her mother had been the catalyst for the gifts but not necessarily gifted themselves.

The room held the glass container that once imprisoned Lexi. Unlike the lab down in D4, where Zuri was held, the nineteenth floor hadn't been fully destroyed. Plus, it was closer to Dr. Harold's office. The two other doctors working with him, Dr. Saylor, a biologist, and Dr. Hutchens, a neurologist, had never worked directly with Lexi and Zuri, but had been tasked to study the data gleaned from the girls. Their recent promotion, however, changed all that.

"Sir, this is incredible," Dr. Hutchens said, in awe of the new data. "We've increased the atmospheric pressure tenfold, which should create more than just the bruising we see on her body. Essentially, it's as though we've placed an adolescent elephant of three hundred pounds on the subject's body."

"Enough to break bones," Dr. Saylor added, battling a sense of guilt. "Yet apart from the ecchymosis bruising and some hematomas, her body is not responding in what would be considered standard duress to it."

Dr. Saylor and Maya had become friends over the years. She'd always been in awe of how on-point Maya's forecasts were. What they were doing to her felt wrong.

"Okay, let's increase pressure again by ten pascals." Dr. Harold's tone was professional and cold, as if he was talking about increasing pressure on a block of wood.

"Ten, sir?" Dr. Saylor asked, rubbing her forehead.

Catching the flutter in her voice, he turned. "Something wrong, Dr. Saylor?"

"No, sir. Just… wanted to make sure I heard you correctly."

"You did."

Turning back to her computer, Dr. Saylor increased the pressure. Within seconds Maya's body responded ever so slightly. It was both intriguing and devastating what Maya was capable of withstanding, and she knew that if it was her in that glass unit, she would have already expired. "Heart rate increasing. One-fifty-five over eighty-nine," she said.

"Okay, let's see if she can adjust again." Dr. Harold was notably pleased that Maya was doing so well.

"Oxygen level eighty-eight." Dr. Hutchens' eyes were glued to his tablet. "Eighty-five and dropping fast."

"Sir, maybe we should let her rest," Dr. Saylor advised, her hands hovering over the keyboard, ready to cancel the testing.

"Hold steady. I want to see if she can adjust."

"Seventy-nine, sir. She's probably going to lose consciousness," Dr. Hutchens added.

"Do you smell that?" asked Dr. Saylor, glancing across the room. "It's metallic."

Dr. Hutchens stopped what he was doing and took a deep breath before turning to Director Harold. "It smells electrical. Where is it? NO!"

VISP

God! Help me!

What is happening? How is this happening?

The pain!

Breathe… just breathe… okay. Focus on what you can control.

I see… pink. Everything looks pink. Alright. That means… it means my eyes are hemorrhaging from… from the pressure.

Agh! The pressure is crushing me!

Is this what my mother endured? Those girls? Did I help them do this to them? Was Aidan in this position?

Don't cry. Keep focusing.

My hearing is muffled, as if I'm standing beside an ocean, catching bits and pieces of the doctors' words. His words. Holding him in my line of sight. The devil. That's what he is. A demon among men.

"Increase pressure again."

Can they hear me? Am I screaming or is it all in my mind?

Why isn't the pressure growing? Maybe I—

Agh… the pressure, like a vise, is suffocating.

Black dots float through my vision.

No! I won't die from this!

Tingling washes over my skin as the crushing sensation consumes every inch of me, rapidly amplifying the stinging buzz of electricity coursing from my head to my toes.

The ringing in my ears is deafening.

Pinpricks of burning flesh.

A scream rips from my lungs as a shockwave explodes from my core.

As if in slow motion their bodies rise from the floor.

Electricity. I smell it.

My fingers! I can feel my fingers brush against one another. Glorious hope! Wait. WAIT! Not again! The pressure is back-filling around me, binding me in place. How?

No! Please, God! Please help me. Please don't let them find those girls. Not Aidan. Not my little boy. I'll do whatever they want.

Stop… please stop.

I feel the slow glide of a tear slide down the side of my face.

As I watch the three doctors stand back up in confusion, staring at me with fear and awe, I know there's no way out. And I can't die.

My death would mean they'll have to search even harder for the others.

I know they're searching for me. I've seen their beautiful faces. How do I convince the girls to stop? Aidan to stop!

Do not search for me! Stay away! Stay safe! Aidan, I need you to live!

Florida  

As the door clicked shut leaving Elias to tend to Dakota, Levi gestured for the others to follow him down the hall. Just above a whisper, he said, "She's changed. I know you guys can see it. Dakota's not capable of leading anymore."

111

"What are you saying?" asked Captain Varrecchia, Dakota's mission operations leader.

"I'm saying, she doesn't see our purpose any longer. We can't trust her."

"So what are we supposed to do? It's not like we can actually put up a fight against her. And you're talking about mutiny!"

"No. It's not mutiny if your leader is the one turning on us!

Captain Varrecchia shook his head. "She's not evil. She's not planning to hurt us." His words bit out.

"No? You saw what she did to me!" Eli argued.

"She got mad, you were confrontational."

"Enough for her to hurt me?!"

"She grabbed your arm, not thew you across the room. You're weak," the captain's words almost in disgust at Levi's overzealous reaction.

Levi ripped his sleep up past his shoulder to show the raised red handprint. "This is weak?! You didn't feel it. The burning pain."

They stared at his arm with disbelief.

Captain Varrecchia cleared his throat. "I… she did that?"

Levi recognized his moment. "Yes. What do you think will happen to the next person that says or does something she doesn't like?"

The captain pulled his eyes from Levi's shoulder and up to his face. He questioned his own beliefs before trying to pull himself back together. "Stop! It's… it's not enough to provoke this sort of talk!"

"Maybe not, but she's keeping us from doing any actual work. And what about her broken arm? She's never so much as bruised her shin and won't even tell us the real reason for it!

Maybe she wants to leave us? Not fight for our cause anymore. We can't let her do that! Or hurt us!" He pulled his sleeve up again.

"You're making a lot of assumptions right now."

"Possibly. But maybe you should all pay more attention. Something isn't right."

Chapter 15
Keep Breathing

Thomas made his way to the makeshift prison. It was time for the three prisoners' weekly rations. The apartment in Zoey's old building had already been set up by Joe as an interrogation room, but they added barred windows and installed a cage door behind the apartment door. He could hear them grunting and swearing before he walked in.

Pulling his gun, he aimed it directly at Oakley. "Step back! Step back now!"

Out of breath, Oakley and his right-hand man, Long, moved away from the bloodied heap of a man on the ground.

"What are you doing?"

"Just taking care of some business is all," muttered Oakley, raspy and breathing heavily.

Thomas unlocked the cage door and stepped in, his weapon trained on the two men. Reaching down, he felt a faint pulse on the third man's neck. Still alive.

Oakley and Long slowly stepped in opposite directions, working their way around Thomas.

"Stop moving!" he ordered.

Neither man stopped. Thomas, rising, alternated fixing his weapon on each one. "I. Said. Stop. Moving."

Oakley, grunting an awkward laugh, said, "I don't think you can hit both of us Thomas."

Holding his gaze straight ahead, Thomas, without warning, fired a shot that grazed Long's leg before immediately training his weapon on Oakley. Long squealed, grit his teeth and squeezed the bloody wound.

"Do you really wanna try me?" said Thomas, straight-faced and somber.

Both men paused for only a moment then continued to move in opposite directions.

"I don't think this is the way you want to go down Oak." Thomas grabbed the shirt collar of the kid on the floor and began dragging him toward the door, forcing the men to stop.

"It's either him or us, Tom. We're not going to give you both," said Oakley, pulling a broken and splintered chair leg out from behind his back.

"You really don't want to do this, boys. You won't be making it out alive."

It happened fast. Thomas looked down for a millisecond at the sound of Keeps groaning and Long was on top of him. He got off one shot before hitting the ground as Oakley broke for the door.

"Long! Now!" Oakley yelled.

Springing to his feet, Long shoved Thomas down with a solid boot on his back. By the time Thomas righted himself, he could hear both men running down the stairs.

With his back tweaked from the surprise hit and follow-up kick, he knew he'd never catch them.

"Dammit!" he growled. Looking back at Keeps, he slammed his palm on the floor. Thomas yanked the long-range radio from his belt and yelled, "Joe, this is Thomas. You read?"

After several seconds, static crossed the line and Joe's voice responded, "Here. Over."

"We got a problem."

"Come on!" Aidan whined. "It's been months since we've seen any action. Please let me come with you! I can track 'em just as well as Brandon."

"No. You're more valuable here protecting the girls." Joe's matter-of-fact tone would've ended the conversation with anyone else, but Aidan wasn't anyone else.

"But you know I'm good! Brandon taught me everything he knows!"

Brandon grunted, "Learning and doing are two different things, man."

"Aidan. Seriously. There's no fight. Those guys are in the wind. We're just taking Sheila to check out the kid and bring him back here."

"First of all, the girls are more than capable. Besides, what if they didn't run and they're just waiting in the bushes to pounce? Or you run into Breakers?" With puppy dog eyes,

Aidan implored, "I need this Joe."

Joe sighed, shaking his head.

Aidan didn't need powers to read Joe's mind. "I'll be fine! In case you haven't noticed, I don't fall out the way the girls do. In fact, I make them stronger."

Joe looked up to see the humor drain from Aidan's face.

"I need to go, Joe. Please. Let me do this. I'm suffocating here." Since finding out his mother was alive, Aidan had grown more anxious, his body like a tightly wound spring. They hadn't allowed him to run off to find her, determined to have a plan first, to know what they were walking into. He was convulsing with unspent energy.

"But!" said Joe, still shaking his head. "If you fall out, I'm not carrying your dumb butt back here. I'm leaving you to fend for yourself."

Aidan's eyes grew wide as he pumped his fist in the air. Standing up straight he shouted, "Aye-aye!" with a firm salute.

Justin, Lexi, Maddy, Grant, and one of the girls they'd saved from Oakley, volunteered to go to the hospital to conduct MRI scans. The rest stayed behind to finalize the plan.

The events of the day before dramatically affected all the girls, and with the escape of Oakley and Long, all were on edge.

Despite the urgency, they came across a functioning MRI machine at the hospital and decided to get several scans done. The data would be beneficial upon their return. The idea of losing anyone wasn't something voiced, but they were intelligent enough to know collecting as much individual information was necessary just in case.

Maria stood at the whiteboard, her hand stained with various colors from the dry-erase markers. Using her hands to wipe the board instead of taking the extra moment to grab the eraser drove Gavin crazy.

"Two missions. One to find girl number eight. The other to find what we believe to be Aidan's mother. According to Rice Jahnsen at LIMIT, we know the personnel at VISP, cowards, recently ventured above ground like the moles they are. With Jones dead..." Maria said, pausing at his memory. She never really liked the man, but the way he died continued to foster nightmares. "And of course, Maddy is with us now, which means Jahnsen lost his connection to the current inner workings of VISP. But it would make sense that Aidan's mother might be there based on the visions of the girls. According to what the girls are collectively feeling, it's reminiscent of what Zuri and Lexi experienced confined in their glass prisons. VISP is the most plausible location to search first."

Gavin quietly listened as Maria sketched out her thoughts. Walking up to the board, he added, "They've been underground this whole time, so it's unlikely they've put back together our old lab. Floor nineteen, where Lexi was held, is the most logical location to keep Maya. So that's the goal. We'll have Jahnsen's operator team from LIMIT meet us at Joe's predetermined location."

"It's where Aidan, Joe and I positioned ourselves to do recon before going in back in August," observed Zoey. "VISP didn't see us coming the first time, so it should still be secure for us to post up there again. There's also, or there was, a safe house five miles out from VISP. Joe found it during our recon. Rundown, but empty and could serve our purpose for a fallback location if needed."

"Okay, so it's decided? We're going after Maya first?" asked Zuri, beginning to pace. "Are we sure we shouldn't go after the eighth first? We'd be stronger with her."

"Maybe, but not knowing what she's capable of, or whether or not she'd help or hinder the operation could jeopardize the safety of the rest of us," Addie said. "We know how to work together. We've had time to learn about each other."

"True, but when push comes to shove, we all seem to unify," Zuri countered.

"Also true, but we didn't have time to think ahead. This time we do... to an extent."

"Plus, we don't exactly know where the eighth is located." Joanna's cinnamon eyes twinkled as she thought about her connection to the final girl. "I mean, I know with Zuri we can find her, but it would be a slower search. I think Maya is in the most danger right now."

Joanna's words carried a lot of weight, considering it was her other half they were talking about. And Addie's buy-in added to the certainty. Bringing a new girl into the fold without knowing her capabilities could be a disaster waiting to happen.

"Alright. I have a proposal," said Maria, glancing toward Gavin. His eyes grew wide as they made eye contact. "You okay? Do I have something on my face?" she asked, lightly brushing her cheeks.

"Yes. No. Sorry. Just a fly buzzing. Continue on, I'll just..." muttered Gavin, shoving a small item back into his pocket and swatting the air.

Maria watched him with curiosity, "Uh, alrighty then. So, I think Joanna's right. We need to find Maya first, then chase down the eighth. It's gonna take the girls some time to locate her and we know Maya's in imminent danger, but with Jahnsen's help, Joe's plan to extricate her safely and quickly should work."

As Maria walked through the details Joe had put together, Macie interlaced her pinkie through her brother's. Gavin looked down to see a sly smile on her face. "You should ask," she whispered.

Gavin side-eyed her with raised eyebrows. Macie's eyes flicked to Maria, then back to him. He didn't need special powers to read her mind. He knew there was never going to be a perfect moment in their crazy lives.

Suddenly, Maria's voice interrupted their wordless interchange. "Something you'd like to share with the class, Gavin?"

Taking a deep breath, he turned and strode toward her. Scooping her hand into his, he began to open his mouth when Maria blurted out, "What are you doing? We're in the middle of a meeting."

Sweat beading and cheeks flushed a deep maroon, he whispered, "Maria?" Reaching into his pocket, he took a step back.

"Incoming!" Aidan bellowed. His booming voice, followed by the slamming of the door as he whipped it open, took them all by surprise. "We need the bed!" he cried, carrying a makeshift stretcher that held a man they barely recognized as one of the prisoners. Drying blood was smeared across his puffy, bruised skin, staining his clothes.

Maria and Gavin jumped into action. Racing to grab the hospital bed kept in the shop, they cleared it of medical supplies.

Sheila followed closely behind Joe at the foot of the stretcher.

"They beat him good. Some broken ribs and contusions. We need to check for internal bleeding and treat for a concussion." She stepped aside while Joe and Aidan hoisted him onto the hospital bed. Maria, grabbing a syringe, moved to inject him with hydrocodone for pain.

"No sedatives," said Sheila. "We need to keep him as lucid as we can." Grabbing the wet rag from a bowl of clean water, she began wiping away the blood and examining him more closely. "Looks like your left zygomatic bone and, yes, definitely your nose is broken."

"Zygomatic?" The man's puffy lips awkwardly released the word.

"Cheekbone," Sheila clarified. "Glad you're with it enough to ask. What's your name?"

"Keeps."

"Good. That's good. Do you remember my name, Keeps?"

Straining his one good eye, he managed to focus on her. "Sheila?"

"Yes! Great job. Now, Keeps, I just need you to stay awake, alright?" Looking toward Maria, she asked, "Can you keep him engaged?"

Gavin, nearby, once again shot a wide-eyed look in Maria's direction at the sound of Sheila's question.

"Keeps, my name is Maria. Where are you from?"

Blinking his good eye several times, he responded, "Florida."

"Oh, fun! Where in Florida?"

"Cape Canaveral."

"Nice. Did you work for NASA?"

He attempted to shake his head, but the dizzying movement

caused his eyes to roll back.

"Wait. Wait! Stay with me, Keeps," Maria exclaimed, placing her hands on either side of his face and looking into his eyes.

"Er, no," he finally answered before his head dropped to the side.

"Hold on now, buddy," said Gavin, grabbing a syringe and a bottle of adrenaline. Flicking it a few times, he quickly inserted the needle into Keeps' arm.

After several anxiety-laden moments, Keeps inhaled with a start. Everyone followed suit. "Good job! Good job! Keep breathing, Keeps. How many fingers am I holding up?" asked Gavin, holding two fingers in front of the man's face.

"Uh, two."

"Excellent!" Without hesitation, Maria inserted an IV in his arm. "Keep him talking."

"Keeps, right?" asked Gavin. "We've talked a lot about you lately, my friend."

Keeps' eyes darted from person to person as his hands gripped the edges of the stretcher tight.

"Hey, right here. My name's Gavin. I'm a doctor. Look here at me. Don't worry about everyone else."

When his eyes finally landed on Gavin, he held them as a lifeline.

"We've heard you're not like the others. Is that right?"

"Yes," he whispered.

"Do you work for someone else? Or are you alone?"

His eyebrows scrunched and his stare grew more intense as he struggled to think. "Dakota," he declared, his voice louder.

"Dakota? Like North Dakota? So not Florida?"

He shook his head, but the effort left him spinning.

"No, no, wait. Stay with us. Is Dakota a person then?"

Closing his eyes, he gripped the stretcher even more tightly, trying to avoid the spinning. "Yes," he whispered, wincing at the pain in his cheek.

Sheila, stepping in to examine, replied, "That's good. You're doing great. Just keep talking. Where's Dakota? Did he send you there to help the girls?"

Despite the adrenaline rush, darkness was pulling him under as his mind continued to spin. "She didn't."

"She? Dakota is a she?" Gavin clarified while tending to the swelling around the man's ankle.

"Breakers. We're… Breakers." His words were barely audible, but they heard him clearly enough.

"Of course," Gavin mumbled.

Maria shot Gavin a stern look that seemed to say, not the time, before cutting in to keep the man with it. "Keeps, stay with us. I need you to stay awake. How did you end up here? With Oakley?"

"Investigating." His breathing grew shallow. "Increased energy signatures."

"His lungs are filling with fluid," noted Sheila. Turning to look Keeps in the face, she said, "Hey, this might hurt. We need to release the pressure building in your lungs." She put her hand out just as Gavin handed her a scalpel and what looked like a metal straw. "Okie dokie, here we go." Feeling for the space between his ribs, she began making a small but deep incision. Quickly, without hesitation, she pushed her finger in and heard a wet hissing sound. After a few seconds she inserted the straw. Dark, thick fluid began leaking from the open end of it. With a grunt, Keeps lurched, sucking in a full breath before slumping over onto the bed, mumbling, "Dakota doesn't know. She's not the only one."

Chapter 16
Truth

Dr. Harold had exhausted all his excuses to keep the rest of the compound oblivious to what had happened to Maya. But she was a staple. Everyone would see her on a daily basis, whether it was her weather update on the network or their twice-daily briefings. For her to be missing the previous two weeks had people talking.

On top of that, after Maya's show of force, Dr. Harold needed the full support of VISP in case he lost control of her. Rotating his sore shoulder, thinking about the power she'd displayed, he was thankful none of them had been seriously hurt. However, he knew Dr. Jessica Saylor was fearful of continuing their work. While he hadn't taken steps to replace her yet, he was prepared to if it came to it.

Calling a compound-wide mandatory briefing for all personnel, he stood in front of them with a confidence only a narcissist could muster. "Hey everyone, please get seated. There's a lot to talk about." They had worked tirelessly for so long. While he was thankful, he also knew it was time to adjust the mission of VISP in order to protect the future. "I know you're all wondering why we're having this meeting. There's been some speculation and more than a few rumors floating around.

"As you know, our mission has always been to seek out individuals with exceptional skills, training, or experience that could help us rebuild the future. As in all of you!" Dr. Harold stood tall, looking over the compliant mass of personnel. "And while that's true, VISP has also had a secondary, albeit more important, goal with our search. We've kept the information I'm about to share with you compartmentalized. Up to this point, it's been imperative that we mitigate the interests of outside eyes and ears who would seek to thwart our mission, steal our research or, worse, abduct the individuals we've found.

"Last August, sadly, the worst came to fruition due to several VISP insiders sharing information beyond our compound. The result? Two of our very important individuals were abducted."

Gasps and raspy whispers broke the silence among the crowd.

"What I'm about to share with you may be hard for some of you to believe, but I'm asking you to keep your mind open. Listen to what I tell you before asking questions or dismissing this information as mere fantasy." Scanning the room for his core doctors on the project, he watched as Dr. Saylor shifted nervously and Dr. Hutchens held a firm gaze. They knew more than anyone else in the room what VISP's true mission was, but even they didn't know all the details.

"So, let's rip off the bandaid. First, I know you've been wondering what happened to Maya, our meteorologist. She is alive. We have her in the lab and we're taking good care of her."

"What's wrong with her?" asked Maya's meteorological assistant, eyes wide with confusion.

"For me to answer that, I'll need to start at the beginning." Dr. Harold cleared his throat, relaxed his stance, and took a deep breath. "Maya and I worked together in the OB department at a hospital between 2003 and 2010. I was a gynecologist back in those days, and she was a nurse in my ward. In 2009, a child was born with the umbilical cord wrapped around her neck. We tried to revive her, but she didn't make it." Clearing his throat again, he shifted his weight, recalling the event vividly. "After the mother spent a little time with her lost child, Maya carried the infant girl out of the room to the nursery to call the morgue. Roughly twelve minutes later she returned to the room with that same baby, only she wasn't deceased. This baby was a hearty pink, breathing deeply and more alert to her surroundings than any child I'd ever delivered." He watched as the room of highly intellectual individuals shook their heads and scrunched their brows.

"How do you know it was the same child?" asked one of the techs.

"I wondered that same question, but the child was still wearing the security ankle bracelet I'd placed on her at birth. And no other child in the nursery went unaccounted for. What was even more fascinating, however, was her eyes. If you analyze the iris of an eye, for the non-medical-doctors in the room, if you look closely you'll see striations that come from the pupil outward like the rays of light around a sun. Upon closer inspection, you'll also notice that it looks like the iris is made of tiny crystals. The closer you look, the more colors you'll see. Regardless, there are dominant colors that, from a distance, make up the overall eye color in a person's iris."

Caught up in his biology lesson, Dr. Harold failed to notice the impatient shifting and shuffling among the members of his team.

"When Maya returned with this resuscitated newborn, I could see very plainly the crystals in her eyes were exponentially more vibrant," he exclaimed, finally taking in the discomfort in the air. "Her coming back to life after so much time had passed was reason enough to want to study this child, but the exacerbated crystalline irises looking like diamonds made her even more compelling."

A medic from the main clinic raised her hand. "Dr. Harold, I apologize for interrupting your fascinating iris exposition. Without belaboring the previous question, don't you think it's very likely this baby was switched? I mean… what proof do you have? Of any of it?"

"Again, I would have agreed with you initially. However, we had video cameras throughout the hospital and several in the nursery. I studied the footage second by second. Maya is clearly seen leaving the delivery room with the infant. She is captured walking down the hall and into the nursery without deviation. Once inside, she can be seen walking up to the doors at the back of the room. One led to the clean room where she would've washed the baby thoroughly, called the morgue, and waited for them to arrive to take the deceased child. The other door led to a quiet room consisting of several rocking chairs."

Dr. Harold's eyes veered up and to the right as he imagined the scene unfolding.

"She hesitated at the doors, then, rather oddly, she chose the second door. Once inside, she could be seen sitting and rocking the child, crying. It bears noting that Maya was eight months pregnant at the time. It's quite reasonable to note that being pregnant and holding a deceased baby was likely an emotional event.

"She kissed the top of the baby's head and can be seen sitting like that with the child for several seconds before Maya suddenly jerked backward, looking the child up and down as she watched the baby squeeze her little fists and kick her legs."

The room remained silent as the doctor continued.

"For over a year, I attempted to study the child as much as possible without raising any flags. I just wanted to understand how she'd been revived, without brain damage or any other disabilities with the lack of oxygen for roughly forty-two minutes. Out of curiosity, I combed through previous deliveries looking for any similar notations. You know what? I found six others where there were noted oddities in their eyes during post-birth examinations."

"Sir, I don't understand what this has to do with MJ or why we're here." With the medics comments, the crowd began to murmur.

Dr. Harold, holding up his pointer finger, nodded. "I'm getting there. Over the course of the following eighteen months, I interviewed every mother who had given birth during the time I'd been an OB at the hospital, as well as conducted an exam of each child. An eighth child was also born after that particular birth. She, too, had the same exacerbated crystalline iris abnormality. What was interesting in that case was I was able to determine that she was not born with it. Twenty-four hours later, however, during another examination, those striations had formed. This was essential data as it nearly confirmed that these children changed post-birth."

The audience listened, speechless. An air of unease began to grow. Dr. Harold, caught up in his story, brushed off the growing impatience.

"Upon physical examination of the eight girls, I found that, beyond color, their irises had similar characteristics. In the interviews with the mothers, I learned that each child was exhibiting odd behaviors. Some were already five and six years old, and their parents, wary of sharing, felt as if they were, and I quote, "going crazy." Household objects would go missing, only to be found in unreachable locations for a child, like a pacifier on top of a fridge. Or the child in the tub now dripping in the doorway after a mere turn to grab a washcloth," he said, his voice softening to a reflective whisper.

"At that point I'd done as much review as I could and decided to start testing my theories. Which meant I needed direct, unimpeded access to the children."

"Dr. Harold," said Dr. Saylor, voice cracking as she interrupted. "Years ago, I read about several children who had been abducted from their homes. Some of the parents died during those abductions. The children themselves were found a year later, overseas, in the desert of Kandahar. Was that you?"

His eyes bounced to individuals throughout the room, watching as mouths dropped. "Yes. Dr. Saylor, I did take those children. It had become necessary to fully grasp what they were capable of and—"

"You killed people. You destroyed families," she said, rising to her feet, her eyes locked onto his. "What does this have to do with any of us, or Maya being confined to that glass box on nineteen?"

The room filled with whispered disbelief upon learning of Maya's current reality.

"Please. Dr. Saylor. Please sit. Everyone, what Dr. Saylor said is true. It was very unfortunate that people died. I tried to talk the parents into allowing me to study them, but they refused. I deeply regret what happened, but it was many years ago, and I cannot change the past and we have a lot to do to get back our future." He paused as the group slightly calmed. "Maya is in a lab but for very good reason." He watched as Dr. Saylor slowly descended into her chair, the flush of anger lingering on her face. "I recognize that many of you probably think what I've done is unethical, but what I learned about those children could change the world. Those girls were capable of doing things you've only ever seen in movies. If I'd been able to nurture them into adulthood, they could've been, and could still be, a means to change our lives, the world, for the better."

"So that's who we've been looking for all this time?" asked one of the analysts.

"Yes."

"Have we found any of these children?" the analyst prompted.

"Yes. Two of the girls were with us from right after the grid failed in 2023." A sharp murmur filled the room.

"I don't understand," said Dr. Saylor. "If we've had them all this time, then why are we still here? Why isn't the world better?"

"That's the tricky part. We were trying to study them while in an induced coma. Your previous director, Director Jones, would not allow them to be awakened for further study as he feared they might overpower us and cause harm."

"Little girls. You're saying he thought little girls might cause us harm?"

"Sadly yes—"

"Wait," Dr. Saylor demanded, standing up once more. "Is that the reason we ended up in the bunkers? Was there ever a bomb?"

Staring her down and shaking his head, he replied, "No. There was no bomb."

"So what you're saying is… one of those girls caused that explosion on D4?" Dr. Saylor's voice dropped to a whisper as she covered her mouth. Having witnessed Maya's power that morning, coupled with this new information, she desperately wanted to leave the compound.

"I'm not sure. There was an explosion, though it may have been from the individuals who broke into the compound and successfully removed the two girls from our labs."

"How did they manage to get past security?"

"It's my belief that Director Jones provided the information for the abduction." Cries of disbelief rang out as members stood, ready to walk out. "I know this is a lot to take in, but the bottom line is that we need to find these girls. They can help us fix what has been broken."

Dr. Hutchens, having patiently listened, spoke up, "It may help if you explained how Maya came into play with all this."

Dr. Harold nodded, "I only recently connected the dots. As

I stated before, Maya was with me during my years as an OB. She had been present at every one of those girls' births. She held them, touched them, cared for them."

"But she would've held countless babies during those years. You've mentioned only eight children with the abnormalities," the eager tech spoke up once more.

"True, which is why it took me so long to conduct the interviews with all the parents. But there was one indicator I failed to take into account until, like I said, very recently. Pregnancy." He took a deep breath. "With each of the eight children, Maya was pregnant when she cared for them."

"Even pregnant, she would've held far more babies than eight."

"Agreed, though I believe there was yet another element involved. The problem is, I've not yet found that piece of the puzzle."

"This is ludicrous," a man interjected from the back of the room. "Sir, Maya only ever had one child, and he passed away."

Dr. Harold cleared his throat, avoiding sharing the truth about Aidan. "Yes, she only carried one child to full term and delivered. But she conceived a child six times. And sadly, she lost five of them. My theory is that whatever she did to those newborns, however mysterious, it caused her to miscarry."

"This is science fiction—"

"Yes! It feels that way. It very much does. But this is real. As real as you and me standing here."

"How can you possibly expect us to believe this garbage? You're clearly deranged. You abducted children, killed their parents, tested these babies like lab rats!" another man shouted.

"Please, please let me show you something." He walked to

his computer and pulled up a video, mirroring it on the large screen behind him. The paused image revealed three doctors surrounding a glass case with a young woman standing inside. "This is from August ninth last year." Dr. Harold stepped to the side with a remote in his hand. "As you can see, one of the girls, whom we called Calla Lily, is standing inside the case. She'd been in a coma since arriving and, without warning, was suddenly alert and upright." He pressed the play button on his remote and let the scene play out.

The members watched as Zuri rose to her feet, visibly angry. Even pixelated, they could see the white glow on her face. While the camera faced the glass case head-on, she was turned to the side, and it was unclear what exactly the glow emanated from. Without apparent provocation, chaos erupted on the screen. The three doctors were blown from their standing positions and suddenly strewn across the floor. Oddly, nothing else in the room moved so much as a millimeter.

Dr. Harold watched as some of his team members covered their mouths, leaned forward, or turned away. "Let me replay this a bit slower for you." Hitting play at half-speed, they watched more closely this time. Gasps indicated that they took notice of the nearly invisible force that knocked the doctors from their feet.

"I know you're all trying to make sense of what you're seeing, but before we discuss it any further, there's another video I want to show you." Pulling up the second video, he put it on the big screen, stepped back, then hit play.

The lab looked similar, though the doctors standing around the glass case were different. The girl lying inside the glass unit also differed. They watched as the doctors on screen argued while the girl inside the case began to move, eventually rising behind the glass just as the previous girl did. Only this time, she pressed her hands against the glass. Fear immediately betrayed the doctors' faces. With no audio feed, they watched as one of the male doctors immediately walked toward the case while the second male doctor lunged toward him.

Amidst the chaos, the girl dropped to her knees, eyes wide with fear. The approaching doctor pulled a lever before being tackled by the other two. Only a handful of seconds ticked by before the glass surrounding her shattered into a million pieces.

The impact knocked out the video feed, leaving static in its wake.

No one said a word.

He pointed at the timestamp on the bottom of the screens. "If you look here, you can see both videos happened simultaneously. These two girls had been our primary project. All of you have contributed to the research in one way or another. You were compartmentalized so as not to put those girls, or VISP, in jeopardy. But why Maya?" Dr. Harold pulled up one final image. It was a retinal image of a set of eyes. The coloring was spectacular. At first glance, the irises simply appeared white. However, as Dr. Harold altered the image contrast, glinting diamonds and various colors emerged.

"Whose eyes are those?" asked the compound's optometrist. He had recently been given the image to analyze, though who they belonged to he wasn't told.

"Maya's," Dr. Harold revealed with pride as if he was responsible for their shimmer. He then pulled up the images of Calla Lily and Rose, placing them alongside Maya's.

The group studied them, almost forgetting the horror the

girls had endured to obtain these images before an analyst broke the silence. "Why are Calla Lily's eyes colorless? Like the clarity of a diamond?"

"That's an answer we have yet to find."

"There's nothing in the footage directly linking either girl to the physical chaos that erupts. How do you expect us to believe that they have... what... extrasensory capabilities? It's fascinating, even concerning what we've seen, but not proof. Not a reason to contain them."

"Your statement is precisely what I was hoping for. Think about what Maya has shared during some of her briefings regarding the weather. She's told us in her own words, 'You don't analyze the data for all the factors that would *support* your forecast. You're looking for that one factor that would make it fall apart.' I don't want you searching to prove they are special. I want you searching to find reasons they aren't so we can truly determine if their capabilities are real," he declared, smacking the table as the audience jumped at the sound.

"I don't want you to push the believe button. I want you to focus on the story the information gives you. This is why I'm sending all of you the data from my early research on the girls. I want you to pick it apart and put it back together."

"So what's the end goal? What's Maya supposed to contribute to all of this? And what happens if we're unable to locate these other girls?"

"Excellent questions. Very good. Ultimately, I want to understand the trigger. How did these girls gain their gifts? Is it something we all have within us? Can we essentially enhance our own capabilities? I want to find the girls and bring them here, not to hurt them, but to strengthen our chances of a new life. To strengthen these young women. To build a new world!"

Wide-eyed, Dr. Harold took a deep breath as a rather quiet analyst stood up, head-shaking, and said, "Let's be honest, you want them here because if they are what you say they are, and they're with us, then they're not against us. You're afraid."

Dr. Harold stared at the defiant pundit. "I believe they are very strong. As you've witnessed. Maybe even stronger now. Yes," he paused, cheeks flushed. "While we can't afford for them not to be on our side, my intentions are greater."

"And if we can't locate them? What happens then?"

"Then we try something outside the box."

Chapter 17
The Switch

"**H**ow's Dakota?" asked Captain Varrecchia.

"She's good. Slept through the night." Eli stared at his computer. He didn't want anyone to see the worry in his eyes. Especially their operations team commander.

"So, she'll be good for the mission tomorrow? Minus the broken arm of course."

"Yeah. Yes, she'll be good to go. She just needed some time to herself this morning. Should be out shortly to go over the plan."

"Okay, cause yesterday was a little… disconcerting."

Eli finally looked up. "Everyone's entitled to a bad day, man. She's good. Just got lightheaded. We'll be good to go tomorrow."

"What are we talking about?" Dakota walked in to hear the last bit of their conversation.

"Hey Boss. Just checking in to make sure we're good to go for tomorrow," said Capt. V, not relaying his concerns about her health.

"Why wouldn't we be?"

He looked to Eli, but found no help there. "Uh, yesterday just seemed a little rough is all. We can push back the mission if need be."

Dakota took a step into his personal space. "And that need would be?"

He paused, not sure how to answer, "No need on my end." He leaned back only an inch but she noticed his subtle retreat. "Whenever you're ready, ma'am, we can walk through the brief for tomorrow."

"Let's get to it then, Captain."

This time he took a step back and said, "I'll round everyone up in the ops center." With that, he stepped quickly out of Eli's office.

Eli had watched the interchange with concern. Something had definitely changed with Dakota. "D?"

She whipped around to face him. Her eyes glowed behind her darkened glasses, and her features were taught. "What?"

"Hey, are you okay?"

"Now *you're* going to treat me like the enemy?"

"What? No! No. No one thinks you're the enemy." He stood up and went to reach for her shoulder but pulled his hand back when he noticed the intense flashing in her eyes. "Something's not right Dakota. What's going on with you?"

"Going on with me? Are you serious? I can hear their

thoughts. Plotting against me. And you think something's wrong with me?" she grabbed the side of her head almost as if feeling pain.

Eli didn't want to provoke her further, but gently asked, "You can hear their thoughts?"

"What? No. I… I just know they are." She turned away as if searching for something.

"What are you looking for?"

"Pain meds. I need… just find me something for this headache!"

"Okay. Okay. Just sit down for a second. We can do the briefing la—"

"No! We're doing it now. Just find me something so we can get this over with." Her brain felt like it was being squeezed. Even thinking was painful. She just wanted it to stop. The pain. The voices.

Levi stood outside the door listening in on the whole thing. Knowing they'd be delayed a few more minutes, he left to find Capt. V. and a few others.

Standing apart from the main gaggle of personnel gathered for the briefing, he whispered in a low, gravelly voice, "Do you still think I'm crazy for thinking she's turned?"

Capt. V. stood quietly.

"I know you've seen it. How she blew up yesterday and now what she said to you in Eli's office."

"Eli's right. Everyone's entitled to a bad day."

"And you think that's all this is? Six months of no hits, breaking her arm under questionable circumstances, threatening us repeatedly?"

"Look. I see what you're saying, but maybe she's sick. Or maybe she's frustrated about something we don't understand." Capt. V. was still trying to give her the benefit of the doubt.

"Stop defending her! She's a terrible liar and she's definitely lying about her arm. And her scare tactics with us? With you? She can't be trusted anymore. We need to do something before she destroys everything we've worked for!"

Levi dug into his pocket, pulling out a syringe. "Propofol."

"Did you do that to her yesterday!?" growled one of the others through gritted teeth, glancing at the door to the building.

"No!" he stammered, shoving the syringe back into his pocket. "Whatever happened yesterday, I didn't do. I'm just saying we can use this to subdue her... when the moment arises." Levi stared at their skeptical faces. "You need to wake up and realize she's no longer on our side. We haven't gone after any targets in months. She's not with us. We have to do something before she turns on us."

"But we're literally leaving tomorrow!" barked the captain.

"Finally! Which gives us the window we need if we'll ever stand a chance against her. Especially with one arm. We have the advantage!"

Silence engulfed their small circle.

Capt. V. stared at Levi, took a deep breath, held it, then exhaled shaking his head. "Okay. *IF* we need to, how do we do it?"

A smile spread across Levi's face. "Assuming she's well enough to travel tomorrow, we'll wait until after the mission wraps. Use the propofol to subdue her," he paused, "and bring her back here. Keep her locked up without her book. Only let her use it when we need her."

"What about Elias? He'll never stand for it."

Levi's expression told them all they needed to know.

"If she's alive, one way or another she'll hurt us." Capt. V. said aloud what they were all thinking.

Levi smirked. "We have plenty of sedatives to keep her down… for a very long time."

Chapter 18
Get Ready

"What's taking her so long?" Levi stood by the four vehicles—two Jeeps, a van and a Humvee—frustrated that it was hours past the time they should've gotten on the road.

Typically, he didn't go on missions, but this was one he couldn't resist.

There were fifteen of them going. With each mission, they'd send a reconnaissance crew first to assess the location, security, weaknesses, strengths, and movements. Once they had solid data on the target's activity, they'd determine the necessary force. Fifteen members were more than what a typical recon required, but with Dakota's arm broken, they added several more to assist. Plus, with the distance being traveled, they wanted to be able to hit the target once recon was completed. Dakota wasn't in a waiting mood.

Dakota would utilize the assessment period to sketch anything about the target she deemed pertinent so they would be ready to go if she needed to provide help during the mission.

Levi would often stay hot and ready behind a computer, ready to release the assault team should they be needed. But with the assault team going, he wouldn't be as useful. So instead, he convinced Dakota of his desire to tag along in order to expand his skillset by seeing the team in action.

When all eyes were elsewhere, Levi pretended to inspect his backpack, confirming the essentials. Quietly, he unzipped an inner pocket to verify that the hidden syringe and propofol were safely secured.

"Levi?"

The sound of his name from just over his shoulder made him jump. Closing his bag with more force than intended, "Yeah?" he said a little too loud.

"You okay?" Elias stood behind him, glancing between him and the bag.

"I'm good. Just checking my supplies." Sweat beaded on his forehead as he fumbled with the outer zipper.

"Okay, uh, we're about to hit the road. Ally has everything she needs on this end, right?" Ally was taking Levi's place as the home base point of contact.

"Yup. She's good to go. Dakota ready?"

"I'm ready," she said, coming up on Levi's other side with her own bag hanging from the shoulder of her broken arm. Her good arm bore a drawing pad, which she held tight. No one had ever been allowed to touch it, let alone look through her book.

Of course, certain pages that pertained to specific targets were fair game at her approval. It was a book all Breakers desired to peek inside.

Levi had snuck into her room once to find it, but even Elias didn't know where it was hidden. He couldn't wait to get his hands on it when they subdued her.

Dakota watched his eyes flick toward the book under her arm. "I'll be in the second jeep napping. Wake me when we stop for a bathroom break."

Elias remained a step behind, staring Levi down.

"What?"

"Nothing. Just a little odd that you're coming on this trip."

"And?"

"And, if there's something other than knowledge you're hoping to get out of this, you'll have to go through me first," Elias added with a look that made Levi clear his throat and grip his bag tight.

Levi watched as Elias climbed into the jeep after Dakota. "I'm counting on it."

 Sanford, NC 

"What did you mean, Dakota's not the only one?" Now that Keeps was finally awake, Justin could interrogate him.

Keeps glanced at him and the others. "Uh, well, there are things she can do that people like me can't."

"People like you?" Maria pressed.

"Like, regular people."

Maria wanted to throttle him for not spelling it out, but aside from her eyes, she stayed calm.

When no one spoke, Keeps started again. "She can, like, draw things? And then they happen."

"As in?" Maria prompted.

"As in… anything, really. If we needed a door unlocked, she'd draw the lock in an unlocked position."

"So, she just draws things and they magically occur?" Justin asked, his curious tone betraying his impatience.

"Well, yes, er, no. She would place her hand on the paper, and then it happened."

They all looked at one another trying to gauge his sincerity.

"That's pretty much it," said Keeps, taking a deep breath.

"So, door handles?" asked Maria, raising an eyebrow with eyes wide.

"Anything. If we were looking for food, she'd draw it out and then track it down right away. Kind of like an old dowsing rod, I guess. This one time, we tried to get out of a building where we were dismantling communications, but we were stuck. I mean, really stuck, you know? So she drew a doorway and it appeared." His eyes, full of amazement, bounced from one person to the next.

Justin shot a look at Zoey.

"He seems to be telling the truth," she replied, stepping toward Keeps. "You said she could draw something like food and then she'd be able to find it? Couldn't she just draw food to make it appear, like a door?"

Keeps chuckled. "Nah. We asked the same thing years ago, but she said she wasn't a magician or anything like that."

Zoey, looking back at Maddy and Maria, said, "What do you think?"

"Sounds like maybe she can manipulate something if it's

a physical thing in front of her, but if it's something that's not there?" Maddy turned and walked to the other side of their makeshift lab, "Maybe she can only guide herself to that particular thing. Like Keeps said, a dowsing rod."

"Do you think it has to do with living and nonliving things? Like, she can physically manipulate a door, but when it comes to something living, plants, people, raw foods, these things can't be altered in a physical way. Like manifesting an apple from the air. It won't work because it's a living thing?"

"Plausible theory," said Maria, staring down Keeps.

"Okay kid," said Justin, softening his tone. "What else do you know?"

Chapter 19
Proposal

"Maria?" Gavin's voice cracked as he called out. "Girls, don't forget to pack plenty of snacks. We'll have a cooler and supplies in our vehicle, but you all need to have additional sustenance at your disposal in your own packs."

"Maria—" Gavin tried again.

"Maria, did you grab the medical bags with the first aid and pain medication?" asked Lexi, brushing past Gavin. Like Maria, she was focused on her preparations. Worry, with a hint of excitement, filtered through her mind, wondering who they may find at the end of this journey.

Maria nodded at Lexi and, trying to see around Gavin, said, "Sheila's got all that. Hey, Grant, did you pack the MRI scans so we can review them on our way up?"

"Yes, ma'am! That and the most recent blood analysis."

"Maria? Hey, can we—" Gavin started, gently touching her shoulder. Without looking, Maria shook his hand free and continued ticking off items from the packing list she was holding.

"Gav, could you hand me that bag—"

"*Maria!*" Gavin shouted.

Everyone in the room stopped and turned toward the two of them.

"Gavin? Where did you come from? What's wrong?" she replied, startled by his aggressive tone and immediately concerned for his well being. "Are you okay?"

"Yeah, yes. You see. There's just… before we go on this trip, with all the possible outcomes and danger we might be in..."

Glancing between his eyes and the startled faces of everyone else, Maria froze.

Taking a deep breath, Gavin looked over at Macie as she gave him a wide smile of encouragement. Reaching into his pocket, he pulled out a little black box and stepped back to get down on one knee.

"*Wait!*" Maria cried, causing him to choke down his next word.

He had tried to prepare for the possibility of rejection but didn't expect it to happen before he'd even popped the question. Maria, frantically turning away, released her hair from its tie, and rapidly fluffed it as Gavin silently watched. Pulling chapstick from her pocket, she swiped it across her lips before yanking her lab coat off and tossing it to Grant nearby.

Spinning back with a sparkle in her eyes, she declared,

"Okay, now I'm ready!"

"Leave it to Maria to pause a proposal to do her hair," Grant said under his breath, causing a few snickers to break out. Gavin blinked hard and exhaled loudly before a vast smile spread across his face. It was all he could do not to laugh out loud.

"Ready?" he questioned, raising his eyebrows.

Large, natural curls bounced as she nodded with fervor.

"Maria, from the moment you walked into our lab, with your sarcasm and sass assaulting us, your intellect monopolizing ours, and your class and beauty peerless… I have loved you. I have always believed I was the smartest person in any room," he said, chuckling, "Until you arrived and, from day one, began deflating the air from my ego." His smile revealed that it wasn't an unwelcome collapse. "I know that the life we're building together isn't cookie-cutter. That we may never see normal again. But, regardless of what happens in our future, no matter where we end up, you are the one I want to share this crazy life with. You are the one I want to grow old with. Maybe one day… if the stars align... maybe we can raise our own children. No doubt they would be as beautiful, kind, intelligent, and feisty as you are. I don't want to live another moment without you. Will you marry me?"

Through his whole speech she struggled not to cut him off and shout yes to the heavens. Now that he was waiting for an answer, she couldn't find her voice, choked up by a lump in her throat.

"Maria?" he whispered, eyes pleading for a response.

Swallowing hard and looking over his shoulder, Maria caught Macie's gaze as she mouthed "sister" with a smile.

Dropping her eyes back to Gavin's, with tears forming, she

opened her mouth to speak but hiccuped instead.

With everyone in the room giggling, Maria finally shouted, "Yes! Yes, you fool. What took you so long?!"

Sliding the ring onto her finger, he rose to his feet and scooped her up off the floor. Spinning in circles, he paused, looked into her eyes, and kissed her with gusto.

"Congratulations!" were shouted as the whole gang mobbed the two of them, hugging and crying and laughing all together.

Aidan, squeezing shoulders and shouting for joy, breathed deep as the sharp edges of the internal depression he had been feeling since the revelation of his mother began to wane. And, in true Aidan fashion, he strode up to Gavin and Maria. Changing the expression on his face from joy to defeat, he said, "So, you're doing this thing, huh? You're one hundred percent sure this schmuck is the one? Cause I mean, well, hello, I'm right here."

Maria laughed, squeezed him tightly, and said playfully, "Oh, Aidan, you'll always be the one that got away." With an exaggerated wink, she sent everyone into a fit of laughter.

Chapter 20
Morality

Maya jolted back to the present. Her eyes flew open only to realize it was the worst part of her real life Happy Death Day movie. Only it wasn't early morning, which is when such bodily functions typically occurred. The act was degrading and mortifying. She tried to transport herself into another memory, some other place or time, but with Jessica looking on, she was trapped.

When Dr. Jessica Saylor returned from their meeting, she was different. She wouldn't make eye contact with Maya. Even kept her distance from the glass. Of course, it was likely from the unfortunate mishap that morning, which Maya still hadn't been able to wrap her mind around. She had been so angry. Her skin vibrated with rage. Then, without an ounce of internal awareness, an unexpected release laid all three doctors out on the ground. Maya was glad they weren't hurt, though would not have minded if Dr. Harold had been injured or worse. Maybe even Hutchens, too. Okay, so maybe she wasn't all that glad.

The only saving grace in her current state of humiliation was that Dr. Saylor was a woman, someone she'd known for years. Though, she couldn't imagine having to look this woman in the eyes ever again.

"Almost done," said Dr. Saylor, speaking into the small microphone at her desk. The unit Maya lay in was exceptionally high-tech, capable of cleaning her body as needed. While fully autonomous, one doctor remained during the ordeal as a safety measure while the others left to provide some semblance of privacy. To her credit, Dr. Saylor often took the job.

In recent weeks, Maya had observed Dr. Saylor's internal struggle develop. She kept a professional face when Dr. Harold and Dr. Hutchens were present, but her expression displayed a sense of sorrow and shame when alone.

"Alright, Maya. You're all set." Dr. Saylor made her way to the glass unit after wrapping up her notes. "I'm going to let them know they can return."

Maya's stare and subtly furrowed brow pleaded with the doctor. She couldn't move or speak, but she could open her eyes and ever so slightly manipulate her expression.

Staring at one another, Dr. Saylor shifted her weight while wiping the wrinkles from her coat. "Maya, I…" her voice trailed off as moisture filled the corners of her eyes, "I, uh… this is going to be a rather difficult afternoon. I wish… I'm going to do everything I can to reason with him to stop this, but I don't know if I can." Looking away, she used her sleeve to dab her eyes. "I don't know how it's come to this so quickly, but Dr. Harold—"

"Afternoon Maya!" Dr. Harold's voice boomed through the room as the door flung open. "This is an exciting day! You're well on your way to making history." His footsteps thumped like a beating heart as his rapid steps took him to just outside her reach beyond the glass.

"Afternoon Dr. Saylor. Everything ready?" he asked.

Dr. Saylor nodded, cleared her throat, and quietly replied, "She's been cleaned and prepped, sir."

"Is something wrong?"

"Sir, I was just thinking... is this something we really need to do? It's only been a day since you mentioned finding the other girls. I mean, this… procedure, well, it just doesn't seem necessary yet."

Half-listening and reaching for his tablet, Dr. Harold paused.

"Whether we find them or not, the amount of data and subsequent research that can be done through the success of this application could be astronomical," Dr. Hutchens interjected, clearly drinking the Kool-Aid Dr. Harold was dishing out. "This could get us to the very root of how their capabilities manifested."

She couldn't speak. His tone brushed off her obvious discomfort over the unethical and immoral act about to be done to Maya in the name of Science. Though enraged and devastated, she wouldn't allow the men to see her as anything less than professional. "I understand, but with others out there, including Maya's son, if we're patient, we would not need to be so invasive. At least not so quickly."

Dr. Hutchens began to respond when Dr. Harold gently

placed a hand on his shoulder to quiet him. "I understand how you feel, Dr. Saylor. I feel the same way." His words didn't match the glint in his eye. "This is hard for us all, but it's a broken world. We don't know when or if we'll find them. Starting this procedure now gives us options in the short term. I know that Maya would gladly agree to this for the betterment of humanity."

"Don't you think that should be her choice? That she should respond to the request directly?"

Dr. Harold's face twitched as he struggled to maintain the placating smile. "Dr. Saylor, if you're uncomfortable with this course of action, you're more than welcome to work on data analysis today in the other room."

She wanted to jump at the chance to get as far away from this moment as possible, but as her eyes caught Maya's, the fear on display planted her firmly in place. "No. I'm fine. Let's proceed."

As they prepared the room, Maya's heart rate increased. Despite the pressure, her body began to tremble noticeably.

"Sir," said Dr. Saylor, hoping to put Maya to sleep as quickly as possible so she could at least avoid the emotional trauma of what they were about to do. "I'm going to administer the sedative so we can bring her out."

"Proceed. I'm heading to cold storage for the sample," he noted, placing his tablet down before leaving the room.

As soon as he was out of earshot she quickly turned to Dr. Hutchens."Steve?"

At the sound of his name, Dr. Hutchens turned toward her. She had never called him by his first name before, and he wasn't sure how to respond.

"Are you fully on board with this? We can't take it back. We'll have to live with this for the rest of our lives."

Looking down at the paperwork, he sighed, closing his eyes. Dr. Saylor leaned forward, but whatever consideration caused him to pause disappeared as soon as he looked at her. "We don't live in that world anymore. If you don't have the stomach for this, I suggest you do what Dr. Harold said and go work on analysis for the day." His stare was cold and cut through her.

Dr. Saylor calmly pulled in a deep breath. With one last look at Maya, she punched in the code to release the sedative, then stood watching as Maya's eyes drifted shut. She couldn't stop what was coming, but at the very least, she could bear witness for Maya. It was clear she was alone in her morality.

With Maya asleep, they depressurized the unit, opened the glass door and maneuvered her onto a gurney. Rolling her to the side of the room, they gently placed her onto a hospital bed and hooked her up to an IV, heart monitor and various cables designed to track every aspect of her unconscious being. Dr. Saylor covered her with a crisp white sheet before arranging her feet pointing up and her legs spread apart.

"We ready?" Dr. Harold asked, walking back into the room.

"Yes, sir. She's prepped." Dr. Hutchens said with no more feeling than a rock.

Dropping onto a stool near Maya's feet, Dr. Harold opened the plastic sheet covering the syringe needle and began to fill it with fluid from a small glass bottle.

"Let's begin."

Chapter 21
Enroute

Being on the road again felt strange to Aidan. He watched the passing trees, overgrown fields and rusted-out vehicles that had spent years wasting away in the elements. His usual jovial self was buried beneath the weight of the reality that his mother was alive. All this time. He'd never considered the alternative.

"Are you okay?" asked Zuri. Her gentle question slowly crept into his mind, breaking up the nightmarish images forming despite the calm landscape.

With a subtle grunt, the corner of his mouth lifted. "Yeah. I'm good. How are you? Have you seen anything yet?"

She knew what he was asking. "No. I'm sorry, Aidan."

Taking her hand, he gave a gentle squeeze. "Don't be sorry.

If it weren't for you, all of you, I would've never accepted the idea that my mother might still be alive."

"You said you thought she died in a fire?"

He nodded his head.

"Joanna told me she saw your memories. I can't imagine you carrying that alone all these years." Zuri hated seeing him in pain. He was the one person who could always pull her out of despair. These past months of being together all the time, she sensed he was changing. Even Zoey had noticed that his personality had changed since the rescue.

He wasn't upset that Joanna had peeked into his mind, but wished he'd been able to hide it better. She didn't need to see the images that had plagued him since he was a teen. "I've just never been one to dwell on things I guess." His words were light, but his deep breath gave him away.

"What do you think we'll find when we get there?"

"I dunno. I'm anticipating it to be a big shock, though. Finding the two of you was a crazy surprise we could never have foreseen. So hey, I'm up for a humdinger of another one!"

"Humdinger?" Zuri giggled. Which made Aidan chuckle. It wasn't so much the word that made them laugh, but all of it. Before they knew it, they were both gasping for air and holding their stomachs in laughter.

"What in the world is going on back there?" barked Zoey before succumbing to the contagion.

For just one moment, the strain of the world upon them eased.

Sanford, NC   👁   5:00 p.m.

"We're going to stop for the night," said James, touching Dakota's shoulder to rouse her.

Pushing herself upright in the passenger seat, Dakota readjusted herself upright. "Where are we?"

"Right around the halfway mark in North Carolina," he replied, flipping on his directional, following the lead car down the exit ramp.

"Good. I need to use the restroom." She stretched her arm out, wishing she could stretch the other, but the sling pulled it tight to her body.

"We'll be stopping about two miles off this main road."

With a deep yawn, Dakota reached over the seat to poke Elias. "Hey. We're about to stop."

Elias stretched, smacked his cheeks, and then sat up. "Cool, my bladder's about to explode."

Rubbing her eyes clear, Dakota looked out across the open fields growing vegetables. It was an odd sight to see. Most open land they'd passed was overgrown. The exit road was also fairly clear of weeds, which meant there was an active community there. Her heart leapt at the promise of active life in the area, which made her question her crew's motives all the more. This community was trying to rebuild their lives, yet here was her team, callously on their way to destroy someone else's.

"What town is this?"

"Uh, we passed a sign back there that said Sanford."

Her heart sank. *Why would Levi bring us here?*

Elias caught her reaction then grabbed his radio. "Levi, this is Elias. Come in. Over."

Several seconds passed before static broke the silence. "Go for Levi."

"Why are we stopping here? Over."

"Camp for the night. Over."

Elias caught Dakota's eyes. "Right, but our plan shows our stop in Mt. Airy, North Carolina."

"Yes, however, I altered it yesterday. Did you not receive the update?"

Dakota and Elias looked at one another with skepticism. "You did not provide me with one. So, clearly I did not."

"Oops, sorry. James should have the bed-down location."

His less-than-apologetic tone grated on Dakota. She knew there was an ulterior reason for stopping in Sanford. Turning to Elias, she said, "This is no accident. Sanford was the location of the energy spike."

Elias nodded, cut his eyes to James, then back to her.

With a subtle huff, Dakota turned to face forward, attempting to memorize the landscape as they passed.

She knew they had taken a right turn off the exit and kept an eye out for what road they were on. Shortly after, she caught a small sign that read *421 S*. As they slowed their pace, she caught another sign that read *Cox Mill*, where they turned right. With every passing second, her unease grew, along with an odd pressure in her chest and tingling on her skin. She could feel the rage building. Something that had never plagued her before, yet was becoming her new normal.

Coming upon a small strawberry farm that appeared active, the crew pulled into an adjacent dirt parking lot. Without a word from James, the driver, Dakota and Elias exited the car, beelining it to Levi as he left his vehicle.

"What are we doing here?" asked Elias, his eyes offering more than a question.

Ignoring the question, Levi signaled to the drivers to refuel. "Go ahead and get it done, guys." As if alone, he watched in silence as they untied the emergency gas cans stored on the back of each vehicle and filled the tanks.

"That gas is for emergency purposes. What happens if we don't find another fill-up station?"

"Calm down. We'll refill the cans in Mt. Airy. We know they have a station."

"Levi, what are we doing here?" Dakota growled through clenched teeth.

"It's all in the plan. Here." Levi reached into his bag and pulled out another folder with a smirk. "You should've grabbed the updated version yesterday. Oh, right. You were recovering."

Elias set his hand on Dakota's shoulder, waited for her to take a deep breath, and said, "Okay, so why here?"

"After going over the travel plan, it occurred to me we'd be going right by the origination point of that energy surge. Being the inquisitive animal that I am, I thought it incumbent upon us to do a quick recon of the area, ya know, since we'd already be passing through."

"That wasn't your call to make," breathed Dakota, swallowing hard.

"Well, with you not fully up to par due to that injury, not to mention what happened two days ago, I thought I'd take the initiative."

Elias grasped Dakota's shoulder as she stepped forward, her eyes burning into Levi's. She said, "Considering I'm on this mission despite my injury, I'd say that mentally, I'm still up to the task of making decisions."

With an odd smile and an abnormally high level of

confidence, Levi turned to face her and replied, "Are you?"

Dakota squinted as a sly grin spread across the man's face while he slowly backed away. It was clear he knew something they didn't and wasn't afraid to play his hand.

"Team, rally up!" Levi called. Without hesitation, the rest of the team encircled Levi. "Somewhere nearby, we tracked an atypical signature. It's got to be within three miles of this location. Keep in mind, this is just surface-level recon to see what's around and if anything is out of the ordinary. Based on satellite imaging, I saw no large structures, so keep your eyes peeled."

Pulling up a zoomed-in map of the area, Levi dictated the different routes for each recon unit. "Take pictures of anything you see. Move slow, but not in an obvious manner that would draw suspicion." After distributing pre-drawn maps, he said, "We'll rally back here when your route is complete."

Dakota and Elias stood outside the circle, listening in. Throughout the briefing, Dakota made eyes with several members with confused expressions, though no one spoke up.

"Okay, let's roll! Mark anything on the map you deem pertinent, and we'll investigate later." Without another word, Levi rolled up his map and made his way back to the vehicle, not bothering to address the two of them.

"Something's not right here," Elias said in a hushed voice. "This is not protocol."

Dakota, staring down Levi, nodded—her mind was racing.

They watched as a Jeep and the van pulled out heading north. Jumping into their humvee, James turned south, following the second Jeep. After a quarter mile, the Jeep in front carrying Levi turned right down a side road with a gated entrance as Dakota and Elias kept straight on. Elias pulled out the map to see they were following a yellow highlighted track straight down Cox Mill. After a short hike, they would turn right onto Pickett Road.

"James, the map shows us turning onto Pickett, in little over a mile." Dakota swallowed the heat in her throat and mustered up her professional tone to keep him from suspecting she was anything other than in-the-know about the mission at hand.

"Yes, ma'am," he confirmed, his own map taped to the dashboard.

"Strange, there's a dead-end side road up ahead on the left. Looks like Levi missed a route. We should have time to do a quick pass-through and verify anything out of place."

Elias gave her a questioning look, but she ignored it, not wanting to tip off James.

Every second since turning off the exit ramp she'd felt the tingle on her skin heighten. It had turned into a vibration and she could hear a not unpleasant hum in her ears.

Turning down the lane, Dakota instinctively knew something about this property was important. She immediately noticed a series of large trees blocking out the corner lot. Spying between the branches, the field on the other side was open and manicured. A strange latent hum filled her ears as she strained to continue to focus. Toward the back of the property, she could see a large metal shop along with a smaller building in the center of the lot, and an old farmhouse up front by the main road. A large and fruitful garden sat near the tree line with several women tending to it.

The pull of energy reminded her of something buried deep inside. Flashes of faces crossed in front of her eyes. Foreign yet familiar.

Following the narrow road, they passed several more

overgrown properties that had likely been abandoned over the years. The further they got from the bustling property, the weaker the hum in her mind.

"Looks like we're coming to the end. I'm going to turn around in this driveway down here."

Elias and Dakota briefly locked eyes, but Dakota quickly shook her head not to do anything yet.

As they returned to the corner lot, she felt the strange pull once again and quickly marked the map.

After completing a full circle back to the strawberry farm, they pulled in to see the other three vehicles in park and the rest of the team standing outside in discussion.

"Did you find anything?" Levi called out as Dakota stepped out of the car.

"Nothing of interest, you?" she said, tucking the map into her back pocket.

"Just a few farms and some buildings we can investigate later," he said, showing them on his map where he'd marked some locations of interest.

Dakota's mind, however, drifted elsewhere. From the sight of the property and the wild hum, she had begun to envision grainy memories of white walls and doctors, sand and dirt intermingling in a confusing pattern. Shaking them off, she said, "Alright, set up the tents. We'll get an early start, three a.m. tomorrow." She looked at Levi, "Is there anything else on the schedule that's changed?" Her words held a bite to them that the others definitely caught.

"Nope, that was it," offered Levi, his eyes boring into hers with a coldness that held the truth.

"Okay, get to work."

Chapter 22

Premonition

*B*lue skies held cotton colored clouds. Birds played tag in the sky, chirping their joy at the warmth in the air. The gentle sun held the promise of a beautiful day without worry or fear.

Maya laid back on grass so green it seemed to shimmer. She held up a single blade in front of her face. The green, in stark contrast to the blue sky, made her feel as if she was a young girl again, lying on the ground like a child, enamored with the sweetness of the air she could taste on her tongue. As her eyes shifted from the grass to the sky, the light began to dim. Shades of blue turned gray. Dark clouds stretched across the vast expanse above her.

The blade of grass, pinched between her forefinger and

thumb, began to wilt and brown, quickly decaying into a slimy mess on her skin.

What's happening? Her mind begged as her lips remained still.

The clouds rolled in, thick and angry, lifting her hair and blowing it across her face.

Struggling to sit up, the swirling air wouldn't allow it. Rain poured down, pelting her face, her arms, her exposed legs, flooding the field around her. Maya feared she might be carried away with the surge, instead, her body remained tethered to the mud beneath.

Trees swayed fiercely as their thick limbs skirted the ground. Water rose above her ears drowning out the raucous thunder.

She pleaded for the rain to stop, convinced she'd drown if it continued to rise, but the skies refused to hear her muted calls.

A flutter in her stomach briefly distracted her. Nausea rose in her throat and settled under the weight of water on her chest.

This is a dream. It has to be a dream. Wake up! she screamed, suddenly able to view her body from above, watching as it lay still under the lapping water. *We'll drown! What are you waiting for?* She stared helplessly as her lips succumbed under the charcoal waters and the air in her lungs burned for reprieve.

"Mom?"

His voice. She would have recognized it anywhere. It was deeper, but it was his.

"Mom? I'm coming. I'm coming! Please, just hold on."

She so wanted him to be there. Save her from this nightmare. The craze of it almost making her lose her mind.

"No!" she finally managed to cry out only to choke on the flood entering her throat. Enraged that her words wouldn't be *heard from beneath the raging water. She didn't want to die, yet the fear rising in her heart was more for him than for herself.*

She prayed, Don't come here! Please. Please God, keep him away. If you could grant me just this one prayer, keep him away. Keep him safe.

Her salty tears blended with the sea now washing over her as a deep darkness filled the edges of her blurred vision.

"Maya?" whispered a young woman, her soft voice drifting by like a breeze. "Maya, hold on. We're coming."

Finding her voice as if the seas above had parted, she said with ferocity, "Listen to me… whoever you are… do not come here!"

Recon Location  Outside VISP

Releasing hands, the girls choked on the air filling their lungs as they sucked in huge breaths.

"What happened?" Maria crouched next to Zoey, checking her pupils and wiping her face with a cold rag.

The others followed suit, handing the girls bottles of water as the fear cleared from their eyes.

"I don't know. Maybe she was dreaming?" Lexi offered.

"It felt so real," said Maddy, wiping thick sweat from her face.

"The storm was so strong, and the waters rose so fast. It had to be a nightmare," Addie said as Joe put his arm around her waist to steady her.

"Whatever they've done to her, she's fighting some unbelievable nightmares," Maddy said under her breath. "Nothing I've ever seen."

167

"I have," Joanna whispered. They all turned to look at her. "That storm, I've seen it before. Or something like it. Several weeks ago, I had a dream... well, I'm not sure whether it was a dream or not, but it was surreal. Just like this. It was different in that I could feel the sting of the rain and the blinding white of the lightning. This? It was like I was watching it instead of living it. I knew at the time that it was from my counterpart, that she was living through it somehow and that I could feel what she felt. When she hurt her arm, that was real. I knew it was real because my arm hurt so horribly. It still aches now, though not as much.

"But this was different." Joanna looked down in thought.

"That's because it came from my mother." Aidan had his back to them. He hadn't been part of their circle, choosing instead to stand back and safeguard their endeavor.

They were positioned at the same location where Zoey, Joe, and Aidan had set up camp prior to rescuing Lexi and Zuri. VISP was a short distance away. Aidan may not have been part of their circle, but he witnessed what they had just as clearly. Since accepting the reality of his abilities, he had begun to see things so much more vividly. In fact, he didn't have to be physically involved with what they were doing to be a part of it. Both a gift and a curse.

While he longed to rescue and reunite with his mother, for the first time in his kick-down-the-door preference for action, he understood they couldn't just rush in. Too many lives were at stake. "I could see it. As if it was a mirage in the air around the seven of you. I think she's okay. It was just a dream."

"I think you're right, Aidan," Addie said. "It was definitely a nightmare. But also... I think it was something more than that."

"What do you mean, Addie?" Gavin asked, holding Macie's hand.

"As it unfolded, I watched our tethers reach out to her. But the colors weren't like anything I've seen up to this point. Iridescent and woven together. And just like with the other colors, I feel like I know what it represents. It just felt like... part of the future. Something that hasn't happened yet."

"A premonition," Justin muttered, longing to see what they were seeing. He was convinced he could be more useful if he only saw what they did.

"Any chance you caught a date in that dream?" Brandon asked.

Joanna patted his chest and said, "If only one thing could be that easy." Smiling, he bent down and kissed her forehead.

"No date, but I get the feeling that it's not too far into the future," Zuri offered.

"Well then, let's finish our recon and finalize the plan. We're going in tomorrow night." Joe pulled out his well-worn blueprints of the building. "Aidan, put in a call to Jahnsen. We'll need his team here by morning."

Chapter 23
Calm

July 1, 2030 | 11:30 p.m.

Zoey sat on the back bumper with a blanket draped over her shoulders. The night sky was awash with a million stars illuminating everything around her. The last time she had been in this location, pain had dropped her to her knees in connection with Lexi. Shivering, she mulled over their previous decision to enter the compound immediately following her episode rather than wait until morning.

She wondered what might have been different if they had waited to infiltrate. Would they have ever found Lexi? Would they have made it in time to save Zuri? The what-ifs had plagued her after things calmed down, but now, on the cusp of another infil, she felt them brewing. Would they regret not going after the eighth girl before returning to VISP?

"It's peaceful out here." Zoey startled at the sound of Zuri's soft voice. Taking her hand, Zuri sat down beside her.

"I was just thinking about you." Zoey smiled. Looking back toward the stars, "It is. Like the calm before a storm, I suppose."

"What do you think that storm premonition was all about?"

"I'm not sure. I've been thinking about whether it was a symbolic dream or a literal premonition, like Aidan said." She chuckled as she said his name.

"What's so funny?"

"Nothing. It's just, thinking about Aidan. I've known him for what seems like forever," she said with a sigh. "All these years, he was more like a brother than I even imagined." Her voice trailed off as thoughts of him drifted through her mind. "If the nerd-pack's theory is right about his mom, I guess I'm just curious why he didn't know he had gifts all along. And, how? How did she give them to us? Or bring them out in us? I dunno."

Zuri sat quietly at her side, struggling to resolve the same impossible questions when Lexi walked up. "Is this seat taken?"

Zoey, reaching out her other hand, grabbed hold of Lexi's as she sat beside them.

"It's funny, now that we're here I can't tell whose eyes I'm looking through."

"What do you mean, Lex?" Zoey asked.

"I can remember exactly how it felt, and the space around me from inside the glass box. It's just... I can see it so clearly again now through Maya, but I'm not sure if it's a memory or if it's her reality I'm seeing."

"Might be a little of both," Zuri offered.

"You guys should be sleeping." Maddy's hushed voice preceded her appearance.

"We thought we'd have a midnight party!" Zoey quipped quietly.

Maddy sat on the ground in front of them. As she settled in, Joanna arrived, pushing Macie in her wheelchair, with Addie not far behind.

"Definitely a party now," Zoey laughed.

"You know, we should probably all be sleeping," she said to the sound of half-giggles all around.

They sat quietly together for a while just allowing the hum in the air to build then settle, build then settle. Addie could see what the rest of them couldn't. Zuri was pulling energy from the ground at her feet. It was so natural that Addie didn't think Zuri even knew she was doing it. Threads of gold seemed to wrap around her ankles, tethering her to the ground without immobilizing her. They moved with her when her feet shuffled in the dirt. Just being near her allowed those same threads to spread to the rest of them. Addie watched as they made their way toward her, wrapping around her wrists before disappearing beneath her skin. The hum they could feel more than hear was coming from those threads, making each of them stronger.

"I never really noticed before, but the color of each of your eyes seems to match the colors surrounding you," Addie said.

Each one looked around at the others before Zuri asked, "What do you think that means, Addie?"

Shrugging her shoulders, she replied, "I'm not sure. Maybe nothing."

After several moments, Joanna asked, "Do you think we'll find Aidan's mom in time?"

"Yes. We have to. If for no other reason than to do it for Aidan. My senses tell me she isn't in imminent danger... more like despair," Zuri's words held a sense of sorrow.

"I feel that too. It's like she knows we're coming," Maddy agreed.

"But doesn't want us to," whispered Zoey.

Zuri raised her fingers, lightly pulling on a few threads Addie could see coming from the compound beyond the trees. "I think she's trying to warn us. She knows something, but can't communicate it to us. But yes, I think you're right, Zoey. I don't think she wants us here."

"What should we do?" asked Joanna under her breath.

"Leaving her here isn't an option," Addie replied. "As much as I didn't want Joanna in danger searching for me, I'm so glad she never stopped. We're not leaving without Aidan's mother."

Aidan, restless himself, had been sitting on the other side of the vehicle listening to them. Hearing their determination, he stood and walked around the car.

"She doesn't want us here because she's trying to save us," he said, breathing heavily. "She knows they're looking for us and that if we go in there, we might never come out." Even beneath the bright starry night, his cheeks appeared flushed. The shimmer in his eyes caught them all by surprise. "But... uh..." he cleared his throat. "I don't want to put any of you in danger for me. Maybe I should do this alone."

Zuri stood up. "Lucky for you, you don't get a say in this matter." She took his hand. "There's nothing that would stop us from saving someone you love. Because we all love you."

He held back the lump in his throat and squeezed her soft fingers.

At the sound of a voice so soft and sweet they all turned. "We go in and get her. I would not have wanted any of you to come for me at the risk of you being captured and tortured as well. But," said Macie, swallowing hard but with strength in her voice, "if you hadn't I would likely be dead by now. You saved me. And I'm so grateful you did. So… we save her."

Addie watched as the colors around them amplified with their resolve. As they did, she saw a thread she had not seen in several weeks. The red and blue vines were getting thicker as she focused. As if a door had opened somewhere allowing the colors to flow more freely.

Zuri felt them and reached out her hand. Everyone saw her movements and held their breath.

"It's her—the eighth. I think… I think she's in trouble."

Dakota waited until everyone was either asleep or convinced she was letting her guard down. Eli had positioned their tent so they could sneak off without being seen. The night sky shone bright enough for them to quietly slip away without using their flashlights.

She planned to hike back to the farmhouse less than a mile from their position. The energy she felt made her internal rage feel almost calm. She had to know what was there.

Once far enough away, they picked up their pace to a light jog and flicked on their lights. Eli, who Dakota had intended to leave behind to keep watch, though he refused, asked, "So now tell me, what do you think we're gonna find?"

"Not sure. All I know is there's energy there. It made the hair on my arms stand up when we went by. This may sound crazy, but it reminded me of when I was a child. Dark memories I've been recalling more and more these past months. It's like a pulling sensation. I felt it grow stronger the entire trip here. But now..."

"But now?"

"That pull has been diminishing since we made camp. Almost like it's moved." Shaking her head and groaning in frustration, she continued, "Maybe I'm imagining things, but I need to see if I can figure it out before Levi makes a play to investigate."

"Alright. Any idea who's there?"

"None."

He let her answer hang in the air as they drew close to the property. Light filled the windows of the tiny homes, but the main house was dark.

"What do you want to do?" Eli asked.

Motioning for him to follow, they crouched low, following the treeline along the street. After several minutes of silent observation, Dakota determined the coast was clear and moved quickly to the side of the farmhouse.

Peeking through windows, she could tell the residence was actively lived in, though it was empty at the moment. The same was true for the building immediately behind the house. Empty.

The knob was locked on the main door of the small building. Dakota pulled out her notebook, drew the locking mechanism in the unlock position, and swiped her hand across the page.

Hearing the click, Eli pushed the door open slowly. Assessing that it was, in fact, empty, they entered.

"What is all this?"

"Looks like a science lab," Dakota whispered. There were beakers and burners, different contraptions she'd seen at their own headquarters in the medical bay. Only, there was quite a bit more sophistication in the equipment.

Eli cautiously picked up several documents, studied them, and said, "This is like, someone's blood work or something."

"Yeah, there are x-rays over here, but they're strange. I've never seen anything like this before."

Looking over her shoulder, he said, "CT scans, maybe? I had one once as a kid when my appendix burst. Looked a little like that."

Dakota walked around the room. It was clear there were several people living there. Some women's flip-flops under a desk. A pair of glasses that looked more like a man's than a woman's.

"I'm not sure what all this is," Eli whispered. "It feels like Frankenstein's lab. Maybe we should get out of here before they return. I don't want to be here when they do."

"Mmhmm," she replied, half listening while attempting to note the various subject identifiers marking the strewn-about pages on the desks.

"Dakota?"

"Yeah, sorry. Just thinking."

"Look, they're definitely doing tests on quite a few people. Those girls we saw earlier, ya know, tending a garden. Maybe it's them?"

"Could be. But there are more subjects than we saw people." Dakota picked up a file marked Joanna. Something about the name tugged at her heart.

"I hate to state the obvious, but maybe they're disposing of people after they, ya know, experiment on them."

"Nothing like taking it to the darkest place imaginable, Eli."

"Well? Do you see anyone else around here?"

Dakota pushed some papers around on a desk nearby. "That doesn't feel right. I don't know. I don't get the sense there's danger here."

Eli was watching out the shop window when something caught his attention. Snapping his fingers, he directed her attention outward. "There's lights out in the field. We need to go."

Dakota, peering out the window, nodded. "Right. Okay, let's move around the south side of the house to the trees. They won't see us that way."

Eli nodded, then slowly opened the door, gently rolling his feet heel-to-toe while crouching low. Dakota followed suit until they were beyond the treeline.

They'd been gone a few hours and the camp was quiet. They moved cautiously toward their tent. The sound of unzipping the door proved uncomfortably loud. Just as they began to crawl inside, a figure walked out from the opposite side.

"Midnight stroll?" Levi asked.

Chapter 24
Getting Closer

July 2, 2030 | 2:30 a.m.

Dakota quickly closed herself off. She had carefully let her inner walls down while exploring the farmhouse, attempting to sense where the energy was coming from. With the appearance of Levi, however, the walls resurrected.

"Just checking out the area," she said with as little emotion as possible.

"Two-thirty in the morning?"

"Early bird catches the worm and all that," said Eli as he none-too-gently pushed past Levi into the tent.

"Dakota?" Levi asked, sliding his hand into his pocket. "You sure you're up to all this? I mean, after what happened and not to mention your arm."

Levi was a hand-through-his-knotted-hair kind of guy, not

the hand-in-the-pocket type. Dakota noticed little things like that. Observations that had saved her more than once in her unconventional upbringing.

Stepping toward him, she put her face in his and, in a gruff voice, said, "Maybe I should be asking you the same thing, Levi? You've seemed a little off lately. Something you wanna share?"

Carefully putting his hands in the air, he stepped backward. "I'm good, boss." He took another step back. "If you're not feeling well again, be sure to let me know, okay?" His false concern made her skin crawl.

Dakota dropped into her tent. It was almost sunrise and her mind raced thinking of the possibilities for Levi's shady behavior.

He's hiding something.

 11:45 a.m.

Dakota's eyes burned with the lack of sleep. Her mind, however, was focused on the amplifying pull of energy she'd felt with every mile closer to their destination. The same pull that drew her to the farmhouse. The strength of the energy convinced her to let down the barrier once again as the feeling grew in strength. Though discomforting in its electric grip, the sensation gave her a sense of peace.

With unwanted memories still holding her captive, peace and joy were fleeting, always leaving her wanting and in despair when stripped away.

It was an addictive sort of supernatural electricity, though, and despite the looming despair, Dakota wanted desperately to let it take over. Real life, however, refused to let her succumb to it. She erected the walls around her most sensitive feelings. Eli looked at her, and, with a sigh, she fidgeted in her seat until she got comfortable. Letting her walls down not only allowed for the peace to flow toward her but also allowed her own unfiltered feelings to be released. That was something she couldn't allow.

Sleep came fitfully. Her eyes fluttered open and shut at random intervals as the miles passed.

"We're about thirty minutes out," said Levi over the radio. "Keep your eyes peeled for anything out of the ordinary."

Even before Elias opened his eyes he could feel Dakota's agitation. Each had a grim feeling concerning what would unfold once they arrived at their target. A sixth sense wasn't needed to see it.

Dakota glanced over her shoulder at him. Both gave a quick nod. They knew they needed to be ready for anything.

"Levi, we'll meet you there. Need to make a quick stop, but it'll only take a few minutes." Dakota's voice crackled through the radio static.

"We're only thirty minutes out, boss," said James, glancing into the rearview mirror.

"Yeah… female issues," she responded. It was the one thing she always had in her pocket in an emergency.

Elias, watching the other vehicles barrel onward, knew she was making an excuse as they slowed to a crawl alongside a patch of forest.

"Thanks, James. It'll be a minute," said Dakota, grabbing her pack.

"I might as well hit the head, too," Elias said, hopping out and heading further up the treeline apart from Dakota. When it seemed clear, he scrambled back to meet with her.

"What's wr—"

"We only have a minute, Eli. I don't know what Levi's plan is, but we need to be ready. When we get back in the car I need you to restock your bag quietly. Anything you can fit."

"You thinking of running? We could do that now."

"No. I wanna know what Levi's up to first."

"Okay," he said, watching her eyes sparkle brighter than he had ever seen before. "Listen, it feels to me like there's something you're not saying. Your eyes..."

Dakota didn't want to get into it, but he knew her better than most. "That pull I was telling you about last night? All day, the closer we get, the stronger the sensation. Like we're heading right toward it. I feel like..." she said, pausing, dropping her voice to a whisper, "it almost feels like there are people out there searching for me. People like me."

Eli's eyes grew wide. "Good guys?"

"I wish I knew," she said, shaking her head.

"So this is what you felt back in Sanford? You have the same expression you did when we were there."

"Sort of. I don't know. But..."

"But what?"

Lifting her forearm up toward him, they watched as the skin on the back of her arm vibrated so rapidly that it simply looked out of focus. After only a few seconds, with the hum in her ears growing louder, she erected her inner walls once more.

"So... what's that all about? Are we being lured? How is this possible?"

Dakota locked eyes with him until a crackling on the forest floor caught his attention.

"Listen, maybe whoever it is… if we can get to them before Levi does, maybe they'll help us," she whispered, looking throughout the woods.

"And if they can't?"

"Levi isn't running me out of my own home. We'll snag an SUV and haul it back to the station."

"Then what? Fight them when they return?" he said, throwing his arms up.

"I don't know yet, but one thing at a time. Just be ready, alright?"

Squeezing her arm, Eli sprinted back to where he entered the forest. Whatever unfolded, he would protect her.

 12:15 p.m.

"It's gone." Zuri's voice dropped in frustration.

"What do you mean?" asked Justin.

"The eighth. She let me in briefly, then closed me off again. The crazy thing is, she's close."

Joanna stood up. "You're right. Seemed like she was within reach. The vibrations on my skin were as strong as if one of you were nearby."

"Do you think she is?" Maria asked.

None of them knew what to say. Had they been wrong about the direction of the eighth being south of them? They were so far north now that it didn't make sense for her to be so close. Zoey couldn't help but think about the pulling sensation she'd felt before finding Lexi and Zuri. Maybe this girl was doing the same and seeking them out.

"It reminds me of when Joe, Aidan and I were getting close

to this place the first time around," said Zoey, looking at Zuri and Lexi. "I could just sense you weren't far from me."

Gavin added, "Well, we all know not to bet against you, so maybe she is. Maybe she's been sensing you the way you sense her, and she's decided to follow you?" He nodded at the genuine possibility of his suggestion.

Zoey, squinting, nodded in agreement.

"Rick and Phil will be here within the hour, along with the rest of Jahnsen's team," said Joe, eager to get moving. "Once they arrive, we'll brief them and nail down our plan of attack. If we're lucky, maybe the last girl is, in fact, close. Would save us a trip south."

"Wouldn't that just beat all," said Grant, eyes wide at the prospect when he saw a dust plume of a vehicle in the distance. "What's that?" Joe and the others turned around.

"Is that Rick?" asked Justin, trying to catch a view of the source.

"Can't be," Joe replied, pulling his radio from his belt. "They should still be about an hour out."

"Maybe they made good time?" Aidan joked as Zuri smacked his arm with a laugh. "Hey! That's my shooting arm there, Big Guns."

Keying his radio, Joe called out, "Green, this is Black. Come in. Over."

"Black, this is Green. Go 'head," responded Phil, calm and clear.

"What's your ETA? Over." Joe pulled out his binoculars and could see they had only minutes before the vehicles would be close enough to evaluate.

"Forty-eight minutes. What's up?"

"We've got company. I'll update you when we know more. Over."

"Roger. Stay frosty."

Joe returned the radio to his belt and began doling out orders. "Move the vehicles a mile east toward the safe house. Cut through those trees and avoid the roads. I'll sit tight and see if I can gauge who it is. Justin, Brandon, fall back to the treeline and flank me, just in case."

"Wait!" called Aidan, moving toward Joe. "I'll stay with you."

"I want you back with the girls," he responded sharply, gripping Aidan's arm. "If I give you the signal, move everyone to the safehouse. I trust you more than anyone to make sure they're safe."

Sheila asked, "And me? Treeline, just in case?"

"With the girls. They're our main priority. If we need you, one of us will radio."

They all set off to their positions with only minutes to spare.

With everything set in motion, Joe crouched down behind a nearby tree as the sound of tires on gravel rolled fast. Three vehicles appeared from around the bend. Shortly after, they slowed to a stop less than fifty yards away.

Suddenly, Joe tensed at the sound of brush behind him rustling. Cautiously turning to look, Lexi crouched down a few feet away. "What are you doing?"

"I thought you might need an assist."

His eyes grew wide, and he wanted to argue, but the sound of doors slamming shut pulled his attention back to the guests. Gesturing for her to come up by his side, he asked, "Can you tell what they're doing?"

Squinting, she watched them stand, then crouch, point and repeat. "They're looking at something in the dirt," she whispered, pausing to think. "Our tire tracks?"

"That's what I was thinking. Damn!" he huffed, angry at himself for not considering that in the plan.

"What about the eighth, do you think she's with them? You said she was getting closer."

Lexi shook her head. "I don't think so. Her signature is there, but I can't sense she's with them. She's not far though. What do you want to do?"

Joe watched as the men traced the tracks. Lifting his binoculars, one of them pointed the group's attention toward the woods. Grabbing hold of Lexi, Joe pulled her to him behind the tree. "Don't move," he said under his breath, praying that Justin and Brandon were hidden and attentive. Carefully keying his radio, Joe whispered, "No one move. They're attempting to track us. Stay hidden until I give the word."

Radio silence, which he was thankful for.

After several painfully long seconds, Joe peered around the tree, exhaled deeply, and then turned his gaze down at the ground.

"What's wrong?"

"They're not leaving. Maybe they determined like we did that this is the least conspicuous location to breach the compound."

"What? Like they're going to try and break in too?" Lexi's eyes and tone accused him of paranoia. "Seems like a stretch. Maybe they're just taking a break?"

"And happen to be this close to VISP? This far from any main travel roads? They're either part of VISP or planning something. Either way, we need a new plan." He peeked around the tree again and sighed as they pulled bags from the vehicle. Grabbing his radio, he gestured to Lexi, steering her away from the tree to rendezvous with the other two hunkered down further back. "Boys, back to the vehicles. Slow and steady. We need an alternate plan."

Chapter 25
There's Someone Out There

July 2, 2030 | 12:15 p.m.

"Take the map and scout the area," commanded Levi. Looking back in the direction they came, he asked, "And has anyone heard from Dakota?"

The group answered with shaking heads and murmured No's which fueled his frustration. Grabbing his radio, Levi barked, "James, come in, over." Several seconds ticked by. No response. "James? What's your position?"

With a crackle of the radio, James' voice broke the silence. "Yeah, boss, we're about five minutes out. Bathroom break."

"Again? Fine. Hurry up." Clipping his radio onto his belt, Levi paused at the sight of the Capt. V. jogging toward him.

"Dakota?" he said as his pace slowed.

"Bathroom break."

"Again?"

Levi shrugged his shoulders in disbelief. "Yeah."

"Think she knows—"

Levi gave him a look that stopped his next words. "How could she? James isn't in the know. It's why I sent him as their driver."

"What then?"

He looked back over his shoulder and almost to himself said, "I don't know, but something is definitely not right."

Capt. V. let Levi's words hang for a moment before cutting through the silence. " I don't think we're alone here." When Levi turned his head back the captain was holding up a freshly tossed balled up saran wrapper. "It was lying on the ground behind a tree over there."

Levi examined it closely. There was no dirt or mud, and a chocolate smear from a granola bar was still fresh on the wrapper. "Guards making rounds?"

"This far from the compound?" he replied, glancing around at their remote position.

"Okay, bring everyone back in. We might need to set up shop further back."

"Good job, James," Dakota said, patting his shoulder. They had almost regrouped with Levi when she had him pull over.

"I don't understand. Why don't you just tell them you think someone's up there? What if they get ambushed? How can you even tell?" James was not convinced Dakota had the ability to sense others like she claimed. Still, he was afraid to contradict her, considering he knew what else she was capable of.

"Difficult to explain. I can sort of... just... feel it."

"Shouldn't we warn the others then?" James replied, reaching for his radio again.

"From what I can sense," she said, closing her eyes and rubbing her temples, "it would be best to find a way around, maybe get eyes on whoever we're dealing with." Opening her map, Dakota pointed to what appeared to be dirt trails throughout the area. In reality, the energy pull had become so strong she wanted to see them before they saw her if they were already watching Levi's group.

"Looks like we'll be going on foot," said Elias, grabbing his pack.

James really didn't like this plan. "Why don't I head up and tell them what's going on while you two go check it out?"

Locking eyes with him, Dakota got in his face and said, "I think it's better we stick together."

 East of VISP  1:00 p.m.

They were about a mile east of the compound nervously waiting when Zuri saw Joe, Lexi, Justin, and Brandon come into view.

"What do you think?" Gavin asked Joe as they closed the gap.

"Three vehicles. Twelve people. I don't know. They didn't strike me as VISP staff or security. And they weren't just passing through."

Gavin looked at Lexi for confirmation.

"Agreed. There's no telling who they are or where they're from. That signature we've been sensing is definitely stronger, but didn't feel like it was coming from anyone there."

"Maybe they're Breakers," said Keeps. "Should've let me stay back and help. I might have been able to place 'em, even though it's been over a year since I've seen them." He wasn't in the best shape after the beating he took, but they didn't trust him enough to leave him at their home with the girls from Oakley's prison. They refused to come out of their small homes by the garden whenever they saw him.

"He has a point," Aidan offered.

"I already radioed Phil. They're gonna send up a mini drone to get more intel. So for now, we just wait."

The girls were huddled off to the side, whispering. Joe knew them all too well. "What are you ladies planning?"

"We're going to try something. If the eighth is nearby, we might be able to reach out to her. Plus, we need to determine what's going on with Aidan's mom. If there's a way to communicate with either of them, maybe we don't need to physically go in there."

"Can it wait til we get to the safehouse?"

"Wouldn't be ideal," said Maddy. "If the eighth is with the group that arrived, maybe we can get to her before we get any further away."

He hated everything about what they were suggesting, but they weren't wrong. "Fine," he said with a sigh, motioning the rest of the group over. After giving them a quick update on the plan, each stepped into their support positions.

Once in their circle, the girls locked hands. Immediately, everyone felt the hum of energy surrounding them. It didn't take more than a few seconds before Zuri stepped forward into the center and began deliberately waving her arms around as if manipulating an invisible object.

Addie watched as Zuri grabbed hold of each colored rope, one at a time. As if willing them toward her, she would briefly investigate before pushing them away once she recognized who or what they belonged to. "I can see them. The blue and red ropes are thicker than they were before. They're near your right hand."

Grabbing hold, Zuri wrapped the cords tightly around her hand before sucking in a deep breath. "She's here."

"Can you tell which direction?" Maria asked.

They all looked in the direction of the VISP compound.

"You think she's in there?" Maria pressed, praying that wasn't the case.

Justin, Gavin, and Grant shifted uncomfortably. Their minds instantly returned to the days they'd been there themselves.

Addie, aware of what they were thinking, said, "I see the strands moving toward the southeast. She's not in VISP, but Joanna's other half is definitely close. The strands are thicker than before, and bright. Like she's cracking open the door for us."

Zuri was half-listening to Addie when a distinct rope brushed across her hand. Feeling through the vines, she began to will the elusive thread to come to her when suddenly, not only her eyes, but the eyes of all of the girls opened wide. "Maya is pushing me away!" she cried out, her voice hoarse and panicky as she grabbed ahold of the thick charcoal-like rope.

"Can you see her? Talk to her? Tell her I'm coming!" Aidan yelled, grabbing his book bag, ready to make a run for it. Before he could even plant his feet, Joe tackled him straight to the ground.

"Stop! You can't go running in there. You'll never make it by yourself!"

Aidan briefly writhed and pushed, but he could feel Zuri's eyes on him.

"Aidan. Please. Give me a minute and just wait." Her sweet, strained voice stopped him in place.

"I can't be certain, but it feels like she's working to push me out. I'm going to try pushing back and see if I can communicate." Closing her eyes, Zuri focused all her efforts on the invisible black chord in her hand.

Releasing Aidan, Joe stepped back, answering a call on his radio. Talking with Phil, he kept his eyes on both Zuri and Aidan. He could feel the pressure in the air begin to grow, pressing in on their bodies.

"She's fighting me," Zuri's teeth grit together as the pressure grew more and more painful.

"Let it go, Zuri!" shouted Lexi, releasing the hands she was holding.

"Wait! What do you see?" demanded Aidan, pushing into the circle opposite Lexi. "Just tell me what you see!"

"There's... there's something wrong," Zuri said under her breath.

"Enough. Let go!" ordered Lexi. Without waiting, she grabbed hold of Zuri's hands, and that's when she felt it. The pressure. The darkness. The despair. With a stomach-churning surge, the connection broke, sending all the girls to their knees and gasping for air.

"What happened?" Aidan asked, dropping to one knee in front of Zuri. "Please. Zuri. What did you see."

After a moment of silence, she looked up into his panicked

eyes. The edges of her crystal-clear irises were coated in a thin, black ring. "She's going to try and end it."

Without a word, Aidan stood up, turned, and took off for the woods.

Chapter 26
Upset

July 2, 2030 | 1:00 p.m.

*T*hey're *too close. I know they're out there. I can hear them planning. It's going to end badly. Dear God, please... help me stop them!*

Maya couldn't move inside the glass prison. However, it didn't stop the onslaught of the girls' distant voices and emotions flooding her mind. She had no idea how to stop any of it.

The vibrations on her skin had increased exponentially, and she could tell by the tone of their voices that Dr. Harold and the others were witnessing something astonishing on the monitors.

"This is incredible!" Dr. Hutchens kept looking back and forth between Maya and the screen. "I mean, she's not even moving, yet the data reads as though her body were at work under extreme conditions!"

How do I make them hear me?

Shaking his head, Dr. Harold said, "This is very similar to what we saw on Calla Lily's charts before the event you glimpsed in the video of her standing."

Dr. Saylor's stomach turned as she stood up from the desk. "Should we sedate her? Or maybe leave the room then?"

Maybe there's only one way.

"No, no! Wait. No sedation. I don't want to lose this data," Dr. Harold shot back, jumping to his feet. "She can't move with the pressure in there."

Staring helplessly, Dr. Saylor locked eyes with Maya. She could almost hear Maya's pleas for help. "This doesn't feel right."

"These spikes are similar to what I saw years ago with the girls. It comes in waves almost like a pregnant woman's contractions." He clicked on a chart and then enhanced it for more detail. "Look," he said, pointing to a peak on the ever-moving chart, "you can see what appears to be vibrations in the pattern. It's not a solid state."

"What does it mean?" asked Dr. Hutchens, leaning right up to the screen.

"Dr. Harold, this really doesn't feel right," whispered Dr. Saylor, still locked onto Maya's tear-filled eyes.

I have to stop them. If I'm not here, then they'll leave. They'll be safe. They'll go home. Her resolve settling inside her mind showed outwardly as only tears building at the corners of her eyes.

"Print that section so we can study it in more detail. Zoom in by sixty percent."

"Dr. Harold?" Dr. Saylor said a little louder.

"Even with increased pressure on her body, the waves aren't decreasing. They look like they're growing stronger," declared Dr. Hutchens, pulling the pages from the printer.

"Doctor?"

"Pain, both internal and external, is the best motivator," Dr. Harold said under his breath. "Look at what she's capable of withstanding!"

I can do this. I know how to put an end to this.

"Doctor!?" Dr. Saylor called out, her cheeks flushed and her fists clenched.

"Jessica, if you can't handle this, you can remove yourself from th—"

"Maya's moving!" Dr. Saylor's voice cracked as she pointed toward the containment unit.

Both men turned to find Maya kneeling with her hands pushed against the glass. The heat from her body radiated outward in moisture around each finger on the glass pane.

Rising to his feet, Dr. Harold raised his hands, palms out. "Maya? Maya, can you hear me?"

Her eyes were glossy, glistening like black diamonds in the fluorescent lighting.

"I know you're upset. We're going to release the pressure now." He waved his hand at the two doctors behind him, motioning for them to end the procedure. "It's okay. Everything is going to be fine," he whispered, slowly moving toward the glass the way he might a frightened, dangerous animal.

Whether I'm alive or not, they'll still come. I can feel it. I know they'll still come if nothing more than for revenge. Her thoughts of self destruction had morphed into something else.

Just a little closer, Maya said to herself, lucid enough to desire running her fist through the glass. Another voice, however, emanating from that crowd of voices in the back of her mind, echoed *"patience."*

As much as Maya wanted to act on her rage out of self-preservation, she knew it wasn't the right time. Slowly, as if honoring Dr. Harold's request, she slid her hands down the glass and pushed back into a sitting position. Working her jaw side to side and realizing she was free of the relentless pressure, Maya uttered, "I'll cooperate."

"Dakota!" Elias wasn't close enough to catch her when she tripped. Unable to brace her fall with her broken arm, Elias could only watch as her head hit the ground. He slid across the gravel on his knees, stopping beside her. "What happened?"

She was unconscious.

They were about a quarter mile north of Levi's group on foot.

"Dakota? Can you hear me?" he patted the side of her face, then lifted her by her shoulders from the ground and onto his lap. Feeling a warmth ooze across his leg where her head lay, he realized she was bleeding.

"James, bring the med kit! James!?"

Staring at Dakota, James didn't move a muscle, his mouth open yet speechless.

"What are you doing? Bring it now!"

Tearing his eyes away, he glanced at Elias. "We need Levi!"

"No! I think he's out to get Dakota. This is what he wants."

"That's insane! Why would he?"

"We don't have time for this!" Elias cried, jumping to his

feet to grab the med kit off James' shoulder.

Startled, Elias could hear rapid steps and breaking foliage nearby just before a man crashed through the brush moving faster than they could comprehend.

"No!" Elias cried as the man missed crushing Dakota under foot by mere inches before tumbling to the ground.

Without a word, James sprinted off into the woods.

"Dammit, James!"

Aidan's mind was blank. He ran as if pulled by a force beyond his ability to resist. His legs stretched and his chest heaved with a burning sensation.

He knew he needed to get to her. His mother. Guilt and fear were devouring him for not having acted sooner. Something was desperately wrong, and the idea that she was being tortured in the way Zuri, Lexi, or even Adeline had experienced was unacceptable.

Zuri's words, *"She's going to try and end it,"* repeated in his mind. *Why would she do that when we're so close?* He wouldn't let her. Couldn't let her.

Pushing forward around trees and over fallen logs, Aidan was no longer in control as the force pulled him closer to her without letting up. He burst through the overgrown brush on the forest's edge, nearly running over a woman convulsing on the ground.

"No!" yelled a nearby man, causing Aidan to lose his balance. Tumbling to the ground, he groaned as his shoulder moved in and out of the socket.

With the wind knocked out of him, he watched the stranger

race to protect the woman. Gasping, he pinched his eyes to focus on breathing for only a moment when he heard footsteps in the gravel beside him. Opening his eyes, Aidan froze. The barrel of a gun was pointed directly at his face.

"Who are you?" the man asked through gritted teeth.

Aidan's senses had returned in the breathtaking chaos of his fall, and with the best toothy smile he could muster, said, "One of the good guys. Who are you, cowboy?"

Chapter 27
They Got 'em

July 2, 2030 | 1:45 p.m.

"They got him!" Brandon shouted as he burst through the brush amid the trees. The girls, sipping water, jumped at his arrival while Sheila paused in the middle of collecting the cold, wet rags she'd given them to put on their faces and necks.

"What?" Joanna tried to jump to her feet but a piercing headache left her wobbly.

"I tracked Aidan through the woods. By the time I found him, he and two others were being hauled off in an armored vehicle."

"Which way did they go?" Phil asked.

"Northwest."

"Alright, this just went beyond a one-person rescue mission," said LIMIT's lead operator Rick, who had just arrived with Phil. Punching a number into his phone, he dialed up Rice Jahnsen, the Director of LIMIT. "Jahnsen, yeah, we got a problem."

The others encircled Brandon, pressing him to explain every detail of what he witnessed.

"I heard several men yelling just up ahead of where I was running. I hid behind some brush where I could see a woman on the ground and an armored vehicle sitting off to the side. I saw a man shielding her. He was trying to reason with the men beside the vehicle, saying that they were hiking and she fell and hit her head. He told them she didn't need any help, but it was clear she did. Aidan was there, listening. He stood out of the way, glancing toward me now and again, although I don't think he knew I was there. I suppose he was gauging whether he could make a run for it but kept glancing at the woman as well."

"What did she look like?" Justin asked.

"Dark hair. Fair skinned. Hard to tell beyond that... seems she was unconscious. Then they started arguing... couldn't quite make out what they were saying."

Keeps stood taller, shifting from one leg to the other as he heard the woman's description. *Could Dakota really be in the same place as us?* "What did the other guy look like? The one protecting her."

Brandon scowled at the man, still embittered for his part in what Oakley had done to all those women. Keeps stepped back apologetically as Brandon sternly answered, "I dunno. Maybe five-foot-ten with dirty blond hair."

"Elias," Keeps mumbled under his breath.

"Do you know them?" Brandon growled, stepping toward him.

"Maybe. I'm not sure," he muttered, taking another step back. "Your description makes me think it might be Dakota and Elias."

"Who?" Phil asked.

"Uh, Dakota is the leader of the Breakers. Elias is her second in command. They…" he began, clearing his throat, "they find places with high energy output and..." wincing, not wanting to say it, knowing that it wouldn't be received well, "and they dismantle them, retrieving all communications tech they can get their hands on."

Rick and several others unaware of Keeps' involvement with the Breakers listened with disdain.

"So we're not fully invested in saving them is what you're saying. Got it." Phil turned away but stopped as Sheila cut in.

"She might be the eighth, Phil."

"What?" He whipped around.

"She's close, I've felt her," Joanna said with her hand to her head. "It can't be a coincidence."

Phil's face softened. "Why would she be with them? They aren't good people, Joanna. We've run into them before, but they always seem to find a way out of our grasp."

Feeling the need to defend Dakota, Keeps took a deep breath and said, "Dakota was really young when she joined the Breakers. It wasn't exactly a choice she made."

"So they kidnapped her. Okay, that makes more sense," Phil shot back, his anger against the man refueled.

"No, no, no. Uh. She wasn't kidnapped or anything. She chose, *chooses* to be with them. It's all she really knows," he said, his voice soft and hands shaking. "I didn't come to be with them until years after the grid failed. I've heard all the stories, but no matter how she joined, she's pretty much our, *their* leader now."

"So let me get this straight," said Phil, throwing his hand in the air, "Dakota, the leader of the Breakers, by choice, might also be the eighth girl connected to Joanna. Yes?" Several in the group nodded along. "Meaning, she might be a bad guy, but she could be a good guy. Either way, our goal is to rescue her?"

They nodded again.

"Okay then," he said, walking in a tight circle and mumbling to himself. "Let's hope she comes with us peacefully. So tell me... what are her magical powers? We need to be prepared, right?"

Everyone turned toward Keeps. Wide-eyed, he cleared his throat and said, "As far as I know, she draws."

"Draws?" Phil asked.

"Draws. She's an incredible artist. They arrive at a target location and she draws what she sees. Only she draws it in an altered state, like the way she wants it to be. When she touches her drawing it comes true. Like if we have to disable security or incapacitate threats. Once she does her thing, her team goes in and disables any functioning tech."

No one spoke. Chirping birds and trees rustling in the wind stilled the moment before Phil responded, "Humph. That's not what I thought you were going to say."

"Hey, we're not monsters."

"Do the Breakers know about VISP?" asked Grant. "VISP's pretty heavily armed. Do they have enough people to breach VISP's security?"

"They know all about VISP. As for people, they didn't have a large presence when I left, but that was like a year and a half ago. I'm not sure what they have now. Plus, with Dakota, we never needed a ton of people to succeed."

"Well, I can tell you, the dozen people we saw won't cut it with everything they've got going on in that compound," Joe criticized.

"To be fair, there were only three of us when we went in," Zoey added.

"Yeah, but we got lucky. The whole place went underground as we were going in. We had no opposition. Now, we know they're all back topside. Unlike the Breakers, our manpower is considerably greater, including you girls as our secret weapon."

"How many people exited the vehicle to snatch up Aidan?" Phil asked.

"Three. All with what looked like M4s. Military grade. In fatigues."

"Like the ones Oakley's men were wearing?" Keeps piped in.

"No. More professional. Like they were actually in the military."

"VISP security detail. Aidan must've been somewhere near the perimeter security cameras. The last time we were here, Aidan and I made annotations on the map," said Joe, laying that same map out on the hood of a vehicle. "Look, there are twelve cameras around the compound. It's possible they've been moved, but based on the direction you just came from," he said, pointing at the map and smacking it as he spoke, "this is likely the one that caught them. Aidan should've known better!"

"Just got off the line with Jahnsen," Rick interjected. His team arrived only minutes prior. Walking over and tucking his phone away, he said, "He's sending three more drones our way and another team. Two hours before the drones are overhead, but the team won't make it for another five after that. We still have two short-range drones with us. What do you want to do?"

"Well, those eyes need to be on the VISP patrols and the other group out there, Breakers or not. They may not know who we are, but they'll be searching nonetheless," said Phil. Looking directly at Keeps, "I think we should send two of you out to verify if the Breakers are on site."

Keeps nodded at the implied request. "I'll go. Maybe I'll see some I recognize and clarify their roles. Might help determine what they're doing here. Would it be so bad, though, if the Breakers dismantled VISP?"

"Honestly... it would not." Joe bit out the words. "But it seems your ace in the hole's superpowers may not be functioning at the moment. If she's the one Brandon saw. So we may be doing this old school." Joe wiped his forehead. "The rest of us will head to the safehouse and regroup."

"No," Zuri demanded, walking right up to him. "We can't leave Aidan in there. Now that he's like us, they'll do things to him. Hurt him. We can't just leave him there!"

Joe put his hands on her shoulders, looking her dead in the eye. "We're not, Zuri. I promise you we're not. But we'll be no use to him if we go in guns blazing. They're likely expecting someone to come after him, not to mention the two others." Looking across at the expanded team, he said, "We don't know for sure who those other two with Aidan are, and if they're with the group that came up on us earlier, that's a whole other group of people we may have to defend ourselves against. We need a new plan."

Joanna took Zuri's hand and gave it a little squeeze. She then grabbed Macie's hand when suddenly multiple images flashed in her mind simultaneously. Scenes of Zuri hearing everything around her while trapped inside the glass unit. Images of Macie interspersed with Zuri depicting the torture she had endured for years.

Just as quickly as the images appeared, they changed. While Joanna recognized the previous ones, she couldn't understand the kaleidoscope of moving pictures racing by. A woman's body, unconscious. A doctor sitting at her feet in a white coat holding a long syringe.

"Joanna?" cried Addie, trying to infiltrate her mind and break the connection. Placing her hand on Joanna's arm threw a fresh set of images into Joanna's visions that immediately dropped her to her knees.

So much pressure. Joanna felt as if her skull may crack.

There was Addie running down a hall, bruises covering her arms and legs and face. Her small body appeared in a dark room, writing on a piece of paper. Joanna caught a glimpse of her own name at the top of the page for a mere second before it changed. Everything changed. Silver eyes suddenly stared back at her, burning into her own. She watched as the woman backed away, her pale features coming into view. Dark hair whipped around her face with hurricane-force winds. The woman stretched her arms out wide only to bring them together in a sweeping motion to the right. Joanna watched as trees and rain, rocks and debris followed the direction of her swinging arms. The power terrified her.

Without warning the scene altered. She was back looking upon the unconscious woman in that stark, white room. The doctor's face came into view as he turned to place the syringe on a metal tray. It was *his* face. The man that stole them. Killed her parents. The man that changed their lives forever.

Releasing her grip, Joanna collapsed. She was in utter darkness. The images were gone, but the crackling sound of thunder roared in her mind. A blinding flash of lightning knocked her unconscious.

Chapter 28
Please God

"Why isn't she waking up?" Addie sat next to Joanna, her jaw tight with pain.

Sheila quietly took vitals while Maddy worked to calm Joanna's mind in hopes of easing her past whatever it was that had consumed her.

"Do you think something happened to the girl she's connected to? Something that put her in this state, like we went through?" Addie asked.

Maddy squeezed her shoulder. "I don't know. Whatever it was, was significant. I just wish Macie or Zuri had been able to see it too. But then again, if they had, they might be in this condition as well."

The safehouse was roughly four miles from their last

position near VISP. It was clear Brandon treasured Joanna, holding her and whispering in her ear the entire drive there. Addie, undeniably shaken, was extremely grateful he'd come into their lives that day in the woods. The day she had been abducted.

Joe, Phil, Rick, Justin, Lexi, and Zoey sat around an old table, maps spread across as they discussed their next move. "The drones should be on target soon," Rick said. "I've advised them to stay several miles away as they run their patterns around the compound. We can't afford to be found out before we're ready."

"Good," Joe answered. "Luckily, we've got people with us this time who know VISP thoroughly. However, it's only a guess that Aidan's mom is held on floor nineteen based on how destroyed the D4 lab was. Doesn't mean they haven't gotten it back up and running, so we need a contingency plan to get down there if need be." Joe flipped through a few pages before landing on a clear view of the main floor. "With Rick's team, we've got a total of fifteen men going in. Grant, Gavin, Keeps and Maria will stay back with the girls—"

"Whoa!" said Maddy, spinning around. "What do you mean we're not going in?"

"That makes no sense, Joe!" said Zoey, practically yelling. "The whole point was for us to go in as well. You know you'll be stronger with us."

"Too many things have changed. We need to keep you all as safe as possible." Joe's concern fell flat.

"Five of us were going in with you before," Maddy's teeth ground together with her words. "That was the plan. We can most definitely help, more than your guns, that's for sure." Her face flushed at the absurdity of this new plan.

"We all know how capable you are. However—" Joe started.

Maddy attempted to cut him off, but Phil stepped in like a fatherly figure, holding his hand up to give her pause, "however, you are all vulnerable right now. Joanna is down, Macie and Addie were already scheduled to stay behind, and it's clear your connection to Maya is strong enough to incapacitate you. If she truly is the catalyst... if something unexpected happens to her, it could put you all in jeopardy. Which would put us in jeopardy of actually rescuing her."

Maddy, staring him down, worked hard to reign in her anger. "I hear what you're saying Phil, however, I'm combat-trained. Not to mention I worked inside VISP for years, specifically on the nineteenth floor. I've had a lot more practice keeping myself and my gifts in check all these years. If you show up without at least one of us, Maya and possibly Dakota, if she is the eighth, won't recognize you. You'll have an even bigger fight on your hands."

"They don't know you either," said Joe softly.

Several seconds ticked by in silence. Standing up, Lexi said, "They may not, but if Dakota is who we think she is, she'll know us." She locked eyes with Joe. "The only way to make sure they do is with Maddy, Zoey, and I being there."

"Lex—" Joe began.

"That's the deal. Maddy is capable of calming a situation. Zoey is weapons trained, and if we can't find them, she'll know if someone is lying to us about where they are. And I've spent years in that place. If anyone knows the state that Maya, and maybe Aidan and Dakota will be in when we find them, it's me."

"I..." he paused, seeing the determination in their eyes,

"don't know why I pretend like I'm going to win one of these arguments. I haven't yet."

"I think I need to be in there with you, Lex," said Zuri, stepping beside her.

With a hug, Lexi said, "I would love it if you were. You're the strongest of all of us... which is why you need to stay back. We'll need some protection here at the safehouse."

Maria went to say something snappy about not getting to go either but Gavin pulled her in closer to his side.

Lexi could feel Zuri's defiance building and gave her sister a subtle nod. Lexi struggled to reconcile the little girl version of her sister so vivid in her mind, replaced with the adult standing beside her. She wasn't helpless, and Lexi knew Zuri was right. She probably should be with them.

"Settled. The four of us are coming with you," declared Lexi.

"Five." Joanna's declaration was the most poignant they'd ever heard from her.

They all turned.

"No, Jo." Brandon's words came from between his teeth.

"I know what you'll say. I'm a weak link, but if Dakota is not in a good place, with me there... our connection... she might not fight back."

Lexi sat next to her. "You're not wrong, but you also know your connection to her is strong right now. Her pain is yours."

"I know that. But you know," she took a breath and looked around the room. "You know I'll need to be there when we find her."

Maya sat quietly within her glass prison. With a level, unemotional tone, she answered their questions, one after the other. Her heart and mind still reeled from the notion that she was the source of their powers and problems. Despite her cooperation, Maya asked several times for permission to leave the containment unit, trying her best to persuade Dr. Harold that she was fully on board with what they wanted from her as long as they didn't go after her son or the women. Dr. Harold denied her every request, citing the necessity for a controlled atmosphere.

"What else do you recall about your miscarriages? Any specific trigger prior to?" The callous way in which Dr. Harold asked the questions left a metallic taste in her mouth.

"I remember the very same night after holding each of the girls you mentioned... I would begin cramping severely. By the third day, I'd lost..." she cleared her throat, "the fetus I was carrying."

"It's just so interesting because you helped deliver so many babies. On many days we delivered multiple children, yet none of them showed the same characteristics. And none of them caused you to miscarry." He stared at his notes trying to make sense of it. "I mean, is it because you were about to miscarry that you transferred the essence of that child to the newborn you held? Or, a, uh, could it be the transference of said gifts to these girls' caused the miscarriage? And why only girls?"

His questions came one after the other but she didn't have the answers he craved. He might as well have been asking her how the universe started. Everything sounded like it should be in a science fiction movie.

Everything except that she now knew she had certain

abilities most humans didn't. She'd always had a knack for things that didn't come naturally to others, like she could tell when a mother or fetus was about to be in distress before symptoms started, or when she joined the military and became a meteorologist, her forecasts were always spot on. That was how she ended up working classified support overseas. Her mission briefs were so accurate that commanders often requested her for the highest level support operations. Not to mention daily things were just natural for her.

Her reminiscing was broken by the excited voice of Dr. Harold. "What if… okay, Dr. Hutchens, Dr. Saylor… " He stood abruptly and dashed to the whiteboard.

"Facts. We know Maya physically held each of the girls on the day or days surrounding their birth. She was pregnant at the time of each birth, so her HCG levels were high. As were her estrogen and progesterone."

After a lengthy bout of silence, he grunted in frustration. "There's got to be a missing link!"

"Did each of the babies have a death or near-death experience?" Dr. Hutchens asked.

"No. Just the one. Zuriella."

"Did the other babies have some sort of difficult childbirth? Born with—"

"Wait! Wait, wait, wait. Uh," he pulled the stack of folders to a table and opened the first, Zuriella. Pushing that to the side, he grabbed the next, Macie. Flipping through the pages, he found the notes of her birth. "Congenital heart condition… put in an incubator for three days… full recovery on day four with no evidence of disease."

He flipped open the next. "Joanna, symptoms of Leukemia,

surplus of white blood cells, placed in an incubator… full recovery on day two with NEOD."

The door clicked before swinging open as LSO Fisher entered quickly. "Sir? We found some individuals outside the gate. We're bringing them in now. One woman, two men. The woman is said to be injured."

"Uh, oh, alright. On my way." Dr. Harold stood up and grabbed Dr. Hutchens' shoulder with a joyful squeeze. "I think we found a connection!"

"What would you like us to do?" Dr. Hutchens asked.

"Verify the conditions of each child at birth. This is a significant link! And grab lunch while I'm gone. We have a full day ahead of us." Turning toward Maya, sitting in her own adult-sized incubator, he said, "Maya, are you hungry? Dr. Saylor, go ahead and give her lunch. When I return, we'll have several new tests to conduct. Draw another round of labs and put a rush on it!"

As Dr. Harold left the room, Maya rose to her feet. A strange sensation arose that maybe they'd found the girls. Or Aidan. Or both. She knew they were too close, that it was only a matter of time. She prayed they could hear her pleas but knew she was kidding herself that they'd listen.

Dr. Hutchens was vibrating with excitement as Dr. Harold left the room. "What do you think this means?" He flipped through each folder in search of birth defects or diseases, highlighting the information on key pages while scribbling questions. "Fetal Alcohol Syndrome… Sickle Cell… good Lord. They all had something that would have left them with lifelong problems."

Breathing hard, Dr. Hutchens stood up, staring at Dr. Saylor. "This is incredible," he said under his breath.

"It is." Dr. Saylor's mind raced, trying to connect it all, even with the missing pieces. "But it doesn't answer three main questions. How were they healed? Was it Maya that healed them? And how did she give them abilities if she, in fact, did?"

Both turned toward Maya as if waiting for an answer. Dr. Hutchens looked like he wanted to dissect her to find the answer. Anxious at the sudden attention, Maya found herself scooching back until she felt glass press against her spine.

Another thirty minutes passed with his nose buried in files until he dropped the most recent on his desk. "The connection is here. It has to be!"

Startled by his outburst, Dr. Saylor took a breath and cooly remarked, "I'm just not seeing anything."

Shuffling a mess of pages around, he mumbled to himself before saying, "Alright, this is ridiculous. We'll just have to wait til he gets back. I'm grabbing lunch, then running to my apartment for a few things. You good to grab her lunch?"

Dr. Saylor glanced back at Maya with curiosity. "Yeah. Go for it. I'll get it."

Maya remained silent for several minutes after Dr. Hutchens left the room. "Dr. Saylor?"

"Yes? Sorry. Yes, I'm going to get your lunch n—"

"No, no. That's not it," she said, her eyes shifted as an idea began to brew. "A couple weeks ago I saw what looked like potential for a significant hurricane coming across the Atlantic. It could greatly impact us. I'd like to have permission to use my laptop and follow up?"

"I don't know, Maya. I don't think that's such a good idea."

"I imagine you don't have anyone else here tracking it. My assistant isn't qualified to track storms of that magnitude. If it turns our way, it could be devastating."

"You realize we're in Pennsylvania, right? We don't tend to get that kind of weather here." Dr. Saylor's brow wrinkled, clearly wrestling the question.

"Jessica, you've known me a long time. Have you ever known me to not put our people first?" The notion of loyalty as she sat in a glass prison made her stomach turn.

Dr. Saylor glanced at the door and then back to Maya. "How about a compromise? I'll use my laptop while you guide me through the process."

Maya balled her fist yet remained calm. "Unfortunately, that won't work. All my data is on my laptop. I'll be unable to access it from yours." It wasn't entirely true, but Dr. Saylor wouldn't have known otherwise.

"Let's wait til Dr. Harold comes back and asks him. I'm sure he'd want to know as well."

"At the very least," she said with a defeated smile and a sigh, "when you leave for lunch, could you stop by my desk and grab my laptop on your way back? That way it'll be here should I get permission."

Dr. Saylor nodded in agreement before stepping out.

She had never been the best at praying. Losing her son all but shut that door in her heart, but now, trapped without an end in sight, she silently pleaded, *Lord, if you can hear me, bring that storm this way. Please, God, bring that storm here.*

Chapter 29
Got Me

July 2, 2030 | 2:45 p.m.

Elias paced the stark white room while Aidan sat quietly. They'd taken Dakota elsewhere in the building to tend to her head injury, with great displeasure from Elias. His black eye was the result of that displeasure. "They can't keep us here. We haven't done anything," he muttered, with an occasional profane outburst when no one responded.

"Hey man, seriously. What you're doing isn't helping. You just gotta go with the flow." Aidan was shocked at his own words, considering he was usually the hothead. All the more, knowing just how close he was to his mother yet unable to fight his way through to her side. He also knew the others would come for him, that he needed to be patient and wait for the right moment.

Luckily, he'd been in the building before, and since they didn't blindfold or knock them out cold, he knew where he was. Though, he wasn't sure if that was a good or a bad omen.

The only thing he felt for sure was that his mother was in the building. Whether it was a sixth sense or just straight resolve, he believed it, convinced he would find her.

"How can you just sit there calmly? We have no idea where they took Dakota. We need out. Like right now," insisted Elias, red-cheeked and rearing to hit something.

Aidan didn't catch it at first, but then it sank in. "Dakota? The girl that was with you, that's her name?"

Elias stopped in place. He couldn't help but notice the recognition in Aidan's tone. "Yeah? Why?"

"Is Dakota able to, uh… do things? Like, things normal people can't?"

Elias's arms dropped to his side. "That's a crazy accusation, don't you think?" His eyes flicked to the camera in the corner, half-believing that whoever was watching might let them go, convinced they were nothing more than hapless nomads.

"Yeah, no. Crazy. Right?" Aidan replied with a wink.

Elias didn't know what to make of this guy who'd nearly stomped on Dakota in the woods in a fit. Now, he was kicked back with feet up on the chair, strangely aware of something no one outside the Breakers knew about their leader.

Before Elias could wrap his mind around it, the door flung open. A very happy looking older black man in a white coat strolled in.

"Gentlemen! Seems you found our place of solace out here in the countryside. Not an easy thing to d…" Dr. Harold's voice faltered as he approached the opposite side of the room, meeting Aidan face-to-face. Unsuccessfully attempting to hide his shock, he stammered, "To... to... to do. How did you end up all the way out here?"

"We were just hiking north to Vermont. We don't wanna cause any trouble," Elias' words felt forced.

"Sure, sure. I hear your other companion was injured? How did that happen?"

"Haven't had much food the past few days. Guess the heat got to her and she passed out. I wasn't able to soften her fall. Lucky you guys found us, honestly. Not sure what we would've done if you hadn't."

Aidan, following Elias' lead, jumped up and said, "Hey, looks like y'all are pretty busy here. If you could just patch her up, we'll be on our way. And we wouldn't say no to some doggy bags and a few extra bandages if you can spare it?" The most sincere faux smile was plastered across his face, convinced the man knew who he was. He'd bet his life on it.

"My apologies," said Dr. Harold, holding out his hand to Aidan. "I didn't even introduce myself. My name is Dr. Harold. I'm the director here."

Aidan's heart skipped a beat, but he didn't let on. Stepping forward, he shook the man's hand. The handshake was tighter than it should've been and Dr. Harold didn't initially release him as he assessed Aidan's face. Aidan finally said, "Nice to meet you. Dan."

"Dan?" Dr. Harold repeated the name and reluctantly released his grip, turning his attention to the other man. "And you are?"

"Uh, Eli. The name is Eli. Again, so sorry to have intruded. If our friend is doing better, we're happy to get on our way." His nervous impatience was beginning to cut through his confident demeanor.

"I'm heading to check on her next. If she's doing alright, we're happy to give you some supplies and send you on your way." Dr. Harold's eyes flicked back to Aidan.

A thought struck Aidan at that moment. "Actually, you know, we've been walking for quite some time. We'd hate to put you out, but if there's any chance you could let us stay the night? Let our friend recoup? We'll be out of your way first thing in the morning. I haven't slept on a mattress in, well, shoot, I'm not sure how long it's been," Aidan said with a hearty laugh.

Elias, turning away from the doctor, shot daggers at him.

"I think we might be able to oblige you for a night," said Dr. Harold, taking an extra second to assess the two of them. Neither looked like they'd been on a cross-country trek for days, let alone weeks. Their clothes appeared clean, and they didn't smell like they had gone without showers. Dr. Harold wasn't a fool. After looking them up and down one final time, he nodded.

Aidan knew the game as well. He'd been given a decent enough description and recognized Dr. Harold immediately. Rage pulsed through his veins as he sat there with a good ole boy smile. He'd play this faux game right along with the doctor.

"Well, sit tight. Let me check on your friend… what did you say her name was again?"

"Dak—"

"Darla," Aidan butted in, cutting Elias off. He didn't think the doctor needed to know her real name. Granted, all he had to do was playback the footage of their conversation, but Aidan was hoping he wouldn't get around to that anytime soon.

"Darla? Alrighty then. Just a heads up, we'll need to keep

a guard with you while on the premises. And we'll have to lock your sleeping quarters this evening as well. My apologies for all this, but we have sensitive items in the building. You understand."

"Absolutely! You don't know us from Adam. Appreciate it, Doc!" Aidan exclaimed.

"Someone will be here shortly to escort you to the cafeteria. By the way, our chefs are top-notch! Best food you'll find on the East Coast. Hope you enjoy!"

Despite the doctor's smile, his kind gestures never reached his calculating eyes.

Dr. Harold left the room eager to return to Maya, yet there was Aidan, delivered right to his doorstep. It was like he had won the lottery. Talking to himself with a giddy smirk, he said, "If Aidan is here, it stands to reason the woman with him is one of my girls." Catching the LSO he asked, "Where's she at?"

"Med bay, sir. We brought her straight there. She was still unconscious when we left her with the physician."

"Great. Dispatch a team. See if there's anyone else out there looking for them."

"Already on it, sir."

"Don't assume just because you don't find anyone that they aren't out there. Beef up security and enact Plan Z."

The man paused. "Plan Z? Are you sure?"

"Immediately. I have a feeling we're going to have company soon."

"Roger."

"Oh! And have your man watching our guests take them to

room 1419 for the night when they're done eating."

"Next door to you, sir?"

Dr. Harold didn't miss a beat. "Please."

Confused but obedient, the captain replied, "Got it!" Snatching up his radio, he set the orders in motion.

Dr. Harold stood outside the doors to the medical bay on the third floor. Stealing a deep breath, he pushed them open and casually said, "Hey, so how's our newest patient?"

The providers' abruptly stood as he walked in. "Female, mid-twenties probably, head laceration. We've stitched her up and hooked her to an IV with pain meds and fluids. She's still unconscious, but images show no sign of swelling. We're anticipating her to come-to shortly."

"Good, good. Let me get a look at her." Standing beside the hospital bed he stared into her face hoping for even a glimpse of familiarity. With dark hair and light skin, common features, he resigned to thinking it was just wishful thinking on his end. Using his fingers, he opened her eyelids wide, anticipating hazel crystals to gaze back at him. He knew from the documentation Jones' had that Aidan was with a woman named Zoey, one of the women he'd abducted as a small child.

To his dismay, her iris coloring was silver, which was abnormal but confirmed she was not Zoey. They were dull but still more crystalline than the average human eye.

Reigning in his curiosity, he rotated her head to examine her wound. After a cursory check for further injury, he said, "You did a fine job. Let's get her cleaned up and in some scrubs. When she wakes, have some crackers and juice waiting. See if she can keep it down."

"Yes, sir."

After a final once-over, he added, "We may need to bring her to nineteen when she wakes. Let me know when that happens."

Before returning to Maya, he needed to have a one-on-one with Dan.

"How much longer til Jahnsen's second team arrives?" Zuri was antsy just sitting and waiting knowing they could just blow the doors off the building and find Aidan with guns blazing.

"Two hours," Joe answered, giving her a side hug. "I know this is frustrating, but Aidan knows how to take care of himself. We need to wait for Rick's people to get back so we know who those others are. We definitely don't have the manpower to fight two different battles at once." He wasn't much for physical contact, but he could see how much Aidan's capture was hurting her. Truth be told, he needed that hug just as much as she did.

"Nice digs, Doc," said Aidan, whistling as he walked around Dr. Harold's office.

"Yeah? Thank you, *Dan*," replied Dr. Harold, leaning hard on the name.

"Really appreciate you letting us stay the night. And you were right. The food here is spectacular. Maybe the best I've ever had." He was laying it on thick. "Although I didn't get to finish, being called up here and all. Will I be able to get back to the cafeteria when we're done? Long time since I ate this good."

"My apologies. I'll have security take you back when we're done."

"You're the man, Doc!" Aidan shot back, pretending to

be impressed by the books on the shelves. Despite his subtle growth in maturity, he still couldn't handle long silences and, after a few moments, plopped down in the guest seat and said, "So Doc, you asked me to come on in. What can I do ya for?"

"Well, I am a bit curious about a few things. Your friend said you were heading up to Vermont? Mind if I ask what's up in Vermont?"

"Sure, sure. Yeah. My buddy's family used to live up that way. We were going to see if we could track them down."

"Haven't seen them since the grid failed?"

"Nah, he hasn't been comfortable making the trip on his own, ya know? We had to talk him into it. He's a little bit of a Nervous Nelly."

"I get that." Dr. Harold stared at him for a few long seconds. "How long have you three been a crew?"

"Few years now, I guess?" He made a show of looking at the ceiling, considering the question.

"Nice. I'd imagine it's been hard to find trustworthy people out there since the power loss."

"You know it. Yeah, we're tight. Real tight."

"So you know the young lady, Darla, pretty well then?"

"Oh yeah, thick as thieves."

"Was it just the three of you?"

"Yup, just us. The Three Amigos."

"Well alright then. We'll get Darla patched up and you can be on your way in the morning when you're ready. No rush."

Several seconds ticked by. "So? Is that all you needed?"

Dr. Harold nodded, "Yep. Just curious. We're always looking for individuals with special skills to help out around here."

"Oh yeah?"

"Absolutely! Is there anything the three of you might be able to offer? I'd imagine a nice place to lay your head and three meals a day would be a nice change of pace for nomads like yourselves."

At the word choice, nomad, Aidan wondered if maybe Dr. H. had in fact listened in on their conversation.

"Well, I mean, if you call hotwiring cars, and stealing food now and again a skill, but I think we're happy with the open road."

Dr. Harold made a show of tilting his head in dismissal. "Sorry to hear that. A few extra hands around here is always welcome if you change your mind."

Aidan realized that was his cue, stood up and made his way to the door. "Sounds good, Doc. I'll tell the others. Who knows, maybe they're ready to settle! Again, really appreciate the hospitality."

"No problem at all," he replied as Aidan grasped the door handle and pulled it open. "Oh! I forgot one thing, Aidan."

"Yea—" Aidan started, then stopped himself too late.

A smile spread across Dr. Harold's face.

"Ah, got me. Didn't ya, Doc?" Turning all the way around, he closed the door behind him. "So? What do we do now?"

Chapter 30
Blood Work

July 2, 2030 | 4:00 p.m.

“Jessica.”

"Please, stop calling me that." Dr. Saylor was striving to remain calm, but Dr. Harold should've been back by now.

"Dr. Saylor. Please, just a few minutes to check on the storm's status. I promise you, I'm just trying to do my job."

Without notice, Dr. Hutchens entered with a loud slam of the door behind him.

"Where've you been? What's going on out there?" Dr. Saylor asked, her voice a little shaken.

"Uh, nothing? What do you mean?"

"Dr. Harold left to deal with some people that were brought in? Then you didn't return from lunch?" she said, growing more irritated.

"I was picking up some data from the analyst lab. And Dr. Harold, I would guess, is still down there dealing with them. Did you make any headway?"

"No. None. And I'm taking a break," she said, bolting from the room and leaving him dumbfounded.

"Alright, that was weird. How's it going Maya? Ready to tell us how you did it?"

Dr. Hutchens' eyes took on a sinister form, as though he might hurt her to get answers. Maya really did not like the man, but he was the best shot she had at the moment. "I'm good. Wish I had answers for you," she said, feigning her sincerity. Clearing her throat, she said, "Hey, I was telling Dr. Saylor about the potential for a hurricane I saw near Africa a couple weeks ago. She was just getting ready to approve the use of my laptop when you arrived. I would really appreciate it if you would consider letting me gather some fresh tracking data."

"Why would you care about a hurricane near Africa?"

"No, it's... that's where they usually start their formation as they cross the Atlantic to the east coast. If it did, in fact, spin up, then it could be climbing our coastline now. I just wanted to verify it wasn't coming this way. We'd definitely want to be prepared if it is."

"But we're in Pennsylvania."

"True, but this time of year, you can't be too careful. My laptop is actually right there on that desk. It wouldn't take long for me to analyze the data."

"How did your laptop get down here?"

"Dr. Saylor grabbed it for me. She was just waiting for you to arrive so she could open the unit and hand it to me when you entered. She was saying something about stomach cramps."

Holding her breath, Maya silently urged him to consider with her eyes.

"Ah, stomach ache, makes sense," he said, turning toward the office door, believing he understood why she'd run out so quickly. "Time of the month?"

Faking a subtle laugh, she said, "So what do you think, Dr. Hutchens? My laptop?"

"Yeah, I think that's Dr. Harold's call, don't you?" he replied without looking at her.

"Do you know when he'll be returning? I'm just concerned. By my calculations, if it progressed the way I forecast, it could be on our doorstep at any moment. Doesn't give us much prep time."

Smiling as he would to placate a child, in a tender voice, he said, "I'm sure it'll keep til he gets here."

"Dr. Hutchens, let me ask you. Have you ever known my forecasts to be wrong?"

He thought about it for a second, then sighed, saying, "Can't say that I have. But again, it'll keep." Turning his back, she knew he wasn't going to budge.

Instead, he dug back into the pages he had been highlighting before he left. Nothing jumped out at him when suddenly he popped his head up with an idea. "Maya, why don't you take a look at this data? Maybe you can tell me what we're missing," he said, pressing the first page against the glass.

Maya slid over to humor him, casually reviewing the medical data, MRI scan assessments, blood work, and neurological testing. Feigning ignorance, she asked, "What is it I'm supposed to be looking at?"

"Well, this page shows an MRI scan of your brain. See how

the right side is lit up? We've determined that yours is firing almost ten percent more than, say, mine, or Dr. Harold's. This second page is your bloodwork. There's nothing particularly notable to distinguish yours from the average person.

Holding up a second page, he said, "The left side is your bloodwork before our procedure, and the right is after."

Maya had just noticed something about the bloodwork, but he ripped it away from the window before she could truly study it. However, that moment's glance was enough. What she saw stole her breath and made her fingers begin to tingle.

"Ugh, never mind. You clearly don't know what you're looking at. Where is Dr. Harold?" Dr. Hutchens' demanded before storming out of the room.

Alone and contemplating the immensity of what she saw, her mind raced.

That can't be my bloodwork. There's no way that's mine. It can't be true.

Chapter 31
Conflict

Levi watched as his team bickered. After James updated the team about Dakota's fall, three of them, along with James, went out to search for them only to return empty-handed. Their only clue was a set of tire tracks that appeared to lead back to VISP. After a full recon around the perimeter of the compound, they found it to be heavily manned, armed and too large for a team their size to overcome. Even with Dakota's help, they knew they would likely struggle to dismantle VISP.

Levi was in a tough spot and had a fleeting moment of doubt with his plan to imprison Dakota. She was handy to have around for moments like these. Those on the team who knew Levi's traitorous plan for Dakota and Elias argued they should just cut them loose and head back to base camp in Florida. Those

Breakers, however, who were not privy to Levi's mutiny, argued for a rescue plan.

Levi, the politician that he was, knew if they returned to Florida without feigning an attempt at a rescue, the rest of the organization would not look favorably on him as their new leader. Although he hadn't realized he wanted the position until he went on that trip, the taste of power stirred a desire inside him that he didn't know was there. That feeling overpowered his short-lived doubt.

"Gather round!" he called out. "Quiet down. That's enough! What do we know?"

"The compound is secured by a ten-foot high electric fence. Twelve guards were on patrol, with more arriving as we left. We can assume they're fortifying their position as a precaution, not knowing if Dakota and Elias are alone or traveling with a group."

"Assuming they are responsible in the first place," Levi clarified.

"Yes. Inside the compound sit multiple buildings, as we can see on our maps. Impossible to determine which building they might've taken them to. My position on this? We retreat another mile from the compound, send in scouts to collect more intel, then head back to the Station to appropriately plan a rescue mission." Capt. V. confidently shared his opinion and then calmly began to pack his gear for a retreat.

"That's not ideal, Captain," argued one of the lower-ranking intel analysts whose job was to provide the infiltration plan once the recon team collected data. "There are wild rumors about this place and what they do here. If they find out what Dakota can do, they'll never let us take her alive. We cannot leave them here."

"No, it's not, but the only way we'd even have a shot at rescuing Dakota is if *Dakota* was with us. Without her, we'd need at least thirty or more skilled warm bodies, which we'd barely have if we called in reinforcements." As the words left the captain's mouth, he realized just how wrong he was to fall in with Levi. "Without Dakota, we don't have a shot against larger bodies like this. Lives would be at stake. Your lives," he mused, cutting his eyes to Levi.

Just the thought of Dakota's unique strength and allegiance among the members enraged Levi. "I hear you all. You're right. Dakota might very well be in a tough spot. You're also right that they outnumber us. Which means we need to be honest with ourselves. If what's behind that compound wall is what we believe, that they kidnap people and conduct experiments, once they see what Dakota's capable of, they'll slaughter us all to keep her."

"Which is why we need to go in now!" shouted the young analyst.

"And if we had the manpower, we would," Levi snapped. "Again, being honest, we don't. Our best option is to head back to Florida and create a new plan. It's precisely what Dakota would do and you all know it."

"By then, they'll be lab rats or worse," another shouted.

"That scares me too, but we don't have a choice!" Levi yelled back sharply. It was becoming obvious the group didn't trust him to lead, and he could feel it. "Captain, take four of your operators and conduct another reconnaissance. We'll pull the vehicles back another mile south, as you said. Document everything. We'll rally back at 2100 hours. Then return to

Station and map out an appropriate course of action." Looking at the young analyst, he said, "Take Intel with you. He can annotate what you find."

The captain, taking a deep breath, nodded. Before setting off, Levi pulled him aside and quietly said, "Radio in every thirty minutes with your position. If you see anything pertinent, deal with it, then radio only me on channel two with the keyword lightning." As he spoke, Levi slid a syringe into the captain's shirt pocket.

Again, Capt. V. nodded. If he somehow managed to find Dakota, it was clear Levi wanted him to follow their inside plan.

"Roll out!" Levi called.

"They're coming!" Zuri shouted. She had been watching out the safehouse window and saw Rick and his men emerge from the treeline.

Cramming into the tiny living room, they listened to Rick's report. "The two with Aidan are definitely part of that group. We overheard them discussing recovery plans but there seemed to be some discord there. They've sent out a team of six to assess the perimeter of the compound and will report back at 2100. Doesn't sound like they're leaning toward actually rescuing them. Most likely, they'll return to what they called their Station in Florida.

"Keeps was able to positively identify them as Breakers. Keeps?"

"Yeah, uh, the Station is headquarters. Cape Canaveral in Florida. It looks like one of their intelligence analysts, Levi, has taken charge... which I have to say is weird. He's not exactly leadership material. Most don't like him, and he's definitely not a combat operator. From what I recall, he'd never even been on a mission. I guess things change."

"Good job guys," said Joe, quietly processing the information. "Alright, I think it makes sense to wait til they've exfilled. Rick, can you—"

"That's at least five or six hours away," Lexi said. "The longer we wait, the long—"

"I know, Lex. There's a good chance they could be hurt in the next few hours—"

"Not just that. We know Aidan won't go down without a fight. He's not going to just let them do whatever they want to him. Plus, if he's in there, he'll do everything he can to get to Maya. It could get him killed."

"He's strong, and he's smart, and he won't do anything to jeopardize us coming after him. He knows that we're going to come after him with everything we've got."

Sheila, who had been a motherly figure to Aidan, Zoey and Joe, placed a calming hand on Lexi. "We aren't going to leave him behind, but Joe's right. We can't take on the Breakers and VISP. Deep down, we all know it would be unwise to put that many more lives in harm's way."

There was a collective sigh of frustration and common sense understanding. As much as they wanted to tear through the woods and bring down every person on that compound, they couldn't risk more lives doing so.

"So... we wait til they're gone," Rick decided. "Let's go over the plan."

Chapter 32
The Pressure

Aidan's brain was on overload. He wasn't stuffed away and imprisoned like he anticipated. On the contrary, Dr. Harold told him everything. Everything about how he abducted the girls; how he helped build VISP to what it is; how they managed Lexi and Zuri all those years. He even offered some insight into Aidan's mother. That she chose to be there. Chose to be part of his experiments to bring the world to a better place.

Out of character, Aidan had sat quietly, listening to every word without interruption. The man seemed to be telling the dirty truth. Yes, he wanted to rip the man's head from his shoulders, but he frustratingly recognized Dr. Harold was his only shot at getting close to his mother.

She was convinced I was dead. Can I be angry with her for not searching for me? Did she truly believe I had died? I mean, I thought she was, but if she has gifts the way the girls do, maybe even the source of them, how could she not feel me out there?

Dr. Harold had even allowed Aidan to leave his office to go back to the cafeteria. It didn't make sense. He sat speechless in the cafeteria, pushing the food around with his fork. For the first time possibly ever, he wasn't feeling hungry. Still under guard, Dr. Harold allowed him partial freedom within VISP. He had been told that Maya was undergoing a necessary procedure and that as soon as it was complete and she was alert, Aidan would be the first to see her.

Finally going to see her. A woman I grieved so deeply for over the years. I should be ecstatic... but I'm scared. If she'd been here all this time, she played a role in what they did to Zuri and Lexi. Maybe she was clueless. Just like Justin never knew Lexi was alive. Dr. Harold said she only recently started exhibiting extrasensory gifts. Why would he lie? Why wouldn't he?

His head pounding and his heart unsettled, Aidan rose and stared off for a moment before engaging the guard's attention. "I think I'd like to lay down for a bit." Being in the cafeteria again, with people chatting, eating, smiling, it was too surreal. The last time he had been there, it was a tomb. It was as if the apocalypse had happened and everyone disappeared. Now, here he was, semi-freely residing within VISP, but the atmosphere wasn't what he had expected.

The guard nodded and together they made their way to the elevator. Aidan couldn't help but notice that people weren't walking around with devious grins or that no one was screaming behind locked doors. His notion of VISP on the outside was drastically different from what his eyes were showing him.

Is this really such a bad place? Maybe they did want to bring the world back. I mean, my mom is here voluntarily, right? And Dr. Harold seems to believe the ladies are as capable of making the world a better place as I do.

Shaking his head, he internally yelled at himself for wavering. *No! Lexi and Zuri never had a choice! Lexi's deep purple scars running across her body are evidence of that.*

Aidan entered their new room on the fourteenth floor and Elias immediately wanted answers. "What was that all about? Are they going to keep us here? Did you see Dakota?"

"No, man. No. Well, I don't know. I don't think they're locking us up, and I didn't see her." His head throbbed as he lay on his bed.

"So are they going to release her?" he demanded, standing directly over Aidan and peering down at him.

"I'm guessing as soon as she wakes up. They're waiting for her to be alert enough to assess her."

"Why did you ask for us to stay? What's wrong with you!" Elias forced his words through gritted teeth. His hands clenched in fists at his sides.

"Look!" Aidan sat up, his head pounding. "There's a very *looong* story in that answer. The bottom line is we came here to rescue someone and running into you threw off the entire plan. But now that we're in here, I just need some time to gather more info on her whereabouts."

"We?"

"What?"

"You said we."

Aidan stared at him. "Yes, I didn't come alone. I just… it's a long story."

Elias stormed to the other side of the room. Several moments of silence passed as both men thought through their situation. "Who is she?" he asked.

Deciding there was no point in lying, Aidan took a breath and said, "My mother."

Elias stared, his eyes flickering compassion before asking, "Is she special?" Aidan stared at the floor but didn't respond. "You said something about Dakota. Having gifts. She does," Elias offered, plopping down on his own bed. "She can do some pretty incredible things. I've heard rumors about this place... about them kidnapping people for testing. Always seemed ridiculous, but knowing Dakota the way I do, and now being here. I'm scared, man."

"You're right to be scared."

"So if your mother's here. Does that mean you have… abilities too?"

"Honestly? I don't know. Nothing like what the others can do."

"Others?"

Aidan nodded. "Yeah, there are others like them," he said, hesitating to share more.

"They're here, aren't they."

Aidan shifted his feet, keeping his eyes on the floor.

"Dakota said she felt people out there, people like her. She even thought they might be near. That's why we were out there on our own. We could tell our group might have a plan. A plan to get rid of her. Hurt her. I think she wanted to find these other people. Find help. Support."

Aidan dropped his throbbing head into his hands. "Well, that figures."

"Why's that?"

Aidan tried to respond, but a pulsing darkness crept into his peripheral vision. Pressure filled his ears with a loud ring.

"Hey man, you okay?"

He knew. Aidan knew his mother was in trouble. Jumping to his feet he slammed his fist on the door. "Hey! Open up!"

"What are you doing?" Elias stepped toward him.

"Let me out now!" This time he kicked the door before trying to rip it open, but the locks held.

"Stop! Man, stop!"

The door burst open and the guard stood firm as Aidan tried to push past him. "Get out of my way!"

Training his weapon at Aidan's head, the brash redhead finally paused.

"You aren't to leave this room without authorization."

"Then call Dr. Harold. Right now." Aidan's lips barely moved with the threat in his words.

The guard spoke into his radio, "LSO Fisher, our guest is requesting to see Dr. Harold. Over."

The three second pause felt like an eternity to Aidan when they finally got a response. *"Looks like he's on his way there now."*

 5:35 p.m.

Maya sat in her prison, glaring at Dr. Harold.

"What's going on? What happened while I was gone? Dr. Saylor?"

The very air around Maya was hostile to his return and the crystals in her eyes so intense they glistened white, yet she wouldn't speak.

"I'm not sure," replied Dr. Saylor in a hushed voice. "I came in to find her like this. She hasn't said a word."

"Maya, I can't help if you don't tell me what's going on. Was it Dr. Hutchens?" He paused to look back at Dr. Saylor. "Where did he go?"

"I don't know that either. He was already gone when I walked in."

"Maya, if you don't communicate, I'm going to need to put you to sleep. Your vitals are through the roof. Your blood pressure is too high. It's not safe."

Maya wanted to scream at him but her lips wouldn't form the words.

"Can you feel that?" said Dr. Harold, momentarily stunned. "That's coming from Maya." A sinister smile washed over his face. "Can you believe it? We can literally feel the electricity in the air."

"I think we need to subdue her, don't you, Dr. Harold?"

"This is just... it's so incredible! Can you even imagine how it must feel to hold that much power?"

"Sir, I really think we should repressurize the unit," Dr. Saylor urged, her voice shaking as goosebumps formed on her skin like a premonition.

Staring at Maya, he let out a deep-chested sigh before punching the option on his keypad to sedate her.

Both doctors watched as the sedative was released in aerosol form, the safest way they had found for putting subjects to sleep.

"Shouldn't it have worked by now?" Dr. Saylor's nervous

tone reflected Dr. Harold's growing concern.

Upping the dosage, they watched the release once again. Still, Maya remained upright and focused.

"Is she doing this? Maybe the sedative has expired?"

"Maybe the cartridge needs replaced," Dr. Harold said. He watched the hair on his arm rise as the electrical current in the air continued to build. "We're going to need to use pressure."

Dr. Saylor quickly made her way back to the computer as Dr. Harold walked over to Maya. "I need you to calm down. I don't want to suppress you, but I will. I know you don't want that either. Just talk to me. Tell me what's going on."

She couldn't speak. She wanted to, but her skin burned. Her lips pressed so tightly together that she could taste blood as her teeth dug into the backside of her lips.

Shaking his head, he called out. "Alright, do it."

Dr. Saylor triggered the pressurization. They both heard the hiss of the air surrounding Maya.

She didn't flinch.

Dr. Harold signaled to Dr. Saylor to increase pressure. At first, nothing. Slowly but surely, however, Maya's body began to lose the fight as Dr. Saylor continued to increase pressure well beyond anything they had ever needed prior.

"She's fighting. At this rate, we'll crush her." They watched as Maya ever so painfully pulled herself back upright as the shine of her eyes blazed brighter than they had ever witnessed before.

Dr. Harold desperately wanted to see what she might do, what she was capable of, but as the seconds passed he could feel what Dr. Saylor had been feeling. Something dangerous was building in the atmosphere like gas vapors moving toward a spark.

With a loud grunt, Dr. Harold turned toward the door, shouting, "I've got an idea!"

"What? No! Sir, you can't leave me here!" shouted Dr. Saylor as he picked up his pace for the door.

"I'll be right back! Listen... I think I know what'll help," he added, before vanishing from the scene.

Maya, still upright, was losing color as she struggled to breathe. Though her eyes shined, her vision had gone completely dark. The crushing pressure on her brain was beyond compare.

Dr. Saylor looked on helplessly as Maya's body continued to fight with a visible, shaking rage, even as her mind began to give in to self-preservation.

I just want my son.

Chapter 33
Distress

This time the girls were ready. They felt something terrible was transpiring, and without a second thought they came together inside the safehouse living room, seated on the floor in a haphazard circle.

"What's happening?" Justin asked.

"Maya's in distress," Maddy said straight-faced, focusing on the matter at hand.

"We have to help," whispered Zoey, her throat constricted. Both she and Lexi knew exactly what was happening. Only it was unfolding so quickly that the two of them found it challenging to get their bearings. Each could feel the spread of maroon veining radiate on their skin like threads of fire that threatened to pull them apart.

"I need to protect us first," Lexi groaned, sensing the shield form like a bubble around her.

"Can you push it onto Maya?" Addie asked.

"We're about to find out," said Lexi, gritting her teeth and breathing deeply. *I can do this. Of course I can do this.*

The strain in her chest from the connection with Maya was hard to brush off. Even more difficult for Joanna who was in and out of mental clarity as she battled a migraine. Brandon, however, sat close behind, propping her up. Lexi, looking past their physical struggles, spread the shield around them, just as she had done when she and Zuri were children, protecting her sister from wild bees. One by one they felt the compression ease. Sitting up taller, they were able to connect with greater intention.

Addie watched the golden threads emanate from each of them and into Lexi like a braid. As her strength increased, so did the protection around the group as a whole. Sweat beaded on Lexi's forehead as she worked to discern how to transmit it to Maya so far away.

"I don't know how. I can't seem to find the right way to guide it toward her," Lexi cried out, beginning to feel the flutter of panic.

"I can help you," Zuri offered, tugging on the charcoal thread leading toward VISP. Weaving some of the gold-braided threads in line with the charcoal ones, she melded it into a dark golden crystalline rope. Addie, watching the strands twist together, saw Lexi was failing to drive it toward Maya.

Joanna, breathing steady and calm for the first time, felt a separate kind of pressure at her fingertips. "Lex, I think… I think it has to be me." Releasing Addie and Macie's hands,

Joanna crawled across the makeshift circle with no clue as to what she was doing. No plan. Just instinct.

Raising her hands, Joanna covered Zuri and Lexi's gripped fingers. Instantly, a shockwave of energy burst through the atmosphere of the safehouse living room. Following the intertwined charcoal and gold cords and taking their protective shield with it, the wave blew through the safehouse and out of sight.

With the sound of rushing wind, the pressure backfilled the room as it left, forcing the seven of them to the ground, helplessly weighed down. The spider web of veins that had all but ceased moments before now spread across their bodies in intricate, chaotic, crisscrossing lines.

"What do we do?" Joe hollered.

No one said a word, frozen in fear, unable to provide protection against this invisible threat.

"Ma'am?" inquired an older physician as she gently squeezed Dakota's arm. "Ma'am, are you alright?"

Dakota remained unconscious since her fall. Though externally she appeared stable, internally she was navigating an endless cyclone of nightmares and dreams, morphing between her younger and older self. Just as the doctor was attempting to stir her awake, a violent wave crashed over her body.

I can't grab hold of anything. Who is this little blond girl gripping my hand?

Hold on tight!

Everything hurts... I'm not sure I can do this much longer, after all, I'm just a little girl. These crushing waters... the undertow is gonna drown us both. No, no, no... come back!

I can't... catch my breath. The water is crushing me. And what is that... bitter taste in the air. My hands are tingling and so cold.

Does anyone else hear that? Please... it sounds like a little girl whimpering. Groaning, maybe. Wait, is that me? Who's poking me?

Cold, gloved hands struggled to hold her steady while the doctor attempted several times to inject her with something to calm her down.

"Darla? Can you hear us? We need to know where you're hurting?"

Dakota could hear them but couldn't make sense of it.

I'm hurting everywhere! Who is Darla? Maybe they weren't talking to me.

As her eyes cleared from the tears and fog of unconsciousness, it was obvious they were addressing her. Attempting to respond, a searing pain spread across her midsection.

"What is that?" gasped the aide standing directly above her and holding her head steady.

"Do you see it?" came another voice.

"Is it a toxin? Has she been poisoned?"

"Maybe she brought it here. Maybe she's a weapon. A biological poison. You all heard what Dr. Harold said!"

Dr. Harold? How do I know that name?

Suddenly, all hands disappeared, and incessant questions evaporated. The room was empty. Silent.

Alone? Where did you go? You're leaving me to fight this... this horror show alone.

 6:00 p.m.

I'm dying. I can feel it. There's nothing left to give.

Girls, please... please don't come here. There's only one way this ends for all of us.

Aidan. My sweet Aidan.

Save yourself.

Maya was holding onto an image of Aidan as a child when a rush of cool air encompassed her. Instead of crushing pressure, she felt the space around her body soften as if she were floating in a cool current. Air filled her lungs, and her eyes opened wide.

I'm alive.

"What just happened?" Dr. Hutchens shouted, startled by the sudden change in the air not only around him, but he watched the data on his screen show the depressurization around Maya within the chamber. "The pressurization stopped. Her vitals look completely normal. What did you do?" he accused Dr. Saylor.

Dr. Hutchens had returned only moments before to find Dr. Saylor frozen, staring at Maya. He noted the unbelievably high degree of pressure flashing red on the monitor, so seeing Maya's chest heave so casually struck him with a sense of fear he hadn't felt before. Cautiously, Dr. Hutchens stepped toward the back of her tank. "Dr. Saylor, where's Dr. Harold? Dr. Saylor!"

Jarred from her petrified trance, Dr. Saylor looked up to see him nearing the unit. "What are you doing?" she yelled, matching his level of intensity as her fear of Maya had nearly eclipsed her fear *for* her. "What do you think you're doing? Wait for Dr. Harold."

"There's no time! Do you want to be thrown to the ground again, Jessica? Or worse?"

"He'll be here! We'll just leave the room until he returns."

"And if we leave and she escapes? What then?"

"Dr. Harold said he knew exactly what to do. He has a plan and is on his way to implement it. Stop! Please. If you do this, we may never get the answers. And Dr. Harold, no doubt he'll have you locked up for such a careless act."

Dr. Hutchens paused. Looking down at Maya, he couldn't believe how fully at ease she appeared, with eyes open, calmly staring into his soul. "We can't... we just can't risk it." Taking one last look, he was filled with a confusing blend of fear and oddly enough, compassion as he reached for the lever to release the toxin. "I'm sorry, Maya."

The first click increased the pressure again. He watched as she squirmed in discomfort, once again struggling to breathe. Yet her eyes never wavered from his.

Begging him to stop, Dr. Saylor moved closer to the glass unit, freezing at the sight of Maya.

I can be free. We can all be free. It's okay. Let him do it.

Time stood still. Shouting ceased. Maya's eyes, tired and closing, saw only blurred movement in her peripheral. Ready to give up, Maya labored to inhale one final breath.

In the darkness she heard a voice she thought she'd never hear again say, "*Mom?*"

Chapter 34
Am I a Bad Guy?

July 2, 2030 | 6:00 p.m.

"**M**om?" Aidan couldn't believe his eyes.

"Stop!" Dr. Harold's voice boomed throughout the lab just as Dr. Hutchens began to pull the lever to its third and final position. "What are you doing!?"

Releasing the lever as if it were boiling, Dr. Hutchens stammered in surprise, "Sir, s-s-something... you see... the tank lost its pressure. The system shows nothing changed, yet she was mov—"

Without hesitation, Aidan leapt toward the man at the back of the glass containment unit. Grabbing him by the neck, his adrenaline pumping, he pressed Dr. Hutchens up against the wall, nearly lifting him off the floor.

"Aidan! Stop!" Dr. Harold shouted as Aidan's face turned

red. With a calming hand on his shoulder, Dr. Harold caught Aidan's attention and, in a soothing voice, directed him to the end goal. "It's okay, Aidan. Release Dr. Hutchens."

Aidan wanted to squeeze the life out of this complete stranger but instinctively knew he'd never leave that room alive if he did. Slowly releasing his grip, Aidan relented, causing Dr. Hutchens to fall away, coughing and grabbing his throat as he stumbled.

Dr. Harold immediately threw the lever back to its original position, only to turn and find Aidan's face inches from his.

"You were going to kill her," Aidan growled.

"No, no, no. Dr. Hutchens was just afraid. After all, I rushed you up here, didn't I? Everything is alright now," said Dr. Harold in a slow, hushed voice, his hands raised in surrender.

After a moment of letting the adrenaline dissipate, Dr. Harold flicked his eyes toward Maya. That simple gesture instantly broke the spell, and Aidan remembered why he was there.

There was his mother. More wrinkles around her eyes. Silvery white streaks through her auburn hair. She was older, in her forties now, but he knew without any hesitation that it was her.

Quietly, with unclenched fists still red, he placed his hand on the glass. Her eyes were closed and her chest rose in small bursts as she was clearly still alive.

"Mom?"

Dr. Harold, covered in sweat from the intense exchange and mad rush to avert disaster, said, "It's okay, Aidan. She was having an... uh... seizure. We had to sedate her."

It took every ounce of control not to pounce on every person in that lab. As far as he was concerned, they were all guilty of abuse. "Why is she in there?" he said, his words hissing through his teeth. Aidan's eyes were glued to his mother as she lay prone inside the same glass box both Lexi and Zuri were forced to endure. "If she volunteered for this, why is she being kept in this thing?"

"No, no. This is for *her* protection—"

"Looks more like captivity."

"I understand how you must feel seeing her like this. But she had an episode this morning, and this is the safest way to ensure she won't harm herself."

A red sheen washed over Aidan's eyes. His rage began to churn again as his skin vibrated. He'd never felt this kind of fury, and somewhere in the back of his mind, he could almost hear a familiar voice pleading with him. Regardless, he knew there was no way he could release her from the unit, simultaneously manhandle three doctors, and safely make it down nineteen floors only to contend with the rest of the compound. This voice, real or imagined, told him to be patient.

Clearing his throat, Aidan said, "So she's not permanently living in there?"

A subtle smile spread across Dr. Harold's face. "No. No, Aidan. She's always free to come and go. However, when these episodes hit, this is the safest place for her. And she's very much aware of that."

From the corner of his eye, Aidan caught an expression flash across the female doctor's face. It was the kind of quick flicker of a look a person makes when they hear an obvious lie.

"That's good to hear, doc. So..." his words lodging in his throat, "when can she come out? It's been a long time. I'd like to see my mother."

"Soon! Soon. Yes, however, her seizures are still emerging. We can tell by her brain waves that she's still being afflicted. It would be too dangerous to wake her." Dr. Harold kept the information to himself that the second click of that lever Dr. Hutchens pulled released a strong sedative.

As far as he could remember, his mother had never had seizures. But he wasn't about to argue. He needed time, and there was only one way to get it.

"Alright, doc." Aidan took in a deep breath and steadied himself. "How can I help?"

Dr. Harold clapped his hands together. The smack startled everyone in the room. "Good man! You are just as intelligent and courageous as your mother." Motioning to a chair next to a computer screen, he said, "Your mother is going to be just as excited to see you as I was! Let me show you what we're working on."

And just like that, a bitter taste washed over Aidan's tongue. *Is this really the only way? Or have I just become one of the bad guys?*

Dakota felt the rush of relief when the pressure eased. Oxygen pulled into her lungs, stretching her chest, and reignited a painful sting across her abdomen. Once her breathing was under control, she attempted to sit up, only to be halted by the fierce pain on the back of her head.

Bandages? Wrapping around my entire head?

Vaguely, she remembered being in the woods with Eli. She'd fallen. But couldn't remember anything after.

Scanning the room, it was clear that it was a medical facility. *We were outside the VISP compound... were we captured? Am I inside the building? Oh, my head... where is Eli? And Levi? This isn't the Station's med bay... I know that much.*

Slowly standing, she felt the sting across her stomach and lifted her shirt. A spider web of angry veins like purple-blue vines crisscrossed an intricate pattern. Touching it made her wince. Stepping tenderly so as not to jar her headache, Dakota approached a glass cabinet with little vials and bottles inside. *Pain-killer. Thank God.*

Finding acetaminophen, she poured a handful of pills into her palm and looked around for water. A half-empty cup sat on a desk, and she downed the pills along with the remaining cool liquid.

Turning back, vertigo struck her like a semi-truck, causing her to drop to her knees. Feeling the cool tile under her sweaty palms, she sensed she was going to black out. As the darkness closed in, Dakota leaned forward and spread out on the hard floor. Her cheek touched the cold tile and for a second her mind was clear with an image of a petite blond woman staring at her. The woman's lips were moving, but there was no sound. She seemed to be begging her to do something but vanished behind Dakota's eyes as she passed out.

Chapter 35
Now She Knew

"Hand these out," said Maria, giving sandwiches to Joe and Phil for the girls. She knew they'd be hungry after what they'd been through. Plus, it gave her something to do with her nervous energy. Phil grabbed as many as he could muster in his big hands, then left the safehouse kitchen.

Entering the living room, he paused at the sight. The girls were in various states of undress with pale faces and distant eyes. Sheila and the others were helping to hold ice packs on their injuries. It was inconceivable what had happened, but he'd witnessed it with his own eyes. Each one had the exact same reddish-purple lines spreading along various places on their bodies. It was as if the vines had spread from one girl to the next, always picking up on a girl's body right where it left off on the previous.

"This is… it doesn't make sense. How did this even happen?" Grant recalled seeing these same injuries on Lexi's body when they'd had to pressurize the glass unit she was in at VISP. Yet, to watch all of them suffer out of nowhere was more than he could comprehend.

"It's like Lexi and I," Zoey answered. "What was happening to her was happening to me. Only then it formed on opposite sides of our bodies. This is different. It's like we each took a part of what Maya was going through." She held her right arm up next to Joanna. Where the path of the red vines ended on her, they picked up on Joanna's shoulder.

"Maybe we took the pain in her place? If we all got a piece of it, maybe she was spared?" Addie wondered with a sense of hope.

Joanna nodded. "I hope so. Because if it didn't…"

"Her entire body would be covered," Maddy said, staring in the mirror at the chaotic lines climbing up from below her shirt collar and around her neck.

Macie stared at her right leg. Like an intricate tattoo, the vines climbed from her ankle to just above her knee. And she felt it. A pain so severe in a part of her body she hadn't felt in so long. How was it possible? "Do you think Aidan felt it?" she whispered.

Zuri put her hand on Macie's. "I don't know. He didn't seem to feel what we felt any other time. He might be okay."

Zoey set down her ice pack, stood, and asked, "So? What do we do now?" She looked at Joe and Rick. "I don't know if we can wait until dark. Things are happening too fast in there."

"You might be right," Joe replied with a sigh.

"Those others are out there too, though," Phil added. "We can't risk a fight *and* getting noticed by the security team on VISP."

"I've been thinking," Joe said, setting his sandwich down. "We need a distraction. Somehow, we need that building to evacuate early. And we need as many people on that compound out of the way if we're to even get a chance at successfully rescuing them. Without getting ourselves killed in the process."

"I assume you have a plan for all this?" Justin asked.

Keeps stood and, without a doubt in his voice, said, "I can get the Breakers to leave."

Everyone was shocked at his interruption. Addie looked up at him from the floor. She could see little more than his silhouette with her good eye, but what she could see with her alt-vision was a glow of determination wrapped in fear. "You don't have to do that," she said under her breath.

Looking down at her, he wanted to beg for forgiveness a thousand times. When they were at Oakley's, his hands were tied. He couldn't stop what was being done to her, and something broke inside of him. But this was something he *could* do. "Yes. I do."

"No, you don't." Brandon's voice caught everyone's attention. "For all we know, you'll go back and share what you've learned about us all. We'll have an even bigger fight to contend with."

"I wouldn't do that," Keeps quietly said, shying away from an argument.

"And how do we know what you would and wouldn't do?" growled Brandon, stepping toward him.

Zoey stepped in front of Keeps, glaring at Brandon. "Because he's telling the truth. I've watched him since you brought him back from the cell. His motives for going to Oakley's in the first place don't negate what he wanted to do once he saw all those women being tortured. He's got a good heart, Brandon. He's telling the truth. He wants to help us, and I believe he can."

The rest of the team listened in silence. Whether they believed Keeps or not didn't matter. They believed Zoey.

Breaking the tension, Joe took the reins, "Okay. Then let's go make a new plan."

Keeps hobbled forward, using a single crutch to help himself along. The men hadn't wanted to bring him in the first place, but Zoey had pushed for it before they left Sanford. She couldn't explain why at the time, using their need to keep him away from the other girls still at home as her excuse. But now she *knew*. This was the reason. He would help remove the Breakers from the equation so they could rescue their own.

After about fifteen minutes of conversing between Keeps, Joe and Rick, Joe grabbed the keys and handed them to the young broken man. "Take a car, but walk the last quarter mile or so. We can't have anyone see you coming."

Chapter 36
Not Convincing

July 2, 2030 | 7:30 p.m.

"Can I wear this?" Aidan held up a lab coat he found hanging over a chair. He didn't bother to wait for an answer as he whipped it over his shoulders, trying to push his arm into the tiny sleeve. All he could think about was the old Saturday Night Live episode with Chris Farley, and began singing quietly, "Fat man in a little coat," to himself with a few giggles from the female doctor in response. "What? Don't think it'll fit?" he joked with a stern look.

Shaking her head, Dr. Saylor said, "I'm thinking my jacket's a little small for you."

Aidan peeled the jacket from his arm. "I'd make one heck of a good-looking doctor. Just sayin'." While he wasn't in a silly mood, his instincts in situations like this were typically spot-on. He had a knack for disarming turbulent environments. He'd never analyzed it before, but being able to make people laugh made them more apt to be at ease around him and share things they otherwise might not. Maybe it was a gift. Maybe it was just normal psychology. Whatever it was, it was working. The doctors immediately began to trust him. While at first they attempted to conceal what was on their computer screens and cover paperwork on their desks, his loveable, down-home personality quickly disarmed them.

Taking full advantage of the situation, he let his eyes wander to everything visible, floor to ceiling. If it wasn't for the nerd-pack and all he'd learned watching them the past several months, he wouldn't have had a clue what he was looking at. As it turned out, he was a quick study and took notice of quite a bit of intel.

Maya still hadn't woken up. Aidan got the impression that she wasn't actually sleeping. Either she was pretending, or they were keeping her sedated. Nothing on their equipment told him she was still in distress if she had ever been in the first place.

Whatever the case, the longer she remained still, the better for him and his group to rescue her. He knew that if she was awake, Dr. Harold would never allow him to be alone with her. He needed to get out of the lab for a few minutes, find Dakota and Elias, and convince them of his budding plan. He couldn't do it without them.

"Hey, Doc? Mind if I grab a bite? I want to check on my friend as well. See if she's up yet."

Dr. Harold turned from his computer. He paused for a beat before answering. "Sure, yeah. Security will bring you down."

"Come on, Doc. I don't need a babysitter," he whined.

Dr. Harold smiled at the grown child in front of him. "As I said, there's still a lot of sensitive information around here that you don't have clearance for."

Aidan threw his arms out in a comical gesture. "What's more sensitive than this!"

Dr. Saylor giggled once again, catching herself before looking back at her notes.

Dr. Harold gestured toward the door before turning back to his work.

"Yeah, yeah. Alright man. Anyone need anything? Sandwich? Candy bar? I still can't believe you have Snickers here!" he said, backing toward the door as he spoke.

Everyone turned him down while Dr. Saylor gently shook her head, mouthing a polite "No thanks."

"My mind is blown. If I lived here I'd be eating candy bars every chance I got! Suit yourselves." Aidan turned, pulled the heavy door open, and smiled at the guard who had been following him around since he arrived. *Does this guy ever get a bathroom break?*

"To the cafeteria, Jeeves!" Aidan flashed him a wide grin, but the guy clearly did not have one humorous bone in his body. "You should laugh more. Make you look younger, or, ya know, likable." The guy didn't even flinch.

As they rode the elevator down, Aidan said, "I need to make a pit stop in my room if that's cool?"

The security guard responded by pushing the button labeled fourteen.

Reaching the apartment, Aidan turned the knob and opened the door wide. Before entering, he peered down the hall, noting the camera at the far end in the upper corner, but saw no people.

In a split-second decision he spun around, grabbed the guard's arm, flipped it behind him and pulled the man into the room by his neck.

"What are you doing!?" Elias barked, jumping up from his bed.

"Help me!" Aidan grunted as he yanked the guard backward. "Grab that t-shirt."

Elias stood frozen, unsure of what to do. "You're gonna get us killed!"

"Grab the shirt!"

Elias turned his brain off and reacted. Snatching the shirt from the back of the chair, he raced over, twisting it as he ran, then shoved it into the guard's mouth before tying it around the back of his head.

"Okay, grab his cuffs from his belt."

"This is a bad idea Aidan. I hope you know what the hell you're doing." Elias snapped the cuffs on and then took three giant steps back.

After seating the guard on the floor beside the bed, Aidan used a tie-down wrap he had snatched from the lab and secured his feet to the bedpost.

"Please tell me you have a plan," Elias pleaded, already covered in sweat.

"Yeah, sure."

"That's not very convincing."

"Well, it's a plan in so much as I'm improvising as I go along."

Elias slammed his fist on the desk and threw his head back in disbelief. "We're literally going to be killed for this! At the very least, we'll never see daylight again. Dude, what are you doing?"

"Shut up and listen. I found my mom."

"You wh—"

"Shut it! My mom is being held on floor nineteen, and I know where they're keeping Dakota. She's in the med bay. Third floor. If we can get to both of them, then hunker down in D4, it'll be easier for my team to rescue us if we're all together."

"Where's D4?"

"It's the second to last level below ground."

"How do you even know about this?"

"This isn't my first rodeo in this building."

"How do you know there aren't people down there?"

Aidan paused, finally taking a deep breath. "I don't... but the last time we were here, we kinda blew it to pieces. They haven't been above ground long enough to repair it for use... probably."

"Probably? What kind of answer is *probably*? They were letting us go in the morning! What's wrong with you?"

"No. They wouldn't have. I've been in the lab with my mom for the past couple of hours. They're keeping her sedated. They think I'm on their side."

"So, what? You couldn't just pretend a little longer?"

"Pretending doesn't matter. They would never let Dakota go. Probably have her sedated, too. And they sure as heck aren't gonna let you go now that you've seen this place."

"This is insane!"

"Yeah, that seems to be about normal. Listen, I need your help. You can either stay here and whine and then deal with whatever they plan to do with you, or you can help me get my mom and your friend prepped for when the others get here."

"How do you know they're even coming?"

Aidan stepped face to face with Elias, gripped the front of the man's shirt, and growled, "Unlike your friends, mine won't abandon me."

Elias wanted to slug him, but an image of Levi's snarky face sneered back at him. Dropping his shoulders with a sigh, he firmly asked, "Okay, so what's next."

"You're in?"

"My options are limited."

A big smile washed across Aidan's face. "You might be a good guy yet."

Chapter 37
Decide

July 2, 2030 | 8:00 p.m.

Keeps hobbled among the trees. Beads of sweat dripped from his face as the pain from his bruised leg and fractured ribs stabbed at him. He knew he deserved it. He should've done more to protect those girls at Oakley's. He also knew dwelling in the past wasn't going to help him, that all he could do now was make his efforts worth it to those women.

He wasn't even mad they hadn't healed him. He knew they had the ability to. He could even tell some of them wanted to, but he guessed that between Brandon and Joe, they were outvoted, assuming that with his strength back he would do something foolish. Not that he would.

The Breakers were not at their previous rendezvous and nowhere in sight. Keeps noted their tire tracks leading back the way they'd come. *Maybe they left? Maybe I just hiked all this way for nothing. Maybe we'll be free after all.* He stood looking in all directions as if hoping some bit of information would magically spring out of the forest. And walking back to Florida wasn't an option.

Dakota, on the other hand, would probably take him back once she understood his situation. Yet if she was in the heart of VISP, he might never see her again anyway.

Buried deep in his thoughts, Keeps failed to hear the stone-crunching sound of footsteps behind him. Having made up his mind to go back to the safehouse and see if there was any other way he could help, he turned only to run directly into a large man with a gun.

Before he knew it, Keeps was spun back around with his arms pinned behind his back and a knife at his throat.

"Who are you?"

"Keeps. My name's Keeps!" he grunted, the pain in his ribs shooting like fireworks into his brain.

The man didn't move or make a sound for several seconds. Suddenly, and without explanation, he released his hold on Keeps and walked around to face him. "Keeps?"

"Capt. V.?"

"What are you doing here?"

"That's… that's a long story."

"Give me the abridged version. Last time we saw you, you were supposed to be doing recon. Then you just disappeared."

"Yeah. Recon turned into a sort of spy mission I couldn't get out of. Until now."

Capt. V. stared at him, his eyes narrow and lips pursed.

"Not enough? Okay, I got rolled up by a group of guys who

were abducting women and conducting crazy tests on them. I'd planned to get as much info as possible, then slip out so we could rescue them. That didn't happen. The main guy, Oakley, which turned out wasn't even his real name, was crazy. Couldn't get away."

The captain softened his stance as Keeps took a deep breath.

"Then this other group showed up to rescue those girls, and I ended up their prisoner. Turns out the girls with the new group were similar to Dakota. Each with gifts, like she has. Recently, they decided to come here hoping to rescue another one and brought me along thinking I'd be of some use. Had no idea you guys would be here. Really would love to get back to normal."

Capt. V. stepped back and shook his head. "Huh. Sounds like you could write a book."

"Seriously."

"Alright, so where are they? How come you're alone?"

"When we realized it was Breakers out here, they sent me to talk to you guys."

"They beat you? You look like you're in pain. Why would they tear you up like this then just let you off alone?"

"No, they didn't do this… uh… there's a lot to this story. But no, they don't think I'm a threat. Well, at least I don't think they do."

Once again, the captain paused to look Keeps up and down. "Alright, let's get you back to the—"

"Wait! Uh... we think Dakota's in that building. Is she?"

"Yeah. They rolled up on her and Elias."

"So what's Levi doing out here then? Since when does he go out in the field?"

"Also a long story."

"Are you going to try and rescue them?"

Capt. V. looked over his shoulder. His recon team was still doing a 360 sweep of the compound while the rest of the group remained with Levi. "Let me ask you, was there a red-headed guy with you?"

Keeps nodded. "Yeah. He got taken with Dakota and Elias."

"Alright. I'll get you back to Levi an—"

"Here's the deal. I came out here to find you guys and propose joining forces to rescue Dakota, Elias, and their people." That wasn't exactly true, but he improvised.

The man let out a frustrated breath, then looked around him once again. "I'm not sure that's the plan."

Keeps took a step back and said, "What do you mean? As in, you're not going to rescue them?"

"Yeah man, look, a lot has changed since you left. Dakota, well, she's… changed."

Keeps just stared at him, waiting for more.

"We haven't been doing missions and…"

"And what?"

"She's become volatile. Levi thinks it's time someone else was in charge."

"Levi thinks? What?" laughed Keeps. "Volatile? What does that mean?"

"Like she's turned against us, Keeps. Not doing missions. Not since last August. Violent."

Keeps couldn't envision Dakota turning on them. She was direct and commanding for sure. But violent? None of it made sense. "So who takes over for her? Levi?" he scoffed.

Capt. V. didn't laugh.

"That's ridiculous. We wouldn't exist if it wasn't for

Dakota."

"Yeah. I know."

"What? Are you on board with this?"

He didn't respond.

"Wow. I guess things *have* changed. I'd never have pegged you for mutiny. Not after what she's done for us."

"Alright! I get it. Look. I'm giving you one chance," he stated, grabbing Keeps' arm. "You can either go back to where you just came from and you were never here... or I can bring you to Levi. Your choice."

Their eyes locked.

"This is a mistake. I've met the others like her. If you come up against them, you'll lose. Don't do this, man."

"Decide."

Keeps wanted to shake him for being so stupid, but he could tell the captain wasn't going to budge. Ripping his arm away from the man, he started to walk away then turned back, "So, what? You're just going to leave her in there then? Let her be experimented on?"

"It's not up to me. You need to leave before I change my mind."

Keeps made his way to the tree line. Before disappearing into the thicket, he paused and, over his shoulder, shouted, "You have a choice too, ya know."

 8:30 p.m.

"Keeps?" whispered Zuri. She was staring out the window watching the sun as it sat low on the horizon when a car came around the bend.

"What?" Joe said, peering out the window over her shoulder. "What the heck? There's no way." Opening the front door, he, Lexi and Zuri approached the vehicle as the engine shut off. Keeps struggled to exit.

"Hey man, what happened? Didn't figure we'd see you again." Joe grabbed him under his arm to relieve some of the weight.

"I told you I was going to get them to leave." Keeps was confused.

"Yeah well, figured you'd take the opportunity to free yourself from us."

Keeps stopped moving and looked at Joe. "I know you have no reason to trust me, but I owe a debt. Plus, you were right. They *aren't* planning to rescue Dakota and Elias. I didn't believe it when you'd told me earlier, but apparently a lot has changed."

Joanna came out as well and met them in the driveway. Still unsteady, but holding her own.

Joe shook his head. "Well, I mean, that's good for us, but I thought you said she was their leader?"

"That guy Levi that I mentioned? He seems to be running the show now. He was hoping to get rid of Dakota or something like that. VISP just happened to take care of it for them."

Zuri responded, "I don't understand. Why would they want to get rid of her?"

"Dunno. I ran into Captain Varreccia out there. He's the commander of their operator team, and according to him, she's become volatile."

"In what way?" Zuri asked.

"He said she's turned against them. Changed."

Joanna touched his arm. "Changed how?" she asked gently.

He paused knowing he had to tell them what he'd learned. "He mentioned her being violent?"

Joanna's eyes dropped.

Lexi saw Joanna's shoulders deflate. "Did you know?" she asked carefully.

Joanna looked up, unable to lie to her sisters. "I wasn't sure, but… I kind of felt like maybe she wasn't in a good place? Like there was a rage inside her, I guess?"

Everyone stood quietly remembering Aidan's comment about her not being one of the good guys.

Keeps tried to defend her. "She's never been a bad or evil person. What he said doesn't make sense. Levi loves the game of destruction. Maybe she just didn't want to do it anymore? Maybe Levi was tired of not getting to destroy people's lives so he wants to give her the boot."

"But isn't she their ace in the hole?" Joe asked.

"She is. Levi never went out on missions. He never witnessed firsthand what she does for the operators on a target. Without her, we'd never have been half as successful as we were." Keeps cringed at his idea of success.

"If that's the case, why is your old captain going along with it?" pressed Joe, feeling a slight weight lift, knowing they wouldn't have to deal with Breakers on top of everything else. Regardless, something wasn't sitting right.

Shaking his head but maintaining eye contact, Keeps said, "He didn't say as much, but I could tell he had misgivings about it all. I think he agrees they'd be worse off without her, but Levi must've had a pretty convincing argument."

Zuri set his other arm over her shoulder. Together they made their way back into the house.

"So what's the word? Didn't find them?" Brandon asked as they walked in the door. His tone was gruff, but seeing the man in pain did spark a tinge of guilt for treating him so poorly.

"He did," Joe answered. "But they aren't going in to rescue their people. Means we should have a clear path without interference."

"Does that mean we can go in now?" Zoey asked, rising from the table.

"I don't think they'll be here much longer," Keeps grunted, descending onto the couch. "They aren't going to pick a fight with people they don't know when they're preparing to leave anyway."

"Good," Maddy said. "Then I say we go now. There's no reason to prolong their exposure to experimentation any further. What's the first step, Joe?"

"Well… we know VISP isn't keen on explosions."

Chapter 38
Could Get Any Better

July 2, 2030 | 8:45 p.m.

Dakota's throbbing head woke her. Still lying on the hard floor, she pushed herself slowly to her knees using both hands, feeling a slight twinge of pain in her broken arm. She had no idea how long she had been out cold, but clearly, no one attempted to remove her from the floor.

Moving her broken arm freely and observing the sling hanging listlessly at her side, she pulled it up over her head. *Did these people heal me? How long have I been here? It would've taken weeks for my arm to heal so thoroughly.* Her mind raced through the implications.

Though her body ached, her mind seemed very clear. Fear began to rise in her gut, but she knew she needed to tamp it down and get out of wherever she was. Spotting her clothes on a nearby chair, she snatched them up, grunting in anger that her weapons were nowhere to be found.

My book!

Dakota saw her bag across the room and grabbed it. She opened it only to find snacks, water, and medical supplies. No book.

Her head began to tingle with licks of fire that quickly spread to her arms.

Her eyes scanned the room, but it was gone. That sketchbook was her lifeline. Squeezing her fists she felt heat spread through her, amplifying the fire. *Why would they have taken a book of drawings?* Her mind played over all the strange things someone would find in it. Drawings of random places and random items with no rhyme or reason.

She wanted to lash out, but no one was close enough so she grabbed a stapler off the desk and threw it so hard that it flew through the adjacent wall, landing in the next room. The action didn't dampen her rage.

Where's Elias? Did he leave me? Did Levi bring me here?

Her mind twisted with betrayal. She wished there was a window in the room that would offer insight into where she was or whether it was day or night. Her memory of the unfamiliar doctors' voices didn't help, and she never got a good look at their faces.

As her heart rate climbed, the sound of people talking nearby finally registered in her brain. Stalk still, she listened as hard as she could, leaning toward the room door. They were just outside but didn't sound like they intended to enter. Piecing together keywords through the ringing in her ears, she gathered they were trying to contact a Dr. Harold. Something about a biochemical agent or so it seemed.

As the sound died down, she tiptoed to the sink feeling so dehydrated. Splashing water on her face then tucking her head under the faucet for a healthy drink, she finally stood upright. A woman glared back at her.

Dakota, jumping back, let out a stifled scream at the image. She didn't recognize the face looking back at her. Her eyes were an intense glow even from what they'd been the past few months. Even more so, there was a myriad of what appeared to be purplish veins weaving an intricate pattern around her right eye and disappearing into her hairline.

It was her. The woman a reflection of her former self only formidable in comparison. Feeling dizzy, she remembered the pain on her abdomen. Ripping off the hospital gown, she checked the rest of her body, finding patches of the same veining randomly scattered about.

Biological weapon? Was it used on me? What would cause this... this scarring?

Without waiting, Dakota quickly grabbed her clothes and then searched the room for another way out. Nothing. She had no way of knowing what kind of facility she was in, whether it was multiple floors or above or below ground. And every time she passed the mirror, she couldn't help but pause and observe the new face looking back.

Putting her ear to each of the three walls, she listened intently for any sort of life, but there was an incessant whirring of machinery around her that muddled her attempts. Not to mention, her lingering headache wasn't helping, although it occurred to her that whatever head trauma she had experienced was now physically healed as well. With a sigh of relief, Dakota stumbled upon some paper and a pencil and immediately drew a crude door on it. Looking at the blank wall she'd thrown the stapler through, with her hand on the paper, she focused what little energy she had left. As soon as she did, golden sparks in the shape of a door fizzled out of thin air on the wall. The new door took little more than a few seconds to fully form.

She reached for the knob as soon as it materialized. Turning it slowly, she peeked around the edge of the frame into the space beyond.

Empty. *Just an empty storage room. Damn.*

Knowing her time was limited, she hurried into the storage room, quietly closing the door behind her. She then drew an X over the image on her paper and swiped her hand across it. Within seconds, the door disappeared and the wall was whole again. Suddenly, as if on cue, Dakota heard a myriad of yells from the room she'd escaped and people scurrying around. A booming male voice demanded, *"Where is she? How did you let her get out?"*

She remained plastered against the wall in the dark, listening as people raced down the hallway, opening and closing doors as they went. From under the door, she saw a shadow of someone standing. After barking orders at the others to lock down the building his shadow began to move away from her door only to pause at the last second.

Dakota watched as it moved back to the center of her door. Startled by the indecisive shadow, she hesitated to grab her paper and pencil until it was too late. The door swung open and an older, tall man in a lab coat stood over her as she crouched low.

It's him.

His silhouette, dark skin, and the way he stood with that gleam in his eye—he was the one who took her all those years ago, selling her off into a life of horror. The images flashed through her mind, memories buried so deep she didn't know they existed.

"Now, how did you get in here?" he said, his voice sounding jovial compared to the growling orders he had spit out only moments before.

She wanted to fight him, but the circulating images in her mind made it difficult to focus, causing her to drop the paper on the floor.

Picking it up, the doctor uncrumpled it to find a hand-drawn door with a large X over it filling the page. "Dakota." She watched as his smile widened. "I didn't think this day could get any better."

Chapter 39
Could Get Any Worse

July 2, 2030 | 9:00 p.m.

"**I** didn't think this day could get any worse," Justin groaned.

Taking hold of his hand, Zoey said, "How much time do you think we have?"

He shook his head. "I don't know, but I know storm clouds when I see them. No telling how big it is. Maybe a couple hours? Looks slow."

The sun was below the horizon, and the remaining light glowed pink off the incoming string of clouds to the southeast. Rick's team was getting into position around the perimeter as the rest of them stayed back at the safehouse. They were assessing the compound for weak spots so Joe and the others knew exactly where to stage in order to infiltrate.

Shaking his head and wishing for just one thing to go as planned, Joe added, "Which means we'll lose Jahnsen's overwatch when we need them most. Is what it is, time to go. If Keeps is right, Breakers won't be a problem. Rick's team should be in position by now." He touched his earpiece and said, "Black, this is Green. What's your status?"

A few seconds passed before a hushed voice replied, "We've completed recon. No Breakers on site. There was a heavy guard presence when we got here, but they've moved inside."

Brandon looked at Joe. "You'd think they'd have more security at the prospect of Aidan and the others not being alone."

Nodding, Joe answered, "Agreed. Unless Aidan was convincing enough. He'd have thought to tell them they're alone. One thing about that kid, he's a quick thinker."

"And if it's a trap?"

"We'll find out when we get there."

Both men knew the risks.

Joe looked at the odd company assembled around him. Their haphazard group of doctors, military-esque personnel, and fired-up women were unstoppable. At least he hoped so.

He'd constructed an explosive device that Rick's team would place near the propane tanks at the north side of the compound. Hoping that it would create a similar expectation of forcing personnel underground so they could easily get into the target building. He just hoped most of the compound would be bedding down for the night, so the explosive would create more disorientation and panic for personnel to leave quickly.

"Is the device positioned?" Joe asked.

"It's affixed. We'll wait on your go. Time?"

Joe took a last look around and released a heavy breath.

"Detonate in sixty minutes."

Aidan and Elias packed all the supplies they could, stole the guard's radio and weapons, then casually made their way to the fifth floor via the stairs before Aidan heard something over the guard's stolen radio about the med-bay patient. Grabbing Elias, he popped open the door to the hidden stairwell and ducked inside. Elias was astounded at how much Aidan seemed to know about the building.

Radio chatter told them Dakota had gone missing. "They're going to have too many guards searching for her down there." Aidan grunted in frustration, staring down the stairwell, debating what to do next. "Plan's changed. Let's head up to nineteen then circle back."

Chapter 40
Burning

Joanna grabbed her chest and clawed at her throat, gasping for air and wincing with every breath.

"What's happening?" Keeps bellowed, looking around for what might have hurt her.

Maddy and Sheila grabbed Joanna's arms and sat her on the couch while Zuri held her hand as they assessed her.

Joe made the decision. "Something's happened inside the compound. Joanna can't go anywhere in this state. Keeps, Grant, she needs to stay with you. We're out of time." Joe was certain Dakota was in trouble. It was Zoey all over again. As he turned to grab his bag, each girl folded forward right where they stood in what looked like an upright fetal position.

"Oh my God!" Keeps watched in horror, spinning around in

search of the cause.

"It's not happening here," shouted Justin, grabbing Zoey and helping her to the ground. "Joe?" he said through gritted teeth, wondering, *What are we supposed to do now?*

Lexi, able to break from the spell, whispered, "It's okay. We're going to be okay." Slowly standing upright, she closed her eyes and, one by one, the girls' pain eased, each shaking off what it was that overcame them and rising upright.

Everyone could feel the pulsing in the air. "Lexi's doing this?" Keeps asked in awe.

"Yes," Sheila answered in a hushed voice, remaining vigilant.

"But how?"

"We don't have time for this," Joe barked. Pointing to the girls, he said, "We'll go in. You need to stay out here."

"You know we—"

"Lexi! We can't risk you falling out again. There's too much at stake."

"I know!" she yelled back, grabbing his arm. "That's why we have to go. We have no idea what's going on in there."

"Exactly."

Loosening her grip, she stared him in the eyes, "I've got this now. I just need to keep this shield up and we're good."

Straining his jaw as he held in a slew of profanities, Joe released a loud yawp in frustration. He knew it wouldn't do any good to fight her on this. "And how long do you think you can hold it? We could be in there for hours."

"It's not taxing, Joe. I can hold it long enough to push off another attack. We'll feel it, but it won't take us down. Besides, I can go full force if we're desperate."

"Fine. But you need to stay in the rear."

Lexi nodded, convinced she could maintain the shield around them.

Looking throughout the room at their determined faces, he made one final demand as Joanna remained weak and unstable. "Fine. She stays back here, though."

Lexi wanted to argue, but she knew he was right. Even with her protection, Joanna's connection was too strong.

"No!" Joanna cried hoarsely. Then immediately leaned forward in pain.

"This is no longer up for debate. Grant?" said Joe, glaring at him.

Grant threw his arm around her, and gave her a gentle squeeze as Maria grasped her hand. "I'm here with you. We can be the team that saves them when they screw it up," she said with a wink.

"My radio's on channel seven," Grant confirmed.

Joe nodded, turned, and then quietly led the crew outside.

Dakota couldn't breathe.

Her burning eyes followed Dr. Harold as he paced the room. Though she tried, she couldn't utter a word.

"I wonder if your friends are waiting outside the compound. Trying to figure a way in. I'm making it very easy for them this time. Are they here? The rest of the girls?" he questioned, a sly smile growing at the thought. "I hope so. Couldn't have asked for a better scenario... to have all my girls back in my care. Incredible! I wonder, are they Breakers like you?"

She wanted to rip his throat out. Strapped to a hospital bed, she was covered with electrodes. He was using an electrical current to immobilize her. Tears streamed from her eyes with every pulse, her body's way of releasing the relentless tension.

"I have so many questions for you!" he said with a giddy laugh as he pulled her book from his oversized lab coat pocket. "This is fascinating. So what, you draw… it becomes real? You know you didn't do this when you were little. How did you even figure out this gift?" He scanned through the pages. "I mean. You could literally change the world with this Dakota."

Her breaths slowed, growing more shallow with each passing minute.

"I'll turn this off if you promise to play nice."

Her red eyes burned at the offer.

"I can see that's not quite in the cards just yet. That's fine." He flipped a few more pages. "You put an X over most of them. I'm very eager to know what that means." Dr. Harold considered his own words for a moment, then pulled the paper he found in the closet from his pocket and unfolded it. "Wait. This door. You drew this door. This is how you got out of your room and into the storage closet. So the X…" his voice trailed off only to come back with confirmation. "You crossed it off to cancel it. To erase the door. Is that it? This X means whatever you draw, disappears." He laughed in both shock and awe. "This is incredible!"

 9:50 p.m.

"Black, we're in position. Over." Joe whispered through his headset.

"Roger. Ready when you are," Rick responded.

Joe locked eyes with each one in his group. As they nodded in turn, he pulled his eyes back toward the lights of the buildings on the other side of the wall.

"Blow it."

Dr. Harold was in the middle of personally congratulating himself for having Dakota and Aidan now in his custody when a ground-shaking explosion pierced his ears.

His head swiveled at the sound of the door bursting open behind him as security rushed in. "Sir, they've breached the compound."

The doctor's momentary fear dissipated. "Good! That's good. Are our people sheltering?"

"Yes, sir. All moving now."

"Are your men in position?"

"Affirmative. Two on the roof tracking the potential targets. Four around the building. And six on the main floor inside. The rest are in their holding positions."

"Excellent! So there are women in the group?"

"Yes, sir. We count five women."

Dr. Harold's expression fell a little. "Only five? That's too bad. I was hoping all seven might be there."

"Sir?"

"Nothing. None of the women are injured, do you hear me?"

"Yes, sir."

With that, the guard left the room and returned to his post.

"Oh, Dakota! You're about to be reunited with your sisters. We're going to change the world together." The grin on his face stirred in her a sort of violent hatred, a feeling that had been growing over the last six months. Only this felt different. A rage of protection. For who she wasn't quite sure.

"And imagine, you'll all finally meet the woman that made you who you are. What a great day!"

Chapter 41
The Shot

July 2, 2030 | 10:00 p.m.

Elias was just about to challenge Aidan's ever-changing strategy when what felt like the concussive pressure of a bomb rocked the building.

"That's gotta be my Joey," Aidan whispered with a smirk.

Grabbing hold of Elias once again, they reemerged back into the main stairwell as a flurry of activity erupted in the halls on every floor.

I wonder if this is what it was like when we kicked in the door the first time around, he thought. While they hadn't actually been the cause of the panic the first time, he had no doubt that this was Joe's handiwork.

"We need to get to the nineteenth floor."

"Shouldn't we get out of here?" Elias shouted with panic.

"Nope. These are our people, and they're coming for us. We need to get to my mom and Dakota as fast as we can."

Bodies flooded the stairwell, each one frantically racing to the nearest floor with a hidden access door to the emergency stairwell. "Stay with me!" Pushing his way through the throng of VISP staff coming at them, he gripped the handrail to pull himself past the flood. Though clearly surprised by the explosion, each employee clung to their laptop, seemingly the only item anyone cared to protect in an emergency.

Within ninety seconds they were the only ones left on the main stairs, but could hear a hoard of shuffling feet through the exterior wall.

"Where are they going?" Elias asked in confusion.

"There's a bunker below the building. We just need to make sure they don't make it there with Dakota and my mom. We'll never get them back if they do," he grunted, pushing his burning legs to the limit. Upon reaching the next platform, Aidan paused to glance up the stairwell in search of security. His eyes caught something familiar, causing him to stumble back into Elias.

"What are you doing?" Elias growled, throwing his hands up to stop Aidan from knocking him down the stairs.

"That bright... purple... smock. Did you see it? Up there," Aidan muttered, frozen in place with Elias still clutching his shirt.

"Man, I didn't see a thing? Is it your mom?"

"I thought... I don't know," Aidan whispered, looking down the stairwell and then back up again. Straining his eyes, he only caught sight of stragglers hustling down. "Nothing. Never mind. Let's hit it."

The hall door on nineteen was closed, and Aidan didn't

have a keycard. "Damn," he said under his breath.

"What?"

"We can't get in. We need a keycard."

Elias, feeling around in his pockets, found what he was looking for and held it up. "Will this work?"

A radiant smile washed over Aidan's face.

"Snagged it from the guard."

"Forget Joe, you are my new best friend!" Ripping it from Elias's hand, he held it against the card reader until they both heard the click.

Turning the handle and opening the door ever-so-carefully, the two were on guard against possible security. With a sigh of relief, Aidan slipped inside first, pressed up against the wall to listen, and then waved Elias in.

With a look of caution, they overheard yelling at the end of the hallway. Unsure of how far down, it was muffled behind a closed door. Creeping to the end of the hall, Aidan heard Dr. Saylor clear as day in the lab. "So we're just going to sit here and wait? This is ridiculous! We need to get her out of here!"

"You know the protocol." Dr. Hutchens wasn't as loud, but he was clearly frustrated. "We wait here with the patient."

"Maya! Her name is Maya, and you've known her for years. A bomb went off, Steve. Everyone has already left for the bunker. We need to get down there, and we need to take her with us."

"You know we don't leave the lab! Especially her."

"If Maya had caused the explosion, that would be one thing, but she didn't. For God's sake, look at her. She didn't do this!"

Elias mouthed to Aidan, "What do we do?"

"I don't hear Dr. Harold in there. Dr. Saylor already wants to leave. This is our best chance. Stay put til I tell you." Counting down in his mind, on one, Aidan pushed the door open and stepped into the room.

"Aidan?" said Dr. Saylor, sucking in a deep breath, her eyes almost grateful.

"Thought you guys might need some help."

"How'd you get in here?" Dr. Hutchens shot back at him.

"Uhm, hello, I used the door?" Aidan said with a snarky smile.

"You can't be here!" Dr. Hutchens shot back, raising his hands and stepping toward Aidan.

Throwing his hands in the air Aidan said, "Hey, whoa! No need for animosity, Doc. I just thought you could use some help."

Dr. Hutchens paused, his hands beginning to shake. They stared at one another in silence with neither man relenting when Dr. Hutchens ripped open his upper desk drawer and pulled out a gun.

"What are you doing with that!?" Dr. Saylor yelled, her voice trembling.

"You need to get out of here, now," he growled, waving the gun toward Aidan.

"Are you really comfortable using that? I mean, I'm not here to hurt anyone and I think you know that," Aidan said in a calm voice while taking a controlled step toward him.

"Stay where you are. And yes, I have no qualms about shooting you."

Aidan nodded, motioning his hands downward while taking another step.

"I'm serious! Do not take another—"

With that final warning, Aidan lunged forward, tackling Dr. Hutchens to the ground. Like kids in a backyard fight, Aidan struggled to rip the weapon from the doctor's hand when a shot rang out. Neither man moved.

Elias, timing his entrance into the fray, jumped into the room shouting, "Aidan!"

After a long groan, Aidan responded in a gruff voice, "It's good. I'm fine." Rolling off Dr. Hutchens, a pool of blood revealed itself on Dr. Hutchens torso.

Elias pulled Aidan away while staring at Dr. Hutchens whose eyes were wide open. "Oh man, did you kill him?"

Aidan grunted, "No, I think he's in shock."

Turning to Dr. Saylor, who was curled up in the fetal position on the floor nearby, Elias called out, "Hey! Get over here and treat him!"

Laboring to breathe and waiting for the black fog to recede from the edges of her sight, she slowly rose to her feet. Grabbing a nearby towel and dropping to her knees she searched Dr. Hutchens' abdomen. She swiped the blood on his lab coat but couldn't find a hole. "Where did he get hit? There's too much blood, I can't find it!"

"That's because it's mine," Aidan said between his teeth as he pushed himself back to lean against the glass prison where his mother remained peacefully asleep.

"No! Crap. Give me that!" Elias shouted. Slipping on the fresh blood, he yanked the towel from her hand.

Dr. Saylor looked back and forth between Aidan and her counterpart and said under her breath, "What did you do?" Her face flushed with heat.

Dr. Hutchens didn't move. Didn't blink. Dr. Saylor, snapping her fingers in front of his face, caused him to jolt back to reality. Scrambling away, he hopped to his feet, stammering, "I… I didn't mean…"

"Grab the morphine!" she demanded. "Steve! Grab me the morphine!"

He looked down at himself and frantically began wiping the blood from his hands onto his lab coat, only smearing it further. Glancing at Maya, then Aidan, then the door, Dr. Hutchens leaned forward and threw up a little before sprinting through the door and into the hallway.

"Damn it!" she growled, heading for the medicine cabinet.

"No! No, wait. If you give me morphine I won't be able to move, and, no offense, but you can't carry both of us," he said, shifting his eyes to Maya.

"Yeah, well, you won't be able to move in all that pain."

He laughed, coughing at the sharp ache. "It's fine. This isn't my first rodeo at the wrong end of a barrel." He cough-laughed again before straining to pull himself up.

"Here," said Elias, reaching out.

"I'm fine. Get her out of that box."

"But—"

"No buts, get her out!" he commanded, wincing and clutching his abdomen.

Dr. Saylor was torn. This is what she wanted. To get Maya out and to safety, but now she wasn't so sure. "Maybe I should go get help?"

"We are the help! Besides, there's no one else up here." Aidan's voice was hoarse, and his breathing more rapid. "We need to get her downstairs. I've got people coming. And we need Dakota. Find me a wrap, something to hold pressure on this thing."

Dr. Saylor stared at Maya, imagining outbursts and explosions.

"Jessica! Wrap!" Aidan called out, struggling to remain composed.

Shaking her head and blinking as if waking from a dream, she grabbed a bandage and rushed it back to him. Carefully leaning forward, they firmly wrapped the towel around his midsection.

"It went through," Elias said. The blood on Aidan's back confirming it. "That's good. At least the bullet's not still in there."

Once he was wrapped tight, they helped him to his feet and set him in a chair. "Stay here, we'll get Maya out."

Elias spun around to join the doctor when he caught her staring at the woman in the glass unit, frozen again.

"What are you looking at, Dr. Saylor?" Following her gaze, he noticed a small hole in the glass. As his eyes adjusted to see beyond the glass, a red liquid expanding around Maya caught his attention. "No," he breathed out.

"What?" Aidan grunted, catching wind of the panic in Elias's response. "What happened?" Stretching painfully, Aidan strained to see beyond the two of them.

"The bullet passed through you," he said with a hushed, shaking voice, "and hit your mom."

Chapter 42
They're Coming

Joe kept his weapon trained ahead of him as he and the others slowly moved toward the main VISP building. Zuri could feel the tethers of Maya, Dakota and Aidan pulling her toward the structure.

"We've got two on the roof," said Rick, his hushed voice crackling in Joe's earpiece.

"Roger."

Lexi had just caught sight of them as well. The snipers were barely visible, but the business end of their rifles peeked slightly over the edge, giving away their positions.

Raising his hand, Joe signaled everyone to stop.

Whispering, Lexi said, "I'm ready. Everyone's covered."

Trusting her ability to shield the team, Joe nodded, then

gave the signal to continue on.

After several steps forward, Joe and Lexi watched as the dirt just in front of them kicked up, followed by the suppressed thump of a gunshot. Everyone ducked as dirt kicked up all around them, creating a thunderous applause.

"Are you guys seeing this?" Joe said, pressing his earpiece.

The snipers, abandoning their cover, were on their feet, struggling to ascertain how they could be missing. After a short, silent pause in their firing, the two snipers dropped out of view. The sound of gunfire from the direction of Rick's team echoed around the building. They managed several clean shots while the several guards stood out in the open.

Immediately following, clamor erupted behind several cement barriers close to the building. Concealed guards gave away their positions.

"Rick, can you tell how many are out there?"

"The bird is showing only four. Doesn't look like a strong show of force guarding the place."

"I'm guessing the rest of the security are inside. Don't let your guard down."

"Affirmative."

Joe motioned for everyone to stay low as Rick's team moved in from around the sides of the main building. Before the security team saw them, Rick's men had opened fire. Zoey held her breath as scattered return fire rang out.

"All clear," came Rick's voice over their headsets.

At Joe's leading, they hurried to the building and pressed themselves tightly against it next to Rick and his guys.

"Joe, I need you to get everyone around the corner. Looks like the only way in is to breach the door," said Rick, pulling an explosive device from his bag.

"Wait," Zuri whispered.

"Zuri, what are you doing? Stay low. We have no idea who else is out there!" Joe demanded.

Ignoring his command, she stood tall, calmly reaching her hand out toward the door. Suddenly, the sound of metal creaking and latches sliding and clicking rang out as the door unlocked.

"Nicely done, little Red," said Rick, shaking his head with a small smirk as he motioned for several teammates to flank the threshold while he cautiously pushed the doors open. One by one the team slipped inside where several more gunshots rang out. A moment later, an operator leaned out motioning for them to enter.

Once inside the foyer the women found three more guards lying on the ground. Zuri didn't see blood, yet they weren't moving. Her curious eyes looked up at Rick.

"Tranquilizer darts," he said with a wink.

With a sigh of relief, the girls picked up their pace.

"They'll feel it in the morning, though." Rick smiled.

"Alright, everyone know the plan?" Joe asked with a gruff whisper.

They all nodded as two operators headed for the stairwell that led down to D4. Everyone knew to report back any evidence that VISP personnel had, in fact, gone to the bunkers. Two more operators zip-tied the unconscious guards as a precaution, then took up positions in the foyer. The rest of them moved to the main stairwell. Once cleared, they began the climb.

"If Aidan's with it, he'll know we're coming," Zoey said.

"I just hope he doesn't do anything rash before—"

Justin didn't get to finish when they heard movement far

up the stairwell. The sound of a slamming door, followed by stomping feet racing down the stairs, echoed throughout.

"Stop the bleeding!" Aidan yelled.

"I'm trying. I think it hit an artery," replied Dr. Saylor, applying pressure to Maya's leg.

"She's losing too much blood," said Elias. "We can't save her. We need a surgeon."

"They're likely all in the bunker or heading there now!" Dr. Saylor struggled to keep her hands pressed firmly against Maya's slick, blood-soaked leg.

Elias had pulled Maya out of the glass enclosure and laid her on the floor so they could work on her. Aidan watched helplessly, quietly pressing the towel over his abdomen as best he could. He longed to help but knew he was not much better off.

"Elias, grab a stack of those towels and the bandages." Any concern Dr. Saylor had about Maya's abilities dissipated the moment she was placed in front of her. Her medical training kicked in and she was fully invested in saving Maya's life.

"Here."

"I need you to roll that towel up as tight as you can, then we're going to swap positions. Yes. Like that," she said, watching him quickly roll it into a tight ball. "On the count of one we're going to switch places. You'll put that towel on her wound and press tight while I wrap it into place."

He nodded, knelt beside her, then held the towel directly over her hands covering the wound.

"Three. Two. One. Go, go, go!"

Aidan groaned, internally pleading with them to be careful as he slowly made his way to her side.

"This is going to act as a partial tourniquet, but we need to get her medical attention or she's not going to make it."

"Mom. If you can hear me, you can't die now. Not yet. It's not your time. I need you to hold on." Aidan's voice was soft and hoarse. Tears formed as he stared at her face.

Dr. Saylor, as if suddenly prodded with a firebrand, jumped up and ran to an emergency button on the wall by the door. An alarm in the hallway rang out. "Hold tight. I'm going to run down to the med bay. Maybe another doctor stayed behind and will hear the emergency alarm."

"No! Wait. What do we do?" Elias sprang to his feet. "Why don't you let me go. You know more than I do about this."

"It's not that simple. If no one's there, I'm going to need supplies to bring back up here for both of them."

Nodding, he knew she was right.

Calling over her shoulder, she said, "Keep Aidan awake and try to wake up Maya. We need them to be conscious as long as possible!"

"Keep them awake. Keep them awake. Okay." His eyes searched the room for anything that could help when he saw the medicine cabinet. Rummaging, he grabbed several packets of smelling salts. Having never actually used them, he pinched a little pack between his fingers and rolled to release the smells. Without thinking, he shoved it up under his nose to test it. The burn instantly made him cough and his eyes water. "Crap! Ugh, that's horrible."

"Really, dude? Give me that." With his free arm he reached out to Elias. Placing the packet in Aidan's hand, Aidan leaned over his mom as best he could, grunting in pain. "Mom? This is gonna burn a little, but I need you to wake up."

Gently, Aidan placed the pack beneath her nostrils. Nothing happened.

"This should be working." He rolled it in his fingers harder and put it back under her nose. "Mom? Mom!" His eyes wide with panic, Aidan waved Elias over. "Check. Hurry! Is she breathing?"

Elias leaned down and placed his ear over her nose. "I'm not sure. I don't feel any air." Laying his head on her chest, he could hear the faint, slow beat of her heart. So slow that it was obvious she was dying. "Barely noticeable heartbeat. But she's definitely not breathing."

Aidan rolled onto his knees, attempting to perform CPR. "Agh! I can't do it. I shouldn't have let myself get shot!"

Elias immediately pushed him aside and began compressions. "Sit back. I've got this."

"Mom, please. Please wake up. This isn't how you die. You can't go before I've had a chance to hear your voice. Please... please."

Wiping his eyes and feeling dizzy, Aidan pleaded with her to wake up. He sensed darkness pulling at his consciousness. Tunnel vision began to encroach. He refused to pass out. There was too much at stake. Dropping his head, he reached out slowly. His hand hovered over hers as it lay motionless on the floor.

The moment their fingers touched, a flash of light so bright paralyzed him. His senses exploded on overload. He felt everything. Every hurt in his body. Every beat of his heart. But he could also feel hers. The pain, the fear, the joyful awareness of touching his hand.

Her eyes flashed open as she inhaled deeply with a startling groan. Terrifying Elias and causing him to stumble backward, she sat upright, face-to-face with her son.

"Aidan?" Maya's voice cracked. The blinding light in her eyes subsided to reveal his face only inches from her own. "Oh, God. You're here," she whispered, fiercely wrapping her arms around him. "My baby. My child. You're here."

The moment unfolded with tears as they gripped one another for dear life.

"No! Oh no. Aidan. You shouldn't be here!" From joy to panic, Maya scanned the room, snatching his shirt in her fists in fear. "Where is he?"

"He's not here, Mom. He's not here." Aidan stammered, clearing his throat. "But he'll probably be coming soon. I doubt he'd go to the bunker without you."

That's when the pain hit her. Looking down at her leg, Maya saw blood covering the floor, her pants, and Aidan as well. "Aidan, you have to get out of here. Leave me! You need to get out of this building. As far away as you can."

"Listen. We came for you."

"No, this is bad. You—" Her voice broke off when she saw the way his arm covered his abdomen and the blood that couldn't have been from her. "Oh no..." she groaned, reaching down and touching his arm.

"Well, aren't we a pair," he chuckled, wincing in pain.

"As a child, when you'd get hurt, you'd crack jokes to keep from panicking." Maya smiled at the memory, yet wanting to scream. Instead, with a deep breath, she responded in kind. "I guess we are kiddo."

"I hate to break this up, but we need a plan." Elias was practically bouncing on his toes in fear with one eye on their reunion and the other down the hall through the open door. "Dr. Harold and his men could come back any second. We're sitting ducks!"

Aidan brushed off some more tears and said, "You're right. We need to find a place to hide until Zuri finds us."

"Zuri? She's here?" With every revelation Maya's stomach turned. She never wanted this. Never wanted any of them this close. She'd prayed for them to be free of VISP, free of her.

"You know Zuri?"

"No, not exactly. I know about her, and the others. I only met each of them once."

"On the days they were born?"

Maya nodded.

"Well, Mom, you're going to love them. And have faith," he said with a wink, "they're pretty badass."

Aidan pulled his eyes away from Maya, turned and said, "Elias, if the hall's still empty, we need to abandon this room and hide elsewhere. The others will find us."

"How? How could they possibly know where to look in this place?" Elias fought the panic tingling in his legs. For as many missions as he'd been on with Dakota, this entire situation had gone so far off the rails he couldn't see a way out.

"Trust me. They have a knack for these things."

"But—"

"Go!" Aidan barked, his body tensing up with every muscle spasm. Leaning forward, he strained to catch his breath.

"Aidan?" Maya's voice was just as tender as when he was

a child.

"I'm okay. I'll be okay," he breathed out.

Elias did as he was told. Holding his breath he peeked around the corner, listening for any sign of movement. Everything appeared still and clear. He thought it surreal that they were no longer surrounded by guards. "Clear," he said, pulling his head back into the room, quietly shutting the door.

"Alright, I need you to help my mom to another room."

"No! Absolutely not. You need to go first. They can't have you. Elias, he goes first." Maya's eyes crackled like lightning. Aidan was shocked at the mama bear ferocity she unleashed.

Taking her hand in his, Aidan felt the vibration flowing through her touch. Nodding gently, he said, "I'll be right behind you. Go!"

Elias didn't wait for a rebuttal. Instead, he just reached under her arms and lifted her as if she were weightless. Pausing once again in the doorway, he listened momentarily before quickly whisking her out of the room.

Once he no longer heard their steps in the hall, Aidan let out a deep sigh and a loud groan. Sweating profusely, he struggled to compartmentalize the pain into a box within his mind, but it was too late. The wound was all-consuming. There was more damage inside him than he'd let on. For the first time in his life, he wasn't sure if he would make it. Leaning back and clenching his eyes tight, memories flashed through his mind. His mom's smiling face as she kissed his knee after he'd fallen; losing his grip on her hand as the ambulance flipped; at the playground with his memé right before she was taken; Joe picking him up from the side of the road; Zoey coming into their lives from the streets of Sanford; Zuri's sweet face lighting up at one of his jokes. As they continued to flash faster and faster, a purple hue that grew brighter and deeper began to cover each image.

As if settling into a warm bed, he felt warmth surrounding him as he slid to the floor, unable to hold himself upright any longer. Taking a deep breath and smiling with his eyes shut, he felt a hand brushing his cheek and a gentle voice say, "They're coming."

Chapter 43
Oxygen

July 2, 2030 | 10:15 p.m.

"This doesn't make any sense. There ought to be a bigger force to combat," Rick whispered. Whoever had been coming down the stairs veered off onto one of the floors above. Rick and the crew heard a door shut followed by silence.

"Agreed," Phil answered. "Something's not right. Justin?"

"I don't know. Our protocol when we were here was that everyone but the doctors with the primary patient were to get to the bunkers. But… I have to believe they would've changed protocol since then. For this very scenario."

"It feels like a trap," Sheila whispered.

Phil nodded.

"Even if it is, we don't have much of a choice," said Lexi.

"I can feel Aidan. I can feel them all and they're up ahead. Zuri, can you tell if there's anyone else up there?"

Zuri closed her eyes for a moment, feeling Aidan's distinct thread drawing her up the stairs, along with a couple of others only slightly less distinct. "Lexi's right, they're up there. Aidan's hurt. I think badly. So is Maya." Forcing herself not to race to him with every fiber of her being. She scrunched her brow as if in deep thought, and added, "There are others, though, too. It's hard to tell. Maybe it's just all the people down in the bunker, but there's a lot of residual anxiety all around us. It's muddying up what I can feel."

They had climbed to the thirteenth floor when they heard another door open somewhere above them, followed immediately by quick light steps.

Rick glanced at Joe, then bolted up the stairs with two others on his heels. The rest stayed still and silent. For such big men, they were light on their feet, barely making a sound as they traversed the stairs.

Zoey attempted to follow but Joe threw up his arm to stop her.

"Joe, it could be Aidan," she whispered, her eyes pleading.

"I don't think so. His steps are too heavy for that to be him."

Out of the silence, from up above, Rick's voice echoed throughout the stairwell. "Stop! Get on the ground. Hands behind your head."

A woman's voice trembled, saying, "Okay! I'm just a doctor. Please don't hurt me!"

Joe took the stairs two at a time with the rest of them on his heels. When he rounded the platform on the sixteenth floor, he saw a woman in her mid-thirties, wearing a lab coat and covered in blood.

"Who's this?" he asked.

"Says she's a doctor. That there are two people injured up on nineteen she's trying to get med supplies for."

"Please, sir. Please, you can follow me, but I need to go if I'm going to get to them in time."

Joe stepped aside as Zoey made her way forward. "Who are you treating?"

Dr. Saylor paused, looking Zoey up and down and staring at the intricate red lines criss-crossing her face. "I… one is a patient, and the other is... is a newcomer that was helping when he got shot."

Zoey stared for a moment, squinting and looking her in the eyes. "She's telling the truth. I think it's Aidan." As soon as she said his name, the woman's eyes gave her away. "You know who I'm talking about, don't you." Zoey could read it all over her face.

Dr. Saylor nodded.

Rick looked at Sheila and Zoey, along with a couple of his men, and waved them on to find Aidan. "You go up ahead and see what you can do. We'll follow…"

"Jessica. My name's Jessica Saylor."

"I'll follow Jessica and assist with supplies. We'll meet you up there."

"What room?" Joe asked.

"All the way at the end of nineteen." She stood up. "Here, take my key card to enter. We'll be there shortly."

"Where were you going a few minutes ago?" Zoey asked.

Jessica looked confused. "I don't know what you mean."

"We heard someone opening and closing doors. Was that you?"

She shook her head, trying to comprehend when she recalled Dr. Hutchens running out the lab door. "That was another doctor. His name is Steve, Steve Hutchens."

"Where was he going?"

"I don't know. He left us. He's the reason they were shot. We really need to go."

Following Jessica back down the stairs, Joe entered a door on floor thirteen labeled Medical Bay II. In the storage room, she threw gauze pads, IV bags, needles, and other supplies into tubs and handed them off. "If we need more, can I send one of you back down here?"

"Of course," Joe declared impatiently. "Let's go, we need to hurry."

"Wait! I need to see if anyone's next door. We really need a surgeon up there."

"Let's hit it." Rick followed her out the door to check the other rooms. As soon as they did, one of his men motioned for them to be quiet. Rick gave a questioning look, to which his man pointed two fingers at his eyes then at the door.

Ever so quietly, Zuri stepped past Rick and placed her hand on the door. She thought she had felt a stronger connection when they passed by the door to this floor, but now she knew. "I think Dakota is in there."

Gesturing for everyone to stand back, Rick's second in command took a steadying breath and reached for the handle. As soon as it clicked, he pushed the door open in a well-rehearsed maneuver, crouched low and immediately entered, moving to the side and allowing several other operators to flood in behind following the same technique.

The girls remained in the hall with Rick shielding them, but the awful sound of that voice caused them to grab hands.

"Well, hello, gentlemen! I've been expecting you," bellowed Dr. Harold, smiling a hearty smile.

Joe flicked his eyes at Rick, also shielding the girls, and his remaining operators pushed them away from the door.

"Get them out of here!" Joe spit out.

Zoey burst through the lab door on nineteen to find Aidan lying on his side in a pool of blood.

"Oh, God." Racing to his lifeless form, she shook him violently. "Aidan? Aidan! Hey, can you hear me? I need you to wake up." Feeling for a pulse, she checked his neck and wrist and even pressed her ear against his chest. "He's not breathing!"

Rolling him onto his back, she began CPR. "Sheila! What do we do?" Zoey cried as Sheila grabbed a syringe from her bag.

"Stand clear, Zoey. A shot of adrenaline might work." Sheila knelt beside him and jammed the syringe into his thigh, squeezing until all the fluid entered his system. Without waiting, Zoey began compressions again, but before she could finish one round, Aidan's eyes flung open and he gasped for air.

"Aidan, can you hear me?"

Like a wild animal, his eyes frantically searched his surroundings until his vision came into focus. Upon landing on Zoey, he grabbed the front of her shirt and yelled, "Memé? Where is she? She was just here!"

Zoey looked around the room. "There's no one else here. It's just you. Was she hurt?"

"No, no, she was holding my hand," he muttered, struggling to clear the fog in his mind. "No, she… I don't… " He looked around the room once again with more clarity. "My mom. Where is she? Her leg. She was shot!" He tried to get up.

Zoey looked at him and shook her head. "Your memé was shot or your mom?"

"It's… I… my mom. My mom was shot."

"We'll find her. I promise, but you need to stay still," she said, pressing down on his shoulder to keep him in place.

"Just let me see what—" Sheila began, inspecting his wound.

"It's a through and through. Just get me up."

"Aidan, stop! You were dead thirty seconds ago. Just hold on." At Sheila's words, he halted.

"Dead?"

"Doc!" called a voice from the hall. "Need you over here, now!"

Sheila glanced at Zoey and one of the operators. "You got him?"

"Yeah, go," Zoey said, tucking her shoulder under Aidan's arm. With the help of the operator, they got him to his feet.

By the time they reached the hallway, Rick's other man was standing outside a door looking on in silence. With renewed energy, Aidan began to pull Zoey with him toward the room. Inside, Sheila was performing CPR on Maya. Her skin was ghostly white. Elias, covered in blood and panting, sat off to the side.

Aidan staggered to Maya and took her hand in his. This time he didn't feel anything. No vibration. No bright light. No warmth. It was like her soul had left and before him was just a shell.

The hall suddenly filled with the sound of running and within seconds, Zuri, Madison, and Lexi entered the room. Frozen in their tracks, they watched as their friends fruitlessly worked to revive Maya.

Their combined pulsing intensified rapidly as Zuri quietly pulled silver threads from every person in the room, borrowing their individual energies to heal Maya. Aidan felt it begin to flow through him and could even feel his own wounds closing up. Though unbelievably painful, he felt immense relief at the same time.

"It's not working. Maybe we're too late," Madison whispered.

"It's not too late. Mom? Come back to us. You can do this. You always told me to put that pain in a box and keep going. Do that now. I know you can hear me." Aidan's voice cracked as he squeezed her hand. "Please don't do this. Please. Just stay."

Zuri began breathing harder as she guided the strands. "Come on, Maya. Please come back to us. Our strength for your life. Our health for your health." She repeated those words quietly to herself, using every ounce of energy she could without hurting anyone else. No matter what she tried, the threads wouldn't tether to her. She could feel them in her hands, thick ropes of energy, but they simply wouldn't attach to Maya.

"We need everyone!" Zoey yelled.

"There's no time," Lexi said in a hushed voice.

"No. She doesn't die today. Come on! Mom, this isn't how you die."

Dakota had never felt so relieved, despite the fact that perfect strangers had come to her rescue. The burning sensation on her skin ever so slightly diminished as Dr. Harold walked in submission alongside his LSO who was relieved of his weapons and both with their hands zip-tied behind their backs.

"We've got you," the man said as he undid the restraints holding her firm to a hospital bed. "Can you sit up?"

She nodded, a little dizzy from the receding electrical currents that had been running the length of her body.

Getting to her feet, the man helped steady her. "I'm okay." Her voice was hoarse but still managed a gritty, "Thank you."

"Are you Dakota?"

She froze in place, staring the man in the eyes. He didn't seem menacing, only concerned. Yet he knew who she was, which should've been impossible.

"How do you know me?" she asked sharply.

"That's a long story, but you have a lot of friends searching for you."

She wanted to argue, but somehow she sensed he was telling the truth.

"We need to get you out of here, can you walk?"

"Yes, but… wait… my friend might be here too. I need to check." She checked herself to make sure she was dressed then scanned the room for her bag. Seeing it in the far corner, she worked out the knots in her muscles as she struggled to grab for it. "I can't leave if he's still here."

"We'll help you, but first we need to get you to the others."

Once again, she wanted to argue but could tell they had

other plans. One quick nod was all they needed to shuffle her quickly out the door with Dr. Harold in tow.

At the stairwell she immediately felt an energy pulling on her. It was that same peacefully safe sensation she'd felt several times over the last months, only stronger. As it amplified, so did her rage. Her skin began to burn as they climbed the stairs.

"NO!" she screamed, grabbing the handrail as her skin flushed.

"What's wrong?"

"No. We can't. I'm not going up there."

"But… but we have to," the man urged, too nervous to reach for her again.

She wanted to push them out of her way. To run from the feelings waging war within her. *I can't go to them. They'll only abandon me. Use me. Or break me.* Yet the sensation of love clawed at her internal walls. *If I go and they walk away, I won't survive it.*

Despite her bitter judgment, despite the agony within and every fiber of her being shouting no, her muscles betrayed her, allowing them to guide her up the stairs.

Up to what would either be a longed-for destiny or her demise.

From behind, Zuri and her sisters felt another source of energy drawing close. A pulse of rage and resolution. Pain and fear.

Zuri remained focused on Maya. The others transitioned their own energies from healing to protection when suddenly a mysterious woman entered the room with Dr. Harold handcuffed and following close behind.

With both shock and pleasure, his cheeks blushed at the sight of the girls.

The woman stood for several seconds watching the team work on Maya.

"Dakota?" Lexi finally asked.

Dakota looked ready to run, but her feet stayed planted in place.

Lexi stepped toward her but the electrical pulse that struck her violently knocked her back into Maddy, leaving her skin burned from the invisible hit.

"Dakota, stop!" Maddy yelled, struggling to send a wave of calm over the terrified woman.

"How do you know me? How do any of you know me?"

Lexi, knowing they didn't have time for deep explanations, said, "We were with you. Years ago when we were all children. That man," she pointed at Dr. Harold, "he took us. All of us. Tested us." She paused, but Dakota remained silent, her body ready to fight. "You know this is true! We fought for survival together back then, and we need to fight now!"

Maddy was sweating, still trying to push through Dakota's walls.

"Dakota, please. We need you." Lexi could see the pain in her eyes. "That woman lying on the floor needs us. She's one of us. She might even be the reason for us. We need her to live, and we need you to make that happen." Lexi's breathing was labored, praying that this perfect stranger would trust her.

Finally, whatever trepidation had been holding her back, they watched as the red splotches on her skin began to fade and her physical strength return.

Dakota looked around the room, pausing to take in each of their faces with pained familiarity. Grabbing a notebook from the bag on her shoulder, she flipped to a blank page and began to draw. They watched in silence, unsure what to make of her reaction.

Rick stood behind her looking on as she drew the people in front of her with a speed and quality that thoroughly impressed him despite the horrific scene.

As soon as she finished, Dakota laid her hand flat on the page and closed her eyes.

Zuri, still focused on Maya, suddenly felt the tendrils of something new. A new energy she hadn't felt from her other sisters. Her head spun around to see where it was coming from. *Dakota.*

Dakota's vibrations were overwhelming. The energy radiated from her in waves, amplifying the other girls' abilities.

Justin, standing to the side, said under his breath, "Maybe Maya's too far gone."

"No! We can save her. Zuri can save her!" Aidan's voice cracked with pain.

Joe stepped into the hallway and keyed his earpiece. "Grant, can you hear me?"

"Yeah, Joe. I read you. Over."

"Are the girls safe?"

"I think so. Adeline sat down a few minutes ago. Joanna and Macie joined her soon after. They're in some sort of trance and aren't responding to anything I say. Over." His voice gave way to a little fear.

"Roger. Let me know if anything changes," Joe replied,

kneeling beside Lexi. Turning toward her, he said, "I think the others are trying to help. Can you sense them?"

His voice was low and distant, drowned out by the deafening hum in her ears, but she managed a small nod.

Soon after, a static-laced pressure began to fill the room. Rick's team and the others felt it first in their chests, followed by a ringing in their ears that proved disorienting.

Dakota fell to her knees, struggling to keep her hand on the page.

"What's happening?" shouted one of the operators, now covering his ears.

A sheen of sweat formed on each of the women's faces as they strained to push as much energy toward Zuri as they could muster. Zuri's hands were rapidly turning a splotchy red as she pressed firmly against Maya when suddenly Maya's lifeless body lifted from the ground, floating in front of Zuri. The lightbulbs throughout the room shattered and electrical outlets sparked as a pulse of electricity bounced from one woman to the next. The metallic smell of a charged electrical current filled their nostrils.

Joe strained to move to Maya's side. He put his arms under her weightless body.

Suddenly, overtop the ear-piercing hum of electricity, they heard Maya's gasp for air.

Her deep inhale, along with the static and the startling amount of power being channeled through her, managed to steal the breath of everyone else within the room. It was only a moment, but long enough for them to grip their throats in horror as if being suffocated.

"Mom?" Aidan choked out with a groan, clutching her hand.

Her eyes remained shut as her chest heaved. Without

warning, Maya fell into Joe's arms allowing him to guide her to ground safely. With a subtle smile, she winced, feeling the burn of the air moving through her throat and into her lungs.

Leaning close, Adain whispered, "Mom, can you hear me?"

Several more calming breaths steadied her heart rate. In and out. In and out.

He touched her face.

"Aidan?" she whispered, doubting her eyes and blinking as if waking from a deep coma.

"Mom!" he shouted through a sob. "You're alive."

With a cautious smile, Maya reached out and pulled him to her. Squeezing him, she whispered into his ear, "You're alive."

Chapter 44
Nap Time

July 2, 2030 | 10:45 p.m.

"Time to leave." Rick's staunch command brought the room back to the present. Aidan and Maya hadn't fully recovered, but they were no longer in danger of dying.

Dr. Harold sat on the floor with his hands zip-tied behind his back, smiling.

"What do you want to do with him?" Brandon asked.

"I think we need to bring him," said Gavin. "If we leave him, the reality is I don't think he's going to stop hunting them. Plus, maybe we can persuade him to enlighten us of everything he's learned over the years."

"That also means keeping him close to the girls. Not to mention figuring out how to imprison him, keep him fed and everything else." Phil didn't like the idea of him being anywhere near Sheila or the girls.

"Lexi?" Joe inquired, glancing her way.

"I think Gavin's right. We'll figure the rest out when we get out of here."

Joe stared at her for several seconds, wrestling internally with her response. "Okay. We'll bring him," he confirmed, quickly turning toward Dr. Harold and asking, "What's waiting for us when we try to leave?"

"Probably the same as what you saw on your way up," he offered with a smirk.

Joe didn't believe him for a second. He didn't need to ask Zoey.

Maya, holding fast to Aidan, suddenly realized they couldn't leave without Dr. Harold's research. "We need his research. All the data from the lab and the filing cabinet in his office. I don't want anyone else getting it if we can help it."

"Where's his office?" Rick asked, walking toward the door and signaling another operator to join him.

"Floor twelve. Last door on the left."

"On it. We'll meet on the main level. Don't leave the building without us unless you're desperate. If you do, we'll rally at the safe house."

Joe nodded, then looked at Dr. Saylor, saying, "What about her?"

Dr. Saylor didn't waste any time answering for herself. "Take me. Please. I can't stay here, and I can help."

Maya wanted to shut her down, to curse her for even offering to help, but she couldn't find it in herself. Jessica had been opposed to everything that had happened to her, always seeking a safer, more humane way of learning about Maya's abilities.

Though she still went along with their testing, she wasn't quite lost. "She can come."

"Good enough for me. Let's roll," Phil declared.

They made their way quietly down the stairwell. As they rounded the platform on floor sixteen, the door flung open. A man in his forties came bounding out with several bags over his shoulders. His eyes nearly burst at the sight of the operators and crew blocking his passage.

"Don't move another step!" shouted Joe, his gun trained right on the man's nose.

"Wait, wait, wait! I'm a doctor. Don't shoot!" Dr. Hutchens dropped the bags, begging for his safety.

"Steve?" Dr. Saylor was shocked.

"Jessica? Jessica! Tell them I'm nobody. I'm just trying to get out of here."

Shaking her head with her mouth agape, she said, "You're right. You are nobody." Slowly stepping forward, as if vouching for him, she cocked her arm back and punched him square in his face.

He went down hard, and the sound of his body hitting the platform echoed.

"Whoa!" Aidan was impressed. "Nice hook."

Rubbing her hand and wincing from the pain, she quietly said, "Worth it."

Once in the main foyer, they sat Dr. Harold on the floor next to the few guards still unconscious. An operator held him accountable with his M4.

"You know, I understand this need to rescue, but you have all the power in the world to make life better for everyone. If you stayed here, you could do that. I have all the appropriate medical equipment and technology needed."

"Really? Stay here, huh? So what, they can be studied like lab rats?" Gavin chided.

"It's obvious you're already doing that on your own. The fact you sent men back to get my research despite the potential danger tells me you're no different than me."

"The difference is, what we're doing is a choice. We're free," said Zuri.

"Free? You think Justin, Gavin, and Maria are different? Why? Just because you're allowed to practice on your own or agree to be tested whenever they ask? No. They're just as obsessed with your abilities as I am. They want to pick you apart. They want to know what makes you tick. How you gained these abilities. They want—"

With a loud smack that caught everyone's attention, Dakota slammed her hand onto an open page in her notebook. Immediately, his voice went silent.

"Did you do that?" Lexi asked in shock.

"He wouldn't shut up," Dakota said with a subtle smile growing at the corner of her mouth.

"Oh snap!" Aidan cried out with a pained laugh. "That's going to come in handy."

Zoey was in awe, "I thought you could only change inanimate objects."

Dakota shrugged, "It's new."

Zuri smiled. As they found one another their abilities grew. Looked as though Dakota was finding new ones for herself.

A few chuckles echoed in the foyer until they heard the clanging sound of footsteps racing down the stairwell.

"Get the doctor up. We've got company," said Phil, his

voice stern and focused.

Rick and the operator burst through the stairwell door into the foyer with every gun in the room pointed in their direction.

"Stand down!" Phil shouted to the sound of four bolts simultaneously clicking into place all around them. The main exit, stairwell, security room, and hall doors all sealed shut.

"What happened?" Justin asked as Brandon attempted to open the main door.

"I don't have a good feeling about this," Gavin said.

Dr. Harold's sickening smile widened even further.

"What's going on?" Joe growled.

Dr. Harold couldn't make a sound, but his eyes spoke volumes.

"Lexi!" Joe shouted.

Without hesitation, she quickly erected a shield around the team.

Dakota crossed out her drawing and shouted, "What did you do?"

Dr. Harold ignored her, instead turning to Lexi and with a sweet voice, said, "Lexi? Oh my. I can remember the day you were born. Your mother, Veronica, was a spitfire, full of life, just like you. What is it that you're doing?"

"Don't you dare speak to her," Gavin instructed.

"Well, whatever it is, it's too late. The moment those locks clicked, we were all sentenced to a nice nap."

"What are you talking about?" Joe demanded, signaling the others to check each of the doors.

"Can't you feel your eyes getting heavy already? I know I can."

"It's okay, Zuri," offered Lexi, watching her sister's eyes

begin to droop.

"What did you do?" Joe growled, grinding his teeth, wanting nothing more than to pummel the sadistic doctor. Instead, feeling around for a place to sit, Joe leaned against the wall and slid down it before collapsing.

One by one, everyone in the foyer sank to the cold, hard floor. Within a minute, all were asleep, including Dr. Harold.

Once the final attempts at moving and twitching stopped, the loud whoosh of an exhaust fan broke the silence as the vents pulled the gas from the foyer. The subsequent sound of the internal doors unlatching, followed by twenty armed guards immediately entering from the interior main hall failed to rouse anyone. With their weapons in hand, VISP security walked effortlessly through the crowd of sleeping men and women.

"All clear. Zip-tie them all. Bring the girls to nineteen as Dr. Harold directed."

Chapter 45
Miracle

July 2, 2030 | 11:50 p.m.

"I can't raise anyone on the radio. This doesn't make sense. How could they all be unaccounted for?" Grant's hands shook. It had been at least thirty minutes since they heard from the team. Their last communication confirmed they obtained the package and were getting ready to exfil from the target.

"Do you feel anything?" he wondered, looking at Joanna, Macie and Addie.

Feeling anxious themselves, Joanna said, "I don't sense that they're hurt, but it's like they're all…"

"Asleep? I think they're asleep. Like, all of them," Macie said with a furrowed brow, shaking her head.

"Even Rick's team?" Maria was shocked. "How's that even

possible?"

"It had to have been an ambush." Addie was starting to feel more confident in their connection. "We knew it was a possibility."

"Yeah, but between LIMIT's team and the girls, how could anyone get the drop on them?" Grant was pacing the small living room of the safehouse.

Joanna looked worriedly at Macie and Addie.

"Grant, Joe said—" Keeps began.

"I know what he said!" Grant shot back.

Joanna stood up. "Joe said what, Grant?"

"I… Joe explicitly said if this were to happen…" He looked at them, knowing they weren't going to like what he said next.

"What?"

"I'm to reach out to Jahnsen and get you back to North Carolina ASAP."

All four women began to argue.

He threw his hands in the air. "I know! I know, okay. It's too soon to make that call. But we need to start considering it."

"It's only been thirty minutes. When they wake up, they're going to need us," Addie said, furious at the idea of leaving.

"Agreed," he replied, continuing to walk in circles.

"You're making me dizzy. Sit down, Grant," said Maria. "We need to do something. Is there anything we can do to help them?"

"Not without risking getting ourselves caught."

"What if I just go and—" Joanna started.

"That's insane! Not a chance. Brandon would kill me."

"I'm not saying enter the compound! Just close enough to get some eyes on it."

"Nope." Grant was envisioning Brandon choking the life out of him and shuddered. "Aside from Brandon killing me, we can assume VISP is now on high alert."

Addie, clearing her throat, asked, "How about if you reach out to Jahnsen if we don't hear from them at the hour mark?"

"Good! Yes, that's a great idea," he said, jumping to his feet. Before he could finish his thought, his radio went off, causing him to fumble it in his hands.

"Roost, this is Eagle. Come in, over." Jahnsen's voice was crisp and confident.

"Eagle, this is Roost. Go ahead."

"We're having trouble reaching our men at the target. Do you have comms with them? Over."

The girls all shook their heads, pleading for him not to say anything.

"Same here. No contact for the last thirty minutes. Anything from your drone?" Grant looked away from them.

"They entered the building with minor resistance. We anticipated them to be on their way back to you by now. Looks like we'll lose our eyes in the sky in the next thirty. What was your last communication? Over."

"Supposed to be exfilling target at our last comms. They haven't arrived." He glanced back at the girls. "I've got three doves with me and their consensus is a possible ambush. Uh, they think everyone might be asleep. Over."

Several moments passed without a response. Grant assumed Jahnsen would be conferring with his intelligence officers. "Roger. They probably wouldn't have been able to subdue them any other way with what the girls can do. Putting them to sleep was likely their best course of action. Over."

Grant nodded in response before remembering that Jahnsen couldn't see him. "Right. Yeah, that makes sense. So what do we do? Over."

"Hang tight. We're discussing options."

"Uh... Roger." Grant wasn't prone to engage in field operations or hitting targets. He felt like an idiot talking through the radio. Turning back to the girls, he said, "So, looks like we hang tight."

"Or…" Addie said.

"I don't like the way you're saying that."

"Or... we ask Jahnsen's team to track us with a drone. We get close enough to the compound and settle in, just in case they need us at a moment's notice."

"That... sounds like a terrible idea. *And*, that storm will be on us any minute," Grant shot back. "Surprised it hasn't started yet."

"I think Addie's right," Maria said, edging into the conversation. "We don't have to go *in* for the girls to be useful."

"They can be useful from here, too."

"Yes, but I think the closer we are, the stronger our connection will be," Addie added.

"Nope. Terrible plan. If their security is on patrol or their cameras catch us, we'll be sitting ducks."

"If I'm close enough, I might be able to see where they're at. Then maybe we can focus our energy," Addie begged.

"You want to be close enough to see them?" He felt like his head might explode at the degree of risk involved.

"I don't need my eyes to see, Grant. Just my alt-vision. For that, it seems the closer I am, the clearer the image."

"Okay, so far that seems to be the case, but Macie isn't

getting anywhere near them. Which means we stay here. Together."

Macie looked back and forth between Grant and the girls. Setting the cup in her hand down on a side table, she unstrapped her harness and placed her hands on the arm rests.

"What are you doing? Macie, hey, uh, please don't do that." Grant was immediately on his feet, hovering over her, not sure what to expect. Even Keeps took a step closer, his eyes wide with curiosity.

Joanna looked shocked, but Addie's face broke into a subtle grin. She could see what the others couldn't. She'd seen it for some time but didn't let on because Macie needed to decide for herself when she was ready.

Pushing herself upright, and with her arms shaking, Macie planted her feet firmly on the floor.

Grant's hands shook as his eyes darted from her feet to her hands to her legs to her face. "Oh my God. What's happening right now? Holy crap!" He attempted to offer her his arm, but she shooed him away.

Joanna jumped up beside him. "Macie? How are you doing this?"

"I don't know, honestly. I just felt like... like I had strength in my legs. Like they wanted to be used. I really can't explain it."

Addie's smile grew and she began to laugh to herself. Joanna, catching sight of her out of the corner of her eye, said, "Why do I feel as though you already knew about this?"

"For the longest time, when it came to Macie's legs, it was like looking at a table or chair. Something inanimate. But a few months ago, I started seeing strands of colorful energy envelop her hips and knees and eventually her feet."

Macie released one hand, then the other. With shock on her face she found herself upright. She was a little unsteady at first but once she straightened her back, a level of confidence none of them had witnessed on her, blossomed.

She laughed. Her eyes filled with glossy tears of joy.

"Oh my God," Maria breathed out. "You're doing it!"

After several moments of intense joy around the room, Macie finally focused on Addie. "Why didn't you tell me?" she asked, a little shocked that Addie had seen it happening when even Macie's own body wasn't telling her.

"I knew that when the time was right, you'd sense your healing and ability to move."

"But how?" Grant asked.

"I think all the work we've done together these past months. Seems to me that, by default, Zuri's ability to heal others had slowly worked on Macie's nerves indirectly." She looked Macie in the eye. "You just had to believe it and feel it for yourself."

Tears streamed down Macie's face. "I feel like I can breathe deep again, for the first time in... in a long time. Like I'm whole again."

"Gavin is going to lose it!" Joanna shouted with excitement.

The miracle unfolding had momentarily let them escape the present danger, but the fear of the challenge ahead flooded back into Macie's mind. "I don't know if I'm strong enough to do much good though."

"That's your mind putting limitations on you. Why don't you take your new legs for a walk," Adeline smiled.

Macie stood frozen, trembling, yet balanced. She took several breaths, then one big one, and exhaled with a loud release. "Let's do this."

"This would be a lot simpler if you just gave us the information we need." Dr. Harold's joyful facade was beginning to crack.

Brandon, with a smile, looked into the doctor's eyes and spit blood on the ground by his feet.

"Look, it seems to me that the majority of the folks you probably had at your disposal for this mission are in my custody. Which means that, without a miracle, none of you will be leaving here anytime soon. But if you tell me what I want to know, the torture ends with you. You can spare everyone else in your group from suffering. If not, well, then we'll move on to the next. And we'll keep going until only the girls remain."

"You won't hurt them," Brandon shot back, calling the man's bluff. He didn't doubt Dr. Harold would purposefully harm the others, but he wouldn't do anything to jeopardize the girls' health.

"Maybe. Maybe you're right. But! That doesn't mean we won't hurt, ah, Sheila. Right? I know she's not one of my girls."

"None of them are your girls."

"Oh, come on, that's not fair. I took care of them, nurtured them, gave them everything they needed when they were young. Now that they're back in my care, they'll have everything they want and more!"

"So conducting tests on them, hiding them on the other side of the world in conditions unfit for any human, subjecting them to fear, that's you *caring* for them?"

"Now, now... none of that was my fault. When we were in

England, everything was perfect. It was the U.S. military that put them in harm's way."

"Oh, the military that you're currently working with on this compound?"

"Military? Son, we're a research facility. It may have started off as a military project, but we've grown far beyond that." Dr. Harold waved the security guard over to Brandon.

Brandon's right eye was swollen shut and he assumed he had several broken ribs as well. He didn't see the guard coming up on his right side, so the impact of a fist to his ribs was something he wasn't able to brace for.

Brandon folded over, gasping for air and choking on vomit. He couldn't help but recall the situation with Oakley. *How do I keep ending up in this position,* he thought to himself before mumbling, "Nice... one. Is that... all you got? My mother... could hit harder... than you."

Without warning, the guard, grabbing a handful of Brandon's hair, yanked his head backward. He could feel the knife at his throat. Just enough pressure to draw blood.

"How can I persuade you, Brandon?" Dr. Harold wandered around the room slowly. "I'm sure those girls would rather you give us the information we need as opposed to you dying."

Brandon couldn't speak with his head so far back. Acidity burned his throat.

"In about thirty seconds, I'm going to give my man here the go-ahead to take away your chance of breathing freely permanently. Then we'll just dump your body in the burn pit out back. So. Your options are to die or give me what I want. Simple choices." Dr. Harold stepped toward Brandon until he was standing directly over him, looking down, smiling. "Ten seconds left."

Their eyes were locked. Finally, not waiting for the countdown to finish, Dr. Harold sighed, looked at his man and nodded.

The security guard held the knife in front of Brandon's face to give him a good look, then put it to his throat and sank in the knife.

"Okay," Brandon whispered.

Dr. Harold put his hand up to stop the act. "What's that now?"

"Okay, I'll tell you."

"Oh, that's wonderful. Jack, would you grab a bottle of water and give it to the man? He must be parched."

After taking a long, fitful swig of water, choking and coughing, Brandon nodded.

"Alright, go ahead."

Clearing his throat, he said, "Adeline…"

"Adeline? The blind girl?"

Brandon nodded, his only chance at buying time. Lying. "She can move things with her mind."

Chapter 46
Cracking Walls

"**B**randon? What did they do to you?" Joe was tied to a chair in the cafeteria on the second floor, along with the others. None of them had been asleep long. Whatever Dr. Harold had used on them was short acting. When he'd come to, he recognized the cafeteria on the second floor. For once he was grateful he'd been in this building before that moment. The girls had obviously been placed elsewhere.

They'd woken up tied to chairs. Rick's team, along with Justin, Gavin, himself, Phil and Sheila, were placed together. Brandon and Aidan were the only two missing. None of them were gagged, probably because they were being watched on camera, listening for anything they might say about the girls or maybe a secondary rescue attempt.

The door burst open and Brandon was dragged through it and tied to a chair. Hunched over, beaten and bloodied, he was struggling to pull air into his lungs.

When the guard left, Joe asked in a hushed voice, "Hey man, can you talk?"

Brandon's lower lip was swollen and a line of blood trickled down his chin and neck. "Yeah."

"Who did this to you?"

"Dr. Harold's goons." He coughed, wincing at the pain in his side. "They wanted me to tell them about the girls."

Joe's hands clenched, further restricting blood flow from the zip ties. If Brandon was sitting here, even broken as he was, Joe knew he must've told them something or he wouldn't still be alive.

"What did you tell them?"

Brandon could partially see Joe with his good eye and shook his head. "What they needed to know," he stated.

Joe nodded, glancing upward at the corners of the room.

The others started to wake at the sound of voices. Their confusion and fear palpable.

Phil whispered to Joe, "We need to get word to Eagle."

"They know something's wrong by now," mouthed Joe, slightly cocking his head toward the camera in the room.

Phil nodded.

Rick took note and signaled to the rest of his men to keep quiet. Rick and his men had S.E.R.E. training: survival, evasion, resistance, escape. One aspect of their training was learning how to escape from different bindings. He had a pin woven into the fabric of his belt. Careful not to drop it, he pulled it out and used it to push in between the tongue and the serrated side of the zip-tie. Once in, he was able to quietly slide the tie almost all the way out, leaving just enough at the end to make it look like he was still cuffed, yet able to pull his hand out when the moment came.

His men followed suit, trying not to squirm in the process to avoid any undue attention.

As their cuffs loosened, the door burst open. In walked the man they believed to be the head of security.

"Looks like you're all wide awake. Good. We have work to do." Sitting at one of the cafeteria tables, he said, "Brandon gave us some really great information about the girls. Dr. Harold has gone to check on them. We want to believe your man here. We really do. Yet,we felt there were a few mismatched things in his recount of them. So, in order to verify, we're going to have to pull one of you in to confirm. Volunteer?"

"You don't have to do this. I told you everything," Brandon muttered through his swollen lips.

"Of course, of course. I'm sure you did. But maybe you don't know everything? Maybe you're not as close as someone else in this room is." His eyes slowly scanned their body language.

Rick's men were trained in how to react during an interrogation. Phil and Sheila were as well.

"There was one little lady Brandon just didn't seem to know much about."

Joe remained deadpan but knew he was referring to Dakota.

"That just seems odd. Don't you think?" He continued analyzing their body language. "So we got to talking and realized there were three people we picked up just before the rest of you showed up. One of those being an injured woman. So we figure the people that know most about her are probably the ones that were with her. Not rocket science, I know."

Elias quickly looked away from his searching gaze, which was the worst thing he could've done.

"Boys, grab that one," he declared, pointing at Elias. "Eli, I feel like there's more you have to say about all this."

"Wait! No, wait, I don't know anything. I swear," he yelled, fighting to pull away as they cut him loose from the chair and hoisted him to his feet.

"Stop!" Sheila's voice, as usual, held an air of command, causing everyone to freeze.

"Yes, ma'am? You have something to share?"

"There's no need for violence. Please let him be. You already have the girls. Dr. Harold knows about them, obviously. That's why this place even exists, right? So you don't really need to hurt anyone."

"Very astute. Yes, he does know quite a bit. But before we wake up the girls, he would love to know just what we're getting ourselves into. Plus, as you know, not *all* of the girls are here. We need to know which ones are missing and what they can do. Of course, he dreams of the day when all the sisters are back together again. Family reunions are great, aren't they, Sheila? You understand."

"Then take me. After all, I've been with them from the start. I was on the special forces team that rescued them years ago."

The guard looked at her with new interest. Looking back at Elias, then at his men, he signaled to put him back in his chair.

The room erupted with demands to leave Sheila alone. It was as if a storm moved in, and ferocious wolves took the places of the once calm prisoners.

Several guards rose, aimed their guns at the inmates, and

shouted them down. "Calm down! Now. Calm down. We have no problem shooting any one of you. You, my friends, are expendable—"

"Enough!" Once again, the room fell silent. With a deep breath, she said, "I am agreeing to come with you peacefully and to share what I know." Joe started to protest, but the look she gave him stopped the words from forming in his throat. "But *only* if you bring me to Dr. Harold. I'll only speak with him directly."

The guard looked her up and down, then once again around the room before walking over to her. Staring into her eyes, he pulled out his radio. "Dr. Harold, we've got someone down here who says she's the one that rescued the girls. She's willing to talk, but only to you."

Seconds passed before they heard, "Bring her to my office. I'll be there in ten."

"Copy that." Stepping to the side, he cut her loose from the chair. "Lucky you. You get the presidential treatment."

Dr. Harold hadn't stopped smiling since entering the room to see the girls still unconscious. He had tried waking up Lexi, but she wouldn't rouse. After responding on his radio, he whispered, "Be right back."

When the door clicked, Lexi cracked open her eyelids just enough to see her surroundings. The only people she could feel were her sisters, so she knew they were alone. Her neck cracked as she raised her head to look around, having kept it in the same position for so long.

"Zuri," she whispered, "are you alright?"

Zuri looked up slowly. "I'm okay."

As others began to stir, Lexi asked, "Is anyone hurt?"

The girls all shook their heads and glanced around the room. One by one they saw Maya. She sat in silence, watching them, taking in their beautiful but tragic faces. Filled with both joy and terror, she wanted to cry. They were alive. They were strong. But they were also trapped in this horrible place with her.

"Maya?" Lexi wondered.

She recognized each of them from their photos. "Alexi?"

"Yes."

Maya scanned the room, naming them one at a time. "Zuriella. Madison. Zoey. Dakota." Each of their names sounded pure as she spoke them out loud.

"We came for you. You and Dakota." Maddy's voice was hoarse.

Maya nodded. "I know you did. But I wish you hadn't. This is not a place to easily exit from. Especially not you," she said, her voice catching in her throat. Shaking her head and knowing just how crazy her words would sound, she said, "I tried to keep you away. I thought," she sniffed at the absurdity of it, "I believed... maybe you could hear me warning you to keep away from here."

Zuri stood up and pulled her hands from behind her back. She was holding an unlatched zip-tie in her hand. "We heard you," she said as she walked toward Maya.

"How?" Maya gasped at the undone zip-tie.

"This? Oh, I'm pretty good at moving things around when I want to," she said with a smile. "We heard you, but there was no way we'd ever leave you here alone." Pulling a knife from the medical supply cart, she simultaneously undid Maya's zip-ties from her wrists using her gift, while handing her the knife for her to cut the others loose.

Maya rose to her feet, now just a little taller than Zuri, and wrapped her arms around the young woman. The same newborn that she had watched come back to life in her arms all those years ago, was now back in them again. "I can't believe how incredible you are. All of you."

"Turns out, so is your son," Zuri said.

"Aidan?" she said with a flush of panic, scanning the room. "They must have him somewhere else."

"And we're going to go find him."

Maya carefully freed each girl, hugging them as she went while Zuri stood close to the door, listening.

"I don't hear anything," she whispered, "but I know there are at least four guards out there."

Lexi, rubbing her wrists, said, "We can probably take them, but that will alert anyone else watching."

"What are our options?" Maddy asked.

Dakota, having snagged some fresh paper and pencils from a nearby desk, whispered, "I've got this one."

They huddled together and watched their new sister as she drew. As soon as she put her hand to the completed drawing, a golden ring formed on the floor that quickly turned into a tangible, functioning hatch.

"Oh my goodness. That's wild," Maddy said, staring at the newly formed door. "How did you even discover you could do that?"

"Story for another time," Dakota quipped. She could tell by their expressions that everyone had questions.

Smiling, possibly her first genuine smile in her life, Dakota reached down and turned the handle. Zoey jumped in to help her lift the door.

"Couldn't you have drawn something a little lighter?" Zoey said, grunting at the weight.

"Yeah, that would've made more sense. Sometimes you just go with your gut, you know? I was thinking manhole I suppose." Gritting her teeth, they set it down quietly.

Maddy, peering through the opening, said, "Looks like someone's apartment. It's empty."

They dropped through the hatch into the room below.

"Okay, grab anything that could be used as a weapon. Hurry," Lexi ordered, shoving several items into her pockets. "Let's go."

Once all six were safely down, they watched Dakota mark an X over her drawing and then touch the page. The hole above closed up and disappeared, transforming the space to its original form.

"That is just…" Zoey started.

"The coolest thing ever!" Maddy added.

Dakota was used to people being shocked at what she could do, but impressing these women somehow meant more to her. She could feel some of the walls around her heart cracking further, but she'd spent her entire life building those walls that, even in front of these women, she wasn't ready to fully let her guard down. For Dakota, love in any form always seemed to cause pain. Nothing good ever lasted.

Zoey looked at Maya. "What's the plan?"

Chapter 47
Monster

July 3, 2030 | 12:45 a.m.

"Sheila, is it?" Dr. Harold asked, entering his office. Sheila sat zip-tied to a chair on the opposite side of his desk.

"Dr. Harold."

"The one and only."

"I should hope so."

Cocking his head to the side he raised a questioning brow.

"Well, I'd hate for there to be more than one monster like you out there in the world."

"Ah," he chuckled. "That seems a little harsh."

"I don't know what you'd consider a monster if it's not someone who tortures innocent children."

"Torture? Oh no. Not at all. I'd never hurt those girls."

"No, just their parents, right?"

Sheila couldn't tell if the sweat forming on his upper lip was from her goading him or his excitement.

She let the silence hold, knowing he couldn't remain quiet. And she was right.

"I'm curious. They tell me you were on the mission that rescued my girls in Afghanistan all those years ago. Is that true?"

Inwardly shuddering at the words *my girls*, she replied, "Yes. That was me."

"Any of these other guys you're with on that mission as well?"

"No. Just me," she stated as Phil's face appeared in her mind.

"Huh. Interesting. So you all just disbanded after the rescue? Or was it after the grids failed?"

"I don't know about the rest. I got out of the service and focused on medicine."

"So you're a doctor?"

"A medic."

His head nodded as questions rapidly fired through his mind. "So you think you know all about me then."

"I wouldn't presume to, honestly. I only know what our intel analysts had on you."

"Which was?"

"At the time, a middle-aged narcissistic doctor who'd abducted eight young children. Specifically girls. Alleged to be performing experiments on them at a rundown hospital in England until you disappeared. Then, through HUMINT, you were tracked to Afghanistan and forced into hiding until we located you."

"Broad strokes. Okay. I do like the word choice there, though. Alleged. That's a good word. I suppose that, yes, they were experiments. But I never hurt them."

"The scars on their bodies suggest otherwise," she shot back, slowly taking in deep breaths. Remaining calm yet continuing to poke and prod was the only way he'd continue to talk to her, offering the girls time to devise an escape plan.

"I didn't cause the scarring."

"Didn't you? Haven't you been here?" she said, looking around the room. "For years, watching as Lexi and Zuri were tested on endlessly? Relentlessly crushing them in your glass prisons?"

"I wasn't in charge at the time. You're thinking of Director Jones, may he rest in peace."

"Ah. I see," she said with a subtle smile, "so you weren't the one pulling the strings." She knew his narcissism wouldn't allow someone else to be the brains behind it all. "Makes sense. I suppose it would take a near genius to put this operation together."

"Well, now, sure I had help. It was a big undertaking," he replied, tapping his finger on the armchair.

"I can see how it would be. It's impressive." Sheila sighed, shaking her head. "I mean, to keep all of these folks compartmentalized. The right hand not knowing what the left hand is doing." She paused. "Not to mention the concern of someone switching sides. Obviously, that's why Director Jones had to die, right? He'd switched teams."

Dr. Harold laughed. "Interesting how you're working so hard to make me the bad guy," he said in a low voice, tilting his head forward and looking up at her. "You're pretty good. Maybe you should've been in human intelligence instead of medicine. You would've been pretty good at it, I think."

Sheila sat still, confidently staring the man down.

"As fascinating as this conversation is, let's get back to it, shall we? Talk to me about the girls."

"What do you want to know?"

"Your friend, Brandon, I think it was. He gave us some valuable information already, but there seems to be a few discrepancies."

"He did, did he? And what are those?"

"Well now, if I tell you, then I won't be able to discern the truth."

Sheila knew she had to give him something. Change the topic. "It's funny... right after we saved them from you, many of the girls were adopted. Their parents, after all, had been murdered during their abductions." She let that horrific fact float in the air and waited for him to react. When he didn't, she continued, "I tried to adopt Lexi and Zuri. The thought of them ending up in the system was heartbreaking after what they'd been through. I was still on active duty and single, so the state wouldn't approve me to be an adoptive parent because of my deployment schedule.

"I tried to keep tabs on them as they moved from foster home to foster home. None of the parents explained why they didn't want them, just that they were too much to handle. I knew why, of course."

"And what did you know?"

"It was that night we rescued them," she said in a hushed voice, watching him sit forward in his chair. "We'd made it to the rally point, waiting for the helicopter to exfil us. The winds began to pick up. Within minutes, the sandstorm was so thick we knew the helicopter would have to abandon us.

"All the girls huddled together, attempting to block the sting of the sand spray. They were all so tiny. So fragile looking. But then one, the littlest one, Zuri, looked directly into the whipping sand with eyes that shone into the blackness all around."

Dr. Harold leaned further forward with his elbows on his desk, sweat still beading.

"We felt a vibration on our skin, different from the sting of the sand. It was mesmerizing and terrifying. The rest of the girls lifted their heads with eyes just as bright, each one focused on Zuri. The vibration grew stronger as a loud hum drowned out the sound of the storm and the distant chopper. We couldn't believe what we were seeing. Not just that their eyes were glowing with colors the shade of their eyes, but as the vibrations grew, the sand started to clear around us. Within moments, we could see the lights of the helicopter, and despite the storm, we were extracted without incident.

"Leaving that air space, we watched out the window as the sand consumed the ground beneath us." Sheila's neck tensed as she replayed that night, feeling the vibration viscerally on her skin.

Dr. Harold leaned back heavily in his chair. "That's an impressive story," already attempting to put the pieces together. "Did the pilots tell you what they saw as they came in?"

"Yes. They said they were getting ready to turn back to their forward operating base when a clearing opened up in the sand. As if there was a bubble around us forcing the sand to deviate from our position. They could also see a strange glow of light, like a beacon bringing them to our position."

"Wow. That is just incredibly impressive," he said, minimizing his attempt at feigning compassion. "Zuri would've been what at the time? Two? Three?"

"Just a baby, yet with more control than most adults."

"There is, however, just one aspect of your story I'm curious about."

Sheila stared—slow, deep breaths.

"How did our military just let them return to their parents? I mean, surely the pilots would have reported the wild spectacle."

"Again. Not all of them had parents to return to."

Dr. Harold nodded, then flashed a glum smile, saying, "Yes, yes. Very sad. But how did you explain the rescue? I can't imagine the military receiving the mission report and allowing any of the girls to go back to civilian life."

"We didn't. Everyone on the mission, including the helicopter crew, agreed not to speak of it. Those little girls had suffered a great deal because of you. We didn't want the rest of their lives to be the same, just under a different thumb."

"Very noble of you. Hard to keep a secret though with that many people involved."

"And clearly we didn't," she said, her eyes scanning the room. "Jones wasn't on the mission, but he *was* the drone operator. Saw everything. Now I'm curious though. How did you and Jones connect? How could you have known that he was part of our rescue mission? How did you convince him to jump on board with all this?"

"Small world, Sheila."

She cocked her head patiently. Knew how desperately he wanted to share his story.

He feigned a deep breath. "Well, I'd deployed several times

myself over the years. Jones was of the old guard, like me. We'd served several tours together so I'd reached out. It was a one in a million chance, but sometimes you win the lottery."

At this she couldn't help herself. "And he just told you. Without provocation, he just told a man he hadn't seen in years what happened on that mission."

"Shared history, shared trauma. He trusted me, as he should."

"Did he know you were the one that took them?"

His smile wavered. "Not at first. He thought he was just venting out a crazy story to an old friend."

"And that's it? He just followed you around by the nose?"

"Well, no. Like any good friend I had to make him part of my life again."

"You mean, make him believe he needed you in his."

"Eh. The result was the same. It did take some time though. I had to guide him to what needed to be done."

"Which was?" Sheila just needed to keep him talking.

"Get him to show the footage to his higher ups. Create a classified compartmented organization within the military to track the girls for future obtainment and testing. The military already had a small command doing similar things, so he got in bed with them."

"And that's how he got you here I'm guessing?"

"Well, it didn't happen until grids failed."

"When everything fell apart." She whispered under her breath. Then looked him in the eye. "That's how he got you here. During the chaos. No one would've known you had any part in their initial abduction."

Dr. Harold smiled. "Jones had witnessed firsthand what

they were capable of that night in the desert. And while at first he was intrigued and admittedly empathetic to their situation, like a rational person he grew more and more concerned. He knew that unless they were trained to use their abilities for good, like most good things, they would soon be corrupted by outside ideals, power-hungry politicians, and abusive government agencies looking for an upperhand in battle.

"The grid failing was a blessing in disguise I suppose. By the time that happened Jones already had a select group of combat operators prepared to rescue Zuriella and Alexi."

"Rescue them? And Jones just went along with all this. That's all it took?"

"Went along? No. He laid the path forward. Albeit, the downfall was Jones was afraid. He feared that if they were the ones to destroy the power plants, they couldn't be trusted to be conscious."

"So you think those girls are the reason for all this? Those two *little* girls. You think they took down the grids?"

"We have them on drone footage next to the Harris Plant in North Carolina. It's *where* we rescued them."

"Because they were near it when it collapsed? Is that what you're saying?"

His smile faltered before snapping back into place. "Unfortunately, Jones was too afraid of their capabilities to allow them to regain consciousness within the facility. Even after several years of induced coma. He even wrote a protocol in case they grew too powerful for containment."

"But in the end he switched sides again, didn't he? If he was so afraid of them, why would he have secretly worked against you to rescue them from VISP?"

His jaw tightened. "Human beings are fickle. He had children of his own. I could see the way he watched the monitors. They grew into young women while they slept. He didn't like what he saw happening to Lexi. The guilt ate at him. We argued. He didn't like the experimentation practices I was putting in place. But there was no other way to determine what they could do since they weren't conscious.

"I didn't think he would go to the lengths he did though."

Shiela goaded him, "Or maybe he'd been working with LIMIT the entire time and finally found a way to free them. Maybe he kept them subdued so you wouldn't get the information you needed from them."

Staring into her eyes, he thought about all of Director Jones' protocols. The bureaucratic rules he set in place. His smile started to wane as Sheila's words crept into his mind. Jones had been protecting them from him the entire time.

"Seems you know more than I anticipated," he said, spinning away from her in his chair. "It no longer matters. Everything happens for a reason." He sighed and stood up. "At the end of the day, it brought all of my girls back to me."

Dr. Harold placed his hand on her shoulder and gave it a little squeeze. "You know, I do believe you'll be more valuable than I'd guessed. What, with all the time you've spent with my girls, there's so much more to learn from one another." His last few words slurred together as his voice dropped to a gruff whisper. "I'm going to have… I'm going to… what's hap... hap..." Dr. Harold's knees buckled and he hit the cold tile floor with a thud.

"Dr. Harold? Are you..." Sheila watched him fall to the floor when she heard a breathy sound from behind or above, she couldn't tell.

"Pssst."

Swiveling in her chair, she scoured the room before looking up to see Maddy's face peering down at her from the ceiling.

"We've got you."

Chapter 48
Alone

Sheila watched as the girls lowered Maya through the ceiling. Once they were all down she looked around, then up at the ceiling again and asked, "Where's Aidan?"

"We were hoping he'd be with you. Where's the rest of the team?" Zoey asked.

"In the cafeteria."

"He wasn't there?" Zoey said, her voice rising a notch.

"No, I figured Dr. Harold had him with you," said Sheila, shifting in her seat. Maddy noticed and cut her ties.

"Crap. That's not good. Maya, do you have any idea where they'd take him?" Lexi could feel her heart rate picking up.

"Maybe locked in one of the apartments or the bunker with the rest of the compound."

"If he's down there, his rescue just got much harder," Maddy added.

"Let's hope that's not the case," Sheila answered.

"I can't imagine Dr. Harold would do that... keep him so far from the rest of us?" Zuri said. "Let me feel out for him, see if I can find him."

"Dakota," Maddy asked, "are you able to work your magic to get to him if he is down there?"

Dakota shook her head. "I can only draw what I see or have seen before. I don't know what it looks like down there," she said, feeling defeated.

"It's okay. We'll find him," Zoey said in a hushed voice, placing her hand on Dakota's arm. The tingling vibrations between them amplified.

"Oh!" Dakota yelped. Shocked by the feeling, she pulled her arm away.

"It's alright, Dakota. That's just our shared energy. It happens whenever we touch one another. In fact, it makes us stronger."

"Looks like your wound broke open," Sheila said, pointing at Maya and reaching for some bandages.

"Yeah, all this climbing through magic doors in ceilings stuff musta got me," she chuckled. The strangeness of what they were doing wasn't lost on either of them.

"You know, you have a pretty great kid," Sheila told her.

Maya cleared her throat. "So I've heard," she said, glancing lovingly at the girls.

"As hard as it was for you, I want you to know he was a blessing in my life," she said, her voice growing hoarse. "Having helped raise him over the years since the grid failed, well, he's like a son to me."

Maya embraced Sheila fiercely and said, "I'll never be able to thank you enough for taking care of him."

After a tight squeeze and a long sigh, Sheila stated, "Now, let's go find that handsome devil of yours before he gets himself into any more trouble."

With a laugh, Maya remarked, "He may be older, but it sounds to me like he's still the troublemaker he once was."

The girls finished tying Dr. Harold's unconscious body to his office chair and then gagged him.

"How did you break free, Lexi?" Sheila asked.

"The sedative wore off quickly," said Maddy, cutting in. "We just pretended to sleep until he left the room. Dummy didn't leave a guard with us. Dakota's gifts are incredible!"

"You said the others are in the cafeteria?" Lexi asked.

"Any ideas on how to get down to the second floor?" Zoey questioned, taping Dr. Harold's legs together.

"We could do that door thing again," Zuri offered.

"That's ten floors. Not only would we be exhausted by the time we got down there, but the odds of running into trouble are too high," Lexi said. "I'm not sure we'd be ready to rescue anyone after that."

"She's right. So what are our options?"

"Actually," Dakota interjected, "Just give me a second." Pulling out her notebook, she drew another door, this time made of wood. Then she drew a number three over top of it. Placing her hand on the image, they all watched as the golden fibers looked to burn a circle into the floor. A wooden circular door with a handle appeared.

Dakota bent down and cautiously lifted. "If it worked, this

should be the third floor."

"How can you tell?" Zuri asked.

"Honestly, I can't."

"Once we're down, I'll crack open the door and check," Zoey said.

Nodding in agreement, the gang silently dropped down through the hole to the mysterious room below.

With the ceiling closed up and the girls deathly silent, Zoey opened the room door in order to catch a glimpse of the room number. When her eyes lit up, they knew Dakota's plan had worked. They were on the third floor.

"Dang, girl! You're incredible," Zoey said a little too loudly. She couldn't believe this woman's capabilities. Despite the incredible feat, she noticed Dakota's smile of appreciation didn't reach her eyes.

"Not to pop any bubbles here, but if they're in the cafeteria right below us, won't they immediately see us if we go through the floor again?"

"I can feel him," Zuri cut in. "Aidan. He's still here, alive. I think he's alone."

"Can you tell where he's at?" Lexi asked.

She tilted her head in a few different directions, squeezing her eyes closed from time to time. "I think," she said, looking up at the ceiling, "I think he's above us. We must've skipped right past him on our way down."

"What now?" Joanna asked as she, along with Addie, Macie, and a reluctant Grant and Keeps, crouched in the brush outside of the compound.

"Let's see if we can pull a Zuri," Addie said, holding out her hands.

"You want to try and feel where they are?" asked Joanna.

"Either that or if we can increase our energy enough, maybe Zuri will reach out to us."

Macie nodded and, in a hushed voice, said, "It's worth a shot." Once she discovered she could walk, her legs found their place quickly, seemingly ready for any adventure.

"We'll keep watch," Grant said.

The girls grasped hands and almost immediately the men felt the air energize around them.

Addie, with her alt-vision, watched as the different colored ropes circled between them until they started branching out as if testing the air for a place to go.

Grant, with one eye on the surrounding forest and the other on the girls, said under his breath, "Please, God, let this work."

"Oh, man," Aidan groaned. He tried to lift his hand to wipe the sleep from his eyes but realized his hand wouldn't move. Blinking repeatedly to clear the fog, he slowly looked around the sparse room. "Huh. Well, this is new." Suddenly, he noticed the hospital bed beneath him and his arms tied to the sides with feet to the end rail.

The hospital gown left him chilled with no blanket in sight. The room was dark except for what appeared to be a flood light situated directly over him.

"Hey!" His voice bounced off the walls. "Anyone home?"

Tugging at the restraints and muttering to himself, he said, "Where the heck am I? Seems like a good time to panic, but I'm guessing that won't help." Seeing a reflection of the light, he noticed a mirror covering the wall nearby and yelled, "Someone must be watching me like the creeps they are!"

Aidan lay still, listening intently for any sound. Nothing.

Laying his head back on the extraordinarily uncomfortable mattress, he took stock of his situation. There was still pain in his abdomen from the gunshot, though he could tell it was well on its way to fully healing. *Had it been that day? How long have I been unconscious? We were in the foyer waiting for Rick... all about to leave when... when... sleeping gas! They gassed us.*

Though angry, he relaxed once he was clear on what had happened. After all, nothing else could subdue the girls' powers. Gas was invisible. The only person that might have been able to give them a heads-up was Adeline, but she wasn't with them.

Is everyone in their own room? Why am I the only one in here? Would make sense if the girls were individually separated like this, but what am I to these people? Maya's son, yes. The girls' friend, yes. Rick's team, Joe... oh man... Joe! The image of Joe in a hospital gown strapped to a table almost made him laugh. *Nah, that doesn't make sense. Why keep anyone who doesn't hold any special abilities? It'd be easier to just get rid of...*

Okay. Okay. Maybe because I'm Maya's son they think I can do whatever she can, or at least what the girls can do. Makes sense.

Or I'm bait. Maybe the rest escaped. If so, I could be the bait used to draw them back. They'd come for me. No doubt, but do I want them to? YES! And NO! Damn.

"Who's out there!" he screamed until his throat hurt. Once again, silence.

Chapter 49
Realization

July 3, 2030 | 1:12 a.m.

Justin looked around the cafeteria, recalling their last time there and thinking they'd never see that building again. He had spent years hoping and praying for a miracle until Zoey, Joe and Aidan showed up. Now, he was back again, only with so much more to lose and realizing just how much he loved Zoey.

I should have told her. I should have grabbed the opportunity to tell her instead of waiting for the right time. Now I'm here, back inside VISP, and probably going to die. And she is only God-knows-where, having God-knows-what done to her.

Lexi? Zuri? The others. Like sisters. How could I have let this happen? Let them get captured. If I ever get us out of this mess, I'm gonna lock them up in Sanford and bubble wrap each of them! The image made him want to laugh, but his eyes burned instead.

He looked at all of the men around him. Each one deep in thought. Probably trying to come up with an escape plan.

Whatever Joe was thinking, his face was almost purple with rage. He had never seen the man so incensed.

"Joe," whispered Justin, keeping his head still and low so as not to draw attention. From the corner of his eye he saw Joe's nearly imperceptible shift in his seat. "What about Jahnsen?"

Joe knew what he was asking. Did Jahnsen have a backup plan to rescue them if they got caught? He did, but it was a Hail Mary. He didn't have enough men to storm the castle, but he could definitely create a distraction that might help them escape. "Maybe. But it won't work unless we can get free of these chairs."

"How long will they wait before they create a diversion?"

"Maybe two—"

"Hey!" yelled one of the guards. "No. Talking." His command had barely escaped his lips when he used the butt end of his gun to hit Justin over the head.

"Hey, man! That's not—" Joe started, but was cut off when the guard lifted his gun to hit him as well. "Okay! Okay. I got it."

"Don't worry, gentlemen," the guard declared to everyone as one corner of his mouth twisted into a smirk. "You'll be leaving us shortly."

"You know, there is something else I can try," Dakota offered, unsure of her plan. "I might be able to conjure up a storm. A big storm. Big enough that everyone would seek shelter, and, just maybe, give us a chance to swoop in and rescue the others."

"So what's the catch?" Lexi asked.

"I don't exactly know how to control it. Meaning, there's a real possibility we could be hurt too... or worse."

"Weather? You can control the weather?" Zoey asked, shaking her head.

"I've only done it once before. To be honest... it didn't go well."

The girls all looked at one another, eventually turning toward Zuri.

"I've tried controlling an existing storm, or at least the elements. Maybe together we can protect ourselves. Protect the team. Control it," Zuri said, attempting to sound confident.

Maddy, considering the proposition, said, "I know this building was designed to withstand bombs up to a certain extent. Shouldn't it be able to stand against severe weather?"

"But this isn't just severe weather. It's something else, sort of like us and our abilities," said Zoey, aware there was no way to know what Dakota was capable of.

"Does anyone else have any ideas?" Lexi asked.

"I could do what I did with Dr. Harold and put everyone to sleep," Maddy offered. "I think I could work the entire room with an energy kick from you guys."

"Would you be able to avoid our guys?"

Shaking her head, Maddy replied, "I don't think so."

"Which means we'd have to figure out a way to carry, what, about ten people? Oh, and still manage to find Aidan quickly," Zoey said.

The room fell silent as they contemplated their options.

"Dakota's plan is the only one with potential. Either all of

Dr. Harold's security will run for shelter, or the storm will keep them busy while we get our guys." Looking at their faces, Zuri inexplicably grew more confident in the idea.

One by one, each of them nodded in agreement.

"I just want you girls to know… I'm sorry," said Maya, considering the weight of their decision. "I'm sorry that your lives ended up this way. That you're forced into this and everything else you've had to endure. It's all because of me, and I…" Clearing her throat, she said, "I'm just so sorry."

Lexi grabbed Maya's hand and said, "None of this is your fault. The grids didn't fail because of you. If it was truly you who gave us our abilities, it wasn't something you did knowingly and certainly not maliciously."

"Lexi's right," Dakota said quietly. "None of this is Maya's fault either though. It's mine."

They all turned to look at her. Maddy said, "No, Dak—"

"I'm the one that blew up the Harris Plant... which caused the chain reaction that brought the rest down."

"That's not possible. None of us had anything to do with it," Zoey said, trying to comfort Dakota, simultaneously sensing that she was telling the truth.

"You didn't. But I did. I was young, angry, and tired. The Breakers found me and brought me in. Protected me. Once they knew what I could do, they wanted my help. Wanted me to take down the power plant to show the world how easy it would be, and the chaos it would cause."

The girls listened without saying a word. Staring at this sister who suddenly seemed alien once again.

"I stood in a hunting blind up in the trees where I could see the plant in the distance," she continued as her cheeks flushed and her heart raced at the freshness of the memory. "I didn't even know whether or not I could do it. I drew the power plant off in the distance. As I drew, I thought about all the people that had hurt me, and I got angrier and angrier. By the time I'd finished drawing the plant in ruins, flames rising around it, I was more furious than I'd ever been in my life. Always being used. No one loving me for me."

Tears washed down Zuri's cheeks.

"I stared at that paper for a long time. The pressure in my head was unbearable. I didn't just put my hand to the drawing, I... I..." Her face scrunched in realization. "That's why that happened," she whispered to herself as if breathing a breath of fresh air.

"What do you mean?" asked Lexi, moving closer.

Dakota suddenly looked up. "I was so mad I slammed my hand on the page and swiped it across the drawing. I swiped it, smearing the fresh graphite lines across the page.

"I did the same thing with the storm off the coast of Florida a few weeks back. The storm amplified ten-fold. It happened so fast it took me by surprise. The winds and rain slammed into me and I fell, breaking my arm. I wasn't able to control it or stop it once I was injured because I couldn't draw an X across the page. I was stuck, waiting for it to naturally subside."

The girls glanced at one another, not sure how to respond.

"The same thing happened back then. The explosion was so massive it blew me out of the tree. I laid unconscious for some time. No idea that the entire world was succumbing to my anger while I slept."

"Do you think it's possible?" Zoey asked Maya. "Could she have actually done that all alone on such a huge scale?"

Lexi and Zuri looked at one another. They knew. She wasn't alone. "It's because we were there with her," Lexi said quietly.

"But, how? That doesn't make sense." Zoey's face showed her disbelief.

Zuri spoke then. "I remember, we kept feeling the pull of energy. We couldn't figure it out, but we could feel it. We decided to see if we could find it and ended up by the plant. We got turned around looking for it when we felt this wave. Like, pressure before a severe storm hits. We ran in opposite directions and tried to protect ourselves. But…"

"But in order to protect yourself you had to use energy. Which with the three of you so close, amplified Dakota's already strong gifts," Maddy stated.

They stood quietly together, recognition of truth in the words.

Maya was shocked, but resolute. Rising slowly, she limped to Dakota's side and placed her hands on the young woman's shoulders. "You didn't ask for these gifts. You didn't ask to be stolen from your family or abused by Dr. Harold. You didn't ask to grow up without someone to love and protect you. And you were young. We can't undo what you did, or what's been done. But together…" she looked at all the women, "together we can do everything possible to make it better." Maya wrapped her arms around Dakota, who, for the first time, felt loved enough to cry without holding back.

As the girls embraced one another, a hum filled the room that seemed to grow with every beat of their hearts.

Sheila, wiping her eyes, finally said, "Okay, my beautiful ladies. I think we have a storm to make."

Chapter 50
It's Happening

July 3, 2030 | 1:35 a.m.

The girls moved to the furthest room on the south side of the building. When they realized there wasn't a window in the room, Dakota created one. She needed to see details in the skyline to have something specific in her drawing to tether her power to.

Dakota opened the notebook to a fresh page as Zuri, Maddy, Lexi, and Zoey held hands in a circle with Dakota at the center. "What are you doing?"

"We've learned that our energy increases when we circle up," Zoey answered.

"And then we pass it to you so that whatever you're doing will be amplified," Zuri added. "Once I feel the energy is strong enough, I'll touch your shoulder to let it flow to you."

"But do you think I'll need it?" asked Dakota, her hand trembling over the page. She imagined the storm she had previously created. "The last one was pretty strong on my own. I'm not even sure it'll work," she added, more self-deprecating than doubtful. She had been so used to being the confident and controlled one in charge that it was a struggle to let herself lean on their worthwhile input, particularly in a group with so many equals.

"It's not just for strength, but control," Lexi shared with a sisterly smile. "I can help tame someone else's powers. If things get out of hand, I can help reign it in."

Dakota awkwardly smiled back.

She looked out the window and the others did the same. The storm they anticipated coming in earlier in the evening was already overhead. It wasn't overpowering. Some lightning and dull thunder but not significant. Although Sheila noted that Jahnsen's team likely had stopped circulating overhead a while ago as the storm rolled in.

"Okay. Here goes," she said, taking a deep breath before sketching the most exquisite storm clouds, swaying trees, and thick raindrops.

The girls watched as Dakota's artistry was on full display. Despite the violent storm her pencil was creating, it was also beautiful.

After several focused minutes, Dakota looked up. The girls, watching intently, nodded, signaling to her that they were ready for what came next. Glancing out the window, Dakota held her breath as she lifted her pencil from the page. Releasing the air slowly she lowered her heart rate, careful not to add even an ounce of personal anger to the drawing but instead work from a place of calm. Quickly making eye contact with Zuri, she dropped her hand to the page and swiped across the pencil marks, smudging the beautiful work of art.

Immediately a gust of wind shook the window and they turned to see the trees closest to the building, lit up by the outside lights, dramatically sway to one side.

Dakota turned to Zuri. "It's happening."

Joanna's concentration was broken by the gust of wind smacking her back. Her eyes flew open. She knew something was coming. "We need to find shelter now!"

"What's happening?" Macie cried, looking up to the sky, shocked by the quick turn of angry lightning and unexpected winds.

"It's just the storm," Grant answered.

"No. It's Dakota. Did you feel it? They're doing something in there. Making it bigger," Joanna shouted, attempting to block the wind as the sound of swaying trees nearly drowned out her voice.

"I felt it, too. The girls are working on something big. I can sense their conviction to shape this storm for a purpose," Addie said.

"But what is it?" Another gust hit them head-on, pushing Macie over from her sitting position and forcing her to clamor to her feet.

"I knew I shouldn't have let you come out here!" Grant groaned.

"Work the problem, Grant!" Maria sassed. "Whatever they're doing, they're doing for a reason. Let's get to a safe space." As she spoke, raindrops trickling through the trees, quickly turning into the biggest drops they had ever seen.

"This is not normal. We need to get out of this!" yelled Keeps, grabbing Addie's arm to help steady her as they hobbled together through the forest.

"Where are we headed?" Addie asked.

"Back to the safehouse," Grant yelled, muffled by the rattling trees.

Addie stopped, causing Keeps to lose his balance and grip on her arm.

"What are you doing? We've got to move!"

"It's too far. We need to get inside that compound." Addie could see the tendrils of energy flowing through the trees on the wind. She'd seen plenty of storms since her rescue, but they never carried the fibers of the girls' energy flowing through them.

"We can't!" Grant demanded, panic in his eyes.

"We have to."

Staring at her determined face, Grant stamped his feet and shouted, "Crap!" Turning back, he called for Maria to turn back as well.

Stopping to shelter against a large tree, Maria looked back at him as if he were insane. Grant simply stared as the wind whisked away her profane tirade before calling out to Joanna to return as well.

As soon as they were all huddled together Addie shouted over the sound of tornadic leaves, "The girls are doing this and I can tell it's going to get very bad very fast. We need to be on that compound when it does."

Maria, shaking with fear and anger, said, "Okay, how do we

do that?”

“We won’t know til we get there.” Addie’s calm was unnerving.

Aidan felt a vibration ripple across his skin. The girls were up to something and using a lot of energy. Whatever it was, he knew they would need his help. He needed to get out of these bindings.

Are they being tortured? Tested on? Abused?

With every question, his rage grew. He refused to lie there waiting to be rescued. They needed him. Pulling as hard as he could against the straps only enraged him more with the added benefit of bruising.

Dr. Harold wouldn’t kill them. He needs them. Doesn’t mean he won’t torment them to get whatever it is he wants.

As if on cue, Dr. Harold walked in.

“I wouldn’t keep doing that if I were you,” said Dr. Harold, his voice sounding hoarse.

“Let me out of here or I swear... when I’m free... I’ll hunt you down and kill you with my bare hands.”

“Big words for a boy tied to a bed,” he replied dismissively over his shoulder, staring at the weather radar on his laptop.

“Alright, let me go and I promise I won’t kill you.”

Dr. Harold chuckled. “As beneficial as that sounds, I think I’ll take my chances.” He zoomed in on the screen looking at a storm system that had been moving toward them all day. Yet as he watched the timelapse, the last five minutes of the storm cell intensified without explanation. “I think our girls are up to something.”

"Yeah? Well, they do that from time to time," Aidan growled, pulling at his bindings when a thought struck him. "Tell me, what are you doing to them?"

"Me? Absolutely nothing. In fact, at the moment, they don't even require restraints," Dr. Harold smirked, unwilling to let on that he didn't know where they were. His guards had found him tied up, but the girls were gone by the time they did. "Here, look at this," he said, showing Aidan the radar.

"This storm has been heading our way all day. But look there," he said, pointing at the area of the storm that had intensified in the final two images on the time-lapse. "See how it strengthens there at the end? What do you make of that?"

Aidan froze and stared at the doctor. "Are you seriously asking me about the weather right now?"

Dr. Harold pulled his gaze from the screen, blinked a few times, then let out a small laugh. "I guess I am. Is this something the girls can do? Manipulate weather?"

Aidan desperately wanted to feed him a heavy dose of sarcasm but instead kept repeating to himself, *More bees with honey, more bees with honey.* "I've never seen them do anything with the weather. I think that's out of their wheelhouse."

"Mmm. Yes." Dr. Harold was clearly not convinced.

"How 'bout this... you let me go, and we'll chat with the girls together? Like civilized humans."

Dr. Harold smiled at him. "That's a very amicable proposition," Dr. Harold said as he headed toward the door. Suddenly, a booming blow against the outside of the building made him duck.

"Either that storm is bigger than you thought, or I'm wrong and the girls are really mad at you, my friend."

Dr. Harold stood up and straightened out his jacket. "I guess I'll have to calm them down. I think…" he said, taking a small step toward Aidan, "that you can probably help me with that, my friend."

Aidan, sensing the nefarious tone in Dr. Harold's voice, yelled, "Friends don't keep friends tied to a bed!"

Dr. Harold nodded at the large mirror on the wall. Seconds later, Aidan began to feel a tingling sensation on his scalp. He hadn't noticed anything attached to his head until the pinpricks of electricity began targeting areas all across his brain.

Oh man! This ain't— he thought as an excruciatingly painful seizure took hold of him.

Chapter 51
You Are Strong

"**S**top!" Zuri yelled.

The girls released their hands from one another as a sizzling electrical current coursed through them.

"Dakota, is this your work?" Lexi asked.

"No," she said, shaking her head. "But we need to move. Things are about to get ugly."

"It's Aidan!" Zuri shouted as she ran for the door.

"Wait!" yelled Lexi, grabbing hold of her. "We need to figure this out."

"But I can feel him," she replied, pulling at her arm and trying to break free.

"I know, I can feel him too. But we can't just run out there."

"Dr. Harold's doing this on purpose," Maya said. She had

never felt anything like what was coursing through her body. Now, suddenly, she instinctively knew it was what her son was feeling. "He believes that hurting Aidan will bring us to him."

"He's right!" Zuri cried, planting her feet firmly. "We have to go right now."

"We need help. We need to find the team," Sheila said. "The—" she began as the window Dakota had designed shattered, blowing inward toward them. The women tried to cover themselves but couldn't hide from the shards of the glass that chaotically flew.

"Everyone okay?" Maya asked, hardly making a sound over the screaming wind now blowing in. Seeing them all upright, she pushed them toward the door. "Move! Everyone out!"

Once in the hallway they pressed the door shut firmly behind them and did a quick assessment. Besides a few cuts, possibly a few that needed stitches, they were otherwise safe.

"Here," Sheila said to Zoey, "let me wrap this real quick." She ripped off a piece of Zoey's shirt, not wanting to take the time to dig in her bag for a bandage. "This will hold until I can stitch you up."

"Where do we go?" Lexi wondered, looking at Maddy, who knew her way around the building better than anyone.

"I don't think we have a choice. Down to the cafeteria. We need to get our team."

As soon as they entered the stairwell, the lights flickered and then turned off. They paused, listening to the howling winds outside. Once the emergency lights kicked on, Dakota said, "Let's move. We don't have a lot of time before we're going to need a storm shelter ourselves."

"Everyone ready?" asked Maddy as she took the lead.

The cafeteria door flew open and the girls raced in. Lexi held her hands up on each side, maintaining a field of protection around the team.

The room, however, was empty.

"No! No, no, no!" Zuri groaned. "They were just here. I felt them. Where could they have gone?"

"Quiet!" Lexi said in a hushed, commanding voice.

They stood motionless until Zuri slowed her heart rate enough to focus. "They're above us. How's that possible?"

"They must've moved them when we were building the storm," said Maya.

"Where are they, Zuri? Can you tell what floor?" Maddy asked.

Slowly turning in a circle, she focused until she could see in her mind the vision of a floor and door number. "They're back on twelve."

"That's the floor the Director and other high level staff have offices on," Maddy informed them.

"Okay. New plan," Sheila said.

"I don't think I can make it up that many flights," Maya said, holding her wound.

Pulling out her sketchbook, Dakota assured her, "You don't have to."

"You've outdone yourself, Doc." Joe employed every ounce of self-control by not breaking his own hands and fingers to get out of his bindings and grab Dr. Harold by the throat.

"Thank you. Yes, there was a lot of planning involved in all this. Glad you appreciate it."

"How did you know we'd come?" Justin asked.

"Well, in all fairness, I didn't. But I wanted to be ready just in case."

"What's the purpose of separating Aidan from us?" Joe could see Aidan through the one way mirror, tied to a hospital bed and repeatedly being shocked via some contraption on his head. Rick's team was tied up in the room next door. Joe figured the four of them were the only ones that mattered to the doctor anyway. Several guards were stationed within arm's length with fingers on triggers.

"I'll tell you, I wasn't sure how all of this would play out, but it's turned out better than I expected!" Dr. Harold stood in front of the window. "That room was designed similar to the glass incubators we'd used for Zuri and Lexi. We were going to transfer Maya in here once it was complete," he paused to look at Joe. "But you got here before the testing on all of our latest technology was done. That's okay, though. We're pretty confident everything works as intended, and now we have a good test subject."

"How can it be an accurate test, though? After all, he's not one of the girls."

"That's true. However, he doesn't need to be in order to ensure the room functions as we designed it," he said, looking straight at Joe with a smile. "Though it hurts me that you didn't think I'd notice."

"Notice what?"

"I mean, he is Maya's son. She did give birth to him. If she could transfer or bring about the capabilities that she did in Zuri, Lexi and the others, just imagine what powers Aidan might possess."

Joe clenched his fists until his hands tingled. "I've known Aidan a long time, and short of his gift of sarcasm, I don't think there's much there."

"I admire how hard you're trying, but here's the thing… I've seen his eyes. I know there's something there. If you haven't seen what he can do, then maybe we need to find a way to pull it out of him," the doctor said, raising his eyebrows with a smirk.

"Plus," Dr. Harold added, "having him here ensures not just the girls will come for him, but Maya. She'd never leave her own child to suffer in this way. After all, she already lost him once. I don't believe she'll let it happen again. The suffering is regrettable, but pain is the greatest motivator."

"So you've lost them?" Justin realized.

Dr. Harold paused the electrocution. Aidan's body slumped on the bed. His heart rate on the echocardiogram was rapid, though began to slow with each passing second.

"I think next we should try…" He looked at his options and said, "compression. Let's verify that applied pressure is actually sealed in the room." He tapped several different tabs on the screen before finally starting the process.

The men watched as Aidan's body seemed to shift before being pushed downward into the table he lay upon by an invisible force. Once again, his heart rate picked up, and his breathing grew labored.

As they watched his vitals, Justin couldn't take it anymore. "Okay! Wait. There are other ways to do this." His lips barely moved as he gritted his teeth.

Dr. Harold, curious at the outburst, turned to listen.

"Look, we've been working with the girls for a while—"

"Justin. Stop," growled Joe.

"We're trapped, Joe. It's out of our hands. We can, however, make this as peaceful for Aidan and the girls as possible."

"I'm listening," said Dr. Harold, eager to finally have some answers.

"They know how to work together, to draw out the abilities of one another. Making them suffer will only stir up anger and fear, sending their gifts in the dark and dangerous direction, unless, that is, unless you want them to turn on you."

Dr. Harold squinted as if deep in thought.

"I guarantee the girls know what you're doing to him at this very moment. They'll be coming up with a plan to rescue him, which may get you or all of us killed. I've watched them work miracles. But I've also watched them create destruction. If what you've told us is true, then the last thing you want to do is turn them into monsters," Justin said, his eyes pleading his case, begging him to turn around and stop torturing Aidan.

The room grew silent as Dr. Harold contemplated his next move.

The men watched as Aidan's oxygen level on the screen continued to diminish. And just when they thought Dr. Harold would move forward with his plan, he turned back to his laptop and paused the program.

Instantly Aidan's body relaxed.

"Okay. What's your suggestion to bring the girls in peacefully?"

Justin looked at Joe, his eyes now imploring for help.

"Do you know where the girls are?" Joe asked.

"They were in the cafeteria on level two, but the cameras

throughout the building have since gone black. I'm assuming our girls had something to do with that." While Dr. Harold wasn't happy he couldn't track the girls, he was elated at everything they'd done so far.

"Is there an intercom throughout the building? A way to communicate with them. If they could hear us, I think they'd believe us."

"There is!" Dr. Harold's eyes lit up at the idea. "Here's the thing, though. This is one of those moments you might recall in old movies where the captured use codes to warn their people of what's to come. So, just so you're aware, we've increased security measures since your last visit. We've installed steel-reinforced locking mechanisms on all exterior doors and windows. The thing is, they were designed to only be used once. Once activated, upon contact, the steel bars will automatically weld to the frame. There are only two people who know the code to free the welds. I'd love to tell you who the second person is, but… well... that would only increase your odds, now wouldn't it?

"My point is, there are only two ways out of this building. The code," he said, breathing in a faux deep breath, "or death."

"Appreciate the honesty, Professor Moriarty," Justin quipped. "Why don't you let Joe take a crack at this. Out of all of us, they'll listen to him without question."

Joe cleared his throat and puffed out his chest at the unintended compliment.

Dr. Harold looked from one man to the other for any sign of deception. "Alright then. If your plan works, gentlemen, you might all be free men living in comfort on this compound, of course. All we have to do is work together. We all want the same thing, right?"

The men stiffly nodded.

Motioning for a guard to assist Joe, Dr. Harold stood several feet away, cautious of being too close to the man. He pulled up the digital intercom on his laptop linked to speakers throughout the compound.

"I'll handle the broadcast, just in case you decide to say something beyond the spirit of our plan."

Joe nodded in agreement.

"Let me know when you're ready."

Clearing his throat again, he said. "Go 'head."

Joe watched the light turn from red to green. He normally had a plan. Even in a last-minute situation, he'd always been a quick thinker, but this was different. Every person he cared about was currently in danger and he didn't know how to stop it.

Zoey's bright hazel eyes flashed through his mind. He'd believed at one time he was in love with her, but as their lives changed, he realized he just wanted to see her happy. There was no plan. All he could do was speak the truth.

"Zoey?" he said, clearing his throat and hearing the echo beyond the walls of the room he was in. "Zuri, Lexi, Maddy, Dakota... if you're all together, I need you to listen. I know you're trying to rescue us. I know you're trying to rescue Aidan. You can feel his pain and that's the one thing I've always hated about what you can do. From the very moment we realized that you, Zoey, were connected to someone else, could feel her pain to such a degree that it caused you physical harm, that connection has broken my heart.

"There are some things I've never told you, Zoey. Like how I ended up with this white stripe through my hair and beard.

And it's something you never asked. You knew I didn't want to talk about it, and you respected my privacy. It was a form of kindness and caring that you didn't ask. But it's something I want… I need to share with you now.

"Seven years ago, I was in town helping a supplier build a security perimeter so he could protect himself and his produce from thieves. I'd been working all day, midsummer, and it was hot as the devil outside. I put up cameras for him around his fence line. The camera feed connected to a computer inside his office within the storage building. I was setting it up for him, making sure all the cameras were set properly, when I saw something strange. There was a little undesignated shack out back. The supplier said it was where he stored trash until it was full, and then he'd burn it.

"I didn't think much of it at first, but then, through the feed, I saw a chain attached to a steel post outside the shack. It ran into a crudely cut hole in the side of the little structure. I watched it for a while, curious, when all of a sudden, I swore I saw the chain move. At first I thought I was seeing things. Maybe it was the wind or a big dog on the other end. But then it moved again. Pulled taught from something inside the shack before slinking back down to the ground again.

"Turning to the supplier, I pointed it out and had him watch as it happened again. I still thought it was likely a guard dog he failed to mention and that he'd laugh it off, but instead, he almost looked scared.

"Just as quickly, he changed his expression and said, 'Oh that? That's nothing. Probably a raccoon in there. I'll go chase him out.' He picked up his shotgun, headed toward the door, then turned back and said, 'You can change that camera to more important property, like my fields. I'm not worried about that old shack. Go ahead and change it and I'll be right back.' His voice sounded earnest, so of course, as you know," he said with a chuckle, "I didn't change the camera position. I mean, what fool would? I told myself I was gonna keep watch in case he needed help. Really, I sensed he was hiding something.

"I watched as he looked over his shoulder before opening the shack door. He immediately turned to the side and aimed his shotgun toward the ground. I couldn't hear him, but I could see his mouth moving. Raccoons typically don't care to converse. When cornered, it's fight or flight. He stood there for several seconds, then backed up and shut the door. None of it made any sense. Only made the feeling that someone was in there stronger. So, before he returned to the office, I'd added the link to his camera feed to my laptop.

"That night, I snuck back and hid along the fence line. I watched as he brought a plate of food to the shack. His shotgun hanging on his back. He was in there for a good thirty minutes or so before he came out with an empty plate. After I was sure he was out of sight, I cut the chain link fence and the feed to that camera. I opened the door slowly, after all, I had no idea what to expect, and heard labored breathing. After waiting for my eyes to adjust to the darkness, I caught sight. That's when everything changed. That's when my heart stopped.

"It was you, Zoey. Lying on the ground, thin as a rail. Even in the dark, your bruises were visible. Food was scattered around you, uneaten. Dried blood caked your clothing and covered your skin with fresh, bright red splits. It's a bit of a blur after that. I know that I dropped to my knees by your side, and promised to get you out. You were weak but still managed to push me away.

"Then you opened your beautiful hazel eyes. A slight spark in the darkness shone back at me. You stared at me for only a few seconds but somehow knew I wasn't there to hurt you. Whatever he'd done should've made you afraid of anyone that came near, yet you knew... you knew I would save you.

"Not exactly sure how, but I got you unshackled and hoisted you up carefully. As I turned to leave, the supplier stepped into the doorway with his shotgun trained on my head. I set you back down and put my hands in the air. He motioned for me to sit next to you on the floor and as he reached down to grab the chain I hit the gun out of his hand. We wrestled... I wanted to kill him... my hands were around his neck as he flailed. But then... you reached over and put your hand on his head and said, 'Don't kill him.'

"Your voice and request surprised me, but even more shocking was the sharp electrical current that moved from my hands up my arms. I had to let go of him, but it didn't matter... you held on to him as his eyes glazed over.

"By the time you passed out from whatever energy you were expelling, well, it was as if he had had a lobotomy.

"I scooped you up and brought you to our home. Cleaned you up and let you sleep. You slept for three straight days, and when you woke up, it was as if you had no memory of your time on the property.

"I never told you or Aidan what you'd done that night. I didn't know how. It wasn't until we went to search for Lexi and Zuri that I truly understood the gift you have.

"After all this time, I've still never heard you tell your story. I'm guessing you've just blocked it from your mind.

"I didn't plan to tell you about those horrible days, but

now, well, I want you to know just how strong you are. You've watched all your sisters survive inexplicable horror. You've questioned what you have to offer. Truth is, you're the strongest person I've ever met."

Dr. Harold motioned for Joe to wrap it up.

"I need you to listen to me carefully. All of you. Together, we can make this world better. We're here with Dr. Harold right now." The doctor's finger hovered over the intercom button as he offered a warning with his eyes. "That's all he wants. He's assured me that if you all come up to the twelfth floor peacefully, he'll let us, all of us, live freely right here on the compound. He'll work with you to develop your abilities, and together we'll all focus on repairing humanity.

"It's a lot to ask, I know... but we need you to do this. This is the only way to save each other and make a difference." With that, Joe nodded to sign-off, took a deep breath, and relaxed.

"Well said. I'm saddened to hear about Zoey," Dr. Harold said with nearly a hint of empathy. "No one should have to go through something so horrific. You did a good thing. Saving her."

Ignoring the doctor, Joe asked, "What happens now?"

"I suppose we wai—"

A crack of thunder reverberated through the building. So loud and sharp they could feel it in their bones, even causing Dr. Harold to duck.

"What's happening out there?" radioed Dr. Harold.

A voice cutting through static said, "It's the storm, sir. Getting bad fast. I think we need to get everyone to the bunker."

Dr. Harold looked around the room and then back to Aidan. For the first time, he looked concerned. "Find out how long it'll take to pass."

"Sir, Maya would be the one to ask and she's MIA."

"It's just a storm for crying out loud. We'll be fine. The building is rated for a CAT three hurricane."

"Sir, as far as we can tell, all the windows on the south side of the building have been blown in."

He held the radio to his pursed lips before setting the radio down and switching on the intercom once again. "Maya? It's Dr. Harold. I know you heard Joe's pleas, and I want to reiterate that we're willing to work with you. All of you. And right now, I'm going to show you proof of that. There's a severe storm out there and it looks like it's chipping away at the building. We need you... I need you—"

Without warning, what sounded like an incoming freight train derailment caused him to drop to the floor and away from his computer. The tornado shook the complex as it began to tear off the roof.

"Sir, water is pouring down the stairwells. We need to move!" came a garbled voice over his radio.

Grabbing his laptop, he leaned into the microphone. "Maya? Please! Come to the twelfth floor. You're the only one who can help!"

Chapter 52
Speck of Debris

July 3, 2030 | 2:05 a.m.

Maya listened as Dr. Harold's voice echoed through the building for help. She had no desire to assist him, but helping everyone else meant helping him, too.

Zoey wiped tears from her cheeks as long-suppressed memories flooded her mind. Maddy gripped her shoulder, offering a sense of peace while Zuri held her hand tightly.

"What do you want to do?" Sheila asked them.

"Do you think he's right? That I'm responsible for robbing that man of his... his mind?" Zoey asked quietly.

"You, of all people, know that Joe isn't one to gaslight, let alone lie to any of us. I wasn't there, but I have to believe he's telling the truth," Sheila answered.

"Then I think I have an idea," Zoey said after a moment's

consideration. "Dakota? Can you get us into that room with Joe?"

"Yeah, I should be able to."

"Okay. Let's go get our people."

"It's been several minutes. Maybe they're not buying it, Boss," whispered a guard.

"They'll come," Dr. Harold bit out. Then more calmly, almost to himself, "Maya will come." He was staring into the room where Aidan lay tied to the bed.

Another loud crack hit the building, causing everyone to wince. This time, the floor itself seemed to shake and then tilt.

"Sir, we can't wait any longer. This building is coming down!"

Dr. Harold, shaking his head, smacked the desk. "Alright, get them up. We'll have to take the stairs."

"The stairs are flooding!" Another guard had just burst into the room, panting and soaked.

"We don't have a choice. The elevator is out of the question."

After several seconds of mulling it over, they conceded it was their only option. "Up! Get up!"

"What about Aidan?" demanded Joe, planting his feet and refusing to budge.

Dr. Harold, looked back and forth between the two of them, then gruffly declared, "We'll have to leave him. He's too—"

"No! We aren't leaving him. Let me stay. Stop!"

After a tense struggle, the doctor waved his hand and said, "Let him free."

Cutting the zip-ties around Joe's wrists, the guard pushed

him away, keeping his gun trained on him the entire time. Dr. Harold stepped forward and grabbed Joe's shirt in his fist. His first personal show of force. "If you manage to stay alive, I expect you to be true to your word."

Joe didn't take the time to respond. He pulled away from Dr. Harold's grasp and dashed to the testing room as the others raced into the hall, pushing their captives impatiently.

Inside the stairwell, they watched as rain poured down through the roofless building above. With nowhere else to go, they began making their way down, gripping the rail tight as if trying to climb down slippery rocks under a waterfall.

"Will the basement floors be underwater at this point?" Dr. Harold shouted over his shoulder at his LSO.

"I don't know. I haven't gotten a response from my team down there. The security room on the main floor is fortified. Might be the next best location."

"Alright, let them know we're coming."

"What about the bunkers?" asked the LSO with hesitation in his voice.

"There's nothing we can do about them," replied the doctor.

"There's at least three hundred people dow—"

"The girls are essential. We need to find them and keep them safe! Period."

"Yes, sir."

A loud screech of wind bellowing outside the building caught everyone's attention. Frozen in place, they stared at the wall as if hoping to see right through it when suddenly, as if their wish was granted, a vehicle crashed through. Right into the stairwell at the feet of Dr. Harold, taking out the three guards in front of him and separating them from the captives further down, the doctor barely survived as blocks and concrete sprayed everywhere. After pulling him back from the carnage in the nick of time, the guard led him back up to the eighth-floor platform.

"We need to get out of here, Doc!"

"We can't risk losing those men," shouted Dr. Harold, clamoring to go back down. "They're our only leverage."

"Our leverage is gone! Besides, it won't matter if we're dead!" He pushed Dr. Harold through the stairwell door into the hallway and up against the wall with his forearm pressed tightly under the doctor's chin. "My guess is everyone is looking for their own way out at this point. You want those men? You go get them. I'm gonna see if the elevator shaft is compromised."

"The elevator? Have you lost your mind?"

"Listen, if it's intact, we can climb down the ladder inside the shaft."

Dr. Harold cursed every name he could think of as LSO Fisher ran off. He was so close. Everything was finally coming together so smoothly that it instantly occurred to him: *Do they really have the power to cause a storm like this? Is this how strong they are? Would they really risk their own lives pulling a building down on top of them just to escape?*

With his back against the wall, he watched in horror as the stairwell door was sucked open. Winds funneled through the hallway, knocking him off his feet. The sound of twisting metal and the roar of the tornado eating away at the walls terrified him as it began pulling him into its mouth.

This can't be it. This isn't how I die.

With his feet in the air and knuckles turning white as he squeezed what was left of the doorframe, his scream cut through the deafening sound. Nearly blacking out from fear of being sucked into the belly of the demon, images of each of the girls' faces began to race through his mind. He was now little more than a speck of debris consumed by the blackness he once imprisoned them in.

Chapter 53
We Knock

July 3, 2030 | 2:15 a.m.

"What do we do?" Joanna yelled over the screeching winds. They were outside the main building and had just witnessed a vehicle lift from its parking space and whip into the side of the VISP building.

Grant, unmoved by the crashing car, was struggling to pry open the main doors with a shovel he'd found when the wooden pole snapped against the steel door. "We're not getting in this way," he said as the heavy raindrops stung his face. "We need to go somewhere else!"

Addie checked around them for anything her alt-vision might find that could offer shelter. Reflexively, she stepped away from the building, hoping to catch a better look, but everything was black. The only signs of life and safety were the colorful ribbons floating through the air coming from inside the main building.

Keeps, watching closely as she stepped further out into the open, grew concerned and reached out to grab her. As he went to pull her back against the wall, a gust of wind full of debris gripped him, spun him in a circle and took his feet out from under him, knocking him out cold.

"Keeps!" Maria screamed. "Keeps is down! Grant! Help!" She was on her hands and knees, beginning to crawl toward him in order to grab his outstretched hand when roofing from a nearby building ripped free of its mooring. She barely had time to see it coming when Grant pulled her out of harm's way.

"No!" Maria yelled as the metal swooped down and violently scooped Keeps right off the ground and into darkness. He looked like a ragdoll as his head and arms flailed around helplessly.

"We have to go get him!"

"We can't! Maria, we can't!" Grant wrapped his arms around her waist and yanked her back to the side of the building. "We're going to end up just like him if we don't find shelter!"

The five of them were pressed up against the cinderblock when Grant recalled the manholes all around the property. "If we can make it to one of those manholes, we can survive underground until it passes!"

"How far?" Joanna yelled.

"Maybe a hundred yards?"

"We'll never make that!" she called, her voice growing hoarse with fear.

"We will!" He locked eyes with her in determination. "We have to!" Then, pulling a rope from his bag, he tied one end around his waist. "Hold onto this! Whatever you do, do *not* let go!" They passed the rope between them.

Dropping to their knees, they began to crawl, one following the other until they were in a line. Moving slowly, it seemed to take forever as rain and small bits of debris pelted their backs. Somewhere off in the distance they heard a thunderous roar followed by the shriek of breaking metal when suddenly large chunks of the building hit the ground all around, nearly crushing them.

By the time they made it to the manhole, they were soaked to the bone. Cuts and bruises littered their bodies.

Exhausted, Grant struggled to lift the cover but it was firmly in place. He howled with every last bit of energy as it refused to budge. "I can't get it!" he called out as he dropped to his stomach alongside the girls.

"What are you doing?" Maria yelled, her eyes wild in fear.

"It's either wedged or bolted shut!"

"So what do we do?" Joanna asked, her voice drowned out by the wind.

Macie's adrenaline was soaring. She kept seeing images of the five of them in a tunnel and instinctively knew it was right below them. Her visions had been unreliable after all the years of abuse by Oakley. This was the first trustworthy one she'd had in so long it took her a moment to realize what she was seeing.

Taking a deep breath, she low-crawled on her stomach until she was right up next to Grant. "I think I can do it," she said, motioning toward the manhole.

Too exhausted to argue, he shouted, "Okay! Let's see what you got!" Through the flashes of lightning, they watched as she placed her hand on the cover. For a moment, nothing happened.

But just as Grant was about to pull her back for another try, Macie felt her body pushing its energy down her arm, through her hand, and into her fingertips. The cool, wet steal began to vibrate and move, but it just wouldn't lift. All of a sudden she felt a hand on her ankle and a boost of energy. Seconds later, another jolt surged through her. Without a sound, the manhole lifted from its iron perch just enough for her to push it to the side.

Once there was enough clearance, Macie pulled her hand back, letting the cover fall to the ground with a thud. Within moments, they were all safely underground, shaking from the cold air of the tunnel and the waning rush of fighting for their lives. They had no way to close the cover and no strength left to try.

Taking Macie's hand, Grant squeezed it for only a moment before guiding them down the corridor.

"How do you know which way to go?" Joanna asked.

"I'm just heading in the direction of VISP's main building. There's gotta be a way in from here," he urged.

They trekked through the darkness, cautiously sliding their hands along the wall. After some time, with no particular success, Addie requested that they stop and said, "Let me lead. I can see far better in this than any of you can. Besides, there's a door up ahead. I can see slender filaments vining out from that direction. There are people on the other side."

"Any sense if they're dangerous?" Maria asked.

Addie shook her head.

"Alright, go ahead." Grant stepped to the side and helped her to the front.

Upon reaching a cold, damp metal door, they felt up and

down for a handle. There was nothing on their side to unlatch or grip.

"What do you think?" Grant said quietly.

Though no one could see her, Maria stared him down, put her hand on her hip and said, "Well, obviously… we knock."

Chapter 54
Whatever Happens

July 3, 2030 | 2:30 a.m.

Zuri looked at Dakota and said, "If I concentrate on Aidan, can you make us a doorway straight to him?"

"At this point, anything's possible. Usually, I have to see something or someone, or know them well enough to guide myself. I've never done it this way... so I can't guarantee."

"All you can do is try," Maya said, smiling and lightly squeezing Dakota's arm.

They stood huddled together as Zuri focused on Aidan's features: his smile, his bright amber eyes and his red hair. In fact, they all did as they circled Dakota.

Soon, the hairs on Dakota's arms began to rise as flashes of Aidan's face intruded into her mind. Drawing quickly, she was able to capture his likeness across the blank page in front of her.

When she sensed her ability was reaching its peak, she sketched a crude door beside Aidan. Tucking her pencil into her hair, she looked at each of the women surrounding her. "Ready?"

Dakota placed her hand over the image, took a deep breath and lowered her hand to the page. She could feel pushback as if the image was repelling her. "I don't know what's wrong," she gasped, flashing a glance at Lexi.

"You're weak. We've asked too much of you."

"No... I... I should be able to do this. I can feel it."

"It happens to all of us when we push too hard," said Zuri.

"So... what do we do?" Dakota's heart raced in frustration.

Maddy placed her hand on Dakota's shoulder. Instantly, Dakota's heart rate slowed while Zuri began to pull as much energy from the rest of them as she could. Zuri could feel their strength coursing through her and into Dakota.

When she was ready, Dakota put her hand back to the drawing. They watched golden strands in the shape of a door begin to burn through the wall before them. It only took a few seconds to appear, just as real as before. This time, however, none of them reached for the handle.

"We don't know who's with him on the other side of that door. Are we ready?" Maddy asked.

Lexi, taking Maddy's hand, said, "Whatever happens, we're together."

Dakota turned the knob and gave it a slow push. The door ripped from her fingers before she could stop it as a panic-stricken face stared back at her.

"Joe!" Lexi shouted.

"Quick! We don't have a lot of time!" he cried.

Aidan was unconscious on the floor behind him. Half of the

ceiling above had been ripped away, and they could see the sky raging. The top eight floors appeared to be mostly gone.

"How do we get out of here?" Sheila yelled.

"I was hoping you might know!" he shouted back.

"Where are the others?" Sheila asked. Phil and the rest of their group were nowhere to be seen.

"Dr. Harold took the rest downstairs. He was going to abandon Aidan so I stayed. But that door locks automatically from the outside and I couldn't break the glass window to get us out!"

Sheila's eyes glazed over at the thought, having already seen the collapse of the stairs. Pushing the fear from her mind, and choosing to believe Phil and the others survived, she said, "This building is being torn apart. We need to get out of here!"

"We need to stop the storm!" Lexi demanded. "It's just getting worse. Dakota? Can you calm it?"

"I don't know. I don't know! Whatever I draw usually comes to an end when the vibrations on my skin stop, or I cross out the image on the page and swipe my hand across it. But… but this feels different."

"You've got to try," Maddy shouted over the raucous sound of an approaching tornado.

Flipping back several pages, she found the storm. They all watched as she drew a large X across the page, took a deep breath, slammed her hand to the page and smeared the granite markings left to right.

The storm raged on as she looked around. Nothing changed. She tried it again to no avail.

"It won't stop!"

"New plan." Lexi pointed at Aidan. "Joe, throw him over

your shoulder. Time to go."

With that, a loud crack echoed all around. They watched, silent and still, as the building shifted on its foundation. Lexi flung her arms out to the side, creating a bubble around them like a shield as debris fell from the floors above, stopping short of crushing them and instead rolling off to the side.

From somewhere far below, Zuri felt a surge of energy weaving its way to them and knew Addie, Joanna, and Macie were sending them strength. Placing her hands on the ground, she willed it to come to her quickly. As she grasped the ropes, she envisioned Addie's face. The energy pulsed through her, forcing her to jolt upright with her arms to the sky. Without hesitation, the girls, even Sheila and Maya, gripped hands and surrounded her. They'd never felt this amount of energy, as if it had a heartbeat all its own. The protective shield Lexi had created spread out further and further from them until the winds no longer impacted what was left of the main building. The dome continued further out, encompassing the entire compound.

With the energy continuing to build among them, the shield yielded its tether to the ground below, shifting toward the sky. It engulfed the storm, removing its power and exhausting its fuel until the last few drops of rain had been wrung from the rapidly dissipating clouds.

As far as anyone could see, the stars shone brightly without a cloud above. The last of the rainwater streamed down their faces. Without the screaming winds the silence was only broken by the creaking of the building, water flowing from broken lines, and the sound of their heavy breathing.

"You did it," Dakota whispered under her breath.

Zuri slid down to the ground, eyes glowing so bright in the

darkness it drowned out the shining stars above.

"We did it," she said, looking up at Dakota and beginning to laugh. "Together."

One by one, they joined in with a mix of laughter and crying as Joe set Aidan back down on the floor.

"Aidan!" shouted Zuri, noticing him begin to stir. Sliding over to him, she knelt by his side. "Aidan? Are you okay?"

With his eyes half-cracked open, he looked around to get his bearings. "Wow, Z. You really know how to bring the house down," he whispered as a wry smile pitched at the corner of his mouth.

Her instantaneous laugh was music to his ears.

"I'm so glad you didn't die," she said, staring into his eyes.

"Yeah. Me too," he said, his cheeks turning red.

Leaning forward, only inches from his face, she softly said, "I think it's time we go home."

"I can be down with that," he replied, turning to close the gap between them. Their kiss amplified the remaining energy around them as the girls looked back toward the clear night sky, giving them their moment.

Chapter 55
Love... and a Little Bit of Revenge

July 3, 2030 | 3:00 a.m.

Dakota used what energy she had left, with help from the others, to bring about a door on a section of wall still intact. Upon entering, they found themselves in the foyer on the main floor of the VISP building.

"Where do you think everyone is?" Zuri asked, tucked beneath Aidan's arm, both for support and because he wasn't going to let her out of his sight.

Scuffling could be heard coming from within the security room. Joe put his finger to his lips and walked slowly to the door. Just before he could grab hold of the handle, the door swung open and several operators fell forward onto him.

Instinctively, Joe started throwing fists but quickly recognized the grunts of the one taking the blows. "Phil? Is that you? Thank God!"

"Phil?" Sheila shouted from the other side of the foyer. Scrambling to right himself, Phil embraced her as she rushed into his arms.

"Oh, God. I thought I'd lost you," he said, his words muffled in her hair as he gripped her tight.

"You guys are okay. How did you get down here?" Zoey said, giving Rick a hug.

"We were in the stairwell when a vehicle smashed through just above us. Took out several guards. I'd heard one of them mention the security room down here as a shelter point. It's a miracle we made it. It's a miracle you made it!"

Their chatter was filled with the last remnants of fear giving way to the giddy relief of surviving.

"What's wrong, Aidan?" Zuri asked as she watched Aidan's smile fade away.

"Where is he?"

"Who?" asked Zoey, catching the concern in his voice.

"Dr. Harold. Where is he?"

Everyone took a moment to look around.

"Maybe he's still up there," Sheila offered.

"Zuri? Can you see where he is?" Lexi asked.

Closing her eyes, she struggled to find the strength to search. And with so much emotion surrounding her, she was too exhausted to push through. "I can't."

"It's okay. It's alright. If he is anywhere nearby, we'll find him," Aidan reassured with a smile.

Joe's face fell. "Quiet!" he barked, throwing his arms up. Without hesitation, the others formed a barricade in front of the girls.

"What is it?" asked Justin.

Joe pointed toward the stairwell to the D levels.

Whoever it was, they weren't concerned about stealth. They could hear talking and even laughing as the noise drew closer to the door that led down to floors below.

Pressing up against the wall, they waited for whoever was about to come through that door. With a loud bang, the stairwell door flung open as Grant burst into the room.

"Whoa! Hey! It's just us!" he cried and raised his hands over his head.

Joe dropped his head into his hands, took a deep breath, then looked up at him. "You are so lucky I'm not armed," he said with a loud sigh before walking over and embracing him with a bear hug.

"Whoa, big man. Since when are you a hugger?"

"Since we almost got swallowed up by a land hurricane," he said, chuckling at his reply.

As Joanna emerged from the basement door, her eyes were immediately drawn to the dark-haired girl on the other side of the room.

Dakota, too, felt the sudden pull and locked eyes with Joanna. It was as if the room had gone completely silent around them. With tears forming, she watched as the demeanor of the woman across the room shifted from anxiety to joy. She froze as Joanna took several long strides, jogging to close the gap between them.

Not waiting for an invitation, Joanna wrapped her arms around Dakota, as a broken sob released from her chest. "Dakota?"

Dakota, with a lump in her own throat, gently nodded.

"I can't believe it's you." Joanna squeezed even tighter.

Moving past the shock, Dakota squeezed back. "Is this real?" she wondered aloud, her voice hoarse with emotion.

"More than you know," Joanna leaned back, smiling wide as all the girls latched on to the two of them in any way they could so Dakota could feel the family she was born to be a part of.

"You're one of us, Dakota. Family," Zuri said.

"You never have to be alone again... if you don't want to be," Lexi added.

"But if you do want to be, let me tell you, it's gonna be hard to find that with these women around!" said Aidan, snuggling into the group hug and receiving a much-deserved smack on the shoulder from Zoey.

One by one, VISP employees began to appear from the lower levels. The foyer got so crowded Sheila started looking for a way out of the building. Still, the front doors wouldn't budge.

"It's a security feature. They were welded shut after we arrived," Joe clarified.

Her expression turned sour.

"Yeah, exactly. Dr. Harold said there's one other person with the code to unseal the exterior access. We don't know who it is or if that person even survived."

"Hey! Joe!" yelled Aidan from across the room, repeatedly wagging his head toward the stairwell door.

Justin turned to Joe. "Does he think we're going to get out going up?"

Maria piped in, "We can go back through the bunker and out the tunnels. That's how we got in."

"Joe!" Aidan shouted over the noise of the crowd, causing everyone to finally look his way.

With a deep breath, Joe rolled his eyes. But he wasn't annoyed. Infact, despite the chaos and pain, he was actually feeling pretty light-hearted as he worked his way through the crowd to see what had Aidan bouncing on his toes. As he got close he called out to him, "Sounds like we can exit through the bunker under the building, Aidan."

"Ooorrr," he said with a long drawl as he slowly opened the door. Fresh night air washed over them as bright stars shone down.

"Well, holy crap. I guess that works, too." Joe patted Aidan on the shoulder. "Well done, kid. If nothing else, this was worth staying back to keep you safe."

"Glad to hear my life has some value. Though it's not like I personally ripped out the wall or anything, I'll happily take the credit," he said with a wink.

One by one the crowd exited the foyer, carefully climbing overturned vehicles, building debris and downed trees.

Upon Addie's exit, the gang noticed the determined look on her face as she slowly turned in circles, peering into the dark with her alt-vision.

"What's happening, Addie?" Lexi asked.

Suddenly, Grant appeared, grasping Adeline's hand. Looking at Lexi, he said, "We lost Keeps out here."

Lexi spun back toward the emerging crowd as if he might somehow be in the mix. "How?"

"The storm. A blast of wind ripped him away from us."

Zuri found her way over having felt Lexi's energy spike. "What's wrong?"

"Keeps. We need to find him." Lexi grabbed Zuri's hand. "Think you can locate him?"

Immediately, she began to block the energy of all the people surrounding her in search of his singular thread. Without asking, she grabbed ahold of Addie's hand, which amplified her search. That's when Addie caught a glimpse of his strand.

"There!" she yelled, pointing toward the treeline.

Grant took off at full speed, jumping over and dodging debris. The closer he got, the more he recognized the section of roof that had struck Keeps, now folded up around a tree. "Keeps!" he called out, and ran with a fresh burst of energy, followed closely behind by the others.

"Grant," Justin called, "where is he?"

"He's gotta be over here somewhere. That's the roof that hit him when we were trying to find cover," he declared, stopping short of the section. Justin and Joe walked around one side and Grant went the opposite direction.

Everyone paused when they heard a groan.

"Keeps? That you buddy? Call out so we can find you," Justin yelled.

They heard another groan from the heap coupled with a faint, "Here."

"He's under it! Help me pull roofing from the tree," Justin directed. They all took an edge and slowly pulled the debris away, grunting and struggling as tree limbs attempted to hold it in place. Once removed, all they found were more branches and debris.

"Keeps? Say that again so we can find you," Joe said, carefully dragging building pieces away from the base. "Keeps?"

They heard another groan. A disembodied ghostly sound.

Slowly, Joe scanned the trunk of the tree up to its damaged branches. There he was, draped over a tree limb.

"Well. Damn. How'd you manage that?" said Joe, shaking his head.

"Just thought I'd hang around, waiting for you all to arrive," Keeps said with a laugh, then coughed, straining to contain the pain he was in. "Think y'all could get me down, maybe?"

As Sheila looked him over and bandaged him back together, the rest of the group caught sight of the girls walking slowly toward an overturned vehicle in the parking lot.

"What are they doing?" Justin questioned, then with an all knowing sense, his head swiveled to Joe. "Harold."

They took off at a sprint.

The girls formed a circle around something on the other side of the car.

Gavin, the first to arrive, gently touched Zoey's shoulder and asked, "Hey? You okay?"

Zoey turned in response, but it was obvious that she wasn't really looking at him before turning back toward the ground.

As the rest of the men arrived and stepped forward, they caught sight of a mangled man lying on the ground.

Sheila came up behind them and gasped, "Dr. Harold!"

Maya, stepping into the circle, confirmed, "He's alive."

Her voice startled him awake and his eyes flashed open. "Maya? Maya, please. Please help me," he said through clenched teeth, attempting to rise only to discover that his arm hung at a grotesque angle. Collapsing back to the ground, he whined, "I need help. Please. Zuri?"

The expressions on the girls' faces remained stoic. Justin turned around to the growing crowd and motioned for them to move back.

Dr. Harold could feel the electrical current building in the air. The hairs on his arms stood up. His adrenaline pumped through his veins, masking the pain as he pushed himself upright.

"Maya. Please. I just wanted to help," he pleaded, trembling as she stepped toward him. "Maya, please don't do this."

Towering over him like a windblown angel, she said, "Do what, doctor?"

"I tried to do right by you. I didn't take you. Or your son. I only wanted to make the world better!"

"Did you do right by these girls? By my mother? Is the world any better off from your experiments?"

His eyes bounced from one girl to the next, begging for mercy.

Addie watched as a purple hue started to glow around Maya.

"Well... I'd say you failed. Failed beyond measure to make anything better for anyone."

Maya reached over and took Zuri's hand. One by one the girls clasped hands.

"No. Wait. Hold on, just, just hold on!" he stammered.

Zoey, touching Maya on the shoulder, quietly asked, "Would you like to do the honors?"

Maya smiled. "I would, but I think I'll let you take this one."

It was then that Dr. Harold realized what Joe had really done by telling Zoey that story. He'd given her a different angle. A different plan of attack. "No! No, no. Hey, I saved you. I saved all of you!" Changing tactics he focused on Dakota, "Dakota! I told you a very long time ago that I'd find you. We're together again! Save me and I— I'll leave. I'll leave you alone! Please, Zoey! Maya? Don't let her do this!"

The intensity of the hum continued to grow despite his pleadings.

Despite their exhaustion from the last hours, the girls grew stronger. Fueled by the people around them.

As the doctor broke down, Aidan stepped forward and took Zuri's hand. As he did, the harshness in her eyes softened. "Dr. Harold. I want to thank you," he said to the shock of everyone, including the doctor.

Addie watched the purple hue move toward and surround Aidan. His cheeks flushed from the warmth that had suddenly overcome him.

"If it weren't for you, I may never have met the most incredible humans God put on this earth. And for that, we want to share with you all we've been through because of your efforts."

Holding eyes with Zoey, her expression suddenly went from confusion to understanding.

Once again, Aidan could see the path forward before they did.

With pursed lips and a subtle nod, she stepped into the circle, allowing them to close the loop around her. Kneeling over the broken doctor, she shut her eyes and, thanks to Joe, traveled back in her mind to that now very vivid memory of what she'd done to that monster that hurt her in that old shack all those years ago. Pulling power from the hurt, the fear, she thought further back to the monster that killed her parents, stole her, and robbed the others of their families and childhoods.

The air around them sizzled with electricity from the dissipated storm and now captured amongst the girls. Zuri, pulling that energy from the ground, the air, and the people around her, leaned forward and placed a hand on Zoey's shoulder. As Zoey opened her eyes, focusing solely on him, the hum grew until it became the only sound Dr. Harold could hear.

"Please. Don't do this," he begged to deaf ears. "I can help you. We can make the world better together. All of us."

Grabbing the side of his head with his unbroken arm, Dr. Harold's words jumbled together and his vision blurred as the pressure compressed his head as though in a vise.

Addie watched as the purple smudge in the air expanded to encompass all of them. Then pulled together in the ethereal shape of a woman. She watched as a gentle smile on the being's face formed as if this woman knew only Addie could see her. Her ghostly hand reached out and touched Addie's face. Their eyes locked in understanding. Then moved to touch Aidan, then Maya, and finally placed her intangible hand on Zoey's.

Zoey leaned forward to meet the doctor eye to eye. "What does it feel like?" she asked gruffly. "Are you in pain, doctor? Confused? Unsure of where this pressure is coming from and how to stop it?"

Addie looked on as their colored tendrils formed into thick ropes, then into a hurricane of light. Every emotion, every hurt and memory, all combined, racing faster and faster around them.

From deep inside herself, Zoey realized she could take all the memories, experiences of pain and loss, terror and confusion, everything that each of them had felt throughout their lives, and place it all on him. Staring into his eyes, she reached her hand out toward him. His eyes widened in panic.

As her fingertips touched his forehead, every horror-filled experience downloaded into his mind in a single moment.

The scream that left his lips was unlike anything they'd

ever heard. His lungs caved in as the air around him compressed his body the way Lexi and Maya felt within the glass prison. Bright red and purple lines spread across his body. His vision, blurred from the pressure, quickly turned to black from all the blows that Addie had experienced in the iron prison. He felt the emptiness of despair crush his heart in the way Dakota had felt time and time again.

Each and every horror they had faced alone over the years, he now felt at once. His mind, soul, heart, and even his bones broke under the weight of it all.

The girls felt his terror combine with their own. Reliving those moments in a matter of seconds, only this time they were together. The pain of those fear-filled events were released, swept up into the violet hue surrounding them, leaving their hearts whole again. So much so that even their physical statures changed as the weight of the past dissipated.

When his body finally stopped twitching, laying flat on his back, his eyes appeared permanently fixed upward. As if looking for the same light Lexi saw so many years prior in that glass prison as she searched to understand where it came from, where she was, and if she was even alive.

Addie, startled at the sight, stood still as a dark mist left his body. The ethereal woman wrapped herself around the darkness as a purple hue caused the darkness to fold in on itself repeatedly until, like smoke, a breeze caught it and carried it away.

Maya crouched down beside Dr. Harold's lifeless form. "Pain isn't the best motivator, Doc. Love is... and, well, maybe a dash of revenge."

Chapter 56
Deadline

"So... you're saying you swallowed up a storm and snuffed it out like a candle?" Aidan's eyes were big as saucers trying to digest it all. "I can't believe I missed all the good stuff! Freaking Cirque du Soleil breaks out amongst my family and I miss the entire thing?"

They were back at their old farmhouse in Sanford, sitting outside around the firepit, watching the sun drop behind the trees. His groan of disappointment was so dramatic everyone burst out laughing.

Several new additions joined them upon their return. Phil had made the move permanent, which left Sheila over the moon. Keeps had shown his true colors and the girls he had once entrapped forgave him. One of the girls now living in a small home next to the garden seemed to be particularly sweet on him, something he could never have imagined. Dakota and Elias had permanently abandoned the Breakers, leaving their people at the Station to turn on Levi and floundering for purpose. Most of the VISP employees decided to work with Jahnsen at LIMIT. Others went off to find family and friends. But a few of them even moved to Sanford to help out the nerd-pack in any way they could, trying to give back to the girls, and experience a new type of community.

"Well that's what happens when you decide you'd rather nap," Zuri chided.

"Nap! Nap? I was strapped to a bed!"

"Excuses, excuses," she said before losing her composure.

Macie walked over with a plate of food and plopped down on the outdoor wicker couch beside Zuri. "Move over, girl. My big butt needs room!" Her voice, though familiar by now, was as magical as any could have imagined.

"Dakota," Aidan yelled over the commotion, "listen, I've always wanted to visit Jamaica. Think you could draw me a door?"

Lexi watched as Dakota rolled her eyes. "She catches on quick!"

They were awash in joy as they ate some of Maria's delicious paninis together. Not one to sit still, Maria was already working on a plan to have the girls visit the local farms around Sanford in hopes of helping them expedite crop growth. Her work and her vision offered everyone another layer of hope for the future. Without question they adopted her as the best fit to lead them into a better way of life.

They'd never felt more free, and encompassed with more love than the family they'd created together.

Joe, polishing off his meal, heard a ping from the computer he seemed to bring with him everywhere. He was taking his newly heightened concern for their security seriously. Ambling over, he checked the camera feeds. Able to make out two dark shapes in the woods, his back straightened abruptly.

"Joe?" Maya asked.

He threw his hand up, silencing everyone.

"What's going on?" Brandon whispered, leaning over to look at the screen.

"Two bodies in the woods."

Lexi felt the shift in the atmosphere and immediately surrounded them with a shield.

Joe motioned for Brandon and Aidan to follow him. Cautiously, they ducked into the woods in hopes of circling back to the two figures.

Several minutes later, the girls heard scuffling and shouting. Unable to see anything on the camera, they ran toward the sound, with Lexi arriving first. Brandon and Joe had Oakley pressed against a tree while Aidan pinned Long to the ground.

"You made a big mistake coming here," said Sheila without an ounce of mercy in her voice.

Oakley grunted in pain as his arm was yanked further behind his back. "We have some unfinished business," he spit out.

Addie, Joanna and Macie walked forward until Oakley and Long could see them clearly. Oakley, blinking in disbelief, said, "You're walking? How is this possible?"

Macie looked at both men then turned to Addie, "May I?"

"By all means," she said, waving her hand. The men pressed Oakley to the ground beside Long and held him in place.

"You know, you hurt a lot of people," she said with a deep

breath, sitting on the ground beside them and casually crossing her legs. "We'd be well within reason to offer you similar treatment. Let you feel what we felt all those years."

"Oh yeah?" Oakley growled, then glared at Sheila. "You're the one that left me behind." Glancing back at Macie, he said, "She left both of us behind! You want to be mad at someone? Look at her."

Macie looked over at Shiela. Her loving, motherly figure. The woman who admittedly felt the guilt of not saving her all those years ago. A woman she could never blame for the evil done to her.

"So that's what this is? You were wronged, so you decided to do wrong?" Macie asked with pity in her voice.

"Call it what you want. I protected you when none of them did," he shouted, grunting as he struggled to free himself from Brandon's grip.

"Is that so? Well, I think it's time I returned the favor." Macie put her hand up and Aidan pulled her to her feet. "We recently decided that living for revenge didn't make us much better than those who have wronged us. It can't be the way forward. So we want to thank you."

He paused, "For?" then groaned as Brandon applied more pressure to his neck.

"For giving us this opportunity to make things better. Pain does not have to equal more pain," Macie replied, glancing over at Zoey who then stepped forward to place her hands on their foreheads. Expecting the worst, the men had winced when they felt a warmth come over them as a gentle electrical current flowed into their minds. Addie could see the amber threads weaving through their bodies.

"Zoe?" Addie warned as she watched the threads grow dark and the men begin to writhe.

"Sorry, it's just so tempting to give them a little something to remember us by," she breathed out. "I know, I know." Zoey sighed and readjusted the current she was using to break down within each man all the hatred, vengeance, and destruction that made up the fabric of their minds.

Over the course of several moments, each man slumped to the ground, releasing the fight.

"Are they dead?" asked one of the women from the iron prison, feeling pensive at the sight of Oakley.

"Just give them a moment," Joanna said as Zoey stood back up on her feet.

With their lifeless bodies offering no resistance, Brandon and Joe extricated themselves, leaving the men prone on the ground.

"Oakley? Long? Can you hear me?" Zoey asked.

The men pushed themselves to their knees and nodded slowly as if in a dream.

"Guys, I need you to listen clearly, okay? You're going to head over to Thomas's farm."

They nodded with childlike confusion.

"He's gonna put you to work in the fields. It's time you put your muscles toward a worthy cause. And you will never, ever, as long as you live, hurt another human for any reason."

Without saying another word, Oakley and Long rose to their feet, faced the direction of the farm and meandered into the woods.

"Are you sure they'll do it?" Macie asked.

"I rewired their minds. They'll remember what they've done

but perceive it as a horror not to be repeated. I've taken away any ability to feel hatred or desire revenge and I've replaced it with compassion." With a wry smile, she added, "I may have also given them child-like acceptance and a touch of intellectual paralysis. Outside of planting crops and digging holes, they won't be spreading their scholarly wings. ."

Zoey squeezed Macie's hand and with a smile, said, "Come on." Together, along with the rest of the group, they headed back to the fire.

Joe picked up a freshly filled plate and sat down next to Maya in one of the wicker chairs. Out of the corner of his eye, he watched her place her hand on her stomach. "Maya? You okay?"

She looked up at him. Her smile created a low hum that all the girls felt and slowly turned her direction.

"Maya?" Maddy asked. "What's wrong?"

"I'm just grateful," she sighed.

Some of the girls nearby placed their hands on her, causing the hum to grow louder. Addie noticed a thin golden-pink fiber weaving its way between their fingers and gave a small gasp. The other girls felt the new tiny vibration at the same time.

"Are you?" Zoey asked with hesitation.

Maya nodded. "We'll have to work fast to bring about a better world. We're on a deadline now."

Aidan, completely out of touch, leaned forward. "Deadline? For what?"

Zuri, looking up at this red-headed man she loved, said, "Well, it looks like you're going to be a big brother."

Also in the PRISONER SERIES:

Glass Prison | Book One

Iron Prison | Book Two

ABOUT THE AUTHOR

MJ Thompson is a retired Combat Weather Forecaster who occasionally jumped out of perfectly good airplanes. During one such jump her static line failed to release, dragging her body begind the plane. Her injuries plunged her into darkness for months where she learned her only light was the ability to write. And that is where her novels began.

MJ and her husband, both retired from the U.S. Air Force, live in Sanford, NC. She owns her own real estate company, renovates houses, has worked with non-profits, and expects she'll learn and do more in the future. She is reminded daily that every day is a new day to learn from the past, careful not to let it dictate the future.

www.ingramcontent.com/pod-product-compliance
Lightning Source LLC
Chambersburg PA
CBHW020327010826
48973CB00005B/1157